# ELEMENTAL RUIN

ALX CHAN YEE

Content/Trigger Warning List

Explicit sexual content, Knife play, Blood/graphic torture, Mentions of disordered eating, Image issues (not explicit), SA mention (not explicit), Mental health issues, Family problems (i.e. generational trauma), Alcohol and drug use, Slight body shaming (not explicit)



Elemental Ruin
Book 1
Cover Design: kiajaelyn.com
Edited by: Julian Baet
Formatting: An Inkwell of Nectar

ART MADE BY:

Family portrait: kiajaelyn.com
Ball scene: Anamin Dario (@Sketchesanmin on instagram)
Six of Wands: (@avoccatt_art)
Other Magik Friends: (@ya_ariart on instagram)
Map: Saumya (@saumyasvision on instagram)

FIRST EDITION: FEBRUARY 2023

Legend
Settlements
Estate/House
Border
House of
Smoldris
HEARTHIS
WINDWY
AQUATIUS
Shopping
Center
House of
Chauvet
House of Oris
ENTHAR
Market
Aeon
Estate
Shopping
Center

MINDAE
Inn
Lake Mindae
us Estate
Phantom Tower
Darkened Forest
IFAERIS

# A Pronunciation Guide
## POSSIBLE SPOILERS! READ AT YOUR OWN RISK!

NAMES:

DISARIS: De-sare-is
AEON: A-yawn
ORIS: Or-ehs
CHAUVET: Show-vay
SMOLDRIS: Smol-dress
ZEPHYS: Zeh-phees

LAND/AREAS:

IFAERIS: If-fur-is
CREATURELANDS: Cree-ture Lands
SEARUCKS: See-rooks
MAGIK COVE: Mah-gik Cove
GIGANTIA: Jeye-gan-teeah
HUMAN LANDS: Hue-man Lands
MINDAE: Min-day
ENTHAR: Ehn-thar
AQUATIUS: Ah-kway-shus
HEARTHIS: Har-this
WINDWYRD: Wind-word
LAZIPEUS: Lah-zeh-!s

BLOODLINES:

AIRLIUS: Air-lee-us

FLAMELING: Flame-leen
ROKUS: Rock-us
WATERIEVER: Water-reever
SPIRITUS: Spirit-ous

OTHER:

OKKARING: Ah-ker-een
LASIALIC: Luh-zye-lack
VALSKULL: Vahl-skuhll

## *Prologue*

Arabella

Having to bury your first love is hard, but it's even harder when you're the one who killed him. Or at least that's what everyone says.

I didn't kill him, at least not directly. I've been trying to convince myself that for weeks, but it doesn't stop people from blaming me. Not his family, not our friends, not my unending thoughts convincing me that they think that.

He was coming to me. We had been fighting all week, and everyone knew it. We used to have an on-and-off relationship, mostly due to him trying to help me and me having unresolved issues, which tended to result in me pushing him away. I was working on myself, and we had gone over a year without risking a breakup. Until that week.

*It was at a party when we ran into one of his ex-girlfriends, Delphi. I went to the bathroom and returned to see her throwing herself at*

*Luka. Her long, brown hair was tied up, green eyes complementing her eyeliner, and a crop top under her red flannel with blue, ripped jeans. She wrapped her arms around Luka, spewing something about how much he must miss her. He tried pushing her off, but as I saw him cast his head in my direction, I walked out.*

*I never thought I was his type. I wasn't thin like his past girlfriends, and after seeing the events that had just played out, these doubts were further enabled. I knew I was too drunk. I was being irrational, but I didn't care. I had my friend Reyna bring me home, and I silenced my phone immediately so I'd be left in isolation with no one to bother me. I woke up to messages and calls from Luka, who was extremely worried. And after two days, I messaged him, saying I needed space.*

*Despite my request, he would still message me to check in, and whenever I looked at my phone, I was secretly hoping it was him.*

*About a week passed, and one night I called him apologizing while he was out with our friends. He said he was coming over, but I could sense the frustration in his voice. I tried telling him it was okay if he wanted to just stay with them, but he insisted on seeing me.*

*An hour went by, and he still wasn't at my house. He wasn't picking up his phone, and it wasn't until I got a call from our friend Violette that I found out he was in the hospital.*

*Stabbed. He had been cut eight times. Two by the heart, three times in the stomach, once by the ribs, once in his back, and one slit to the throat. Overkill. There was nothing I could do to save him. Everyone knew he was coming back to see me. I didn't kill him physically, but if I had just waited until morning, he might still be alive.*

Now here we are, at my boyfriend's funeral, everyone watching me as I try to keep from throwing myself into the casket with him.

His sharp features are even more defined in death, skin paler than when he was alive. Death doesn't change his hair. Still a blond with barely more color than his entire body. If there's one thing that followed him from life to his funeral, it's his all-black clothing.

A sigh escapes me as I remember that people will never joke about the dread of our clothing again.

*It was supposed to be us until the end.* He is–*was*–my everything. Nothing's going to be the same anymore.

I notice our friend group across the room. Violette's short hair is pulled back by a headband, her face buried in Damien's suit. He's changed his hair since I last saw him. It's no longer in locs, but now a lined-up, nearly shaved head. Juliette's red, tight, curly hair in a ponytail matches her swollen eyes. Grayson's the only one from our group missing. *Probably somewhere at the food table.*

Violette and Damien make their way towards me, immediately pulling me into a hug. For the first time in two weeks, I let myself shatter. I fall into their arms and sob. Violette runs her hand through my hair and grabs my face between her hands, pulling me down to meet her. "It's not your fault, you know. No one blames you."

"You don't know that. Just 'cause you say you don't, it doesn't mean that Luka's family thinks the same. They had one son, and because of me, he's dead. If I wasn't so jealous, if I was more firm that he stayed with you, then maybe–"

Damien cuts me off. "He chose to leave that night, Ara. No one could have known he would be killed."

"But Delphi," I croak. "She said if it weren't for me forcing him to leave the party–"

"Fuck Delphi," Violette fumes. "She doesn't speak for any of us, and she *sure as hell* was never our friend. She followed Luka to uni, she couldn't handle their split, so she hated *you* for taking what she thought was hers."

I take a shallow breath in and stiffen when I feel someone putting their arm around my shoulder. It's Grayson, pulling me in for an uncomfortable side hug. "Hey, Ara. How are you feeling?"

"As well as you can expect, I guess." I sigh. "Also, you have finger sandwich on your mouth."

He laughs, wiping the crumbs onto the black of his shirt. Juliette joins us, closing her hand in Grayson's. For a second, I'm surprised, raising my brows at her, her cheeks immediately blushing.

Her big, round cheeks and fair complexion turn a bright shade of pink. "What?" she mouths.

I just shake my head, smiling. *One day they'll figure it out.* One day.

The five of us go up to Luka's casket, my friends holding me as tears stream down my face. When we reach Luka's parents, his mother grabs me into a hug, telling me how much Luka loved me. How they still look at me like their future daughter-in-law. I start to break down, rambling how much he loved them, though it mostly applies to his mom. He and his father may have had a lot of problems, but I want to believe that somewhere, he cared for his son.

The five of us sit in the first row, but I can't keep my eyes on his casket. I turn back, seeing my other friends, Evie, Amber, and Reyna looking at me, their faces asking me if I'm okay. I nod to them, forcing a lazy smile. They mouth an "I love you" to me, and I force myself to return looking to the front.

I'm numb through the whole service, my mind fading out until I'm called up to read the eulogy I know I'm not ready to give. Delivering this means accepting he's really gone, and I'm not sure

I'm ready for that. I make my way towards the podium, taking deep breaths to keep me from crying.

It's ironic. I thought eight was supposed to be a lucky number for Asians, but all it brings is grief.

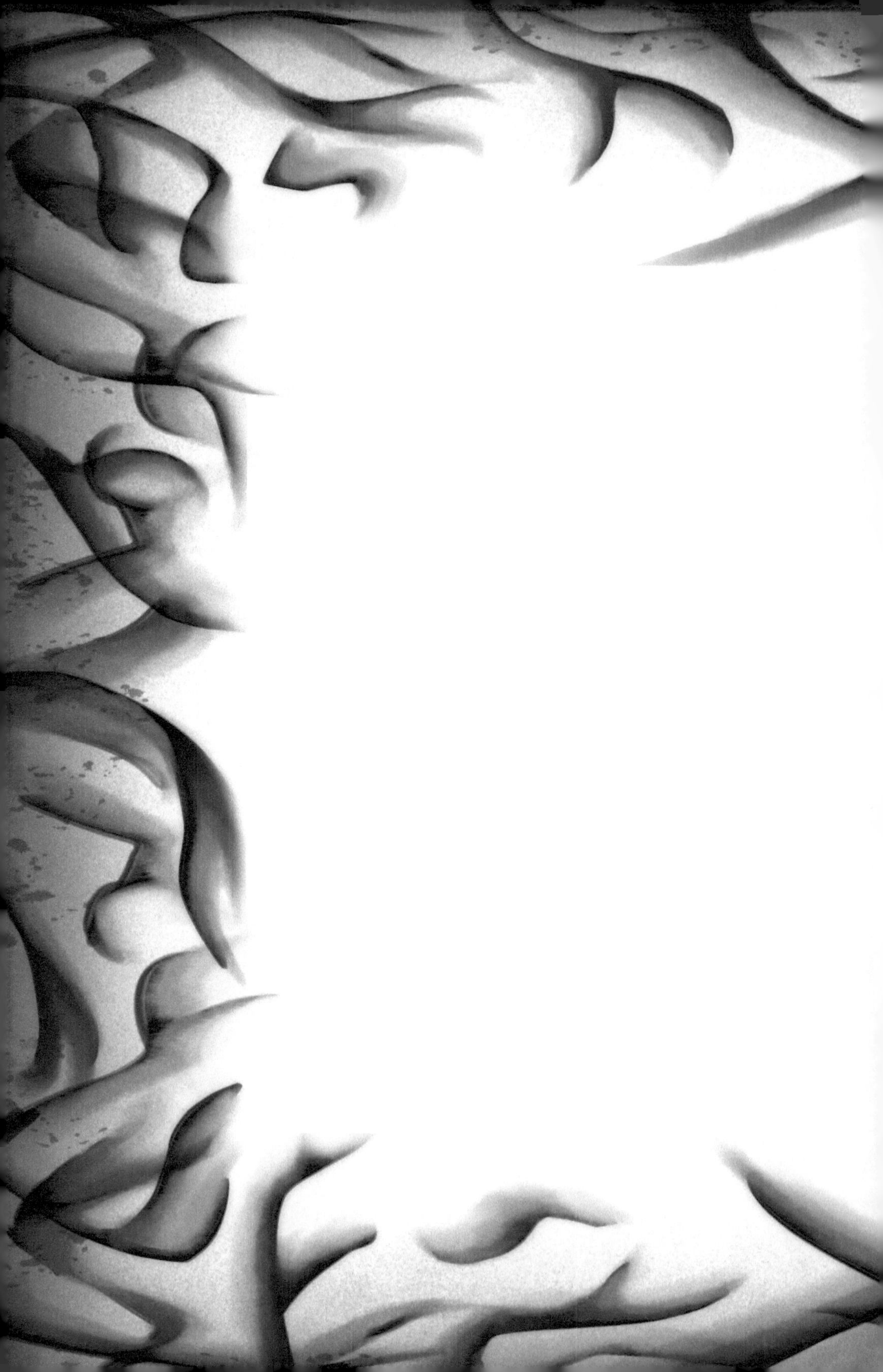

Part 1
The Duty

# I

## Accidents Happen

Four Months Later

Arabella

I'm always late. The morning sun outside touches me warmly, but the garbage truck collecting the trash is what really confirms it for me.

*Shit.* I grab my phone from my nightstand and check the time. *10:15.* That gives me fifteen minutes to get ready and pack for my day at school.

I have a missed call and two messages from Violette asking if we're meeting up for breakfast before class. To save time, I *could* just skip my entire routine, buy food, and head straight out the door, but I need the routine, or it'll probably make me anxious all day. I dash to the bathroom. Quickly, I brush my teeth, wash my face, and finish my skincare before combing my hair. I'm still not used to its length above my shoulders, despite having this hair for months now.

Magiking on my makeup when I finish, I run downstairs to pack food for the day, but when I check the fridge, all I have is some bread and a week-old burger I haven't thrown out yet.

*Gods I need to start eating more than a piece of bread and calling it a meal.*

I check the time again. *10:25*. Five minutes until class starts, and I've already missed the bus. Now there's two options: drive and risk an extra forty minutes in Los Angeles traffic to get to the park's museum, another possible twenty minutes trying to find parking, then rush to the Magikal area hidden from humans to enter the college, or I can okkar to class.

Do I understand why we use the word *okkar* to mean teleporting? Not really. Do I care enough to waste time in my brain questioning it? Also no.

You'd think being an educated witch since fourteen would make this so much easier than it is, but no. Okkaring is the *one* thing that I can't figure out. Well, that and how to stop myself from accidentally starting a fire when my emotions are out of control.

Being that I'm now five years older than sixteen, the legal age of Magik, I no longer need a wand to contain my powers. But maybe, *just maybe*, I should've paid more attention in classes teaching us about okkaring. Because now it's my last semester at the University of Lazipeus, and I'm running late for my senior course class.

I think hard, really hard, about where I want to go. I imagine the school grounds, the class being on the fifth floor, my seat in the back of the class next to all my friends, and hope–*pray*–that I end up at the doorway into the classroom. The image of the classroom starts becoming clear. I'm just about to okkar, when suddenly, I hear the sound of someone's car alarm going off. Concentration now broken, I open my eyes, getting a glimpse of the dark tree that stands outside my window right before I feel myself being pulled to a different location.

*Shit. Where the fuck am I?*

I'm surrounded by nothing but trees. The sounds of branches cracking from nearby animals stepping on them echoes the forest. I pull my curved dragon knife from my bra, preparing for anything.

Exhausted, I rest against a tree, remembering how much energy it takes to okkar when pulled to a place you can barely visualize.

I need to figure out where I am and how to get home before anything happens. I don't trust these woods in the slightest, especially not when I'm alone in them. Grabbing my phone, I open the map GPS in hopes of finding my location, but there's no signal. No way to determine how far away I've gone from my targeted destination. My phone hasn't even changed time zones to clarify the difference.

Deciding the best option would be to walk until I find help, a realization occurs. *Finding a random stranger in the middle of a forest might be worse than coming across a wild animal.*

The only positive note is that since it's still daytime, I don't have to waste any of my phone battery using the flashlight to get out of wherever I am. It seems like midafternoon, which means I have three, maybe four hours to find civilization.

After exploring for about twenty minutes, I hear three voices. I hide myself, crouched behind a bush to watch them before revealing myself, just so I can ensure my safety. There are two men and a woman. One man is extremely tall with tan, darker skin, long, curly hair, thicker eyebrows, and a deep, raspy voice. The man next to him is pale. Shorter and wider than the other, but still much taller than me or the woman. He has an eyepatch that clearly needs replacing, an extremely muscular build, and a bigger stomach.

The woman, on the other hand, seems like the one in charge. Or at least someone of higher command than them. She has warm, olive-brown skin and a pixie haircut. Her eyes, a vibrant shade of blue, and such beautiful bone structure that I could probably develop a crush on her on the spot. All three are captivating, holding me in my place.

"Princess Esme, we *must* insist that we escort you back to the estate for your protection," Eyepatch says.

"Oh don't be so antagonizing towards me," the woman scorns. "I know you and father don't believe me capable of defending myself, but I assure you, I am fully able if needed."

She hits Curly with her shoulder, whipping him around. The sweat from his forehead begins making strands from his hair stick diagonally across his face.

*So whoever these people are, they have to be really important if they're calling her princess.*

Curly hustles in front of the supposed princess, grabbing her arm. "Pardon me, princess, but if it were not for us following you, we'd both be out of a job and likely killed by your father."

Her body jerks, her eyes blazing. "And whose wrath do you fear more? My father, who likely hasn't bothered to learn your names? Or me?"

*I like her.* Putting away my knife, I move from the bush, making my appearance known. "Excuse me, sorry to bother you but–"

I'm given no time before Curly cuts me off by pointing a sword at me. My eyes widen, legs backing off. "Witch, you are trespassing on Disaris grounds. Surrender peacefully, and you will be taken to the king for trial."

"No, you don't understand," my voice shakes, "I'm not trespassing. I just got lost and–"

Eyepatch steps forward, his height towering over mine. "Silence," he commands, putting his hand up. "Either come with us now, or face your death."

I shut my mouth and begin following them in a line. *How did they know I was a witch?* There's no way the men will let me walk behind them, and there's less of a chance they'll let me near the princess to explain myself.

No words are exchanged for minutes before I hear the princess begin to speak. "Are you really a Magik?"

"Princess," Eyepatch says, "I must ask that for your own safety, you do not talk to the vermin."

If I wasn't so scared he would follow through on his threat of killing me, or maybe if I was confident enough I could okkar somewhere else, I might say something back. Instead, I just mutter, "Yes."

We finally reach a château-like palace with a dark, stone construction and sections looking more like a castle. The grounds are the most elegant thing I've ever seen, but we're moving at such a fast pace, I can barely admire it. My mouth drops. I've been to big houses, mansions–hell, Luka's family owns a giant manor and smaller houses on their estates in England and New York–but this is something like I've never seen before.

I continue walking in silence, but when we near the entrance, the princess is escorted first before I'm taken inside.

There are chandeliers hanging. Clicks of my boots hitting the marble floor sound with each step, making everything louder. I feel the beating in my heart rapidly escalating. So rampant, I swear it's risen to my throat. I need some type of release, some outlet from my body to stabilize me. So I start doing my finger counting against my thigh. *One. One Two One. One Two Three Two One.*

"What are you doing, witch?" Curly demands.

Usually, when counting, I go up to eight and then reverse it to fully ground myself, but somehow this asshole thinks I'm bothering people by touching my fingers to my leg.

Fine. If this is how he's going to treat me, I'll play this game. And I'll play it better than he can. "I'm obviously putting a curse on you."

"Well, stop that. You're about to plead your case to the king. May he grant you a swift death," he mocks before opening the doors that are surrounded by royal-like, golden framing.

Taking in the beauty of the room, I am at a loss for words. The elegant walls, surrounded by drapery, parallel to the windows and its matching gold-rimmed, white curtains. There are two wide-seated thrones, side by side with gold framing and red, velvet cushioning that sit adjacent to windows. The marble floors, now black instead of an off-white, are mostly covered by a scarlet rug that goes up the stairs and leads to the thrones. Behind it sits an archway that curves into a point at the top with gold trimmings and a black walling.

While slowly making our way towards the thrones, I see two men and the princess surrounding who I assume are the king and queen. The princess gives me an apologetic look while both Eyepatch and Curly bend to kneel.

"Rise. What news do you bring? Why have you brought a

witch?" the king questions. He's aggravated. Like if someone's just torn him from something of utmost importance.

"My king, we found this creature wandering the Darkened Forest and trespassing upon Disaris land. If it had not been for us, there would have been a chance of it harming Princess Esme," Eyepatch says urgently, tail twitching, as if his life depends on it. It probably does.

"And *why* was it possible the princess could have been harmed in the first place?" The king asks, turning to the princess.

"Father, I was just walking around. I had no intention of stepping foot outside the royal grounds," the princess answers, obviously lying.

*Is this just how all royalty speak?*

It's weird hearing these people talk so archaically. So proper. I listen to the king and princess bicker about why she should be allowed to have more freedom, to which he responds about how he's just trying to protect her with everything going on. Whatever that means.

I look around the room to distract myself from their repetitive exchange and realize that everyone has pointy ears, which tells me I'm not in the presence of humans. I think.

Bringing my eyes to the people surrounding the throne, I take notice of the two men that are at the sides of the king and the queen. One has a warm, beige skin tone with medium-length, slicked, black hair, similar to the king's, but some facial features like Curly. Unlike the king, he has more stubble on his skin, but it's light. I can only assume this is his son, based on how intently he's clinging to the king's every word. Though the man looks like the king in how he holds himself, he's much more tan with fuller lips, a more square face, and darker gray eyes.

To the left of the queen stands another, much paler man. He's taller, but more slender than the other, looking to be the same age. He also resembles the king but shows no similarity facially to the one by the king's side, so they can't be identical twins. This one has an oval-shaped face with defined bone structure in his cheekbones and jaw.

He looks like he was sculpted from a religious myth.

My lips part. I can't take my eyes off him. His nose, lips, and eyebrows are a bit thinner than who I think to be his brother's. His slightly curly, jet-black hair falls just below his right brow, the part leaning towards the left and the back seemingly falling to almost the bottom of his neck. One side of his hair is tucked behind his pointy ear, and his dark, carbon eyes are smoked with eyeliner.

He almost reminds me of Luka. Their facial structures are so similar.

This makes no sense. How are all three of the king's children the same age, yet have vastly different features? While I know it's likely they all could have different mothers, the king must have gotten them all pregnant at the same time. The only clear thing is that the princess is the daughter of the king and queen. She has the exact same, wider nose as the queen, along with similar hair texture, though the princess seems to have slightly looser curls.

As the fighting carries on, my attention keeps going back towards the men by the throne. I must be staring because the one with wavy hair begins to glare at me.

"What are you staring at, you leech?"

When the words leave his mouth, the arguing stops. Everyone's attention is diverted towards me, expecting me to speak. This is one of those rare instances when I know to control my mouth and not say something that would land me in deeper trouble than I already am. As much as I am looking forward to death, I'm not planning to die from my idiotic mouth.

"Well?" the king orders. "Speak, witch."

I hesitate. My mouth goes dry, not knowing if this is a trick. "Your Majesty, this has all been a misunderstanding. I wasn't trying to trespass or invade your land. I was simply trying to okkar to my classroom, but there was a fire, and I lost my concentration and ended up here. I really didn't mean to intrude, I promise. If you just showed me the way ou–"

"Your Majesty, if I may," Curly interrupts. The king nods, giving permission to speak. "This creature was lingering in the bushes before approaching us. If not to attack in some form, why would she hide?"

"That's a good point," the king replies. "Any explanations?"

I scoff. "You can't actually expect me to have been taken to a forest, *by accident,* and for me to just trust the first people I saw without making sure they wouldn't kill me first. That's like sprinting straight into the arms of a murderer." I turn to Curly, looking into his eyes. "But I guess it happened anyway, since you're practically sending me to my death."

The whole room stares at me in astonishment. Probably for speaking with confidence, or because they didn't expect me to defend myself at all.

Taking a deep breath, I try to keep myself from exploding. "Look, all I want is to get back to my house because at this point, class has to be over. I don't care about harming anyone here. I just. Want. To get. Home."

"Father," the princess calls. "I trust that she is telling the truth. She hadn't done anything that would have warranted any suspicion she was trying to harm me or anyone here. I beg you to excuse her and let her go."

The king listens to his daughter's words, seeming to take them into consideration. "Very well. You will not be sentenced to death at this time. However, until I decide on the consequences for your actions, you will henceforth be held in Phantom Tower for your low crimes against the crown. You will be granted bathing privileges, as well as food three times a day. Consider yourself of luck that you had my daughter here to speak on your behalf." He rises from his seat. "Guards, take her to her cell."

Within seconds, guards start constraining my arms. There's no way I would be able to fight my way out of this. I struggle, twisting my body to the king, my stomach coiling like a pretzel. "No! Please just let me go home. I just want to leave."

I pull away from the guards just long enough to see the queen and princess looking at me with empathy, while the curly-haired son looks at me in disgust. And when my eyes meet his, he smirks.

I continue floundering all the way down to their prisons in a separate extension of the palace. Tired of my refusal to cooperate, Eyepatch decides it best to carry me. They have me stripped from my bag before cuffing my wrists in metal and throwing me into a cell far from the other prisoners. My body is numb, tingling until I'm hyperventilating. My throat tightens, and I want to cry, but my body physically won't produce tears.

There's no sunlight that reaches here. And if there weren't a few lights between the cells, I would be surrounded by darkness. I can hear the guards rummaging through my bag, intrigued with everything they find.

This is it. This is what it's like to be at my lowest. There's no way for anyone to find me, no way for me to get help. I'm alone. Maybe if I had just reached out to my friends more, I'd have someone worried that something's wrong. But instead, I've practically isolated myself from everyone.

Since Luka died, I've barely seen any of them. We meet up every now and again, but it's rare when I am *actually* present. They've all been so worried about me, but I keep pushing them away. They'll all probably think I'm in one of my moods again and assume that's why I'm not at school or why they can't see my location.

Drowning in my thoughts, I realize the day has slipped into night because a guard announces dinner. He doesn't bother to hand the food to me. Just drops it on the ground, kicking it into my cell. The meal, if you can call it that, is barely edible. But I'll take that over starving to death. It might be some form of mashed potatoes and meat, though I'd rather not think about where the meat came from.

This is pathetic. My magik doesn't even work from this cell, not that it would help me when I can't okkar. The entire place is disgusting, and I miss my bed. All I have here is a foam mat and a thin blanket.

*So help me, when I get out of here, I'm finding a way to kill everyone.* I know there's a hex that can kill. Luka taught it to me from some restricted magik book his dad snuck from the Coven archives. It bends the cells in their blood so that you can stop their circulation and end them. I just need to get out of this prison.

I'm bored. There's nothing to do. I don't have a book or my phone. Dissociation and daydreaming only go so far. It seems late enough where I could sleep. At least in sleep, I can dream. Or at the very least, I'll be unconscious without badgering thoughts and fears.

It takes maybe another hour before I can fall asleep, and when I finally do, I dream of the princess. We're having lunch in some cafe I recognize by my house when she tells me she's coming.

I wake up in a panic. Half of me hopes when I open my eyes, I'll be in my bed and this would all be a horrible dream or some wake-up call from my subconscious trying to push me to talk to my friends. But when I see where I am, I'm quickly filled with disappointment.

Loud clanking on the cell doors wakes me. They're so irritating, my ears clog themselves, and my body shivers. Guards are letting us out one by one for bathing while handing out breakfast. Like last night, they just kick over my food. Considering yesterday's dinner, I don't have high expectations for breakfast, but I'm surprised when I see what's on my tray. There are eggs, rice, and a few pieces of meat. It reminds me of childhood breakfasts at my grandparents' house. I gratefully savor the food as someone's feet stand outside my cell, the door unlocking. It's Curly.

"You must feel like a prisoner blessed by your gods. You have the privilege of eating leftover food from the royal's breakfast." He laughs, adding chains onto my cuffs. "It's bathing time. You have ten minutes to wash yourself. Personal soap is provided in the bucket with your towel."

We start ascending the stairs, my hands touching the uneven texture of the walls. Smelling my clothes, I crinkle my nose in disgust. "Am I going to be given a change of clothes?" *Nothing.* "Is this a shower or bath situation? 'Cause I really don't feel like bathing in my own filth and scrubbing my body in dirty water. And I *will* need to change 'cause–"

"Do you ever shut up?" Curly complains, clearly agitated.

*Does everyone really just stand in silence, accepting their punishment with no questions asked?* After the thirtieth step, we reach a door that opens to the bathing room. *Thank fuck there's a shower here.*

Inside the bathing area, he unchains me. I feel on my skin that something about this room must also keep me from using my magik.

For something meant for prisoners, this is decently clean. The floor is stone, and the walls are covered in old artwork. I grab the bucket with soap and a towel. It's new and has the label 'Witch' on it. *At least they're decent enough to not force prisoners to share toiletries.*

I jump into the shower, turning on the water. Not only does the water heat up quickly, but the water pressure isn't the worst. There aren't any products to wash my hair with, so I spend the remaining ten minutes letting the water run down my body after using the soap. Once the time is up, the water shuts off, and the guard calls for me to come.

Wrapping myself in the towel, I decide to ask again, "So is it possible I can get a change of clothes? I really can't be in the same underwear that I was in yesterday, and I think I might have honestly bled through them. Some of us get these things monthly called periods, and I think that mine might have started yesterday."

He looks at me with revulsion. "Fortunately for you, we have been ordered to give you a new set of clothes. Including new undergarments."

After handing me the clothes, he turns around, giving me privacy to change. I definitely lied about having my period, but I was hoping it would gross him out enough to give me new clothes. And it worked.

"Thank you. I know working must be difficult," I express with a new tactic, hoping pleasantries will give me access to more privileges. "What, with having to deal with rude prisoners all day. But I appreciate you turning around, giving me privacy."

Taking my time changing before being back in chains, I remain in awe of the room. When I finish, I tap Curly, signaling he can turn around. He looks exhausted, like he didn't get any sleep. Bags permanently set under his eyes, barely able to look anything less than determined.

Once exiting the room, we go back towards the cells. Halfway through the stairs, I decide to try my luck talking to him again. "So, since I'm sure I'll be seeing a lot more of you, I think it would be better to know each other's names. Y'know, so I don't keep referring to you in my mind as Curly. What is it?"

"Kabir." He treks on, walking with no follow-up or asking me what my name is. I guess that's fair since he has no obligation to be kind to me.

"Well my name's Arabella. I noticed you looked tired. Did you not sleep? Did the king give you shit for putting the princess in danger?"

"I liked you better when you did not talk out of fear," he says while continuing down the steps.

What does he expect from me? This is the first source of contact I've had in almost a day. "Well, one of my many talents outside of magik, is my inability to shut up in uncomfortable situations.

Sometimes I can, but being that I've had nothing to do for the past however many hours, I think you'll do for company."

As we reach my cell, he unchains me, not turning or saying a word.

Left alone, I think of my dream from last night and wonder if it was something that was actually happening, or if it was my silly unconsciousness imagining things that carry no meaning. I'm still confused as to why the men at the throne looked at me like that yesterday. Possibly, like the king, one was curious about my presence, whereas the curly-haired one looked like he wanted me dead.

I spend a long while playing scenarios in my head about how I would escape, what I'll do when I'm out, why everyone by the throne was so attractive, how I'll make everyone regret putting me in here. There's no one in the neighboring cells to talk to, therefore no one to share my thoughts with. It's not like Kabir will come here to have a conversation, so I just accept my probable spiral into madness.

A door opening from the top of the stairs can be heard. I'm hoping it's time for lunch, but instead, I hear what sounds to be the princess' voice from the guards' table.

"Princess, you're not to be down here. If His Majesty knew you were, he would have our heads," Kabir says in a paranoid tone.

Footsteps start to become louder, approaching my cell. It's only when they reach me that the princess responds. "Don't worry, Kabir. My father himself asked me to talk to her since I was there, after all. There's no need to fret. Besides, she's behind a cell in a prison that stops any of her powers from being useful. How much harm could she really do?"

Kabir's lips thin before nodding hesitantly and leaving to grab the princess something to sit on. She looks at me to give me a smile and wink, telling me that she definitely won't be asking questions for the king.

When he returns with a blanket for the princess, he sets it down, and she thanks him before he walks off. When he's out of view, she pulls something wrapped in a napkin from her jacket and hands it to me. It's a piece of bread.

*I knew there was a reason I liked her.* I immediately thank her, then begin devouring the food.

"So..." she says, a long pause causing silence, "you're really a Magik, huh?"

"Yeah. I'm a witch." Looking up from my bread, I give her a look. "Why do you keep saying Magik instead of witch?" I ask out of curiosity, but also because everyone knows females are called witches.

She thinks about answering as if this is a sensitive topic. Like it's a minefield and any misstep will cause an explosion. "Well your people are called Magiks, are they not? Males are sorcerers and females are witches? I would assume not everyone wants to be categorized as one or the other, so I tend to just use your proper name until I know."

I look at her without saying a word. It's never occurred to me how much being referred to as one or the other could be so limiting. Even if people don't identify as a man or woman, they just tend to call themselves whichever term they're more comfortable with.

"Well, I'm a witch. But, I also don't care if you call me a Magik." I take another bite of the bread and swallow before speaking up again. "How'd you know? There's no way you took one look at me and knew I was Magik. I didn't do any spell that would have shown any remnants of my magik. So, how?"

"We're Fae. We can sense magik on creatures. You didn't seem like a Merfolk since you don't have colorful hair or bright eyes. You're a normal height, have two eyes and legs without hooves, so you're not from Gigantia. There was really only one logical explanation. Can you not sense magik on people?"

Moving my head from side to side, I look around, wondering if this is some kind of trap. If she's setting me up for a bigger question. "No. At least I don't think we can. Sometimes I get gut feelings about if someone has any magik in them, but that's really all it is. Intuition, I guess."

She nods. "We haven't been properly introduced. I'm Esme. And you are?"

"Arabella."

"You're not very talkative, are you?"

Sucking in my cheeks, I bite them, trying to resist from saying something without thinking. I take another bite of the bread, keeping my eyes on the floor. "You were in my dream last night." I pause, waiting for her reaction. "You told me you were coming to me today, and I thought it meant nothing, but you're here now."

Her eyes flicker towards the guards' table before looking back at mine. "I have the ability to appear in people's dreams. My family all have abilities. I figured you were lonely, so I wanted to join you. It was the least I could do after my father sent you here with no reasoning. Plus, it helped that my father asked me to."

More moments of silence pass as I finish my bread. When I take the last bite, I turn to the princess. "Why do you talk like that?" She looks at me with knitted brows. "I just mean, there's no way you don't know how most people talk. You speak so proper. Is that a royal thing, or a Fae thing, or?"

"It's more of a performance," she responds with a breathy laugh. "I don't normally talk like that, but being a princess, there's a certain level of expectation people have of my speech, especially my parents and the guards. Most of my family don't speak so articulately. Sometimes, a few of us go back to the Human Lands to see what's new. It's mostly the boys that actually speak with such mannerisms. Our father tends to send them to the lower courts' rulers, but he forbids the daughters from leaving the grounds. It pretty much just resulted in a bunch of rebellious daughters." She sighs, then turns to me with a faint smile.

If there is anyone who would likely be my ally, it might be her. We bond for hours about shared family experiences, and when dinner is called for her, she promises to come back tomorrow.

Repeating the routine of yesterday, the morning consists of breakfast and a shower. The only difference is that today, I know for a fact I have company to look forward to. Kabir brings me breakfast and actually hands it to me this time. I leave him to his peace, but for once, he decides to say more than a few words to me.

"The princess seems to have taken a liking to you," he comments out of nowhere.

"Uh, yeah. She's very sweet. It was nice having someone to talk to again, even if it was for a few hours."

He waits for me outside the door while I shower. As he's rechaining me, I toy with the possibility he will carry a conversation with me. "Are you her personal guard or just in charge of the prisoners? I know you were with her when I found you, but it seems like since then, you've just been down here with us," I say as he takes me back to the cells.

Letting out a heavy breath, he speaks. "It's punishment. I failed my duty of keeping her on the grounds of the estate and put her safety in jeopardy. So as such, the king thought it right for me to watch you. If you harm me, it's fitting to show you were capable of doing that to the princess."

My mouth opens for a response, but I immediately shut it. What can I really say in response to that?

I sit on my mat, fidgeting with my hands as he locks my cell. It's nice to have someone to talk to and keep my mind from falling into despairing thoughts.

By the time lunch rolls around and Princess Esme isn't there, I start to worry she isn't coming. *Maybe I said something wrong.* I immediately snap myself out of that. I have to keep reminding myself not to indulge in these thoughts, or my stay here will be a lot harder than it already is.

Just as I'm about to take a nap, I hear the door open with three female voices coming from the top of the stairs. Giggles and loud steps are echoing as they make their way down. I recognize the princess' voice telling Kabir she's here once again to see me.

"Why have you brought Lady Dyana and Lady Isadora?" he asks, giving her time to come up with an excuse.

She's putting on her proper princess act again. "I assume if there are more girls, the prisoner will likely share more. It's important to find out all the details, is it not?"

"*Uh-huh,*" he says, unconvinced. "Just make sure you're not caught. I refuse to endure more punishment from your father."

They thank him, shuffling towards my cell.

I send a small wave to the princess and the two others. One of the women is taller than us all, with pink hair and brows. Her eyes light with a pale blue and full, rosy lips. The other is the shortest of the three with dark, aqua-blue hair and eyebrows. She looks shorter than me by maybe three inches and has bright white eyes with golden specks in them. Both wear a curved, T-shaped pendant with an orchid charm dangling from the bottom.

"You don't have to stand there awkwardly, Arabella. I brought my cousins here so you'd have more people to talk to since we don't know when you're getting out of here. This is Isadora." She points to the one with pink hair. "And this is Dyana," she says while motioning to the girl with blue hair and round ears like mine.

"Hi, I'm Arabella. Sorry, I know this is probably a weird question, but Dyana and Isadora, are you both Merpeople? Princess Esme told me yesterday that they tend to have bright hair and eyes."

Isadora lets out a blithe laugh before catching her breath and tucking her hair behind her pointed ear. "Dyana is. She's a Mermaid and was adopted into our family. I just change my hair," she says, combing a hand through it. "Hair dye being created is one of human's best creations, but it's even better when Fae have a way to make it permanent." She reaches out a hand through the cell bars to shake mine. "And please, call me Isa. Mainly the guards call me Isadora. Or my father when he's upset with me."

The princess chimes in. "Also, please do not call me or my siblings by our titles, Arabella. If we're going to be friends, I don't want you treating me like I'm a higher rank than you. It's Esme. Just Esme."

I nod my head and reach my hand outside the cells towards

Dyana. "Do you have any names you prefer to be called, or is Dyana okay?"

"Dyana's already short for something. My true name is Dyandraina, but no one other than my family knows that. Them and you, I suppose."

Kabir hands lunch to all the prisoners before returning to us with specially made food from the kitchen. Sandwiches made from meats, cheeses, and sweet fruit on the side. They all begin eating as Esme hands my food through the cell bars. "Did you like the clothes you have for today, Ara?"

*Why did she call me Ara? She doesn't know me like that. Only my Magik friends call me that. Was she the one who gave the orders to give me fresh clothes? It wasn't like I saw other prisoners getting clothes as nice as mine.* I nod. "Yes! Thank you so much! They're really comfortable. How did you know my sizes?"

"I just guessed honestly," she responds with a smile.

Isa looks at her and lifts her brow, prompting Esme to confess. "Okay, fine. I stole them from my sister's room after guessing your size. I know it's a bit tight, but I figured it was better than staying in the ugly clothes they give the rest of the prisoners."

"So I'm not just a prisoner, but a *high-class* prisoner," I joke.

Prisoners don't receive this type of hospitality, and I almost feel bad for them. They've been in here longer, meanwhile, I've been here for about three full days getting fresh clothes, visits from the royal family, and food made for me from the kitchen. I shouldn't dwell on it, because why should I care about them? They're strangers to me, and I didn't *technically* do anything wrong.

When we finish the food, Kabir comes by to collect the remains, telling us that there will be a guard change before dinner. He suggests they leave before the change since they likely won't be as lenient as he is.

"So you seem to have met enough of our family. What's your family like?" Isa asks before taking a drink of her water.

"Well uh, like Dyana, I was adopted, but I honestly look enough like my parents that unless you really knew me, you probably wouldn't have thought otherwise. I don't have any clue who my birth parents are, but it's obvious at least one was Asian. Maybe Chinese, based on my last name and features." I take a drink of water. "My foster dad's Filipino, and my mom's half White, which is why no one asks about me being adopted, since I'm so pale. People just assume I got my dad's features with my mom's complexion. My older brother somehow looks close enough to me, but he's pretty tan like my dad. It's probably why no one ever questions us being related." I laugh awkwardly. "My mom's a witch, so she always knew what I was when she adopted me. She gave up living with Magiks to live a normal life with my dad. I guess she knew my parents. When they died, I was a few months old, so she took me in."

I take in a breath before continuing. "They tried to keep me from using magik 'cause my brother somehow ended up with no abilities, but as I got older and unable to control my emotions, I couldn't control my magik either. I'd accidentally set things on fire, send books flying off shelves, make other kids fall down flights of stairs. When I was fourteen, they decided to put me in this Magik school in San Francisco. It was like a boarding school, so I'd see them on holidays and some weekends, since we lived close enough. But other than that, I'd live with my friend Juliette on campus."

They all listen to me very carefully, absorbing every word. It's possible I'm oversharing, but not enough is being said to have anything used against me. I don't know them well enough to confide in them or tell them things they could use against me in the future. I learned my lesson on that topic. Only share things that won't hurt you unless you really trust that person, and even then, proceed with caution.

Keeping in mind that we don't have much longer together, we laugh about how fun it will be for them to take me into town when I'm let out. I play along since they're being so kind, but I know when I'm free, I'll never see them again.

After bantering for hours, Kabir comes back to tell us the guard change is in ten minutes, so the girls need to leave. I say my goodbyes to them as they promise to return tomorrow. At the close of the door, I call Kabir back over to my cell.

He walks over, offering nothing, so I look at him and smile. "I just wanted to thank you for letting them come talk to me. I know that by now, you knew they were coming down for their own fun and not for information. I appreciate the nice gesture."

The Fae doesn't respond. He doesn't even acknowledge what I said as he walks back to the desk.

Maybe I won't kill everyone here when I leave. Maybe I really can just go back home.

# II

## Family Rankings

Cassius

Supper is running uncomfortably long. The entirety of our family sits in the family dining hall at what's usually an empty, long table. With five siblings, four cousins, my uncle, mother, and father, there are thirteen of us joined.

We eat the first course in a long silence until the main course arrives. Father had said that tonight we must dine as a whole. Rarely do we eat together unless someone dies, or there is important news being delivered. For the sake of not having to spend more time together, I'm hoping it's the latter.

After the main course is served, father rises from his chair. The clinks from a fork hitting his glass turn our attention, waiting for him to speak. "I'm truly glad everyone could make it tonight. As we know, there have been some problems within Ifaeris."

*Fae have been going missing, and some have turned up dead. "Problems" is putting it lightly.*

My father continues. "However, I have now come to a decision that may benefit us all. We have a witch at our disposal." He pauses, raising his glass. "It is no secret Magiks and Fae have not gotten along for millennia. They have taken issue with our people, so there is reason to believe they are the root of our missing Fae. I propose we use this witch to our advantage and have her solve who is behind the kidnappings."

The weight of his announcement is met with quiet stillness. The only ones who knew of the witch are mother, father, Esme, Ezra, and myself. I'm thoroughly surprised that father would announce her existence to the whole family. In fact, until he spoke, I had been under the impression that she was dead, and we would never hear of her again.

I mumble under my breath, "And why would she help us?"

"She'll have a choice. By aiding us, I will grant her freedom," he returns, scowling at me.

"Well," mother interrupts while sipping her wine, "if that is all settled, may we enjoy this lovely dinner together?"

"Of course. Eat children, for tomorrow we work towards ending this issue."

While eating, the women giggle about their day. How they snuck around behind father's back, tricking guards. *Must be fortunate to speak of rebelling at the dinner table without father reprimanding you.* Not that it troubles me much since I lost his favor long ago.

Being a prince has its privileges. I can do whatever I wish due to my title alone. Father thinks me rotten, the common fae think I'm incapable of kindness, my eldest brother thinks me weak. With a reputation such as that, I have no need to be disingenuous.

"Were you going to finish that?" a voice asks. I look up from my plate, my younger sister smiling up at me.

"No. I'm not that hungry tonight, Cel. If you want my corn, take it."

While I pour my food onto my sister's plate, I sit in solitude as everyone socializes. As I take my eyes from the table, mother is watching me, sending a look to ask if I am okay. I nod my head, and she returns to eating. Despite not actually being my birth mother, she cares for me.

At dinner's end, I stroll outside into the back garden to wander with my own thoughts, only to find Esme, Isadora, and Dyana talking. Just as I am about to turn back inside, I hear Esme calling for me. I groan, begrudgingly moving towards them. Dyana is laughing as I approach them, Isadora asking for my thoughts on the witch.

"Why would I have any thoughts on her? It is not as if I know her."

The mortal is nothing to me.

Dyana, now calm, responds. Saying, "Yes, but you were there when she was brought in, weren't you?"

I let out a breath. This meaningless talk has nothing to do with me. Better use–or rather, more entertaining use–of my time ought to be had. "I suppose."

"And she's pretty," Esme responds immediately.

Isadora joins in. "Like really pretty."

"Honestly!" Dyana squeals.

"How would you two even know?" I raise an eyebrow in suspicion, to catch them in their own befalling. "You weren't there, so how would you know of her likeness?" I pause. "*Unless, of course,*" I say, grinning at them, "were you three sneaking down to the prison cells to see our prisoner?"

They stop in their place, realizing they unintentionally revealed their foolishness to me without even thinking, though that much I already knew. "You know, father might not be thrilled when he finds out the precious girls were acting sisterly to someone who possibly intended on killing one of you."

"She wasn't going to hurt me and you know it. She was terrified in the throne room," Esme snaps, eyes shooting at me. "Wipe that shit-eating grin off your face, you worm. I know you're not going to rat me out to father. You know he wouldn't believe you anyway. Not when he's too worried about the safety of the women in this family." At the end of her statement, furious, she storms back inside.

Perhaps my sister is right. No, I know she is. Those of us remaining now stand awkwardly for a long moment before Isadora and Dyana decide to go to their estate.

Rather than following my sister, I stroll around the garden, basking in the moonlight and privacy away from the clatter that is my family. I pick one of the roses from the bush, bringing it to my nose before tossing it. Laying my body on the grass, I stare at the sky for minutes before getting up and making my way towards my friend, Korine's, estate.

Time moves sluggishly as I wait for her to answer the door, freezing from the night temperature. At the sight of the door opening, I rush inside and up the stairs to her room. To give us privacy, Korine closes and locks the door before asking what is going on, to which I explain the events of the past days.

She holds my hand as I tell her about what happened tonight.

When she starts to kiss along my jaw and slips her hand inside my shirt, I halt everything I am saying, and press her into the bed, mounting on top of her. Lifting her shirt from her body, I trail kisses down her chest towards her stomach.

"Do you really want this?" she whispers softly.

I climb up, putting my lips on hers, shoving my tongue into her mouth while unfastening my pants.

"I need this." I breathe heavily into her ear. "I need a release, and you are going to give it to me." I grind my hips into hers and squeeze her breast, eliciting sharp whimpers.

*This. This is what I need.*

Korine and I lack a conventional friendship. We had one, until we became lovers at seventeen. She was always the one who had been at my side, and I thought we understood each other. We cared not for the responsibility of power and shared contempt for others in Ifaeris.

Our affair ran harmoniously until one night when we were twenty, and I saw her with Ezra.

*My family wanted to take a trip to the seaside of Aquatius, so I invited her to come. Uninterested by the events of the day, I left to acquire us wine, but when I came back, I saw the two of them. His hand was around her neck, kissing her lips, her fingers gripping his cock. I smashed the bottle on the rock beside them, which seemed to startle only her.*

*Korine jumped up and begged. "Wait, Cassius, we are not romantically involved, I promise!"*

*I laughed, sneering at her. "Oh really? Because it seems quite obvious you two are involved, considering he's still stuffing himself back in his pants. Why play on the specifics of being romantic? How long has this been going on?" Silence. "HOW LONG?"*

*"Five months," Korine choked.*

*"FIVE MONTHS? So for the past five months, while you were saying you loved me and we were planning a life together, you were bedding my brother?"*

*Ezra got in between me and Korine, creating a barrier. "Cassius, you know better than to compete with me."*

*Pushing him down, I erupted. "You do not get to speak."*

*When Korine grabbed his arm to make sure he was okay, I could only stare in disbelief.*

*I turned from them, willing my wings to summon and take me far from them.*

*"Cas, wait. Please." Korine ran up to me, trying to catch her breath.*

*"What?"*

*"I love you, I do. But I care for him. You and I know we just aren't working."*

*"Very well. But when he breaks your heart, when he chooses someone else or discards you like rotten fruit, when he makes you hurt in a pain so excruciating you cannot bear the sight of him, you are not to come back to me. I will laugh in your face and slam the door." I flew into the air, heading home to Nexus Palace.*

Korine is not what I want anymore, but our friendship has remained the same. After Ezra inevitably left her without so much of an explanation, she came sobbing to me. I did exactly what I promised and shut my door in her face. Over the past year, we've reconciled our friendship, and tonight was the first time that we had been intimate since we had ended our courtship.

I knew I would regret this from the moment I did not stop her mouth from moving along my jaw, and yet I still took her. I should have just found another woman to satisfy my problem, but Korine is simple. With her, I know I can do this with no hesitation. She's familiar.

I wait until she drifts off into sleep before flying back home. It is well into the midst of the night, so I trudge up the stairs and make my way towards the bedchamber, but am stopped by my eldest sister, Maude.

"And where were you?" she asks me in the same manner as a mother catching their child sneaking in.

"At Korine's. We were talking."

"Talking, huh? Then why is your shirt inside out?" She cocks an eyebrow with the corner of her mouth lifting.

"It matters not. If she misinterprets whatever occurred tonight, that is her own doing, not mine," I say with no regard to tonight's events. "And why are you wandering in at this hour? You look as if you've just returned as well. Were you perhaps with Gideon again?"

"That- That doesn't matter either," she stutters. "If I wanted to go out on a date as a grown woman, I am allowed to do so."

I laugh at her remark. One we both know our father would disapprove of. "I'm sure our father would be thrilled that his first daughter is courting a man with long hair on half his head and a shaved half on the other. Is it serious? Should I wake him and inform the wondrous news?"

"Whatever, you roach. If you don't tell, I won't question

whatever fucked up ordeal you're putting Korine through." She stares me down.

"I have already told you," I say, meeting her stare, "if she still has feelings for me, that is her own issue. I have made it perfectly clear that I want nothing romantic from her after Ezra left her. I'd say a little torment is justified." I begin walking towards my room. "Goodnight, dear sister. I hope you enjoyed your night with your miscreant plaything."

Shutting the door, I grab my underwear, bringing it with me into the bathroom. I step into the shower, relishing the hot water falling on my skin.

Slipping into my black, silk bed sheets, I am reminded that we are sending that witchling to her death by having her track whomever is taking the Fae. *That is not my problem to worry about.* I just so happen to be granted the privilege to enjoy when the news is being delivered to her.

Consistent knocking breaks me from my slumber. I rise from my bed and drag myself to the door, rubbing my eyes.

*It is far too early for anything important to be occurring.*

Upon opening the door, I find Isaak, one of the guards, waiting. "Excuse me, Your Highness, but the king has requested that you, Princess Esme, and Prince Ezra join him for breakfast."

"Is it a request or a demand?"

"Request, sir. Though he said it in a way that felt more like a demand." He stands in his place, but it is evident that he is afraid to deliver this message to me.

"Very well," I say. He continues staring at me, lingering for a verbal dismissal. "You may go now."

I close my door, throwing on sufficient clothing before walking from the hallway and down the stairs towards the dining hall where my father, mother, brother, and sister are waiting. Company of this size cannot present itself as pleasant news for myself.

"Well, well, well," Ezra ridicules, "look who finally decided to get out of bed and join us."

"It's barely past nine," I shoot back. I turn to my father, who does nothing to inform of this early gathering. "Why were we all called? Is this about the witch?"

My father glances up from his plate, unsurprised by my tardiness. "Yes. As we discussed last night, we are going to let her out of the prisons today and inform her of the conditions of her freedom. Since you were all within the room when she was brought in, I want you there when we inform her of the situation at hand."

I roll my eyes to the back of my head. *This couldn't have been told to us at a later time?* I truly had to be woken up early for this?

Taking a sip of water, my father reads my mind, glaring at me and opening his mouth once more. "I'm telling you this now because I want you to free your schedules of anything you had planned today. To ensure you are free when I send the guards for you. Is that clear?"

Ezra turns his head towards me and back to father. "Yes, sir. We will not be late." He looks at me. "At least I know I won't."

"Good boy."

Esme turns to me and raises her eyebrow, letting out a stifled huff instead of laughter. Smiling at her, I snort in agreement.

As we continue to eat our breakfast, father discusses the agenda for the day. He rambles on about how this will aid in bringing him more respect from the Fae and goes on to say he is sending more guards into town to question the common fae. I sit in silence, attempting to avoid the gaze of my mother and any trouble I could cause with my father.

Lost in my own thoughts, I am shaken when I hear my father's booming voice from the end of the table. "Speak, son. You have yet to comment on our plan. Or have you decided that you are above contributing to your family duties as a prince?"

"I did not think you cared for my input."

"Do you expect to thrive off your title for the rest of your days? To live off luxuries without paying any mind to responsibilities?"

"I have no care for what is going on. It affects me not, so why should I share my ideas when you are not going to pay any mind to what I have to say?" I respond casually.

"You take that tone with me and do not show any ambition towards anything you want," he scolds. "You may be a prince, you may be able to get away with things with our subjects, but you are ungrateful and a waste of the Spiritus bloodline."

Tension fills in the room. Blinking feels as if it would cause noise. Father and I have yet to break eye contact.

After what seems like minutes, my mother clears her throat, breaking the silence. "What your father means to say is that we worry for you. You spend all day drinking and entertaining yourself with common fae, seeing us only when absolutely required. We want you to show some effort in royal duties."

"No," our father silences her. "I stand behind what I said. He needs to start showing he's worthy to carry on the bloodline. If he cannot, he may leave this palace and live amongst the common fae like his brother."

"Elliot," mother reprimands, "that is *enough*."

"No, mother. He explained his thoughts on me quite well. I

think I'll take my leave." I exit the dining room, walking up the stairs and nearly stepping into my bedroom, when I hear Ezra's footsteps behind me. I stop. "What do you want, Ezra?"

"I know father can be harsh with you at times, but he's trying to push you to live up to your potential. He wants you to mature, but you keep disregarding everything he says. You become too defensive, and rather than heeding his advice, you act out as a child would." He puts his hand on my shoulder, turning me around to face him. "I know you are clever. I've watched you charm everyone when you were in lessons. You once persuaded Lord Tanzin in father's favor. You are capable of being what he wants you to be."

I shrug my shoulder back, removing his hand from it. Lord Tanzin was only swayed into father's favor due to my relationship with his daughter. "And who says I want to be anything like what our father wishes me to be? I am not going to kneel to his every word, just because I want to be king. I know it is why *you* kiss the ground he walks on, but that just makes you a desperate son, begging for attention."

His face turns hardened, grave with controlled anger. "Perhaps your attitude is why he will never pick you to be his rightful heir."

"You fail to realize, a title does not a king make. I care not for the crown, nor have I for a long while, but you might want to take that into consideration when he chooses you to be his successor."

His eyes scan up and down, sizing me up. "I'll make sure to take note of that, brother. Just be sure you're at the meeting today. We cannot have this witch undermining our father's power. Your absence may prove him weak if even his son cannot be bothered to show up for important meetings."

"If he is so distracted by the absence of an individual who does not care to hold power, does it truly give him credibility to take charge of the missing Fae?"

His face has yet to change expression. He is in a better mood than most days. "Just give me your word you'll be there."

I glare at him. From his posture, I know he will make sure I am in that throne room, even if he has to carry me in himself and secure me to the floor. "Fine. But I make no promise to support everything father says, nor will I offer any suggestions that would cause him to chastise me in front of everyone in the room. I've had enough of that for one day."

"Just keep to yourself, and it should be fine."

"You have my word. Now if you will excuse me, I have sleep to return to, after it was so rudely interrupted." I tread into my bedroom, stripping from my clothing and climbing into bed. Casting shadows from my hands towards the curtains, I shut out all light that enters the room.

# III

## Choices That Aren't Really Choices

Arabella

It takes a few seconds for my eyes to adjust when the cell door is opened, and when they finally do, I notice Kabir reaching out a hand. The expression on his face looks somewhat concerned as opposed to his counterpart, who shows nothing but indifference.

"The king has requested to see you," Kabir says. "You are to be sent up to the throne room post haste after their lunch. We are to have you bathed and made presentable."

Just like the previous days, the guards chain me before letting me exit my cell. Kabir leads the two of us up the stairs, and rather than stopping at the usual bathing room, we go through the doors, out into the sunlight, where my eyes aren't taking it too well.

"Am I finally being let go?" I blurt.

"Not that I am aware of. The king hadn't given much detail, other than you were to be taken to him after his lunch."

*If he is ordering for my release, that might explain why he wants to see me.*

I drag my feet along the grass with the chains weighing heavy on my body. Rotating my head in every direction, I take in the details of the grounds that I hadn't been able to appreciate during my last walk through it. The abundance of green grass, the forest that I had been brought from, a garden with a small, flowery hedge maze on my left, and a fountain mirrored to its right, where a woman pours water from a vase. It smells like the freshest spring I've ever lived through. Finally, we get closer to the stone road walkway that leads up to the back entrance.

Kabir takes me past the main staircases and through a hallway before we ascend another flight of stairs on our left. Thoughts rack through my brain as to what's going on, but I can't really give any answers to myself. Once at the top, he brings me into a bathroom.

"What's this? Why are we in a bathroom?"

"Like I said earlier, you are to make yourself presentable before your consultation with the king."

"Yeah I get that part, but why didn't you just take me to the usual shower room?"

"You must wash your hair and be rid of your current garments. The prisoner toiletries aren't enough. You have twenty minutes to shower and change into these," he says, handing me a new set of clothes. "Knock when you are ready to be taken to the waiting room."

After freeing me from both my chains and cuffs, he closes the door. As I look around, the bathroom is full of scented body soaps, lotion, and hair products prepared for me in the shower. In the corner, there's a small bag with my makeup. I remove my clothing and set my new set of clothes onto the toilet when a note falls out.

*Remember to use the washcloth*
*+ skincare products we put in*
*there for you*

*-Esme, Isa, and Dyana* ♥♥♥

I smile at the note, setting it down to turn on the water, gathering myself as I wait for it to heat. After stepping in, I let the water rinse me for several minutes before applying shampoo and lathering it by massaging my head.

*Fuck, it feels good to wash my hair again.* Washing off the last bit of lavender soap, I step out and wrap a towel around my body, going towards the sink to brush my teeth.

*Knock. Knock. Knock.*

"It's been twenty minutes. It is time for you to be escorted down," Kabir's voice informs from outside the door.

"I'm almost done. Just changing into my clothes. Give me like five minutes, please."

"Five minutes is all you get."

Dressing myself in my crop top and miniskirt as quickly as possible, I magik on some makeup before grabbing the hairbrush to the right of the sink. When I attempt to fix my front bangs as best I can, I realize I need a finer tooth comb, so I give up. I gather my dirty clothes and towels before opening the door and handing them to Kabir.

After he rechains me, we start towards the stairs. A million things are going through my mind. My heart is beating faster with each step. *Imagine if I just fell down this flight of stairs right now. That would probably hurt.*

"You're being uncharacteristically quiet," Kabir mentions offhandedly.

"Well I'm about to talk to the king and see if he's letting me go or not. There's a lot on my mind."

"When has that stopped you from voicing your thoughts since you got here?"

*Fair enough.* When we reach the bottom of the steps, he guides us into a space that stops to the right of the throne room.

I'm sat on a couch by Kabir before he pulls up a chair by the door. The heaviness of the metal beginning to take a toll on my wrists, I try adjusting them in any way I can, but it's pointless.

"Is this really necessary?"

Kabir shoots his head in my direction. "Pardon?"

"Do you really need to keep these on me? I mean, I haven't tried to escape in the four days I've been here, and there's no point in me trying now when I see the king soon. Don't you think that if I wanted to try something by now, I would've?"

He examines my face, deciphering if I am being serious or not. "Are you under the impression the suppression cuffs keep you only from okkaring?"

I stare at him.

He smiles at the ground and lets out a *hmph.* "The cuffs are a restraint to keep you from using magik. With them placed on you, you are without your power." As he glances at me, he grunts with irritation. "Oh, don't look at me like that. It works on all. Abilities do not work when these are placed upon anyone."

While I burst into a fit of laughter, Kabir rushes towards me. "What? Do you need a healer?"

"No, it's not that." I wheeze. This is good, too good. "It's just, you went from calling me a creature and insulting me, to *possibly* enjoying my company and being lenient with me in the prisons."

He turns away, defensively. "I do not."

"Yeah? Then why did you give me extra time in the bathroom? Or let the girls sneak down to talk to me when you knew by the second time they did it, they were coming down to befriend me?"

Narrowing his eyes, he faces me, arching a brow. "Perhaps I believe you to be as innocent as you say you are."

A sharp gasp slips, and giggles break out from me. He sends me a lazy smile, and due to my struggle of controlling my facial expressions, I unintentionally send one back.

Towards the end of lunch, Eyepatch comes into the room to tell us that the king is ready to see us. Kabir stands from his seat, helping me up. "Thank you, Gavin."

*Gavin?* Not exactly the name I was expecting from Eyepatch. At least he has a more stylish one now.

Placed between the two guards, we enter the throne room, where I'm met with the king, queen, Esme, and the two men from before. The shorter one with straight hair watches me like I'm a piece of meat, whereas the curly-haired one still looks at me with disdain.

*What is his DEAL?*

In contrast to my last appearance, there's now about eight other guards stationed around the room, some standing near the statues by the door. Gavin and Kabir, upon us reaching the bottom of the stairs, bend their knees to the floor to bow. At the king's signal, the two men beside me rise. The king shoots his cerulean eyes in my direction as his mouth widens into an eerie grin. "Hello, witch. How have our guards been treating you in our prison? With respect, I hope?"

*Gods, this man likes faking manners.* "Yes, Your Majesty. They have all made sure I am taken care of, and there have been no problems between us."

"That is a delight to hear. I have a proposition for you, my dear witch. But first, your name."

"Arabella. Arabella Huǒ, sir."

"Airabella, I have a–"

I cut him off immediately. I just said my name, and he already mispronounced it in disrespect. "Arabella. As in, 'Are uh you letting me go'?"

"Ah, well Arabella, I have a proposal." He announces this with such vigor, you'd think he was making a deal he already knows is closed. "In exchange for your freedom, you are to help solve an issue that has been going on within the lands of Ifaeris."

Curious, I eye him with suspicion at his tranquil reaction to my outburst. "What's the issue?"

He stands from his seat and begins to pace back and forth. "You see, Fae have started to go missing within the past few months. Considering you are a witch, and given our history with your people, we have reason to believe a Magik is behind this, with a personal agenda." He pauses for a moment before stopping to face me. "We want you to aid in finding who this Magik is and put an end to their terror."

"And if I say no?"

"That has quite the easy solution. We kill you right now. In this room. Guards?"

All the guards surround me, drawing swords and pointing them at different parts of my body. Kabir looks at me with hesitation.

*TRAITOR.*

"Father, *no!*" Esme shrieks. She runs down the stairs towards me, trying to pry the guards away. "She's done nothing wrong. You cannot mean to kill her."

"I had not intended to," he replies nonchalantly. "I'm giving her an offer to choose her own fate. She may choose to help us and gain her freedom, or she can end her life right here."

"That's not much of a choice," I backfire. "You're sending me to my death with both options. It's a double-edged sword."

He chuckles with a planned sadism. I'm terrified of what he would do if I made a sudden move. "Maybe. But at least this way you may die as a guest within the Disaris grounds."

What feels like minutes pass as I take every word into consideration, weighing every option. "Fine. I'll help you on your little kidnapping quest."

"Wonderful! Now, you will be given a bedchamber on the second floor within the west wing with my other children. You're to be treated as a guest and therefore are free to roam the lands, coming and going as you please, so long as you are back here every night. You are to wear these earrings at all times, as it is a tracker to ensure we are aware of your location. If you break these rules or make attempts to escape, we will hunt you down and end you in your place. Do you understand?"

"Yes, Your Majesty."

"Fantastic. Guards, please remove her chains."

As the guards unchain me, I feel two of them pierce small, hooped earrings into each side of my upper earlobe. Some blood drips, a bit trickling down my ears onto the floor and making them throb slightly. The king turns to me yet again as he sits down on the throne. "One more thing. You are to work with Cassius on this. He will help you adjust to our lands and be my informant on every move you make towards fixing this issue."

The man on his left snaps his neck towards the king. "*What?*"

This is the first time he's shown any emotion, outside of disgust for me. He clearly wants to get out of here and wasn't expecting to work with me. His body goes rigid, eyes filling with rage.

"You heard me," the king scolds. "You are to work with Lady Arabella. You had said this morning that I do not heed your opinions, so I am offering you an opportunity to remedy that."

While they argue, my attention is captured by the queen. Now I'm sure she's Esme's mom. They share many of the same features. While Esme has a lighter bronze and golden tone to her, the queen has a dark, ebony complexion that glistens beautifully as the sun shines on her. I am pulled from my thoughts when Cassius storms out of the room, smirking at me as he passes me. Like he has horrible ways to torture me in store.

Meanwhile, the other man at the king's side won't take his eyes off me, making it clear that he does in fact see me as someone they can use at their will.

When the king dismisses the room, I'm given back my belongings, immediately putting the knife in my bra. I ask for the rest of my things to be brought to my room as I step outside for some fresh air.

It isn't until I'm by the garden's entrance that I hear my name being called. Glancing behind me, I see it's Cassius coming in my direction. Being that he isn't someone I want to be in the company of, I try to ignore him, walking faster, past the gardens and towards the forest. A hand grips my wrist, stopping me in my tracks and twisting me in his direction. I don't know how he reached me so quickly.

"Don't touch me," I warn as I turn my head. My body tingles, going numb in his grip. Cassius is staring at me, finding entertainment in my discomfort.

He tightens his hold on me, and I respond by twisting my right hand around, squeezing his wrist that holds mine. I swiftly switch my left hand to grab his wrist and take my knife from its place. My right hand holds it tight, the blade's tip up against his throat, while my left keeps our arms against his chest. At the knife's base, it presses near a black birthmark on the side of his left neck that appears like foggy mist. I'm still nearly half a foot shorter than him, even with my heels.

The sound of running can be heard in the near distance, accompanied by Dyana's voice.

"Arabella," she pants.

"What?" I yell, not taking my eyes off him.

"That's Cassius."

*Breath.*

"My cousin."

*Breath.*

"The king's son."

His lips lift, starting to form a smirk as he tosses his head back, brushing away the hair that fell to his right brow. There's a scar at the arch. One I didn't notice before.

I roll my eyes and push him away, accidentally cutting the skin just below his neck. "Don't ever touch me without my permission again."

He runs his finger across the cut, collecting blood onto his finger and sucking it clean off. "Worry not," he purrs, coming closer. I can feel the heat from his breath as he brings his lips to my ears. "Next time it will not be me asking permission to touch you."

My eyes widen slightly as he turns back to walk into the palace. I'm frozen. Extremely grateful he doesn't see my reaction.

"Aren't you supposed to give her a tour of the grounds?" Dyana yells at him.

Not missing a beat and without breaking his stride, he responds over his shoulders, "Since you are such good friends with her, why not take on my responsibility?"

Dyana groans. "Sorry about him. He's not the most pleasant person to be around."

"Well unfortunately for me, I think I'm going to be spending most of my time here with him." I sigh through bared teeth. "The king ordered us to solve the missing Fae situation together."

She looks at me with her mouth lowering. "Wow, that is unfortunate." For a while, the air is filled with nothing but birds chirping. Breaking the silence between us, Dyana asks, "Shall we get this tour started?"

Inside, after showing me the front door, we turn our backs to it, and Dyana points to the hallway I walked through this morning. "So to our right is a hall that takes you to the onsite servants' quarters past the kitchen. It's where the chefs, healers, and maids stay. Most in the servants' quarters have no young children, and any that do, reside in the larger rooms. There's a staircase that leads to a separate section of the palace, which was made for servants' bathing only. It's where you showered earlier."

"How did you–"

"Did you not see the note? We got Kabir to tell us when you were being brought to the king, so we arranged a better bathroom for you."

As we walk back towards the throne room, Dyana continues. "Anyway, as you know, that's the throne room, and the room to its right is the waiting room, where people await their time to speak to the king. There's two main dining areas. The one by the kitchen towards the east wing, outside of the throne room, and another on the west wing outside the ballroom. Next to the ballroom are training rooms and libraries that carry books of every genre from all parts of the world."

We take the left of the two white, curved staircases, which face the back entrance. Once on the new floor, we both turn towards its hallway. I take in all the art that's hung on the walls of the palace, ranging from flowers, to mythical creatures, to portraits of what seems to be their family. *How the hell are they all so beautiful?* "So what's this part?"

"We're in the second story of the east wing. It's the floor where all family and invited guests stay. The third floor is reserved for the king and queen, along with rooms for knights to keep watch over them. Fourth and fifth are mainly storage, with other rooms in the tower areas. I heard you're staying in the west wing, so uh, good luck."

"That was ominous. Care to elaborate?" I say while my brows furrow, then immediately shoot up.

"It's nothing. Cassius' room is just on the west wing."

*Great. Another thing to add to my inability to avoid him as much as possible.* As we descend down the stairs, I realize she hasn't told me where her room is. "Wait, where's your room?"

"Me, Isa, my brothers, and parents have our own estate. It's a manor a bit from here. You just have to go out the back and keep walking to your left. It's a white building. If you see a light brown estate, you're in Enthar at the House of Oris, and you've gone too far."

She goes off, giving me time to wander the palace without her guidance. I walk through the pointed archways that frame the hallway entrances, the space near the ceiling having intricately carved crown moldings made from porcelain with swirling shapes and elegant designs. I explore the ballroom, the multiple music rooms, and the art rooms before she returns to my side.

By the end of our tour, we're called to dinner by a servant. I sit at the table, noting how many people there are. The king and queen sit at the head, with the queen sitting to the king's right. Across from me sits a woman who's barely taller and a bit smaller than me in size, with small horns like a goat. I assume she's the sister Esme spoke about. She seems very reserved around new people. In contrast to the king, she has dark-brown hair and looks nothing like him, other than her eye shape. To her right is the other man from the throne room, who is sat next to two identical men with bright, copper hair. One has longer hair, a thin scar on his bridge's nose, and a bit of a wider face, whereas the other has a thinner nose and shorter hair that ends at the top of his neck. I sit between Isa and Esme, Dyana sitting on Esme's right.

While in the middle of dessert, Cassius sits in the chair next to his sister across from me.

"Ah." The king smiles. "You've come to join us at last."

The queen calls for one of the servants. "Can you please get a plate for Cassius?" She glances over to me with her bright, violet eyes, smiling while tucking her falling hair from her updo behind her ear.

"How rude of us." She simpers. "We haven't introduced ourselves to you. Arabella, I'm Queen Helena, and this is King Elliot."

Now that I can observe their faces without the stress of facing possible death, I notice how young they look. The queen looks like she could be in her mid-twenties, late at most. The purple in her eyes makes her look even more youthful, complementing the dark of her skin. The king too looks like he's thirty. His beauty is evident in all his children. I swallow another bite. "Nice to meet you."

"You'll have to forgive us. Two of our children are missing tonight. Our twins, Maude and Atticus. You know Cassius, Esme, and Ezra already. Our youngest, Celeste, is across from you. I also saw Dyana giving you a tour, so I'm sure you know who she and Isadora are. They are my sister, Zielle's, children, along with Xavier and Montgomery Aeon," the queen continues.

The twins look at me, nodding upwards in acknowledgment.

For a while, the dessert is eaten in silence. Then, Ezra makes a show, bringing the attention to him and sipping from his glass. "So Arabella, you must be excellent with a sword. From what I have heard, you were nearly ready to strike Cassius for touching you."

*I don't like being touched. What's so weird about not wanting a stranger to touch me?* "Yeah, I'd be happy to demonstrate on you if you'd like."

The whole table breaks into laughter and "ohhhs". My eyes shift around as I join in, thinking it's probably how they interact.

"Well let us hope you're as talented with a sword as I am," he says, raising his drink.

I glance off to the side quickly, brows knit in confusion. "Are you planning on stabbing me?"

"Perhaps," he responds while bringing his cup to his mouth.

When the servant clears the plates, we remain seated as the family exchanges light-hearted jokes between them. And once the king and queen leave, the twins and all the women go to the courtyard, beckoning for me to join them.

Outside, the weather is chilly. The winds are lightly blowing, which shake leaves from the greenery around us. Suddenly, the weight of my shoulders becomes heavier when I feel a coat being placed around me by the long-haired twin.

"You appeared cold. Take my jacket." I try to argue, but he already takes two steps down from me. "It's fine. Just don't fall in love with me," he jokes, immediately winking at the end of his words.

"I think *you* should be worried about not falling in love with *me*. You know, since you've known me for less than two hours and you're already stripping," I tease.

The man turns towards the girls, leaning his back against a railing. "Oh, she's fun. Your father sure knows how to pick a prisoner."

"Only the finest for you, sir," I laugh while giving a mocked, shallow bow.

He takes a seat on the steps, placing his arms on one a few above where he sits. "Do you have a nickname? Or should we stick to Arabella?"

"Why, Xay? Arabella too hard for you to pronounce?" the shorter-haired twin taunts.

"I'll show your mother too hard!"

"We have the same mother, you idiot."

Isa comes up to me, laughing at her brothers' stupidity. "I'm so sorry about them in advance. They're twenty-five but still act like children. They're," she pauses, watching her brothers wrestle, "a lot, to say the least."

"We heard that," they object simultaneously.

It's the first time in days where I feel unguarded enough to relax. "It's fine. They actually remind me of my friends back home. Xavier feels like he's the me of your family."

Xavier gets up from where is and pushes himself between me and Isa. "What did I hear about me being inside you?"

My mouth drops. I take in a short breath and close my mouth before responding. "I- That definitely isn't what I said."

"Tomato, tomato," he ignores while shrugging.

We all huddle in a circle for warmth. Despite the smartest solution being to walk inside and warm up, we bring ourselves closer together to share body heat. We're all probably stupid for this, but it makes me think of my friends from school.

That thought in itself reminds me that I should probably message them. "Oh Esme, is there any place I can get signal? I've been gone for like almost five days, and if I don't check in with my friends soon, they'll think I'm dead."

*Although, I almost was.*

Esme giggles, shaking her head. "Arabella, there's signal everywhere in the land."

Deciding I like them enough to use a nickname, I say, "You can call me Ara or Bella if you want. But anyway, in the forest there wasn't–"

"Why would there be any signal in the middle of the forest? Even I know that's not common in the Human Lands," Esme interrupts.

I turn my head towards her, surprised she knew this.

"Magik leaders usually operate from Magik Cove, but I know a lot of you tend to reside in Human Lands, which is what we refer to as every land that is not concealed from the humans."

I nod, checking my phone to see my battery's dying. "Uh, I know you probably don't have phones, but are there any outlets here? My phone's at six percent."

"Actually," Esme smiles, "I managed to get some smart Fae girl in town to make charging gadgets. They're powered by the energy that was taken from lightning. I had her make some when I snuck to the Human Lands and got a phone from a friend. She's also the one that's established signal for cell phones throughout the land."

"Wait a minute." Isa breaks our attention, grabbing my phone. "Who is this with you?"

Still not wanting to reveal too much, I think carefully about how to respond. "Oh, that's me with Luka."

"*Ou*! Is Luka someone special?" Dyana asks with insinuation in her tone.

"No!" I bellow too quickly. I instantly feel regret. Like I'm disrespecting Luka's memory. They all stare, looking afraid they might have offended me. "I mean he is, but it's not what you think."

Esme turns on my phone again. "You had really long hair here. Why'd you cut it?"

"About four months ago, I decided to chop off my hair. Cutting my hair felt symbolic to cutting out the negative things that didn't serve me anymore." I pause, thinking about how pathetic what I said came out. "That probably sounds really corny."

"Actually," Celeste chimes in, "I think that is amazing."

"Well I think it's time we all retreat to the comfort of our beds. We'll see you all later," Esme pipes up, going towards the door, followed by Celeste.

"Are you coming, Arabella?" Celeste questions.

"I think I'm going to stay out a bit longer. I'll see you in the morning. Goodnight!"

They say their goodnights, followed by Montgomery, Isa, and Dyana deciding to go back to their home. When I start to take off Xavier's jacket so that he can go with them, he stops me. "Keep it on. I'd prefer if the king's new witch didn't become sick when I could've prevented it."

"Aren't you going home?"

"I think I'll stay for a little while longer."

We sit on the steps and spend the next two hours laughing about the things we have in common, specifically our adoration of how fire seems to follow us everywhere. And when he doubts my gymnastic abilities, I seek to prove him wrong. So I do a cartwheel into the splits, which he then attempts. Not to my surprise, he fails and yelps so loud, I'm sure he wakes up the whole palace. I feel weirdly comfortable around him. *This feels normal. Like I've known him as long as my friends at home.*

Sitting back on the stairs, he looks to the stars before turning to me. "So why are you so terrible at flirting with others but so natural with me?"

I climb up next to him and take a seat. "What do you mean?"

"You don't really mean to tell me you didn't notice Ezra flirting with you."

"Was he?"

"You said you'd stab him the way you almost did Cassius. And then when you *did* finally catch on, you asked if he'd stab you in front of the whole table, basically asking him to fuck you." He laughs. Harder when he must realize I had no idea.

"*Oh*. I didn't know he was flirting. Considering he was willing to send me to my death not six hours before that, I thought he was making fun of me. Sometimes I'm terrible at picking up social cues. For the most part, I'm decent, but it's not just flirting. I say things that I think are casual, but it gets misinterpreted as flirting or me being unnecessarily rude. Or I'll overexplain things–"

Xavier turns, cutting me off. "Like you are right now?"

I turn away, embarrassed. "Yeah. That tends to happen when I don't wanna say the wrong thing and have them get mad at me."

"I have a similar issue where I say things without thinking first. Same goes with actions. Usually, Monty's having to apologize and clean up my mess," he admits.

"Yeah, I get that." Feeling my eyes becoming heavier, I check the time and see that it's 2:34 in the morning. "Hey, it's getting pretty late. I think I'm gonna head to sleep. Thanks for letting me use your jacket though. Get home safe."

He pushes himself from his place, walking up the steps, motioning for me to join him. "It's too late to walk back home. I'll just stay in one of the spare bedrooms. We do it constantly anyway."

Once we get inside, I ask the guard on duty if he knows which room I'm staying in, and he leads me up to the third door on the right of the west wing.

Inside, the room is covered in a cream-colored wall. A desk stands a few feet left of the door, and a bed is pressed to the back wall. Over the bed hangs a black, see-through canopy, paralleled to the pearl sofa on the other side of the room. At the edge of the bed, past the space of the wall, there's a huge walk-in closet. Across from that door, down by the couch, there's a spacious bathroom with a standing shower, bathtub, countersinks, and a toilet.

Xavier walks through the room with me before rasping a lazy "goodnight" and shutting his door. I quickly wash my body through another shower, messaging all my friends before going to sleep.

> sorry ive been mia!! been going through a mood and needed space. So much to tell you. will text again soon. love u!!!

# IV

## *A Romantic Charade*

Cassius

The mere thought of having to work with the witch turns my slight irritation to a grand headache. *We need to finish this with haste.*

After changing into an open, black shirt with breeches and boots to match, I exit my chamber, drifting down to the dining room. I search for the witch through the first floor and the gardens, but to no avail. As a final attempt, I ask a guard posted at the door if he knows whether the witch has woken up or not, to which he states that she has yet to come down and must still be in her room.

The best course of action would be to wait and find her at lunch, which ought to be served soon. With more time free, I move up the stairs so that I may return to my bed, but while walking through the corridor towards my room, I clash with the witch exiting hers.

Regrettably, it's next to mine.

This is the first time I have seen her in such an open state. The sight of her bare face in contrast to the sharp lines that had painted her eyelids in the previous times I have seen her holds me in my place. It is raw, nearly vulnerable.

My presence is unexpected to her, her flat, black hair falling forward as she jerks back. "Oh sorry. Didn't realize you were there."

"Perhaps if you were looking where you were going, you would not have this issue," I counter, though in honesty, neither of us had been paying attention.

She gives me a look. Raising her eyebrows slightly, she rolls her eyes. "Yeah, okay. *I see you're polite in the morning.*"

"And you are just as observant," I reply wryly.

I glimpse down at her body, noting she is in nothing but an ill-fitting, relaxed brassiere and loose pajama pants borrowed from Cel. She wears the same silver and diamond-framed onyx marquise necklace that she wore before. The skin from her large chest is pouring out of the bralette, visible for all to see. I am stopped in my place with little to say.

She breezes past me, descending down the stairs, something urging me to call her. "Put a shirt on. The whole kingdom may see you."

"Then they should take a picture if they care that much," she yells back.

*She would have every servant see her like this?*

Quickly, I race into my room, grabbing an old slept-in shirt from my closet and following her. What she wears makes no difference to me, but I would rather not know the undergarments my sister keeps.

At the time of reaching the witch, she is in the dining room, questioning one of our servants about what time lunch is going to be served.

"Servants bring food out at noon," I say while leaning against the column next to the doorway.

She turns from the servant, narrowing her eyes in my direction. "And will everyone be here for lunch, or am I enjoying your company alone?"

"We don't normally eat together. Unless it is a special occasion." She grins in relief, but I only let her have this satisfaction for a small moment before I go on. "However, we currently have matters that need discussing."

"*Ugh.*"

"Follow me, if you might, to the council room. I'll have lunch brought to us." I turn, starting towards the west wing. "Lizette," I motion to the Dryad in charge of food service, "will you ensure lunch is sent to the council room for Lady Arabella and myself, please?"

She nods.

We make our way into the council room, where the witch gapes at its size. I move past her, taking the seat that I usually pick during father's meetings. I hate this room. Memories of the many drawn-out meetings held in here trickle into my mind, most of which were unending due to father enjoying hearing himself speak and weighing out every single option before deciding on his initial suggestion. I grow impatient with her fascination. "Are you intending on sitting?"

"Sorry. Not every day do I get to wake up in a palace after being held hostage for four days," she shoots, scowling.

"Yes, well you'll grow accustomed to it."

The moment she sits across from me, I throw my shirt to her, and she grabs it. She looks at the shirt, then back at me, dumbfounded. I move my hand in a circular movement, motioning for her to put it on. The top just barely fits her, hugging every extra curve. She peers down at herself and says nothing.

*Is she nervous?*

She starts fidgeting with the paint on her nails. "So what did we need to talk about?"

My mind still focused on her initial reaction, I attempt to bring myself to the matter at hand. "Well, since you are unaware of what has been occurring within the lands, I thought it best to inform you of the situation more extensively and see if you had any knowledge or theories of your own before we begin."

Her lips thin, forming a line. "*Hmm.* Okay, well let's hear it."

"You see," I begin, "over the last few months, Fae have gone missing. Initially, my father ruled it to be of no significance, being that some simply wish to leave the lands, but after six were reported to disappear and one lord had turned up dead within the Darkened Forest, we began to suspect there was something bigger at hand." I pause, allowing the information to process.

She looks around the room, attempting to form her next thought. "Were there any links between those that went missing? Maybe family, or they did something that pissed someone else off?"

It's troubling how little this phases her. She was just told that multiple Fae had gone missing in such a short period of time, and yet she speaks as if she has had experience with something similar. "We had royal guards look into it. From what they were told, the common fae knew nothing of any link, and when asking the families about any odd habits their loved ones had before disappearing, they refused to speak. When another lord was found dead, we came to the conclusion that the victims had less and less of a commonality."

Scoffing at my words, she stares directly into my eyes. "And you only started worrying about your missing people when those that went missing were closer to your status?"

"We do not know every Fae personally," I respond. "We have rulers of the lower courts to govern over the common fae. Of course my father wasn't going to recognize it was a problem until it affected us. We hadn't even been properly informed of this issue until after Lord Theodore's death! It has only grown since then, and now there are almost thirty who have disappeared, eight found dead."

She looks down at the table when the doors fling open and crash against the walls, Lizette and one of the new servants coming in to bring lunch. We eat in silence, nothing exchanged between the two of us with the witch looking at her handheld device she brought in, snickering with every few bites she takes. Her laugh reverberates around the walls before it is immediately replaced by the sounds of her tapping.

When she finishes, though still fixated on the empty plate, the sound of her voice fills the room. "So Fae have gone missing, a few turn up dead, and from the information your guards gathered, the common fae know nothing. Am I correct?"

I nod.

"That's not possible," she states with finality. Her posture straightens, eyes directed at me. "There's no way in hell that about thirty people randomly disappeared, and not a single Fae knows anything."

Crossing my arms, I look at her inquisitively. "Well, then what are you suggesting?"

Once again, she is glancing around the room to collect her thoughts. Her tongue pokes around different areas of the inside of her mouth, formulating her next words. "I think the common fae know more than they're letting on. It's obvious they don't trust the crown if, even after you sent guards to collect information, they come back with nothing." She looks back at me. "It's impersonal."

"What do you think we ought to do then?"

"*Hmm.*" She brings her hand to her mouth. Leaning forward, her elbow rests on the table, her chin placed on her palm, curling her knuckles inward. "Maybe if we go around asking what people know, they'll be more likely to give answers. After all, it makes them think that the crown cares if they sent the prince. And those that don't trust your father, well they don't know me, so they wouldn't expect me to have any underlying motives, other than wanting to know town gossip."

*Clever. Unorthodox, but cunning.*

"That plan is sufficient, but what of when they realize you are not Fae and withhold from telling you anything because you're a witch?"

She opens her mouth to speak before immediately shutting it again. "Why would me being Magik be an issue?" she asks as if I have offended her.

"Fae and Magiks have not been at peace for millennia. My father does not care for them." If she knew her history, she'd understand why. She would hate us just as much.

Licking her lips lightly, she takes a deep breath, clicking her tongue. "Uh-huh... Well then, we cross that bridge when we get to it. I'm sure there are Fae who would rather trust a witch over the entirety of the crown that did nothing to help their missing loved ones."

"We—"

"Prior to this past month."

Even if I will not admit so, her statement is fair. My father had heard claims about the missing Fae, but nothing was deemed worthy of action, until the lords had been murdered. It became something that could put him in imminent danger.

"Okay," I begin, "tomorrow we shall go through the lands and start asking people what they know." I look at her. "You are not to leave my side."

"Wouldn't dream of it." She shoots me a sarcastic smile, rising and moving towards the direction of the door. Pausing at the door, she turns to me. "Actually, I would."

In the past two weeks, we have gone into Mindae's town, attempting to gather what the common fae know. If we are not met with deliberately rehearsed or surface-level answers, dirty looks and whispered insults are hurled in our direction. Though I do not care one way or another of the thoughts the common fae have of me, their fear brings us no closer to answers than if we were to send another guard into town.

Today, as we travel into the Enthar town center, the common fae continue to show their hatred towards the witch. A hatred rooted from generations that suffered the Magiks' slaughter so long ago.

In the crowded market, I catch the eye of a woman that I remember from my youth. I squeeze through the many Fae who refuse to move, making my way to her.

The witch, not far behind and lost in the crowd, calls out to me. "Where are we going?"

Without turning back, I answer loudly so that she may hear me over the bustle. "Asking that woman a question. She was a teacher from my schooling days."

When she finally catches up to me, we walk towards the woman who hasn't aged since the last time I saw her seven years ago.

"Madam Ophelia," I shout, attempting to pull her attention.

She turns in our direction, smiling, giving a wave and stopping in her place for us to meet her. "Prince Cassius. I have not seen you since you were fifteen. I hope you are well."

I send a smile back, hopeful of where this is leading. "I am. I was hoping we could speak with you and ask a few questions."

"Oh dear boy, I would love to, but unfortunately, my husband is waiting for me at a tea shop. If I can talk to you any other day, I will be more than happy to–"

"As your prince, I demand you answer our questions," I cut her off. She is stunned into silence, antennas rigid. "Now, I know you've heard about the Fae that have gone missing. There are far too many that have disappeared for the whole town to not be aware."

Her body retracts. Tears start to form in her eyes. "Yes, I have heard about them. My brother was one of the many that have gone missing, not that your father cared about that earlier."

"How dreadful," I reply without remorse in my tone. I am not to be blamed for the actions of my father. "Well, if you do not wish yourself or your children to be next, you will tell us all that you know."

A gasp leaves her mouth. "Is that a threat, Your Highness?"

"You mistake me for my brother. It is a demand. Nothing more, nothing less."

She takes a sharp breath. "Those that have gone missing can only be faulted by the crown. Now if you'll excuse me, I must attend to my husband."

That interaction was unhelpful. I had hoped that the woman who had taught me, my favorite tutor, would have offered us something that would assist us, but instead, we are given the same, generic answer as each time before.

The witch and I continue through the street, side by side, attempting to talk to anyone who looks in our direction.

After long-standing silence, she says, "You're vile, you know that?"

"Oh?" I chuckle. "Pray tell, why is that?"

"You've done nothing except be rude and arrogant to the people we're trying to ask for help. You demand to be given answers because your dad's the king, and you don't show any empathy for people who have lost their family members or loved ones."

I step in front of her, staring into her eyes. While her statement holds true, it does not bring us any closer to finding the missing Fae. "And what have you done? For weeks we have gone around *together*, and it has only been *me* speaking with them. All the while you stand by my side with nothing to say."

"You're the one who said they wouldn't trust a witch! Besides, these are *your* people!" she asserts, arms extended and filled with tension. "*You* should know them better than I do."

"Oh ho! Says the witch who held a knife to my throat for trying to get her attention."

Her eyes are on fire. If she could shoot daggers at me with them,

I have no doubt in my mind that she would. "I'm not apologizing for protecting myself when a random man tried to touch me."

I bend down, meeting her cold scowl. "I never said you should."

"Whatever," she mutters. "Let's just try approaching this differently." She pushes past me, heading towards an inn with vines creeping their way up its outside walls, flowers the color of an ocean's sea foam blooming.

My feet pick up speed so that I may return to her side. "How are we to do that? The Fae know I am the son of their ruler, and I am not exactly known for my kindness."

She seethes through her teeth. "Just follow my lead."

Standing in front of a disorganized desk, scattered with metals and torn parchment, we wait for someone to help us. The innkeeper approaches, a scowl hidden under the smile shown in her direction. At the sight of me, it is immediately replaced with a bow. "Hello, how may I help you?"

Her voice suddenly jumps octaves higher. "Sorry to bother you sir, but my boyfriend, Prince Cassius, and I had heard about how delectable the food from your restaurant was, and I had begged him to take me. Do you think you have an extra table so that we may dine here?"

*Boyfriend?* What strategy is this?

He looks suspiciously between the two of us. "Of course, madam. Let me go check with our staff." He walks to a servant by the nearest table and whispers in her ear so that she may hear him more clearly, and after a few minutes, he returns.

Before he reaches us, I snake an arm around the witch's waist, bringing her closer to my side.

She glares at me. "What are you doing?"

"Just following your lead," I say through a feigned, innocent smile.

The innkeeper returns with two pieces of paper. "If you'll follow me, please."

"Thank you so much." Unwrapping my arm from her waist, the witch trails directly behind him.

Once sat at our table, I gaze at the piece of paper and see it is full of food items. The witch studies hers, becoming lost in the words on it, while I am befuddled by the lists of food, price, and ingredients. I tear my eyes from the page to see her looking at me, giggling. Her eyes close, the hoop pierced through the right side of her nose moving up with her as it scrunches.

Seldom have I heard her laugh, but never has she done so in my presence without it being from her device or at the expense of myself.

"What?"

Her laughter plays on, stammering through her words. "Y- You look so lost. Have you never seen a menu before?"

The tension in my body eases. "I've never ordered from one, no. Is that common outside of the palace?"

She waits for me to continue before her eyes widen. "O- Oh, you're serious. Uh, yeah. You have a waiter take your order after choosing what you want from their menu." Her face relaxes. "I guess when you're royalty, you never have to worry about choosing from a menu when you can just have anyone make you whatever you want."

At that, I am baffled. She assumes that I am waited on hand and foot. While my father receives that treatment, he only expects the servants to do the same for the women in our family. "You seem to think I'm a lot more demanding than I am."

"Are you not? You're pretty spoiled and pretentious."

Snorting at her statement, I reply. "All very true, but when you grow up around the finer things in life, you tend to enjoy a little pampering."

The servant comes to take our order, but rather than deciding for myself what I want, the witch orders for me, saying I cannot go wrong with what she calls "basically chicken tenders".

As the servant writes down our order, I ask for two glasses of water to hydrate us from our long day. The witch adjusts her shirt, her knife popping out by her chest. I quickly avert my eyes in a different direction, relieved the servant is returning with glasses of water.

After delivering our food, the witch thanks the servant before asking if she could refill our refreshments. As she pours into our glasses, I assume it would be a good time to resume our romantic charade.

"So," I drawl, "*are you well equipped with handling a sword?*"

A fit of coughing comes from her while she chokes on the bread she eats. She takes a sip of her drink, leaving colored marks on the glass. "I'm sorry, what?"

"You are fond of knives. I figured that perhaps you must know how to handle a sword."

"First of all, I have magik, so I don't really need a sword. Knives just make a better physical threat. Secondly, swordsmanship isn't that common among Magiks or humans. It's more of a hobby. There are other weapons that people use."

"I see."

While continuing to eat her pasta, the witch grabs one of the pieces of chicken off my plate, putting it on her own. Though I know we are playing the role of a couple, what right does she have to take from me?

"Your pardon?" I look at her.

"What?" she laughs. "It's only *one* piece of meat. If you want some of my pasta, you can have some as a trade."

She takes some of her food and splits the bread in half before putting both on my plate. We continue our meal while eavesdropping on the conversations around us to see if there is any information we can use. Most of it is nonsense that she giggles at for entertainment.

The witch grabs my hand, placing hers in mine as the servant comes to deliver our sweets. With how busy the establishment is, the witch ensures to get in a "thank you" before the Fae takes off to another table.

Perhaps the witch is unaware she mindlessly keeps twisting one of the gold rings around my finger. How she holds it in mine while no one is looking, with eyes drifting past the faint scar on the back of my left palm.

When one of my fingers twitches, she jerks her head up, as if she had been interrupted from her thoughts, and removes her hand from mine, placing hers under the table.

To make it more comfortable for the two of us to move on, I decide to speak. "So why play a romantic relationship for everyone to see?"

"Oh, that's easy. You said it yourself, the common fae don't see you as kind, and they know the king doesn't like Magiks. Those that, for some reason, don't know who you are will assume we're a normal couple interested in current affairs. Those that do, well..." she trails off, stopping herself from speaking faster than her thoughts form. "If they saw you rebelling against your father by showing interest in a witch, they'll think you're more likely to be on their side. And when they see you're dating a nice, *polite* witch, they'll see you as more approachable. The power of suggestion." She smiles deviously. "It's psychology, really."

We exit the establishment, leaving a large amount of Gold Zips as a tip on the table to further display appreciation. We spot a clothing shop while walking along the streets, and before I finish registering the sign, I'm following her inside, holding the extra clothes she cannot hold on her arms.

"Why do you require these clothes?" I question, helping her to the changing room.

She turns to me. "In case you've forgotten, I haven't been able to wear anything other than your sister's clothes for weeks. I need something that would be in my style and would fit me correctly. Besides, I'm sure buying some clothes is a small price for the king to pay when I'm helping his kingdom." She pumps her eyebrows and smiles, her high cheekbones disappearing at the spread of her wide cheeks.

While she tries on the garments she picked, I wander around the shop, lost in the memories of exploring the town with my circle of friends. Suddenly, I feel a tap on my back. I turn to see a woman beckoning for me to come closer. I lean down so that I may hear her voice more clearly.

"I don't think it's a coincidence," she croaks. "They took my husband." Tears are streaming down her face, watering the leaves that grow from her skin. "He was poisoned. Found in the market streets. Dumped there like he was no better than a piece of garbage. Now my daughter, she's gone too."

I look at her, not knowing how to respond. *How would the witch tell me to act?*

As I'm about to apologize, she grabs my arm. "Please," she pleads, "you have to help. Put an end to this."

I remove myself from her before putting a hand on her shoulder. "I vow we will do all we can to stop this."

"Bless you," she cries before exiting the shop.

"*Disaris!*" the witch sings. "*Time to pay!*"

After finishing her purchase, we start towards Nexus while I tell her about the interaction with the woman from the shop. She agrees that it is not surprising that a mother would be worried about her child, but for her to be so public about it and daring to touch me is a sign that the news of our relationship and ultimately, my reformed attitude, has already spread around the town, falling right into our trick.

As we pass through the market again, the eyes of all bystanders turn to us. Some kids wave to her, older Fae glaring but respectfully nodding in our direction, a few bowing.

"Wow," she laughs. "Word travels fast."

"Considering I just spent six hundred Silver Zips on you for clothing in a small market area that is surrounded by common fae, I would hope they take notice."

I catch her looking at me before she immediately snaps her head forward.

"You know," I murmur, "you are a *very* expensive lover to court."

I weave our fingers together, making a point of our relationship to those looking in our direction. She flinches, her body tightening.

Once out of view from onlookers, she quickly removes her hand from mine and marches ahead of me.

It was her idea to act as lovers, so why is she so quick to freeze at any affection that normal couples do? Has she not taken a lover before? I understand none of her actions, but I ought to keep from fixating on this. It is futile to dwell on such thoughts of unimportance.

At last, we reach the hill before the grounds. Not a single word has been spoken since we left the town. Whenever I am at her side, she picks up her speed, leaving me behind. About halfway through the hill, I become irritated by her passive aggression. Even more, I hate that I agreed to her earlier suggestion that we not use a carriage. "It was okay for you to grab my hand for those to see, but when I do so because far more are watching us, *that's* a problem?" I jog, attempting to meet her. "You're quite the hypocrite. You do not get to tell me not to touch you, but grab my hand when it is convenient to you."

She stops in place and snaps her body in my direction. "It's not my job to remind you we have a responsibility. And I was just doing the best I could to make sure people bought our story."

"Might I ask, how is that any different than what I did by grabbing your hand? You are incapable of putting aside your own inferiorities for a few moments to play out an act *you* conjured."

She is being so stubborn.

Her eyes move to the side, down, then back at me. She knows she is wrong.

"Whatever." She lets out a huff in defeat. As she moves her body back towards the direction of Nexus, she turns back at me. "But don't ever grab my waist like that again without warning."

"That's fine." I smirk. "I can wait for you to beg."

She breathes out, rolling her eyes. "I really don't like you."

I take a few steps towards her, closing the space between us, and bring myself to her ear. "I seriously doubt that, sweetheart."

Aggressively pushing me away, I stumble back a few steps, her face returning to a hardened state. "Call me sweetheart ever again and I swear to *any* gods that might exist, I will cut your dick off." She eyes me up and down, raising her eyebrows. "Small as it is."

And again, we remain in brooding silence as we walk the rest of the way before reaching Nexus. Tomorrow, we do not plan on leaving the palace until after lunch. Until then, I will enjoy my peace.

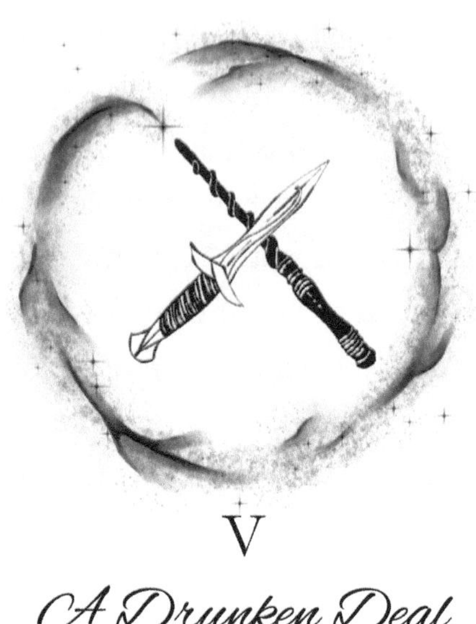

# V

## A Drunken Deal

Cassius

The realization that I do not have any control over my arms occurs only after I unintentionally elbow and slap the witch for jolting my body. The temperature of the ring she wears at all times ices my skin along with her frozen fingers. I had initially assumed it was one of my sisters waking me to tell me something irrelevant. Or perhaps it is natural instinct for my body to react to the witch. Regardless, I am now conscious and *very* naked under my covers in the presence of this woman.

"Ow!" she shrieks. "That hurt, you asshole."

Sitting up against my bed frame, I rub my eyes, keeping sure my lower half is not exposed. "That was your own doing for attempting to wake me." I look up at her. "You are aware you're supposed to knock before you enter a prince's room, right?"

"Oh, I'm *so sorry*, Disaris. I'll keep that in mind next time I wanna shake you from your bed."

*Has she no manners?*

Everything about her is enraging, and yet, she continues to banter as if we are friendly. She sticks to me as if she is a personal disease conjured just for my own suffering.

"Believe me, the next time you're shaking me from my bed, the only thing knocking will be the bedpost," I say as I scan her body. "And will you be calling me by my surname your entire stay?"

She laughs out once before saying, "I wasn't aware I was close enough to be on a first-name basis with you."

Dropping her eyes to my chest for a brief instant, she clears her throat and averts her eyes, embarrassed. Though it's hard to tell if her cheeks are flushed under her cosmetics. She backs from her place and walks towards the door, keeping her eyes to the hall. "Anyway, we're leaving in thirty minutes. I suggest you put on a shirt. Unless you want the whole kingdom to see you like this."

She slowly lingers out, shutting my door. It is amusing to see her so flustered over a naked chest when she herself was so ready to walk around in nothing but a bralette.

As we walk through Windwyrd, I feel the eyes of everyone staring at us. Though I'm used to people looking at me, due to being a prince or hiding from my line of sight out of fear I'll say something cruel, these gazes are for something entirely different. Gawking at me and my false lover.

It isn't long until we hear the shouts of a man cursing myself and the crown. He is clearly drunk, so there is no use in entertaining his outburst. We walk on, ignoring his shouts, when I feel a sudden and dull pain from something hitting the front of my head. I reach down to pick up whatever rubble was thrown in our direction and see that it came from a broken plate.

While trying to comprehend what is happening, I hear the witch screaming at the man who was harassing us moments ago. I hurriedly leave my position to get to her, knowing this will not end well.

Pushing my way through the crowd, I see the witch face-to-face, confronting the man. She is stepping up to him with no fear in sight. At least, none that can be detected.

"You think that just 'cause the prince found himself a whore, it changes his family's neglect?" the man says, barely coherent, followed by taking another swig from a stolen jug.

"Do you wanna repeat that?" she challenges.

We must depart at once, or what comes next may result in death. Not hers, but his. I grab her arm, attempting to take her away. "Pay him no heed. He isn't worth the trouble. Let us depart."

She turns to me, wrath filling her eyes. "No." She yanks her arm from my grasp, whipping around towards the Fae. She laughs sadistically, glaring him down before reverting to a dry demeanor. "Not only did you just insult me, but you assaulted a prince. That's punishable by death. Now you can either apologize, begging for forgiveness, and *maybe* he might give it to you, or you can repeat yourself, risking a *very* public execution."

The man is sweating and beginning to tremble. Magik abilities or not, she could strike fear into anyone. It's impressive how a witch of such average height could bring a man of his size to his knees.

Crawling, he keeps his eyes on the ground. "I- I- I'm so sorry, Your Highness. I beg for your forgiveness."

"You are pardoned." I interlock my fingers with Arabella's. With the point of my shoe, I bring it to his chin, lifting his face so that he must face me. "Just know, I only forgive once," I warn before walking away.

No one dares to follow us.

"What was it that you said of being a nice and polite witch?" I whisper into her ear.

"He shouldn't have thrown something at us and called me your whore," she says unbothered. "I could've done worse."

That much I gathered. For one who had previously berated me for using my title to get answers, Arabella is quick to use it when threatening a Fae.

Being that no one who had witnessed the incident will speak to us, we continue to walk past buildings with more rounded architecture, created from marble.

We stop at a tavern when an elderly Changeling motions for us to join him. When we sit, he takes a bottle from his bag. "I believe you two have been asking about the missing Fae."

"Yes," Arabella responds plainly.

"Let us strike a bargain." He gives a toothy grin, wrinkles and sun spots freckling his fair, purple skin. "I will answer as many questions as you can form coherently, so long as you drink this bottle of lasialic with me."

We speak simultaneously.

"Deal."

"No."

She pulls me aside. "Why would you say no? We can get *actual* answers if we do this."

"You fail to understand." I look down at her. "Lasialic is Fae wine. It's not the regular alcohol you are used to."

"Isn't it the one you're always drinking?"

"Yes, but I am a Faerie. It does not affect me the same way it would you."

I beg that she takes this seriously. It would be a nuisance if I have to drag her back to Nexus, especially at midday.

"Listen," she says, ignoring everything I had just cautioned, "if I can drink a whole bottle of whiskey by myself and *still* not black out, I'm pretty sure I can handle a few glasses of wine."

She strides back to the man, sitting down next to him and pouring herself a glass. "Okay, we're ready."

"No," he denies. "This bargain only extends to you. The prince may watch, but he is not to ask any questions."

Arabella gives me a pleading look, asking me to trust her.

*Spirits help me, she's so stubborn. She's going to get herself sick, or worse, killed.*

"Fine," I grumble, crossing my arms. "But I reserve the right to take her and leave at my discretion."

She leers at me.

"Of course." He smiles, taking a sip of his wine. "Ask away, my dear."

The glass of lasialic reaches her lips, taking a sizable gulp before she asks her question. "What's the connection between all the Fae going missing?"

"There are hardly any. Although if there were, it would only be the blame of seduction," he chuckles.

"That's a horrible answer." She takes another sip. "Other than the two lords who have died, were any of the disappearances people of importance in the community?"

He swishes his glass around, thinking of how to respond to the question. "No. I'm afraid they were just other common fae who had the misfortune of disappearing."

This man has given us nothing. Everything he tells her, we already know or had assumed. This is uneventful. We could be spending our time obtaining real answers, but instead, we are at a tavern and drinking before dinner to question a common fae that likely knows nothing. This, I could have done from the comfort of my bed.

Arabella takes another large sip, finishing the glass. Her eyes begin to droop, closing her eyes longer with every blink. "Are they being taken? Or are they leaving of their own volition?"

The man finishes his wine before refilling their glasses. He looks at her, patting her hand and smiling in an unfriendly manner. "My, you certainly are inquisitive. Unfortunately, I do not have an answer for that one. There is only so much talk that goes around in the town. What I can tell you, is that all those who have disappeared were reported gone between the hours past sunset into the start of the new day."

*So they all were missing for roughly twelve hours before most people took notice.* Those hours are the best time to take someone if they were to go 'missing'. It's when you spend time with friendly acquaintances, drinking, or when one would have late-night affairs.

I watch as Arabella takes another drink of the wine and giggles, her lip paint smudged, her eyes dilating. A length of time passes before she gathers herself together enough to ask another question.

"When... When did... Um... When did this first start happening?

Like when did these people go missing? Were they disappearing all at once or separately?" Her breathing is becoming heavier, words barely coherent. By now, she has drunk nearly two glasses.

"Fascinating," he comments. "You've consumed enough wine to cause a normal mortal to need a healer, and yet you continue. You have a lot of ambition." He looks at her, observing her every movement. *As am I.* "In any case, from what I noticed and have heard, those that have disappeared were said to have gone missing on Mondays, Thursdays, and Saturdays. Those that were found dead were always found on Tuesdays. Other than the lords who were shown to have physical markings, the other dead were poisoned."

Arabella is barely able to hold her head up. I take her arm, pulling her from her chair. She is sweating, yet the temperature of her body is cold. I force my coat around her. "We're leaving."

"No!" she weakly protests.

"Yes," I command while holding her up. "You can barely speak, and if you take one more sip of that wine, you will surely need to be taken to a healer."

"We. Are. Leaving."

"Good talk, witch," he calls as we walk out the door.

Once we reach the exit, the winds are mildly blowing, causing the climate to feel colder than it already is. The sun has been replaced by pouring rain, and if we leave now, we will be back at Nexus in time for dinner. Arabella wraps herself tighter in my coat. Stumbling to walk in a straight line, I steady her as if I am the only thing that will keep her from falling onto her face.

"Can you make it to Nexus?"

"Huh?"

"Nexus."

She turns to me, puzzled.

"The palace."

"*Ohhh,*" she snickers. "Yeah, I'll be fine, I promise!" She shines a wide smile while skipping up the street before tripping on her own foot, hitting the ground with a loud smack.

"You are all but fine. I'll carry you." I stalk to her, helping her up as she climbs on my back. If we attempt to okkar back, there stands a high chance of the witch hurling bile onto myself.

"How are you carrying me? I'm heavy, and you don't look strong," she blurts, her words slurred. She rests her head on my shoulder, nuzzling into my neck.

"I can carry a lot more than you think, sweetheart."

"Hey! I told you if you called me sweetheart, then–"

"Yes, I know. You'll castrate me. Any new threats, princess?"

She laughs, her arms around me holding tighter. It is after uncommon silence that I notice she has fallen asleep. When I hear the sound of her snoring, I set her down and lift her into my arms, summoning my wings to fly us the rest of the way.

While in the sky, my eyes become fixated on the wingless dragon on her thigh. One that is now fully visible from her skirt flying up. I use a hand to pull down on it, but it is of no use when the winds continuously blow it up.

When we arrive at Nexus, I carry her to her room and lay her in bed. "Cassius," she calls. Her eyes open, irregularly blinking and looking up at me. "Why didn't you just let me keep drinking? I could've gone longer."

"Because," I hesitate, sitting on her bed, "if you drank anymore, you would have gotten alcohol poisoning."

Her eyes narrow, her lips forming a smile. "You don't care if I get sick from alcohol poisoning."

Truthfully, I ought to not care, yet for some reason, I had worried for her in the tavern. I angle my face towards the wall to avoid her studying my face as I speak. "I would prefer it if I didn't have to tell my father that you died when we are the closest we've ever gotten to a lead."

Noises still murmuring, she attempts to drag on. "Well we still don't know what we're looking for."

*Perhaps she's correct. This is a good start, but it still doesn't tell us where to look.*

"I also did not want you to die today." I look back at her, attempting to change the subject so she does not return to the man for another game.

Wrapping herself in her blanket, her eyes start to shut again. "*Psh*. You're lying. You don't care if I die. You don't even like me."

I rise to leave, but before exiting, I stop, eyes peering at her. "Even if I wished to lie to you, that is not possible. Fae cannot tell lies."

At that, I shut the door, allowing her to get some rest.

# VI

## *Alcohol Makes for Bad Decisions*

Arabella

Laughter thunders from outside my door. I follow the noise to the first floor and lose myself in multiple rooms before finding Esme, Celeste, Montgomery, Xavier, Ezra, Maude, and an unknown man drinking and bantering.

From what I learned, Maude is the eldest sister and shifts her form the most. She sits in a long, red dress with a low-cut top. The dress is covered in gold glitter, like they were individually placed, one by one. Next to her, on the side of the couch, stands a slightly tan man, who I assume to be Atticus, her twin brother, who I have yet to formally meet. His medium-brown hair is sitting just below his shoulders, his facial hair prominent. He is the biggest of the family, with a round stomach and muscles that are currently lifting the couch as his siblings sit in gaiety.

It feels like I shouldn't enter, like this is their family time and I'm intruding by watching how they interact with one another. Most of what they're doing consists of drunken, idiotic stunts or taking a drink.

Hunger peaks in my mind, bringing about the realization of how long it's been since the last time I ate. I start towards the kitchen but hear Xavier's voice call out to me right as I pass the door of the room his family occupies.

"Ara!" He gets up from his seat and skips to the doorway, grabbing my arm. "Come join us!"

Normally, for the most part, I'm uncomfortable by the touch of other people, but he's not in his right mind, and I doubt any of them are sober enough to understand.

While I sit on the floor between Xavier and Montgomery, Celeste hands me a glass that fills with a glowing, sparkly, bright, arctic liquid. Lasialic. *Fuck. Can I really handle more of this tonight?* I debate between whether or not I should before grabbing the cup, hesitantly holding it in front of me. *Fuck it.* I take a small sip of the strong wine before leaning back.

I've somehow already forgotten the taste of berries and faint honey their wine carries in contrast to the grape ones I'm accustomed to. Wine isn't usually my taste, but theirs is delicious.

"Oh," Esme brings her head up to me, "Bella, this is Maude and Atticus! They're our oldest siblings!" She turns to Ezra. "Next to Ezra, of course!"

I turn to them, politely smiling and taking another sip of the wine. "I've met Maude a few times, but it's nice to finally meet you, Atticus," I say, reaching out my hand to shake his.

"Apologies," he laughs. "You see, I've been busy in different areas helping build houses with my wife's father."

"Oh?" I look at him inquisitively.

"Yes. My wife's father builds temporary homes for those that cannot afford it, and I help fund it." He takes a shot of, well, I'm not sure what. "Usually I wouldn't be away from seeing my siblings this long, but since my wife got pregnant, I've been waiting on her hand and foot to ensure she's as comfortable as possible."

Before I have a chance to respond, Montgomery starts to speak. "He and his wife don't live here. Our uncle doesn't particularly approve of his choice of occupation."

Elbowing him playfully, I face him. "I'm sure that's not true, Montgomery. He's probably grateful that his son wants to help his people."

Montgomery lets out a coughing laugh of some kind. "It's Monty, and he *really doesn't*. Sure, he's okay with funding the houses if it gains the favor of the public, but he only decided that after *months* of going back and forth on the decision." He takes another swig from his cup. "After, of course, he kicked Atticus out for spending two hundred *thousand* Gold Zips on starting up that business."

"In father's defense, Atticus should have just asked before he spent that money," Ezra defends.

Maude laughs in a chortle. "You really think our father would allow that much money to be given freely, without going back and forth for months before ultimately saying no?"

"Well not particularly," Ezra responds. "However, I do believe he wants us to be responsible as possible future rulers." He glances over to his sisters. "Not that the women in our family aren't more responsible than our pitiful, youngest brother."

My mouth parts open a bit. *Does he actually have that little respect for Cassius?* Trying to shake the thought from my mind, I drink more from my cup, listening in while the family extends their opinions on the king.

"You're being quiet, Arabella." Ezra places his hand on my shoulder. "Something troubling you?"

As my eyes glare down to the hand on my shoulder, I take a deep breath to try calming myself down. *Get your hand off me before I rip it off.*

I begin my counting as I take another deep breath, tapping my fingers at my thigh. *One. One. Two. One. One. Two. Three. Two. One...*

Once I reach eight, I see everyone's attention directed at me. How do I even respond? I didn't intend to join them, but I enjoy being in their company after spending over half the day asleep from day drinking.

"I uh... Well I was just thinking about how other than Monty and Xavier, you're all siblings, but none of you look alike, and you all look to be around the same age as me."

"Our father's been a busy man," Esme laughs.

The room erupts with cackles and hollering. Thinking about the mannerisms of the king and how men in power tend to be, I laugh alongside them. "Yeah," I nod my head, "that tracks."

Ezra continues to ask me questions as we drink, and I confess the things that Cassius and I have learned in our time among the common fae. While I know he's likely the only one who is processing what I have to say, everyone tries to pay attention to the words coming out of my mouth.

Subjects are changed multiple times within the span of minutes, and in them, I manage to finish my glass. Maybe I'm building a tolerance for this wine.

Xavier hands me another drink before asking, "So you really spent weeks wearing Celeste's clothes and the four things the tailors made you?"

"Yeah," I laugh. "It was really nice of her to–"

"Them," Celeste interjects.

"Sorry?" I turn, facing the princess.

"If you're referring to me, please use them."

"Oh okay! Thanks for telling me," I respond, my focus returning to Xavier. "Yeah, they were nice enough to let me use some of their clothes, but I needed my own style back, so I dragged Cassius to a store and had him buy me clothes."

Apparently shocked by this reveal, the room falls into laughter and gasps. Some put a hand over their mouth. This quickly turns into mockery of Cassius about him paying. When the room calms down a bit, a question suddenly pops into my head. "Queen Helena." I pause. "She doesn't care about the king's affairs?"

"Only when it calls into question her authority as queen," Esme states while pouring herself another glass. "She probably has just as many affairs as our father. We're all sure they married for strategy, and while I'm evidence that there's some level of mutual affection, neither of them truly loves the other."

No one speaks. Like what she had just said is some unspoken truth. The only thing that could be heard now is Ezra sucking in a sharp breath, which is probably his way of holding himself back.

He needs to be in control, but more importantly, he always needs to be right, which, in all honesty, I could understand to a degree. Our commonality ends at that. He expects people to cling to his every word. His longing for the crown is rooted in its status. Being king represents the ultimate form of power.

"Shall we return to our little game?" Xavier suggests.

"I think I've had enough alcohol in me for one day, but I'll play a round or two," I say while pouring my last glass.

"Boo," Xavier whines in dismay. "Fine then, you're first." He brings a hand to his chin, planning my dare, and now I worry about what insane thing he'll have me do. "I dare you to take a shot... and pour it into Ezra's mouth."

"That's it?" I eye him suspiciously. "That's nothing. Hand me a shot."

Monty walks to the minibar table to pour alcohol before handing it to me. As I make my way over to Ezra, he straightens himself on the couch. Legs still spread, I straddle him, my knees on both sides of his thighs. "You okay with this?" I ask, not wanting to make him uncomfortable.

He responds by tilting his head back and opening his mouth.

I pour the shot down, dropping the glass as I lean my head over his. Opening my mouth, I let the alcohol fall from my mouth into his. He closes his lips and makes eye contact with me as he swallows, his eyes filling with lust.

I start to lift off of him but am stopped by his hands grabbing my waist. I feel a bulge in his pants harden, the fabric looking tighter. Without another blink, he presses his lips onto mine. I close my eyes, kissing him back, sinking my full weight to his lap and grinding into him. His hands reach under my shirt, tracing the skin of my back, slowly creeping towards my bra.

As he sucks on my neck, I let out a moan. It incites him to

chuckle against my skin. His mouth reeks of nothing but alcohol. But then again, I bet mine did too.

It isn't until I hear Atticus groaning that I remember we're in a room of his family. "Get a room. There are literally many to choose from."

Swinging my legs off of Ezra, I stand, holding his hand to help him up. We climb up the stairs that lead to the east wing, and I'm pulled into a bedroom. *His bedroom.*

When we enter, I sit on the bed, silently thanking myself for keeping my birth control spell active while he locks the door before moving in my direction. He strips himself of his shirt and starts lifting my top off.

After throwing my shirt to the side, his hand brushes across the rolls of my stomach. The touch raises every flag of insecurity to spike. My reaction has his cocky grin growing while his hands unclasp my bra and he pushes me down on the bed. If he wants control, I'll let him take it for the night.

Not bothering to take off my skirt, he pulls down my underwear and plunges two fingers inside of me. He's thrusting at an intense speed, but it's not enough.

"Fuck," I moan.

"More," I demand, shutting my lids as he speeds his fingers up, reaching deeper.

He begins sucking on my breasts, eliciting a dire need for him to be inside me.

Ezra brings his lips to my mouth, his tongue entering, twisting with mine. I can feel myself close to coming. I buck my hips against his hand in hopes of release but am met with him removing his fingers from me and his tongue clicking with sadistic disapproval.

I sit up, glaring at him. "*What the fuck?*"

When I register he's moved from the bed, his pants are gone. His cock fully out, he motions for me to come to him. Obeying like the submissive he so craves, I glide my steps towards where he stands. He's much bigger than I expected.

"Suck."

I kneel beneath him and take in his length, teasing the head with my tongue. What I can't fit in my mouth, I wrap inside my hands and pump up from the base. He's well over eight and a half inches at minimum. His length isn't just big. It's thick.

A groan escapes him as I swirl my tongue, taking him deeper. Bobbing my head up and down, I feel it twitch inside my mouth, pre-cum leaking from its head. Swallowing, I continue my movements and apply more pressure, my hand moving in tandem with my mouth.

His hand grips my hair, pulling me up from my place. He extends his arm, leading me to his bed. His naked body on top of me, he repositions his hand towards the entrance of my core.

"You're so wet," he coos in my ear. "I cannot wait for you to drench my cock."

The words are nice, but I feel nothing for them.

He brings his mouth to my nipple and begins sucking me with as much pressure as I had done on him. I can feel my body reacting to the alcohol as he bites down on my piercing. Most of his cock slips into me in one thrust and begins moving, wasting no time for me to adjust. He brings his mouth to my neck, sucking harshly as I run my fingers through his hair, tugging it when he reaches his fingers to circle my clit.

This is a terrible idea, and I know it. But the hunger on his face washes away every logical thought I have. I'm too lost in enjoying myself to care about any consequence this may bring. I want a distraction. A release.

I deserve this.

Taking his mouth from my neck, he gazes into my eyes. Scanning his body, it's no wonder he became the leader of the guards. He has such a muscular, toned upper body, I'm sure he could break me if he wanted to.

When he crashes his mouth onto mine, I bite the bottom of his lip, bringing him back to me when he rudely lifts his head. His thrusting recedes, movement stilling as he removes my hands from his shoulders and pins them above my head with one hand, my neck slightly gripped with the other.

He resumes his thrusting. Harder. I start to feel a coil inside me chasing a high when he takes a hand from my wrists, dragging it down my body back to my clit. He rubs rapid circles, tightening his hold around my neck.

"I can feel you tightening. Come for me, pet," he breathes in my ear.

With his words, I'm brought to the sensation of my release. Through my orgasm, he pistols in and out of me without the slightest bit of calm.

"Fuck!" I scream.

"That's it, baby," he purrs before removing his cock from inside me. He pumps himself three more times before he spurts all over my stomach, his head partially thrown back, face full of ecstasy.

If the alcohol from today hadn't worn me out, this definitely did. I'm fully spent, drunk from the huge amount of alcohol I consumed today, but sober enough to know what I was doing. While catching our breaths, he rises from the bed, getting a cloth to clean us.

"Just so you know," he looks at me, "people will do anything for power, pet." He holds my stare before redressing himself. "Let us return to my family."

A pestering itchiness tingles through my leg when I wake up. I look down at my foot and find the constellation of my astrological sign on my left ankle. *I don't remember getting this. When the fuck did that happen?*

The events from last night replay in my head as I check my phone for the time. *12:55.* I change into a black, lacy tank top and skirt that the tailors had sent up. Honestly, I'm not sure how they picked up on my style so quickly.

After I add an underbust corset to finish the outfit, I magik on makeup and tie half my hair with a scrunchie before throwing on jewelry, a tiara included. When I view myself in the mirror, I figure it's good enough for the day and walk downstairs in my heeled boots.

As I descend the stairs, I'm met with Kabir waiting at the bottom, arm out to help me down the last few steps and ready to join my side.

"Good afternoon, Lady Arabella. Sleep well?"

"Yeah Kabir, I did. Thanks."

Venturing into the kitchen, I grab myself some water, pointing to the glass to ask if he wants any. He shakes his head before I down the glass of water, leaning on the counter. "Why do you call me

Lady Arabella? I'm not noble, and you of all people shouldn't be acting like I am."

"You're a guest at Nexus Palace. As long as the king requires you to be treated as such, you will have the respect of that title."

We stroll back towards the main staircases, and I feel the eyes of the eldest prince. Passing Ezra, he turns his attention to me, the corner of his lips lifting. "Hello, pet." His hand reaches for mine. "Enjoy your night?"

Oh gods, I definitely remember fucking him. It was fun in the moment, but now I'm feeling major regrets. He hadn't nearly met my standard when it comes to dirty talk. "It was decent," I reply coolly, walking towards the back entrance with Kabir.

Cassius is sitting by the door frame reading a book when I plop myself next to him. His shirt is covered in creases and isn't tucked in like it usually is. The puffs in his sleeves are unbuttoned at the cuffs. The entirety of his face is tightened while his hair reflects that of bedhead. Everything about him is disoriented. He looks to me for a second and scrunches his face in dismay, quickly returning to his book. Clearly, he's already fed up with me today. Probably because he had to play babysitter and carry me back yesterday.

"Whatcha reading?"

"It does not matter," he replies coldly.

My eyes widen, brows furrowed, turning to Kabir, who gives me a shrug. "Okay well, I was just wondering if we were going into town today to try getting more intel? Maybe trying Hearthis or Aquatius?"

"You did enough yesterday. I shall search for information on my own. Rest your body after the entangling night you had," he snarls, standing up and going inside.

After he leaves, Kabir and I go down the steps. Our arms are linked, making sure I don't stumble down. "What's his problem?"

He sighs. "The problem with Prince Cassius," he pauses, choosing his next words carefully, "is that he always has a problem. No one can ever tell what offends him."

Deciding not to take it personally, I skip towards the open land, Kabir still following me. "Why are you staying at my side today?" I laugh. Guards are training behind us. He should be with them. "You my personal bodyguard or something?"

His face remains still. My jaw drops, a smile growing on my face. "Oh shit, you are, huh? That's hilarious! Okay, tell me something," I say, clapping my hands together, "why do you really think that no one will tell us anything?"

"I don't have any good answers for you, my lady. All I can confidently say, is based on what I know, the king has not been well liked among the common fae for years now." He gazes off in the distance. "If they aren't telling you anything, it could be because of any association you have to the crown, but that still wouldn't explain the disappearances of both common fae and lords."

I nod my head along. "You're probably right."

Spotting Xavier by the water statue, I rush to him. "Xavier!" I shout, running until I crash into him, tackling us both to the ground.

"What was that for?" He dusts himself off.

"That was for letting me fuck Ezra last night," I say before shoving him again.

"You two almost fucked in front of us!" he laughs in disgust. He readjusts his sunstone necklace that wraps inside a kite-shaped wiring. It's the one that both he and his brother always wear. "I'd rather I *didn't* have to witness you having sex with the kiss-ass cousin."

"As opposed to sex with any of your other cousins?"

"Maybe." He shakes his head at me sarcastically. "Anyway, what are you doing here? Don't you have common fae to interrogate?"

I sit in the grass, patting the spot next to me for him to join. Leaves tangle in his hair, which makes me take notice of its length and how fast it's grown since we first met. Rather than falling past his shoulders, it now sits maybe three inches below them.

"Cassius is being weird."

Xavier laughs at me, like I just said the most obvious thing in the world. "When isn't he?"

I tilt my head, nodding, lips pointed down in agreement. "True. But he said he wanted to do his own research today and left, so I decided to bother you." I grin, shaking my head as I speak.

"*Hmm.*" He turns to face forward for a moment, lips thinned, before looking at me again. "Okay, second question." His head tilts. "Why are you in a tiara?"

"Oh." Readjusting the tiara that fell slightly from its place, I giggle. "If I'm gonna be forced here while being treated like royalty, I might as well dress it." A beat passes before I continue. I'm distracted by the tiny Sprite guards with hair of seed heads that are sparring against Pookas. "Besides, crowns are pretty, and I look powerful."

"Maybe I should start wearing them," he says smugly, grabbing the accessory from my head.

"Well you would be very pretty, if you didn't have leaves in your hair."

"Your fault. Not mine."

Pulling myself up so I can pick the debris from his hair, I feel the tingle on my ankle again. I groan, slapping the area through my shoe.

"What's wrong?"

"It's just my ankle," I admit, taking off my boot. "I woke up with this tattoo, and I barely remember how I got it, other than it happened last night." My eyes narrow, suspicious when he snickers to himself. "Do you know?"

"Oh yes, that was me," he answers whimsically.

I look at him, aghast.

"You said something about wanting a new tattoo, so I grabbed my machine that my sisters got for me in Human Lands and tattooed you."

I blink a few times. "Oh... Well it's pretty good. It's just irritated like a bitch right now."

"You're a witch," he says, slowly. "Magik away the itchiness."

He's right. I can't believe I didn't think about that. I sit down and magik my skin, manipulating away the feeling, though it should be completely healed in a few days.

With the itchiness gone, I finish picking the remaining debris from his tangled hair as he sits between my open legs, hunching over so that his torso is short enough for me to reach his head.

# VII

## *Spite Is One Hell of a Motivator*

Cassius

Peeking from a window, I see Arabella laying her head on Xavier's lap, both full of laughter and animation. The sun shines on the crimson-maroon color that commonly colors Fher lips, highlighting its fullness.

Why does she emanate pure bliss in the company of my cousin? What is it about him that makes her so comfortable?

I entertain the thought of spending my day with Korine and our friend Harrison before ultimately deciding against it. After all, I should make use of my free time collecting information, as I had told Arabella I would.

The halls of Nexus are silent. So quiet you could hear the scratching of a head in another room. I wander into one of the libraries to search for a book on anything that could assist us in any way. The archive section is a good place to start, but the area is mostly filled with useless information that I already know.

Although this task is likely inconsequential, I search for any indication that we are facing a repeat of past events. The past tends to have a way of finding its way back around, so I suspect that perhaps there is a chance of finding an answer.

The remaining libraries are overflowing with words from fiction and novels that serve no purpose at this current time. As I walk from the halls, I see my family gathered together around the foyer. Maude and Atticus are missing. Likely she, with her lover, and he, tending to his wife. Ezra too is nowhere to be seen. However, Isadora and Dyana's loud hair and even louder voices are echoing throughout the palace.

In hopes to avoid speaking with them, I ponder ways to sneak around them. They do not need me to participate in their idle gossip over foolish matters. One would think that with all the frivolities others in my family could get away with, my sisters would make better use of their time, but alas, they'd rather share information about the children of the other high-ranking Fae. I could appreciate such conversation if it did not include speaking poorly of my friends.

Servants are coursing through the floor, preparing for tonight's meal. It's the perfect opportunity to leave without drawing any attention towards myself. Attempting to sneak past, I'm stopped by my pestering cousins, who drag me into their conversation.

"What's with you?" Dyana asks.

"Yeah, why do you appear so upset?" Cel adds on.

*Perhaps it is due to being forced into this conversation.*

I assume they are waiting for an answer. They have no business inquiring about the state of my mood. That aside, apart from spending the past two hours sifting through books that held no useful information, I am perfectly content.

Whether it is due to my lack of response or simply waiting to mock me, Isadora and Esme join in.

"How do you even know he's upset?" Isadora says to her sister.

Esme begins to laugh, curious for herself. "Yeah? He only ever seems like he's looking for his next victim to torment."

Dyana gives an answer to their questions. "He's been scowling all afternoon. Instead of it being directed at everyone, he keeps reverting his head outside. He's clearly pissed with Ara."

"You mad we told you she had sex, little brother?" Esme taunts.

Isadora cracks a cocky grin. "No, he's just upset he can't torture her with his existence."

Cel is the only to say nothing and instead offers a look of concern. The others continue to cackle, exchanging insults as if I am not within two steps from them.

I needn't endure this ridicule, so I laugh. "Do you have anything better to put your attention towards, or will you continue living all your days vicariously through the lives of others? Something which you all so clearly lack?"

The laughing falters. The space suddenly fills with cold stares and frowns. It is one thing to stop them, but I have struck a nerve with them all, aware of how our father holds them to such a high standard. They are furious.

I walk away from them, only to be faced by Ezra. He struts his way over to me in a smug fashion, acting as if he is already king. Presumptuous. As if our father would give up his power so easily.

"Ah, brother," he calls.

*Damn it. Have I not endured enough ridicule from our family today?*

"Yes, Ezra?" I reply, standing my ground so that he may come to me. "Do you require something?"

His jaw clenches, visibly irritated that I don't bend to him. "Do not take that petulant tone with me. Am I not allowed to spend quality time with my own kin?"

"Not when the kin is me," I remark. "So I'll repeat myself. What is it you require?"

A slap strikes me to the ground. The side of my face stinging, I see Ezra rubbing the back of his hand. While he is always pleasant to our sisters, he never shows a glimmer of kindness towards me. Perhaps it is why I return those mannerisms. But he has never been that way towards Atticus. Yes, he belittles and degrades our brother's choice of lifestyle, but never has he had physical altercations with him to such a degree. However, Atticus is larger than us both. Ezra is likely too afraid to behave the same way he does towards me.

Our father is similar. Not towards Atticus, but to me. I am treated as the disappointment of all my siblings, going as far as to say that Cel is a replacement for the sin of my birth. Ezra is an exact duplicate of our father, possibly worse. At the least, our father does not beg for approval.

Ezra looks down at me, calling me pathetic. Laughing before saying another word. "Get up. It was hardly forceful enough to cause you to fall."

Standing from the floor, I fix the hem of my shirt before facing my brother. "How may I help you?"

He smirks, enjoying the power over me that I give him. "Better. I was curious as to the particulars you have received recently."

"Pardon?" I ask through gritted teeth.

Backing away, he distances himself from my body. His arms are crossed, treating our conversation that of a game. "I asked about the information surrounding the missing Fae that you and Arabella have learned. You two have been going into the town for weeks, and I have yet to hear of updates. So," he leans his body towards me, "what have you acquired?"

The egotistical look he has is infuriating. I want to wipe it off his face. "If you must know, many of the common fae are upset that we had not taken their missing seriously, prior to the lords. There are also some who suspect this isn't coincidental. That the days they have been taken, along with when any were found, are of importance."

It will not satisfy him, but it's all we have been informed of.

Unimpressed, his face examines mine. "So in totality, you have learned nothing that my guards did not already know?"

Nothing is going to be enough for him. He may desire answers, but more importantly, he desires to see me fail so that he may come out victorious by solving this himself.

No. There is one thing we discovered. I recall the woman from the store. Something that rallied enough of the common fae to trust us. "We have learned that the common fae are easily impressionable. They are drawn to false acts and are likely to spill their hearts out if they see people of importance showing empathy towards them."

"Interesting," Ezra says. His eyes roam around the hall before directing them back at me. "Dine with me, brother. We ought to discuss this at length."

We walk into the kitchen, where he demands one of the servants to have our food brought to the Head Guard's office–his office. He takes such pride in a role that was handed to him. He did nothing to earn his title but instead was given it by our father. That aside, even I can admit he has a particular taste for strategy. If only he were more thoughtful in applying that to his subordinates.

Inside his office are shrines dedicated to his accomplishments. From his academic achievements to markings of his aptitudes, they are displayed to exhibit the victories he could accomplish as a leader. He rarely invites me in, other than to disparage any accomplishment I have. I sit, tuning out as he explains once more my inability to make headway on our investigation. He takes pride in belittling my weaknesses by comparing them to Arabella's strengths.

"She has been here for nearly a month, and already she seems to overtake father's favor over you with her ideas. Not that you ever really had a position in his court," he chastises while taking a seat.

Leering at him, I spit back, "Have you done anything to help our cause, being that you're the leader of our guards? One who our army general reports to?"

His mouth forms a wicked grin. It's tiresome how someone whose only power is distinguishing lies can hold his stature. Such a useless ability from our blood. "I have been preoccupied with more pressing things." He picks up a stack of papers from the desk, tears through the first few before handing me the rest. "It seems that there may be a connection we missed. The only Fae who have been found brutally murdered were those of higher positions. Those men were the only ones who had any physical markings on their bodies."

I look at him. This we know from the man at the tavern. "And how does that help us?"

"Does that not fall under your duties?" he replies arrogantly. "I am just here to pass along what I know."

There has to be another reason he is telling me this. He would not freely give me this information if it didn't benefit him in some way. "And that is?"

"That if those in power cannot hold themselves, someone, or *something*, will get to them."

With that, a servant walks in with our supper. Ezra dismisses me from the office, calling into question why he requested we dine together if all he wanted was to give me reports on the deaths.

I spend the next few days avoiding Arabella, drawing up excuses about how we can better gather facts alone, rather than together. While I suspect that neither of us has collected much, we must review anything we have discovered, though I'd much rather be off to my own activities. Enough time has passed where neither of us harbors ill feelings from the other day.

Seeking her presence throughout the palace, I have yet to detect her anywhere. The guards are just as unaware of her whereabouts, so I resort to the last measure. The tracker.

When I discover her location, I exit Nexus, okkaring towards an open area past the estate and under a willow tree along Lake Mindae. I observe her movements and understand she is doing a form of training. She works her way through physical exercises, the light winds blowing through the leaves and her barely tied hair. After a while, she shows exhaustion and begins breathing techniques.

I never see her with her hair tied, at least not in this manner. If it is not fully down, there are two sections of strands in the front while the locks that would cover her ears are swept back and tied lowly in the back. The way her face is fully visible emphasizes the red of her cheeks and the sweat that slowly falls.

Frustrated with herself, a patch of grass next to her catches on fire. It is then that I am running to her.

As I'm attempting to extinguish the flames, I pull my coat off and set it on top, stomping so that it may snuff it out. Once it is fully put out, I lift the clothing and see that the fire had eaten its way through the fabric, making it no longer suitable to be worn.

Arabella's panting becomes heavier, though I cannot be sure if it is from the concern of nearly setting the land ablaze or the exercise she had just completed. She sits down, resting her head between her arms atop her knees, not taking her eyes from the patch of grass.

Once she calms and her breath regulates, I sit next to her, asking if she is okay.

She watches me, breath still heavy. "I'm fine. Sorry about your jacket."

"I was quite fond of this piece of outerwear, but I would sooner choose having a new one made over a new palace to reside in," I respond to ease her guilt. She smiles thinly before bringing her eyes back to the ground.

I need to refocus. We have a duty to accomplish if I am to rid myself of her as quickly as possible. We must discuss what we have found from others, yet my mind cannot help but remain curious over how the fire started. "What were you training for?"

She gives a light huff. "I wasn't really training. I save that for my time with Kabir. I was working out and trying to practice a little magik." She takes in another breath. "The breathing is just for centering myself, but sometimes, my brain gets out of control, and when my emotions flare, well... you saw what happened. Fire combusts."

"Yes."

Unable to form a way to shift the conversation, I say nothing, waiting for her to speak again. I lean back, resting my body on the ground, feeling the earth surround us both.

Arabella scrambles to restart her breathing activity before her breath stills. When I turn, her face is puzzled in confusion. It is evident her thoughts have to do with me, but she doesn't know how to say it. Finally, she blurts out, "How did you find me?"

Lifting myself, I sit up. "Excuse me?"

She maneuvers herself so that we are now facing each other. Sweat drips from her forehead and neck, her cheeks still flushed from the activity she had been doing. She combs a hand through her hair and takes a drink from her container before asking again. "I just mean, how did you know where I was? I didn't tell anyone where I was going, so how did you find me?"

I take the device from my pocket that indicates how to find her location. "I have a tracker, if you recall."

"Shit. It actually works?" She takes the device from my hands, observing it by turning it in every direction. "So like... is there a way to shut it off? Maybe take off these earrings?" she asks, her eyes widening while pursing her lips.

"If you want to remove the jewelry, you will have to speak with my father. Only the king has the capability of ordering them off," I say, taking back the device.

Plummeting herself into the ground, she watches as clouds go by. Her eyes shut, and a sigh escapes her lips before opening them back up. She looks so calm. Peaceful nearly. Especially in contrast to her typical angry demeanor that she throws at me.

Rain begins trickling from the sky, prompting us to okkar to the grounds of the palace. Running from the lake would take far too long. The soil, now muddy as we near the stone, causes her to trip, sullying her clothing. She wipes down some of the grass from her black, skintight trousers that hug her skin as she begins lightly laughing at her misfortune.

Once inside, a guard hands us towels and takes our shoes from us so that we may not tarnish the floor. While another servant takes my coat so that she may dispose of it, I ask, "How did the land catch fire?"

She turns her head towards me with a befuddled look. "I told you–"

"Yes, you said it occurs when your emotions spiral. But why? Can't Magiks control when they set fire to things?"

Upset by my question, her whole demeanor towards me changes. Her jaw stiffens, body tight, and she begins tapping her fingers against her body as her expression becomes dazed. I noted previously that this is something she does repetitively when we are in large crowds or our environment is cumbersome.

After seemingly soothing herself, she blinks before facing me. "Most Magiks can control it, but for some reason, I can't. Or at least I've never been able to. It's like with okkaring. I try to focus and center myself, but when I always have a million things going through my mind, it makes it hard to think. My mom didn't let me train properly until I was fourteen, so I was a bit behind in school when I started." She begins to fidget with her hands. "With the whole fire thing, well, most Magiks can do it, but I was only ever able to have a small grasp over it with my friends or someone I trusted. But when you're always on the verge of snapping, there were times fire would sometimes follow," she laughs off as a jest.

It's evident that this is a subject she is yet to feel comfortable speaking about. Something she cannot discuss without making a quip. I avert my eyes from her. Odd that even with lessons and teachings, she is not able to control herself.

"Perhaps," I suggest while refusing to look in her direction. "If there was a way I could help you control it, would you allow me?"

Arabella is never one to ask for help, that much I comprehended from our time together. She feels as though she needs to be independent of everything. But if I don't wish to see myself cooked like our meals after one of her outbursts, I will need to assist her in this.

To my surprise, she does not argue with me on this. "How?"

"I may not be educated in witchcraft, nor able to perform your abilities, but there are powers shared by both Fae and Magiks alike."

"Like what?" she asks, doubting there could possibly be anything that we have in common.

"For example, both creatures have the ability to okkar to different locations by thought."

She begins listening, a blank expression as I speak. In some way, she may trust me, since she makes no objection to my claim.

"And those of us with the Elemental bloodlines have abilities that match our ancestors," I add on. "While some are physical, such as my brother Atticus' heightened strength, there are those of us whose abilities extend to a more mental state. My father can read the minds of Fae, Esme can travel through people's dreams, and Ezra can detect when one tells lies."

Her head cocks in my direction, lips parting before they are once again shut.

"And of course, there is me, who has the ability to summon shadows at will," I say, plunging the room into darkness.

Shadows surround the room, enclosing us in tendrils of smoke. Arabella's body twists in all directions in disbelief. As she reaches her hand to what circles us, I grab it.

"What the fuck, Cassius? Don't touch me!"

"Then do not directly place yourself inside the shadow's hold."

She pulls her hand from mine, putting space between us. "You act like you have such animosity towards me, but you sure do a lot to keep me from putting myself in danger."

A huff of laughter escapes me before explaining myself. "You misunderstand. I am *trying* to demonstrate my capabilities to you, which *include* the dangers of my shadows."

Sucking the shadows back into the skin of my hands, light now shines through the hall once again.

"How did you do that?"

"As I said, some of us have certain capabilities from our bloodline. Some that require us to draw from a mental state."

Walking away from her, she speaks loudly before I can fully turn away. "Show me."

I stare at her, waiting.

She groans. "*Ugh*. Please help me, Prince Cassius."

"Beg."

"Oh, fuck you. I'll just ask Esme or Ezra or something," she spits through rolled eyes, moving away from me.

"We'll meet tomorrow," I call.

Halfway up the stairs, Arabella pauses. "What?"

Tilting my head to her, I smirk. "You have done enough damage to the grounds for one day. Tomorrow, I will show you how to keep your thoughts at bay. It will aid you in your struggles."

Then, I am left in my own company, driven to our storage of lasialic.

Apparently when I said that we begin tomorrow, Arabella took it as starting whenever she so chooses. It is well past noon, and she has yet to come from her own bedchamber. I cannot stand this. How she puts off something that is for her own benefit.

Irritated with her absence, I barge into her room, only to find her missing from her bed. It's after checking her bathroom and going through open areas on the first story do I give up my search.

*Perhaps she is with Ezra.* The thought agitates me. If she does not care for my support and seeks my brother's help, why had she agreed to mine in the first place? She could have rejected my offer, but instead, she continuously finds ways to provoke my displeasure.

At the sight of my brother in the courtyard with other guards, I come to the conclusion that Arabella had not spent the night in his bed. It is both a strange relief and worries me all the more. I spot Kabir, assuming he will likely know the whereabouts of the witch.

"Kabir." I reach my arm towards his shoulder. A Fae, much taller than I, with a build and stature of such largeness, makes him far more intimidating than I could ever be.

He turns to me, neutrality on his face. "Yes, Your Highness? How may I be of assistance?"

"It's Arabella."

Neutral shifts to concern. "What happened? Is Lady Arabella okay? I had left her alone as she requested." He begins marching towards the palace, similar to that of a frightened loved one.

Kabir is so fit that his casual marches are a jogging pace for me, which means I have to go at more of a run in order to grab back his attention. Once we reach the inside, I opt for yelling instead. "Kabir, no." He stops in his place, allowing for me to continue. "I only require to know where Arabella is. Do you happen to know?"

The worry on his face fades, his body settling. "Oh. Yes, Prince Cassius. She is in the second training hall," he answers. But as he leaves out the door, he pokes himself back in and asks, "Do you not have the tracker that could locate her in your possession?"

Right. The device I used to find her not twenty-four hours ago. "I-" I hesitate, quickly needing to think of an excuse, "I left it in my room." With hopes the response warrants no suspicion, I add, "I recently woke, and it had slipped my mind. In any matter, you have been of great use."

Passing through the different rooms that lead to the training halls, I catch a glimpse of Arabella attempting to okkar to different points of the room. She is frustrated, grunting and upset with herself when she is unsuccessful. I take delight in seeing her like this. As her frustration grows and fury enters her eyes, to prevent the palace from being set aflame, I say, "I expected you to meet with me."

Startled by my unexpected presence, a knife is thrown in my direction, hitting the doorframe next to me. I retrieve it from the floor, amused by the unflipped weapon. When handing it back to her, she refuses to make eye contact. "You hadn't opened it."

"Oh, well you scared me. I didn't have time to think." She grabs water from the corner of the room, limping with every step, legs covered with freshly acquired bruises and cuts.

"Your legs," I say.

"I'm fine," she responds as she slides her back along a wall before falling into a seat on the floor. Her arms fling over the injuries, knees near her chest. "So how are you planning on helping me?" she asks with fingers quoting the word helping.

Standing over her, I watch until she groans and forces herself up from her position.

"What were you attempting before I came in here?" I ask, not intending to reveal I was observing her while she was upset with herself, nearly setting another piece of our property ablaze.

"I was..." she trails off. Her lips are thinned, arms crossed, trying to gain the courage to speak without humiliating herself. "I was trying to okkar, and it was pissing me off that I couldn't."

"Interesting." I pace around her, debating what my next move will be. Where we will go from here.

Uncrossing her arms and slamming them against her sides, she grows defensive. "Don't patronize me."

"Do you really believe that was what I was doing?"

Arabella's eyes scan me, backing from where she stands. She must be truly desperate if she is willing to put her pride aside and stay. Despite her stubborn nature, the difficulty outweighs her contempt.

Now standing directly facing her, I tilt her chin to meet my face. She winces. "Firstly, we will work on controlling your thoughts."

She scoffs, lightly kicking around one of the wooden figures scattered in the room. "Easier said than done. Don't you think if there was a way I could do that, I would've tried it by now?"

I sigh at her misunderstanding. The refusal to allow me to elaborate firstly. "We aren't controlling your thoughts forever, just calming them for a minimal time until you have a better grip over your intentions. Tell me," I say, drawing closer to her, "when do you feel the most at peace?"

She ponders the question. "I think it's when I'm reading a book I'm invested in. Or spending time with my friends." Her face beams with joy, eyes glistening as bright as the stars in a clear night sky.

I quickly wipe the smile that inches its way onto my face in hopes she may not notice. "So bring your thoughts to that." She tilts her head, questioning what I just said. "If you want to take hold of your power, think of things that bring you to your most calm. Memories or hobbies." Putting her behind me, I prepare to demonstrate my abilities. "Observe."

Shadows summon from my palms, allowing them to swallow the room into utter darkness. She wanders through it, heeding my warning to not touch the borders.

"You needn't fear. Unlike the shadows of yesterday, these do not have the ability to harm what it touches. It is used as a form of distraction. A way to darken everything around so that sight is difficult. I also have the ability to do this." I bring the shadows back within me as I form a silhouette of a man to stand next to Arabella.

She inspects the figure, circling around it to fully understand its being. When she attempts to slap her hand through it, she is met with a pain that brings her body squatting to her feet. "PUTANG INA!" For a moment, she recollects herself, shooting a glare at me. "Why didn't you tell me the shit was solid?" She shakes her hand through the ache.

"It was more enjoyable to see how you would act."

Standing back straight and shaking her hand from the sting, Arabella runs her other hand along the edges, marveling at its permanence. "Is it able to hold things too? Can it move around?"

"Yes," I reply. "It has the ability to move and fight as I could, without it being physically tied to me."

Her eyebrows furrow, eyelids blinking to have a better understanding. "How?" she asks.

While it is posed as a question, I know she refuses to drop a question unless my answer meets her standards. "I have the ability to summon shadows–"

"And wings, apparently," she interrupts.

I close my lips together. "Yes, and wings. I can summon shadows in one of four ways: darkness surrounding and harming those who touch it, having it drown the light from an area, creating objects that act as they would if created, and casting a silhouette of a man, as you just saw." Her mouth starts to open, but before she says another word, I speak. "I will my shadows based on the intention, and when I cannot control those intentions, I think of the things that ground me the best. Either things I am fond of or what motivates me."

"Huh, that's cool."

Not pressing further about what calms me, I am grateful. If we did not hate each other, there is a possibility I would be open to sharing, but that is not the case. She would think me a monster if she knew that my power draws from my rage.

"So how exactly does this help me?" she questions. For the first time, she questions me without any hint of sarcasm in her tone.

I wrap my arms around her body and grab her hands. She stiffens slightly, but rather than fighting me, she falls into my hold, allowing me to touch her. "Close your eyes and think of something that motivates you the most."

She takes a deep breath before exhaling. "Okay."

"Do you have it in mind?"

"Yeah."

Pulling her hands apart, I lower my head over her shoulder.

"Now think of the fire coursing through you, imagining you have a target in mind." I can feel her lips moving. She's grinning. Letting go of her, I move to the side and take a few steps back. "Allow the energy to move to your hands. When you open your eyes, direct the fire to the target in front of you."

When her eyes open, sapphire flames blast from her fingertips, reaching near the other side of the room.

Squealing with excitement, she falls to her knees. "I did it," she says in disbelief. "I actually fucking did it!" Jumping up from her place, she comes to me. "Thank you! I mean that. Thank you."

"Do not thank me yet. There is still the matter of okkaring. It's similar to what you have just done, but you need to focus on the exact location you want."

Arabella's face now flashes with aggravation. "Can't you let me have *one* thing?"

While chuckling to myself, she disappears from where she was standing and reappears at the doorway. "Of course you can't," she says, exiting the room.

Calling out to her, I ask, "What was your motivation today?"

Down the hallway, her words echo. "Spite."

# VIII

## *Light Stabbings*

Arabella

Breathing in and out, I think back to the memories I have with my friends. With Luka. I think about all the memories we created together and how I never felt safer than when I was with them. Taking one last inhale, I feel the fire burning within me, letting it move through my body and into my palms. Just as I am about to release the fire, Maude screams my name, scaring me and causing the flames to shoot from my hands onto the jacket I left on the dirt.

Shrieking, I try putting the fire out, effectively burning a hole that now matches Cassius' jacket. Maude picks it up and hands it to Kabir, asking that he dispose of it.

"Sorry. I hadn't meant to frighten you," she says apologetically, glancing at the now burnt land. "Or ruin the few clothes you have.

Though I'm sure the tailors would be happy to make you a new one."

Behind her follows the voices of the rest of the Disaris daughters, along with Dyana and Isa. *I guess we're having a day without men.* The thought is quickly squashed when I see Xavier and Monty behind their sisters. *Or not.*

Linking arms with me, Isa and Dyana pull me to the ground, giggling when their brothers pile on.

"How's our favorite prisoner?" Monty asks.

"Yeah, sleep with anyone new?" Xavier jokes as he props himself onto his elbows.

This is so embarrassing. Other than Isa and Dyana, they were all there to witness me with Ezra. It's not like I was too drunk to be unable to give consent, but of all the people in the family, Ezra should *not* have been my first.

"Don't be assholes. It was a mistake. That's all it was. A drunken fling, if you will," I say in hopes they'll drop the subject. But unfortunately for me, I know the ridicule is far from over.

All sitting in a circle, Maude begins teasing. "Oh come now, you can't really expect us all to act as though you didn't fuck Ezra."

"Yeah," Celeste now adds to the conversation. "If it weren't for Atticus, you two would've fucked on the couch right in front of us."

Biting my lip that curls inward, I shut my mouth in response. I can't exactly deny that without lying. We were definitely seconds away from me pulling down his pants in front of them all. I throw my face into my hands to avoid eye contact with any of them. "Why are y'all so comfortable with talking about me fucking your relative?"

Slinging her arm over my shoulder and immediately taking it back, Dyana bursts with glee like she is the sun bringing warmth.

"You're here for weeks and mostly keep to yourself, and the *one* time Ezra decides to spend time with us, you fuck him. Of course we find it hilarious. *We* can barely stand him."

"Plus," Esme snickers, "it's not like Ezra's getting sex from anyone else. You were just drunk enough to want him."

"*Ugh,*" I grumble, falling into the grass. *They're never going to let me live this down.*

The position of everyone must have shifted because my stomach is suddenly weighed down by the pressure of Xavier's head. "I think you've proven that you have the absolute worst luck in our lands," he says.

Lightly hitting the top of his head, I plead, "Can't we just pretend it didn't happen?"

"Nope," Maude states.

"Not when it pisses off you *and* Cassius," Monty declares.

*Why would it piss off Cassius? Is that why he was being weird to me the day after it happened? Does he hate me so much that he'd be upset I slept with his brother?*

I push the thoughts from my head since his opinion shouldn't matter. Cassius and I are forced to work together, and as he stated, Fae and Magiks cannot stand each other. I'm still here because his father refuses to let me leave unless I want to die, and Cassius is working with me because his father demanded he do so.

Xavier drums his hands on my thigh. "I can tell that you're in a daydream. What's up?"

"Nothing," I say, sitting up after Xavier lifts his head from me, repositioning it onto my thigh. "I wasn't daydreaming. Just trying to figure out how to better my training."

No one's convinced of what I said, which only would make them press further.

"What were you doing anyway?" Isa asks. "Y'know, before you turned your jacket into crispy cotton."

"Funny story. I uh, I actually *was* practicing to try to get a better grip over my thoughts. Yesterday, Cassius helped–"

Sounds of shock leave everyone's mouths. Even Xavier gets up from his position just to gawk at what I just said.

Rolling my eyes, I continue. "*Anyway,* he helped me figure out a way to manage my thoughts better so I could master my fire spells and okkaring. I was in the middle of it before you decided to collectively jump me."

This statement is proof to believe my earlier claim about bettering my training. Esme stands, motioning for them all to follow. "Let's leave Bella to her practice. I think she has a lot to do, and she doesn't need us distracting her." She pushes her foot into Xavier to get him to pay attention to her words. "That means you too, Xavier. Actually, it means you most of all."

After about two minutes of the two going back and forth about leaving me on my own, Monty pulls Xavier up, and they all leave. Being that Esme is the one who knows how truly terrified I was my first day here, she knows how important it is for me to master okkaring.

I recenter myself before the thoughts and memories of motivation consume my mind.

For the following two days, all I do is spend my free time trying to manage my thoughts and work on controlling my fire. I'm beginning to have such control that the magik takes practically nothing from my energy anymore. Of the two, okkaring has always been easier for me, so I'm not as repetitive of it when practicing.

Since the explosion I had in Windwyrd, we thought it best to give time for the common fae to forget the incident. Luckily, there haven't been any Fae that's gone missing or found dead within the time that I have been here. At least none that we've been told of, which, to the king, makes it less of a priority.

I take myself back to the lake to exercise, allowing myself a break from the days of practicing concentration. The spring breeze isn't nearly enough to combat my sweating. But it's better than none at all.

Thinking about all the schoolwork I must have by now, I figure that at this point, I might as well drop out, which sucks since graduation is in a few weeks. *Maybe I could still graduate since I never missed an assignment.*

A rustling comes from the Darkened Forest behind me, causing me to turn in its direction as I walk back to Nexus. I debate whether or not to investigate, but I know I'm not dumb enough to go alone. Speeding towards the palace, I move with the intention of finding Cassius or a guard to come with me. It isn't until I feel someone swaddling themself around me that my body is constricted.

The people holding me are in masks. I can't see their faces as they lift me. I scream, calling for help to anyone who could come.

They're having difficulty lifting my body. Good. If they're going to kidnap me, at least I won't make it easy on them.

"Hello, witch," one of them says.

"Would you stay under the thumb of a ruler who has clearly passed his prime?" says another.

Biting down on the hand of the masked figure that holds my

mouth, they drop my body, causing me to fall to the floor. I swiftly move from them, creating distance between us.

I try to calm my mind. Try to remember any spell in order to save myself. I constrain two with my magik, bringing them to the ground. Charging myself with anger, I let the thought of flames circulate through me as I aim to shoot for the one running away. I miss completely, my flames out of control and hitting a tree instead. I'm so lost in my frustration that I don't notice a Fae close to me until a sharp pain rushes through my side. One of them stabbed me, the blade dragging to the center of my torso.

Whoever stabbed me really twists the knife by antagonizing me with words. As if killing me would send a message itself. "The reign of King Elliot must soon come to an end. A new power is upon us." The voice is masculine, but just as I register that, he pushes the weapon deeper before running off.

Screaming in agony, I set fire to the things around me. I drop to the ground, letting one of the Fae I constrained free and burning the other one alive. I can't control my magik. As his flesh chars, I can feel myself breathing unevenly, my vision going blurry. I feel arms around me, and it takes every effort I have to open my eyes. When I do, I see Cassius with a look full of both panic and frenzy. Is it possible for him to show both at once? I take a short breath.

*Is he actually worried? Or am I hallucinating?*

His smell of oak and cedarwood mixed with the fresh berries from lasialic hits me. My shoulder is shaking. Cassius is doing everything he can to keep me awake. "Stay with me. Who was it that did this?" He screams for the guards, who I hear nearing us, not that far behind the Fae prince.

"Ran." I swallow. "They ran into the forest." I'm shivering.

Everything's going hazy. I can't tell what's real and what are my thoughts anymore.

Cassius tells the guards to search the forest as his arms move farther under me. He cradles my neck with one and my waist with the other. Tears are falling from the corners of my eyes. This is how I'll die. *Figures. I'm going to die in the same way Luka did.*

The next thing I know, Cassius is setting me down from his arms onto a bed. *Did we fly or did he okkar us?*

"There was a man," I manage to get out. "He said your dad's reign is coming to an end."

The feeling of blood draining from me is apparent. I'm shaking. My body feels like it's on fire. But for some reason, this causes me to laugh.

"What?" Cassius asks, probably perplexed with how I could find this situation funny.

"It's just–" I lose my train of thought, my body going numb, breathing becoming increasingly difficult.

He pats my face, trying to keep me conscious. "It's just what?"

His voice is barely audible to me. I feel like my ears have been submerged underwater. Taking in a deep breath, I take the last bit of energy I can. I cling to his arm, refusing to let go of his hand. "It's just funny to me that they tried to take me, but I fought. I wouldn't leave you... my other captors." I laugh through a shortened breath.

Cassius rubs his thumb around my hand, my adrenaline fully gone now.

Opening my eyes and letting my head fall to the side, I smile at him. This is too intimate. I need him to bring back some normalcy.

"Remind me." I groan out in pain. "Remind me again how much you hate me."

"I cannot do that."

"Can't or won't?"

Before he has a chance to respond, I am overtaken by shooting pain.

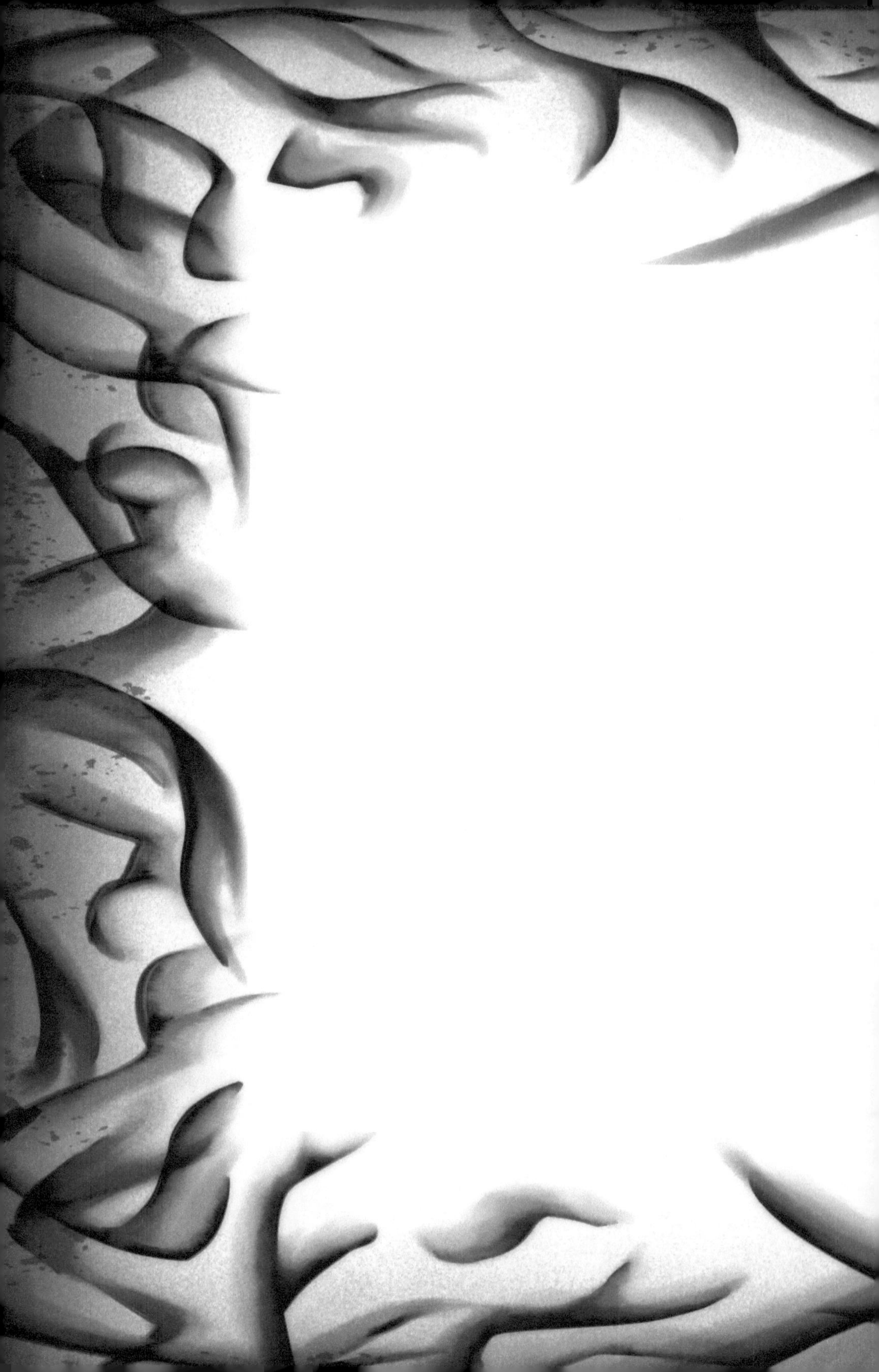

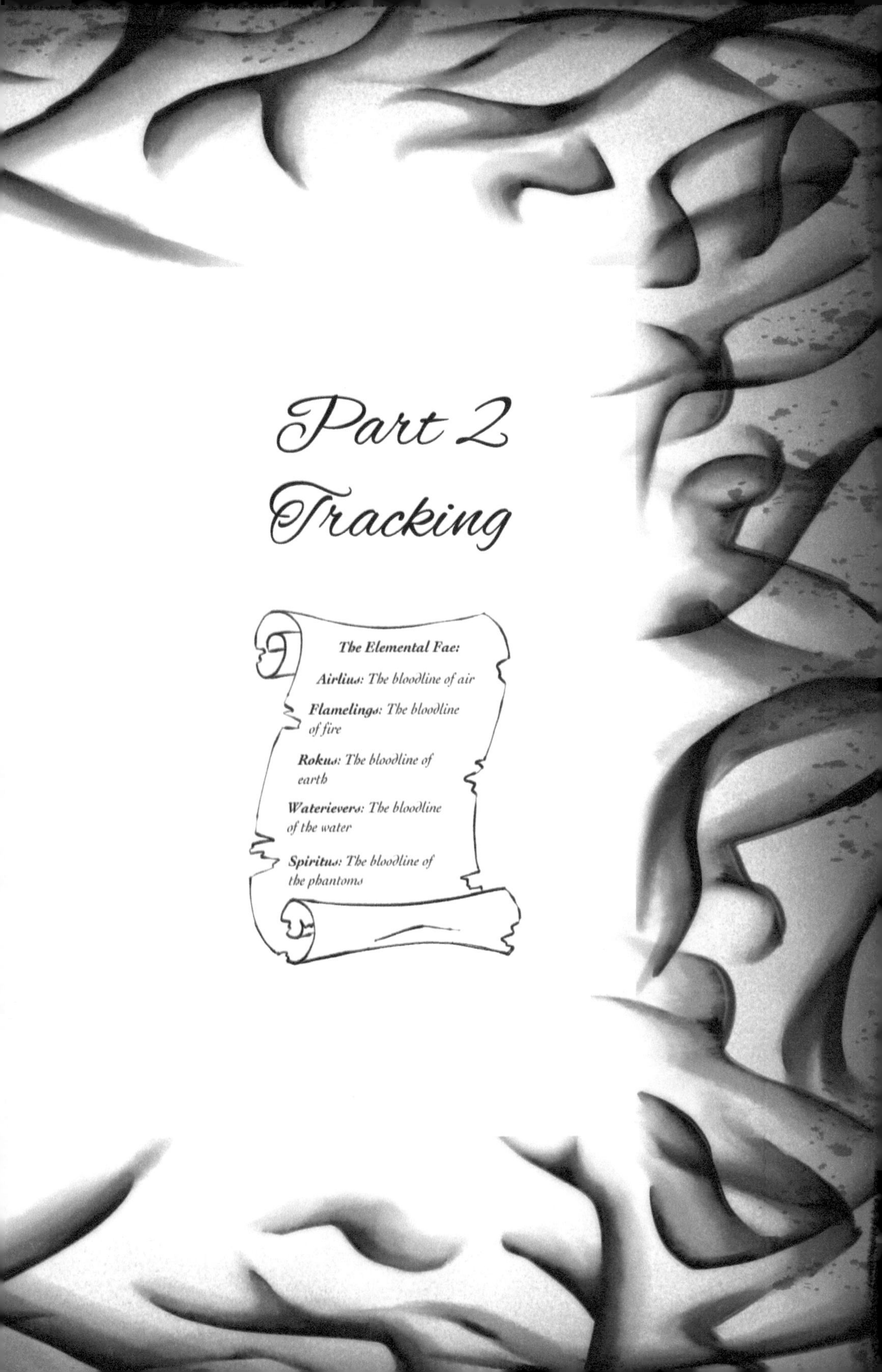

# Part 2
# Tracking

**The Elemental Fae:**

**Airlius:** *The bloodline of air*

**Flamelings:** *The bloodline of fire*

**Rokus:** *The bloodline of earth*

**Waterievers:** *The bloodline of the water*

**Spiritus:** *The bloodline of the phantoms*

# IX

## Torture and Answers

Cassius

Impatience.

It is all I have been feeling for hours as the healers are with Arabella. There have been no updates, no news, no sign from anyone that she is okay.

I'd sent for our healers to care for her, but we're nearing the seventh hour with not a single soul to have left her room. There is nothing I am able to do beyond waiting. Wait for someone to leave and tell me she is just fine. For Arabella herself to walk from the doors and come with me to question one of the men who tried to take her.

*That bastard should count his blessings I refuse to question him until she is with me.*

While I was preoccupied with keeping Arabella conscious, the guards searched the forest. Most got away, however, one was ignorant enough to attempt hiding nearby. Once I left the room to allow the healers to tend to Arabella's wound, the guards informed me that the apprehended was taken into shackles and is now being kept within a private, enclosed cell away from most imprisoned. As prince, I requested that they spare no sympathy in his treatment until we meet with him.

The healers should be gone already. Left hours ago so that we may return to our quest for answers. It does no good waiting by the walls and listening in on the exchanges from the next room. If I wish for a distraction, I should be the informant that my father had asked me to be.

After opening the fourth door in the west wing offices, I find a woman leaving with her blouse inside out. The woman's eyes practically jump from their place when she sees me, casting them to the floor in shame. She scurries out the back entrance, stumbling down the stairs. From what I am able to hear, she tears her dress, alongside twisting a leg.

I knock on the doorframe that the Fae just left, waiting a bit with no desire to subject myself to my father's indecency.

"Come," my father speaks. Waves of his black hair define themselves more from the sweat that coats them.

This room is less so an office and more of a spare bedroom for my father's invited guests. On the wall hang items for pleasure, whether it be for his enjoyment or his guests. I, for one, am hoping to never set my eyes into this room again.

"Father, I have come to inform you about the current state of where the witch and I are in relation to the missing Fae."

He motions for me to sit, but taking into account the activities that preceded my arrival, I prefer to remain in the doorway. I attempt to hold a still demeanor, but my father sees through the veil of my thoughts and walks towards me instead. Closing the door behind us, we keep pace side by side through the halls into the throne room.

Upon entrance, he sits upon the stairs leading to the throne, anticipating my next words. "What is it you mean to bother me with?"

"We have learned from the common fae of the patterns and times in which Fae have been reported to have gone missing from their families," I say, waiting for a reaction from my father. When his face remains unimpressed, I carry on. "We have also learned the only physical violence that was inflicted on those who had died were Fae who were of higher importance. The ones who were closer to our circle of contact."

That piece of information strikes my father. He now is grasping what I have to say. The angle of his head is tilted down, and his lips are held tightly against each other. His body leans forward in interest of the news.

"And does that put myself in harm's way?"

My mouth opens, but for a moment, there are no words that leave. *How is it that this piece of information is what finally made him understand the danger?* As if the lords' deaths in themselves weren't raising enough suspicion to place him in a deadly corner. It's not exactly that which bothers me, but rather the fact Arabella has opened my eyes so clearly to see the selfishness within my father's rulership. "Yes, sir. Lady Arabella and I have been doing all that we can to pull information from the common fae and from different lands, though it has been no simple feat when they do not trust the crown."

"I can understand why. We have not done much in order to

protect them." He rubs his slender fingers around his chin, cradling it between two fingers when lost in thought.

"Also," I add, "if you were not informed, the witch was stabbed today. It was done by a group of creatures, and they had uttered something strange."

"And what was said?"

My father shows no sympathy towards the mention of Arabella being stabbed. As much as Ezra revels in our father's antipathy towards me, I do question if what he said about father showing her bias over myself is as high as he made it to be.

"That your reign is coming to an end. I'm unsure as to what they had meant by that since Arabella had told me when she was barely able to speak herself. We will question the man in custody as soon as she is able."

Immediately, his posture straightens, adapting to how he holds himself when the common fae come to him for counsel. "I do not care for the state of the witch. If there is nothing more of significance you have to tell me, you are dismissed."

"Father, I assure you that Arabella's well-being is crucial to solving–"

"You forget yourself at the feet of the witch. Stir emotions with politics and you will lose yourself." I say nothing, baffled by the comment that carries no real truth. "Out!" he roars.

I bow before him, taking my exit.

Once outside the room, I hear a door close from the second story. I stand at the bottom of the stairs awaiting for the healers to inform me of Arabella's condition. When they reach me, they look uneasy, causing a tinge of knots to form at the base of my stomach.

"How is the witch?" I ask. "Is she to be brought food and water?"

One of the healers holds her frown. "No, Your Highness. We have done all we could. Her heart beats, but she is not waking up."

My throat tightens, a sting circulating. Every bit of impatience I once had has turned to anger. "How is it she not waking up? You have been with her for hours, and yet she still remains injured and unresponsive? You are considered to be the best healers in the lands. If you are not able to heal a simple stab wound, when she herself has magik, might you reconsider your field?"

The other healer speaks. "Prince Cassius, you have to understand, she has lost a lot of blood. It will be days before she wakes up. If she ever does."

"*She will*. And you will see to it that she does. I will be checking on her every day until she is made well."

"No," the same healer denies. He grabs a tonic from his bag and hands it to his partner as she averts her gaze from us. "Until otherwise stated, only those allowed in that room are us. We cannot risk anything from the outside being brought into her room and furthering the possibility of her death."

If this pushes a speedy recovery and therefore a means to have her leave Ifaeris, I will do everything in my power so that it shall be done. Time is of the essence if I am to be rid of her. "I expect nothing less that her difficulty extends to her nearly dying."

With that, they leave, and my wings bring me to Korine and Harrison to distract me from the events of today. A fair play of fun would present pleasantness in my mood.

Hours turn into days, and Arabella is still unhealed. I have done my best to gather any information, but it has resulted in nothing. No matter the lands I travel, the common fae still do not trust

myself alone, and I will not allow to meet with the Fae who made an attempt on her life. Something that I no longer have the privilege of holding off. It is decided. I will have to question the man in custody, whether or not I have Arabella at my side.

A foolish endeavor when it is she who can collect answers far better than I.

In a twist of fate, I feel my sister before I see her. Though she attempts to sneak behind, one cannot attempt to frighten me when I have mastered the art of shadows. There is little I'm able to do to help Arabella. She is a mortal. I should have thought it more likely that her life is in constant danger by aligning herself with my father. For her freedom, she risks everything, while I, all the more, wish her better so that she may go away.

Taking my rest on a marble-carved bench by the garden fountain, I wait for my sister to make her presence known, though I spotted her long ago. "Esme, if you are attempting to get my attention, doing so quietly will not work in your favor."

She groans at her failed attempt to sneak up on me and cuts through the flowered hedge, destroying the garden our mother cares so much for. "Okay, well you need to come with me into the house."

I turn to her. "I do not *need* to do anything you ask of me. That is, unless you will be giving me something of interest in return?"

"It's Arabella," she says. "She's conscious."

We rush into the palace and up the stairs, where the healers are standing outside the witch's door.

"She's awake?" I ask, unsure if Esme's word is current.

Esme pushes past me from behind. "Do you think I would've come to you if she were still asleep?"

The healer closes his bag and looks at us. "Yes she is, but she is in a very fragile state at the moment. We cannot allow her any activity for weeks."

The woman puts a hand on Esme's shoulder. "She'll be okay. Just make sure she doesn't do anything too strenuous."

We both give a curt nod.

"I'm going to walk them to the healer's room. You ought to talk to Ara," Esme says while descending with the healers down the stairs.

I knock, ensuring she is decent. Rather than waiting for her permission to let me enter, Arabella opens the door herself. She stands in an oversized shirt without bottoms, and her hair is wrapped in a towel. There is no color in her face. As if all life had been drained from it. She still holds herself as if nothing had happened, but I can see the glossiness in her eyes. How it shines identical to a jewel submerged in the seas. She's filled with despair, though I doubt she would say so herself.

"Oh, hey Cassius."

"Hi."

There is no reason for this tension. We've spoken four words to each other, and it feels as though all the breath has been stolen from my lungs.

She widens the door to allow me inside. Her shoulders are slumped, posture weighed down heavily, making her appear shorter than she is.

"Was there something I could do for you? Or were you double-checking that I was dead?" she remarks with a hint of humor.

"I have come to inform that the guards managed to capture one of the Fae who had ambushed you. He is in a private, upper section of Phantom Tower being cared for by our top guards."

Every part of her face drops. From her eyes to cheeks to mouth, everything is agape in shock. "You're kidding." When I shake my head in response, she slips on open-toed shoes and speeds out the door. "We have to talk to him now."

I chase after her. "Do you not wish to put something on to cover yourself?"

Arabella glances down at her naked legs and pulls down the shirt even lower to her knees. "Shit, you're right. Okay, uh, give me like ten minutes, and I'll meet you downstairs."

Though Arabella is alive, she is all too eager to jump back into action and further gather information to prepare her leave. It is unsettling. I lie still, waiting in my bedchamber, and as the sound of her stepping out can be heard, I exit from my room, to which she gazes with furrowed eyebrows, eyeing me to the side. "I said I'd meet you downstairs."

Holding my arm out for her, I respond, saying, "You have been courting death for nearly five days. I thought it best to accompany you."

She does not, of course, accept my help. Not even nearly dying will she drop her independence.

"I think I'll be okay."

As we approach the private section where our prisoner is being held, I stop Arabella from entering. "If you wish, I will speak for the two of us. There is no reason for you to overwork yourself."

Her face hardens. "Are you belittling me?"

"Only a fool would belittle a witch who has just survived a stabbing," I reply. "You undoubtedly have the ability to handle yourself. I was only suggesting."

She looks at me suspiciously, eyes narrowing before opening the door.

When we enter, the prisoner is glaring at us. The colors of his knuckles are a shade of white from gripping his own hands, and his body is different shades of brown to purple from bruising from his capture. Parts of flesh on his knees are visible from burns.

The man knew we would be coming. I had informed the guards that I would be paying him a visit prior to Arabella's wake. He must have been waiting in anguish for hours. He sits chained to the wall that barely allows him to reach past the bedding area, much less the cell door.

"I was told you'd be visiting today," he says.

Arabella steps in front of me, staring directly at the man. She still lacks color in her skin, though she carries the attitude of one freshly prepared for a fight. "We will be asking you questions, and you will be answering them, if you want to continue living life as a prisoner instead of living among the dead."

He moves from his corner and stands as close as he is able, eyeing her up and down. A dark patch of black, completely burned skin lies on his upper arms, though not all can be hidden by his hand. "Well hello to you too, witch. How has your cut been healing?"

"We are not here to grace pleasantries," I stop him. "As Lady Arabella has said, we will be asking you questions. And you will answer them."

He walks to a wall and slides until he is once again seated. "Then ask."

"What do you know about the missing Fae?" Arabella asks.

"They aren't." He chuckles. "Why are you so sure they're missing?"

The cuffs on him tighten, turning his body carmine. He attempts to move as much as he can to undo his chains, but Arabella's flat hand curves down, her magik dragging him closer to the corner. "Please. Stop her!"

I bend close to his level and hold his face to mine. "Fae do not leave their families without incentive. Perhaps now you will take this with more seriousness."

When the skin of his neck purples, he confesses. "Fine. I can't tell you much, but I can tell you all I know."

"Arabella," I call. "Let him speak."

She drops her hands to her side, allowing the return of blood circulation to the man. The chains reverse to their original state, the Fae cracking the side of his body. "I do not know a lot. I was told we were to take you. We have meetings, though I don't know the schedule, and I've never seen our leader."

Retreating to Arabella, I once again speak. "While it is noble that you are divulging these details, I find it difficult to believe that this is all you know. Shall I have my witch resecure your restrictions?" I turn to her and she begins raising her hands.

"No!" he shouts in desperation. "Magik! I believe it is somehow involved. Though I cannot tell you how, since I myself do not know, and no one believes me."

Lowering my hand to signal Arabella to stand down, he takes a breath of relief. If this man is as unknowing as he says himself to be, he likely would not be aware of the ins and outs of the missing Fae. Nor would he be able to give us the answers we require.

The Fae's attention turns to Arabella, the look on his face sinister. Plotting something that he hopes will likely spin her out of control. "Tell me something, witch," his voice grates, "do you blame yourself for the deaths of those around you?"

Not only do her eyes blacken, but the entirety of the air turns searing. She is going to set the entire holding aflame. I attempt to call for her, but my voice runs unheard to her ears. There is nothing between her and whatever fury this man has caused.

Her fist clenches, the silver, double-moon ring indenting into her skin, all while the chains constrict the man further, color completely drained from his body. He looks similar to an animated corpse, his eyes bulging, hooves convulsing, but body going rigid. Her hand grips so tight, any bit of blood showing in her cheeks seems to drain from her as well.

The man begins choking on himself, blood spewing from his mouth. He desperately attempts to say something but is stopped by the gurgling of his own gore.

Short, shallow breaths escape Arabella that could almost be mistaken as airy. She takes the knife from her clothing and starts slicing the man's wrist. Slowly and deeply.

"What's the matter? Can't take what you tried to do to me?" She cuts him again.

I must put a stop to this. At her rate, if she continues, he will be of no use to us. "Arabella. He's dying."

No matter what I say, she is unyielding. She twists her fingers, causing the blood to stay in its place, rather than it leaving through the exposed flesh. "At least if you die, it's the only one I'm actually responsible for."

I haul myself from behind her, pulling her from the waist. Her head snaps to me, releasing the hold she had on the man.

"Arabella, stop!" I order. "We are done for the day." I carry her out of the cell.

The man is involuntarily shaking, reacting to the blood recirculating through his body. "You're as deranged as the family you sold your soul to."

Arabella twists herself to escape my hold, fighting harder when I tighten my arms around her.

I call to a guard, commanding, "See to it that there is a healer to mend him."

Once we exit the room, she rips herself from my hold and storms down towards the exit, panting.

At the doors of Nexus, she is calm enough to ask, "Was there anything the healers told me I needed to do?"

It takes a moment to process what just occurred and what is being asked, but when Arabella surveys me, impatiently waiting for my response, I am reminded of the orders they had given. "Yes. They said you were to not take part in activities and not to do anything strenuous. I am afraid we may have already broken their rules."

She smiles. "Then this'll be our little secret."

I shoot up from where I lay. The outside is still dark. I swear that everything I just witnessed was real. Arabella's death, the destruction of Ifaeris, the blood of my family. Images of Arabella's arms being ripped from her body were too much to bear. She was screaming for me. Calling out my name as she was being torn to pieces. Tears were falling upon her face, and the whites of her eyes had become bloodshot. There was no trace of a soul in her body when life left her dark, umber eyes. I could do nothing as I was forced to watch.

*Why was she calling out to me?* More importantly, why was I dreaming of her? Arabella is nothing to me, save a possible way to get my father and brother to leave me to my own merry. She serves no importance in my mind, other than the pestering rush she gives me at every sighting of her being. There ought to be no reason for her to occupy my thoughts, and yet I can never stop thinking of her.

# X

## *More Drinking*

Arabella

Cassius hasn't said a word to me in the days since we visited the man who plotted my capture. Whenever we pass each other, he averts his eyes or doesn't acknowledge me at all. It's annoying. We have a job to do, and how are we supposed to complete it if my partner refuses to speak to me? At first I assumed he was trying to make sure I didn't put myself in harm's way again, but when it turned to avoiding, I knew he was acting out of pettiness for not listening.

*Do you blame yourself for the deaths of those around you?*

The words have replayed in my head several times since I blacked out and lost control. Luka. He's all I can think about. With everything that's been happening the past few weeks, I've been able to divert my focus from his death, but being reminded that I was the cause of it set me off. Logically, I know it isn't my fault, but irrational guilt still gnaws my thoughts. When the Fae said that, all

I saw was rage. All I could think was that I should kill him. I should have just let him die. Used the killing curse that stopped the blood flow and let him die immediately. But no, I'm selfish. I wanted him to suffer. Let him suffocate on the words he spilled.

Is that what it is? Is that why Cassius has been ignoring me? Did I scare him? *Is he afraid of me? No.* I remind myself. *He just hates you, just as you cannot stand him.*

We are a forced partnership, and I'll be damned if I let his own vindictive nature keep me from freedom. That in mind, I let it bring me into Enthar on my own. Without the prince by my side, I'm less likely to draw attention. It'll make hiding in the shadows easier. Or at least make it easier to ask questions without recognition.

I've gone around for an hour with nothing that would help me, until from around the corner of a building in the market, I hear two women speaking about one of their husbands' disappearance. Peeking my head around, I see that one has mid-length, black hair with tight curls, and thicker, arched eyebrows, while the other has long, wavy, green hair with mixed highlights and iridescent, butterfly wings that light shines through. When they speak, it's apparent that their loved ones' disappearances happened recently. I hide back, bringing my head as close as I can to the corner near them without being seen.

The one with long hair wipes tears from her cheek. She looks roughly the size of the tip of my longest finger to the middle of my forearm. "I just do not understand where he would have gone. He promised to be home before bed."

"Didn't you suspect him of seeking the king for help?" the curly-haired one asks. "Maybe that's all this is. It's possible he will return."

The leaf-haired Pixie shakes herself from her friend's attempt at comfort. She throws down the beverage she's drinking and breaks into hysterics. "What if he's gone missing like the rest of them? He was already acting as strange as the others in the days leading up to his disappearance."

Strange? Others? *So there is something that they all shared.*

"That's preposterous, Arlinda," the curly-haired woman's voice penetrates through the claim. "You know as well as I, that Phonellope's talk of her brother's disappearance was based on her own suspicions. She thought he was acting odd, so she assumed the crown disposed of him."

This calms the Pixie down a bit, but not enough for her voice to stop piercing my ears. "Oh Iris," she cries, "but what of the meetings? Phonellope's brother and Ralik had been meeting for weeks prior to his disappearance. And when Kohlai disappeared, Ralik would still run off at the same times."

Just as I'm about to intervene and ask some questions of my own, they are swept away by the busy street and other common fae. As the area clears, they are gone from their spots, and I now have no way of getting answers. The sun now setting over the horizon, I know it's time to get back to Nexus. I can always question them at a later date, and this is enough information to update Cassius.

Once back in the palace, I grab some food from the kitchen and search for the prince. None of his siblings can be found, and I doubt the king would be bothered to know where he is. I search through the gardens, the front courtyard, anywhere I think he could possibly be.

Inside the libraries, there are thousands of texts, but no section has Cassius. There are so many books in these rooms. I make a mental note to return the last book I borrowed. Finally, I ask a guard if they know where Cassius is, to which they tell me that he has been in his room since dinner, hours ago.

I haul myself upstairs with determination from the information I have learned today. At least this is something that will get him to speak to me. I knock on his door a few times but get no response.

"Cassius, I have news. I'm coming in, so you better be clothed." I open the door and enter. It smells like him, but rather than only a hint of the wine he is so fond of, the stench overpowers the room. The decor on his walls is a lot more simple than that of the rest of Nexus. While I was in here once before, I hadn't paid attention to the details. The desk by his wall contains paper and writing instruments, while another room, like mine, is for his clothing alone. His bed sits in the middle against the wall, covered in sheets made of black silk. His headboard is black with gold ridges, and the prince himself is laughing while lying on top of his sheets.

I go to his side, checking if I'm intruding before telling him what I heard today. "Hey, we need to talk. I went into town today, and I heard two people saying–"

His arm reaches up, and I can't help but stare at the faded scars on his back. Ones that match in pattern with the mark on the back of his left hand. When I take notice of the direction he's pointing to, I see an empty bottle toppled over on the nightstand that sits next to the bed. I look around, spotting another fully untouched bottle on his desk next to ink. Not a glass is in sight in the whole room, and I realize he is drinking straight from the bottle.

I flip him from his back. "You're drinking wine? *Again?*"

"Well I thought it best to slow my night of consumption with wine, rather than something of stronger substance," he chuckles.

From his behavior to the smell of mixed alcohols on his breath, it's clear he's finished more than just this bottle. He's acting as drunk as I got when I first tasted lasialic. Though Fae alcohol does not damage your organs, it is more potent. There's no way for me to tell him what I learned. At least not in a way where he would fully comprehend it. I try to put him under his sheets, and he struggles, as all drunk people do when trying to get to bed. He groans and whines and eventually rolls over enough for me to throw the blanket over him. All of this while he is delirious in laughter.

"You know," I say while out of breath from moving around, "we have a word for you in my world."

Cassius lifts himself so that his back is against the headboard. His grin turns flirtatious, and he takes my face with his hand, looking into my eyes, mocking me with false adoration. His eye makeup is smudged down his face, his fingers naked. The rings he typically wears are scattered next to the bottle. The bareness of his abdomen matches the faded scars from his back. He sits with nothing, other than his underwear hugging around his waist.

"And what is that, my evil temptress? The goddess whose ground I worship?" He doesn't pull his gaze from mine. In fact, his eyes lower to my lips, and if I didn't know any better, I'd think he wants to kiss me. That in this moment, we could pretend we aren't enemies. Play the role of lovers that we have the common fae believe we are. But I won't lie to myself. We are who we are, and he will always be the man who was willing to send me to death.

My heart stops. My mind is racing. I'm in no mood to fall into this ruse. How he sees me as nothing more than a witch to do his father's bidding. I can't do it.

"A drunk."

He releases his hand from my cheek. "This from she who nearly drank herself to death from lasialic." Taking his body from the headboard, he leans closer to me, closing the space between us. His pupils widen as he rests his forehead against mine. "You know, I am constantly troubled with your presence. By your absence. Even in my state of unconsciousness. I dream about you. It is unnerving. So even in sleep, you haunt my mind. Now hand me the other bottle."

Panic rises through me. My eyes could be dry from lack of blinking. I've forgotten how to breathe entirely. Not wanting to play his sadistic game of getting a rise from me, I put distance back between us. I refuse to appear weak. I refuse to *be* weak. He isn't going to win whatever angle he is playing at.

I leave his bed and grab the bottle of wine, keeping it for myself. "No. But I *will* bring you back some water."

He responds with a groan, and I am out the door.

Lingering down the stairs and through the kitchen, I need as much time and space away from Cassius as possible to collect myself. It's not like I don't know he's a beautiful creature, but neither of us like the other, so why mock me by showering me with compliments?

*He's just drunk. He'll forget about this by tomorrow.*

Opening his door with my free hand, I see that Cassius has fallen asleep in my short leave. I leave the water in place of the bottle, along with placing a trash can near his bedside table. With the amount of alcohol he consumed, if it was enough for him to say these things, I know he'll likely need it through the night.

Inside my room, I lean against the marbled sink, waiting for my shower to heat. I'm gross and sweaty from the day, and I need a shower. As the water heats, I can't help but think of what Cassius said. I hate his taunting. His teasing and the way he makes me feel so wanted yet discarded at the same time. But I remember what he once said. That Fae cannot lie. Even if he was teasing me, there's a hint of truth to his words.

While he sleeps comfortably tonight, I will not.

Last night was a failure for many reasons. Aside from Cassius being drunk out of his mind, I wasn't able to tell him about what I learned. How could I? How does someone revert the conversation when one is so incoherent, the only words he can get out of his mouth are fed by alcohol? It doesn't matter. I have to explain why I almost killed that man without going too into detail. Find a way for us to get back on track to finding the person who is taking the Fae. I have to tell him today.

After lunch, I find Cassius in the garden with some feminine Fae. She is beautiful, like him, with brittle, wavy, dark hair and freckles along her fair-skinned, nearly pink face. She dresses as posh as Cassius does, without makeup or theatrics. It's like she's a more toned-down version of him.

Her hands are playing with his as her sea green eyes roam the area. She laughs and laughs until she spots me.

On my way to them, I'm tripped by a pile of dirt I'm not sure was there before. I could've sworn the path to them was flat. "Hey Cassius, I needed to talk to you about some things concerning the missing Fae. Is it okay if we talk alone?"

The pretty woman snorts. "Is this the witch you have told me so much about?" She links her arms with the prince, voice raspy as she speaks. It's obvious that she wants to make a show of their relationship, though it's none of my business. "How dare you address your prince as anything other than Prince Cassius."

I throw Cassius a pointed look, brows slightly up while closing my mouth, internally asking if she's serious. "Okay? First of all, he's not *my* prince. If you already know who I am, you'd know I don't serve him. Secondly, I have to speak to him about private matters, so if you don't mind, I'll try to be done as soon as possible."

She looks at me in disgust. "*Ugh*, as if the prince would bend to you just because you need to talk to him. He will come to you when *he* is ready."

"Korine, mind your words when speaking to our invited guest," Cassius warns, his voice dry. It's the first time he's taken his eyes away from me.

Korine cackles, unlatching herself from him. "Oh. *I wasn't aware you cared for a mortal.*"

His face becomes as stone as a statue, nose wrinkling as he snarls. "She is but a means to an end. We both know most Magiks deserve to die. Still, she is the king's invited guest."

This makes Korine smile. Something about her needs his approval. Whether it's his affection or her craving for powerful men, she wants him.

"Of course she is," she laughs sardonically. "Why would someone with your allure desire a witch who has arms nearly as big as my legs?"

Cassius glares at her comment. An interesting approach for her insults, considering multiple of his siblings are bigger themselves.

I make it visibly noticeable when I roll my eyes. *If you hit low, I'll always go lower.* "At least my hair isn't so greasy that potatoes could be cooked with it. Or have eyebrows that look like uneven arrows pointing to a broken nose."

Her mouth opens, fingers shooting to the sides of her nose. "My nose is not broken."

"It will be."

Gasps of horror leave her. Her face scrunches, brightening to a darker shade of rose, the antlers that peak through her hair whipping with the turn of her head. She straightens her posture and lets out a shrieking breath.

"Whatever. Find me when you're in better company, Cassius," I say, putting emphasis on the casualty of his name.

When I turn to walk towards the palace, I feel a rush of air from tripping to the ground. Something hits the back of my head, and it feels like sludge from mud. I turn back to Korine laughing while Cassius, finding amusement in this, is smiling at me, not looking at the Fae who so badly is watching him for his praise. Sharp rocks are flung in my direction, all controlled by Korine. They rise high above me, ready to pierce through my body. I dodge a few, Cassius sending his shadows to hold me down as stones cut marks into my skin.

I'm struggling, punching through a shadow, but it's still somehow solid enough to suffocate me at my throat. My hands grip into the ground, eyes slightly able to peek at the Fae to my side who stares at Cassius long enough to stop pelting me.

This is easy. The earth I can control without problem. I sink the ground from under her, using my magik to bury Korine. The sounds of her screams are so loud, it causes me to shrivel. Then, Cassius' shadows pull from me, and I'm able to stand.

I take one hand and begin summoning fire. Korine's eyes widen, face full of fear. She's no longer trying to hurt me.

Stalking closer, I bend to meet her, dirt now up to her chest. "If you want another fight, I won't start it. But when I finish it, don't say I didn't warn you."

I leave, forcing Cassius to dig out his friend himself. My cuts need to be cleaned and healed immediately. Updating him can wait.

# XI

## Sharp Tongues

Cassius

I must seek out Arabella. She attempted to intimidate Korine yesterday, which I have to admit, I found amusing after Korine continuously condescended her. It took nearly two hours to retrieve her from the ground, long after the witch had left.

We are still working together after all, so the information Arabella had to tell me must have been pertinent to the missing Fae. The training halls are empty, along with the libraries, galleries, and her bedchamber. Only one place exists where she would be. The area she trains within the grounds when she wants to be outdoors.

She is not training. Instead, she is sitting, painting her nails, and has something in her ears. She bops her head in rhythm, raising her chest with every upward motion and humming a tune. Her hair will not keep from falling onto her face, which causes her to flick it back with her head multiple times. It is mesmerizing watching her.

Inviting. I hate it. With each step I take towards her, I hold onto hope she recalls nothing of what I said the other night. Something that I thought was another dream. It hadn't been real, for if it were, she would not have stared into my soul the way I looked into hers. No, my only wish is that she does not mention my confession I made whilst drunk.

I call her name, but she cannot hear me over whatever is in her ears. It's when my footsteps are within her line of sight that she looks up from her nails. Removing one of the instruments in her ears, she gives me a blank expression. She must still be wroth with what had occurred not one full day ago.

"Well," I smile, "you most certainly made an impression on Korine."

Returning to her nails, she makes no reaction to my comment. "I wasn't trying to impress anyone. You two are the ones that tried real-life stoning me."

"Korine must believe that I care nothing for you, lest you wish to have died from her abilities."

Though her parents rule a lower court, to murder Arabella would only result in Korine punished, and I, berated by my father. My shadows that held the witch down had pleased Korine just enough for her to pause her actions, allowing Arabella the opportunity to free herself. I'd much rather the witch be gone with this solved than to take on such an endeavor myself.

"Okay, whatever." She beckons for me to sit across from her. "So she was able to control earth the same way you can with shadows. How's that possible? I thought your family was the one with powers."

"What is it you know about creature history?" I ask.

"I didn't know Faeries were real until I got here. I thought your kind was extinct. At least that's what they taught us," she admits. "But I guess it's similar to how some people don't teach the true history if it paints them as a villain."

At least she is willing to admit her schooling did not inform her of the proper history. "The creature worlds, or Creaturelands, are split up into different sections filled with creatures of all kinds. You know well of Magik Cove being hidden from humans and how many Magiks live among them. The same lands of other creatures are hidden from the eyes of most humans. There is Searucks, the kingdoms among the sea. It is where most sea creatures and Merfolk live."

"Like Dyana?"

I nod. "They live all over the oceans, but the main kingdom lies within the South Atlantic Ocean." I pause, waiting for her to look at me, assuring I may continue. "Then there is Gigantia. The land that is home to most Giants, Centaurs, Cyclopes, and other creatures among that realm. Some of the most generous creatures you'll ever meet. They are located closer to the northeast of the Indian Ocean."

Arabella gestures her hand towards me, pointing at her black, painted nails, as if asking if I would like her to do it to me. I shrug, and immediately, she grabs my hand. "And Ifaeris? Where is that?"

"We are by the North Atlantic Ocean. Between North America and the United Kingdom."

She pauses her activity and types on her device, pulling up a map to view roughly where we are. When she unscrews the painted brush from its glass container, she watches me. "It's a phone, Cassius. You're always staring at it."

I realize then, this is the first time I have seen a phone. I have heard about the device from my sister's conversations, but I had never seen one with my own eyes until Arabella had brought it in my company.

There is still the topic that needs to be addressed. "You mentioned yesterday that we ought to speak. Was there a new discovery?"

Again, she pauses painting my nails. "Oh yeah. I had gone into town and overheard two Fae talking about the disappearances of a husband and someone else's brother. They think the crown had something to do with it."

"That's–"

"And," she goes on, unable to notice I had wanted to speak, "there was something about meeting times. I'm not sure if it really had to do with the missing Fae, but one woman said that leading up to her husband's death, he started acting strange and meeting with another man who had gone missing. I don't think she knew exactly where though." She unseals the paint once more and diverts her attention back to my hand.

Her soft hands caress mine, delicately handling them, as if she is afraid she will ruin the art. "It's possible he was having an affair and found a way to twist his words, saying he planned to meet with your dad, but considering the recent missing Fae, I doubt it."

"Was there anything else you found?" I question, curious to see how she gathered that information from them.

Arabella shakes her head. "No. I was about to ask them, but I was listening from behind a corner, and when I was gonna talk to them, the street got busy and they were gone."

So she managed to obtain this from lurking in the corners. When had she found time to do this on her own? She was meant to be confined to Nexus until the healers gave permission to leave.

"When had you found time to collect this information?"

Her face frowns tightly, and her mood turns sour. "When you were ignoring me after we interviewed that man."

I let out a single breath of laughter at her statement. At the choice of words. It brings a sense of delight that she so horribly misunderstands me. "That was an attempted murder."

"Serves him right," she says while shaking her head. "Anyway, so back to the whole Korine controlling earth. You never answered that question." Before I can speak, she rambles on. "And how is it all your siblings look around my age while your dad looks like he's *maybe* thirty at most? Also, why do you say that Magik and Fae hate each other?"

*Spirits around, she has a lot of questions.*

There is a way to answer them all as shortly as I can. "This would date back to our history lesson. Let us start with the Fae and Magik rivalry. Fae blood can be powerful if you are of the Elemental bloodline. There are five Elemental bloodlines: fire, water, air, earth, and spirit. They are known as the Flameling, Wateriever, Airlius, Rokus, and Spiritus bloodlines. We're unsure how these Fae were chosen, other than them being able to manipulate the elements that coursed within their blood. Descendants of this bloodline are born with abilities that match that of their element. It is why I am able to control shadows, Celeste can manipulate emotions, Esme can travel through the unconscious, and well, you understand."

Her lips part, beginning to form her next thought.

"Before you ask, the original Elementals were not kin," I speed through, watching her close her mouth at my words.

She looks at me, playing around the skin of her fingers. Something she does when she pays close attention to someone speaking. "So that's why Korine was able to control earth? She's from the earth Elemental bloodline?"

"Yes," I confirm. "Thousands of years ago, the five Elemental Fae were at peace with everyone until a witch fell in love with one of the Elementals. The air Elemental and the witch were happily courted until she bore him a son, which the Elemental refused to take claim over. The witch was furious for his treatment but grew vengeful when she saw her beloved bedding another woman. She swore revenge, and being one of the most powerful in the Magik Coven, she declared war between the Fae and Magiks."

Arabella whistles, the sound no different than the wind on a cold night. Her lips purse, forming a small O-shape. "Wow. Terrible choice of lover."

This brings a chuckle from within me. "No creature from the other lands dared to take a side, as choosing one would result in doom no matter what path they chose. While the Fae understood this, the Magiks took that as a stand against them. There was bloodshed and attacks to all from the Magiks until the original Elementals and the son were killed. While their descendants remain strong and carry aspects of the Elemental line, the Magiks went into seclusion, isolating themselves from the rest of the world of creatures, which I suppose is why they never taught you this history."

Leaning back, Arabella now remains overwhelmed by the amount of information delivered. She likely now has more questions but holds them back. Her face becomes easy to read when she is curious. "Okay, well that explains why some Fae are less hostile than others towards me, but that doesn't explain your dad's age."

"As I explained, we're of the Spiritus bloodline. All Fae begin to age slower after we reach twenty years, but unlike common fae,

Elemental bloodlines stop aging completely once we look near what you mortals view as late twenties. We tend to stop physically aging completely around two hundred years. From then on, our complexion stays ageless and immortal, whereas common fae continue to age slowly." I watch the fascination grow on her face. Everything about what I am saying is similar to a fairytale to her. "Some common fae can live to be a thousand. With Elemental bloodlines, unless we are killed, we live on forever. My father himself is nearing three hundred years."

Hands now wrapped around her knees, Arabella only fills with wider curiosity. "And your cousins, do they have special abilities?"

I shake my head. "If you recall, my cousins were born from Helena's sister. Zielle was adopted by Queen Helena's mother. They lived as sisters, but share no blood, and both are considered common fae. Helena is nearing one hundred and fifty years within the coming months."

"That doesn't really make any sense," she argues. "Like I get why you get powers and all, but logically, why is your blood so different you basically become a vampire?"

*Does she expect me to have a reasonable explanation for this?* To humans, our kind should not exist, yet we do. She constantly requires answers to questions that she herself would be unable to answer. "I cannot say why that is. It's comparable to how you're able to do magik when there is no scientific evidence. Or similarly, why I have the ability to summon wings. Things cannot always contain logic."

She considers this and offers no retort, no objection to what I have said. Instead, she changes the subject. "And what about your dad?"

I turn to her, eyebrows knitted. "What of him?"

"Well I'm assuming all the descendants of Elementals are equal, so how did your father come into power?"

Her curiosity is unending. With each answer, ten more questions arise. She, in earnest, wishes to learn of our history and all that she was not taught in her schooling. "After the war against the Magiks, it was decided that the Spiritus Fae would become the High Rulers of the Faeries, lest the lands chose otherwise. About eighty years ago, Ifaeris was at war with Gigantia. They fought for over twenty years, and my grandfather had been killed during it. It was my father that delivered the plan that had struck peace with their land, and because of this, it was agreed my father was worthy to carry the crown."

"*Hmm.* So if your dad's three hundred, that makes you?"

"Twenty-two," I laugh, finding humor at her idea that I am much younger than what she had expected from my father's age. "In fact, my family is considerably young compared to other Fae. Ezra's twenty-eight, Maude and Atticus are twenty-six, Esme, Xavier, and Montgomery are twenty-five, Isadora's twenty-four, and Dyana and Cel are twenty."

Moments of silence pass between us as she finishes my nails, allowing for them to dry. Arabella now lies on her back, eyes closed as the sun touches softly onto her face through the leaves. And she gets that look. *She's thinking again.* A question is inevitably approaching.

Her eyes flicker, turning her head to me. "Hey, Cassius? Have you ever killed someone?"

*What a peculiar segue.* I revert my attention to her. "No, I haven't. However, I could conjure the shadow silhouette to do so if needed. If you continue the threats on my life."

Rather than striking fear into her, her eyes widen, and cheeks blush, lips biting down on each other. "Listen, I know you probably said that to intimidate me, but I found it kinda seductive."

"What?"

"What?" she immediately responds as if she did not just utter those words.

My eyes narrow, attempting to more accurately understand what she has just said. "You must know that what you've said cannot be rescinded by false modesty."

She responds with a laugh and pushes herself upright to face me once again. "Yeah, I've heard something like that before. Try surprising me for once."

This is a dare. A form of trickery. I lean in to kiss her, but all I'm met with is the emptiness of the air around me. She has moved from her place and now views me with pure fear in her eyes. While I normally find amusement in flustering her, this holds a different impact. These movements are caused by my actions, over my words. She cannot stand to look at me.

It is mortifying.

Perhaps it would be better that she stab me and rid me from this moment.

"We need not ever speak of this."

"I can't do this," she lets out slowly. "Not with you."

Suddenly, it becomes all too clear what she means. "Me?" I let out a bitter laugh, throwing my head back. "Is it me you cannot do this with? Or does your vexation not extend to my brother?"

Her face glowers, locking her jaw in place. "It was one night. I wanted him for *one night*."

I lean in, so close that our faces are but a finger from each other.

Close enough that in one breath, I could have her. Taking her in like the oxygen one needs to live. "Believe me, I am well aware women seek the pleasure of my brother."

Pushing herself back, the thoughts in her brain churn so loudly, it is evident on her face. "I know he's shitty sometimes, but you're acting like he's tried to kill you."

The look on my face must give it away. Arabella assumes that Ezra and I are simply siblings who do not enjoy each other's company, rather than him abusing his control over me. Rather than him and father wishing I was never born, due to my wickedness. That I am capable of harming others, due to the nature of my powers. It is not my fault that I was not able to control them as a child. This only led to myself making no defense against their belief that I am now the monster they think me to be. She thinks I hate him for being the future heir to the throne, but alas, I hate him for far more than she will ever comprehend.

"And who here has made efforts to kill you?" I ask, challenging every word she launches at me.

Arabella climbs over me, uncovering her knife from her brassiere. The sharp blade angled against the skin of my throat, I am trapped. It is arousing. More so troubling that I have these thoughts.

Eyes glowing with power, she holds her other hand to my arm. "Besides having a knife ripped through me, how about your bitch of a friend who tried skewering me with rocks?" She pauses, seething through gritted teeth. "Or how you summoned your shadows to hold me down while you watched with joy? I'm not gonna fuck the king's arrogant son. At least not another one."

She is irrevocably convinced that I despise her.

"If you're going to kill me, do so already."

My words are something she did not expect. Her eyes widen slightly, and the hold on her knife loosens for a split second before immediately reclaiming its grip. A detail that I am sure she herself is unaware of.

My hand relaxes on the ground below me, my elbows bent as I study her. "Your empty threats bore me. You have proven you're far more than capable of unleashing pain onto another, so if you are planning on cutting my life short, do it." I lift my free hand, summoning a shadow around us. "Unless you are too fearful of what my shadow will do to you."

Arabella jolts her head behind her. A foolish opening for opportunity. From fear or anger boiling through her, she presses the blade deeper into my skin. She may be unable to detangle her resentment towards me and is unaware that she would be murdering a prince, though I doubt my father would care. I prepare for her worst, but instead, she throws the knife and presses her lips onto mine.

It's unexpected. Surprise falls through every part of my essence as I deepen the kiss. When she opens her mouth, I brush my tongue against the skin of her lips.

Her arms wrap around me, and I pull her to the ground, the weight of her body falling onto me like a source of comfort. I find myself straying further from any cruel remark I could say at this moment. My blood rushes, electrifying me whole, which isn't helped by the grinding of her hips.

It tortures me so.

Fingers reaching her waist, I maneuver her in continuous back-and-forth movements.

She tangles her hands through my hair, only once coming up for air. Moaning against my touch, I am completely under her control.

But all at once, her actions cease. Her eyes shoot open in regret of her choices as she uses my shoulders to propel her from where we are connected. She still remains unmoved, hovering over my chest. As if she is waiting for me to tell her to leave. And when I do nothing, she makes the choice for us both.

"I'm sorry," she murmurs. "I can't do this."

She removes herself from me and gathers her belongings. I am held still, unable to process her reasoning as she starts for the castle in a hurry, running her fingers through her hair as she leaves. Not thirty seconds ago, she was willing to throw herself at my body, yet now she acts as if she wants nothing to do with me. I want her. And I hate every part of myself for these desires.

I yell out to her from the distance, "I grow tired of your conflicting opinions towards me. What in your life has damaged you to where you feel you must consistently attack my character while being defensive when I point out your hypocrisy?"

# XII

## Reminders of Him

Arabella

Shock stops me in my place. I freeze. No, it isn't shock. It's anger. Anger that vulnerability will put me at a weakness. Bitterness that he's right. That no matter how much I say I hate him, there is a familiarity to our interactions. A familiarity I fear because it can only result in heartbreak.

*Luka pissed me off. Why was he with her when he told me that he couldn't stand the thought of me with someone else not two days ago? I hated him for it. I wanted to be the only one he would talk to like that. I was throwing a childish tantrum, and I knew it, but I couldn't stop. He needed me to be his, but I was always in constant fear that he would leave.*

*He stood over the side of my bed as I crossed my arms and sat up. I pulled him from his little conversation into my bedroom. I don't know what I was expecting, but it turned into an argument.*

*"It's not fair for you to sleep with whoever you want, but keep expecting me to worship the ground you walk on. You don't get to do this but be angry when another woman shows the slightest interest," he said in a strangled tone.*

*He was broken.*

*And I caused it.*

*Jumping from my bed, I stood in front of him, refusing to back down. "Considering all it takes is sleeping with you to drag you back, I sure as hell can be mad when someone tries taking you from me."*

*This only enraged him further. He threw his hands to the back of his head and marched to the door. "You cannot act like I am yours without acknowledging that you are mine. That's not how it works, love."*

*I wanted to scream. Everything he said was right. If I weren't so cowardly, maybe a better person, I would've said I stopped fucking others months ago. I would run into his arms and tell him then and there that I was his forever. But I didn't. All I could do was what I did best. I shielded myself.*

*"We're not in a relationship," I stated with finality that I hardly believed. "We are two people who fuck."*

*Luka stepped towards me, backing me into my closet door. His blond hair fell to his face. Something I only ever saw after the gym or sex. He ran his fingers through my hair, stopping at the crook of my neck. Peering his gray eyes into my soul, he could have asked me anything in that moment, and I would've folded to his every whim. I was his, whether I wanted to admit it or not.*

*The thumb of his right hand rubbed in circles along my skin, sinking me into his touch. "Are we?" he hummed. "Then Ari, my sweet blossom, why do you get jealous when another receives the adoration that I only bestow upon you?" He trailed kisses along my jaw. "Why do you know my favorite meal and cook for me when you assume I'm in a mood?" His lips reached my neck, and my breath hitched to a tone I thought could break the sound barrier. "Or how I know exactly what foods to feed you in order to satiate you?" His lips were so close to me that I could feel his skin vibrating against mine. "Even better," he crooned. "Why do I know exactly every place to kiss on your voluptuous body to have you withering under my touch?"*

I need to deflect. Change the subject and separate myself from this.

*Run. Run before you break yourself falling for him.*

Throwing on the most unaffected face I can, I turn back to Cassius, laughing. "First of all, who still speaks like that?"

Cassius appears dazed. Like I'm the one who speaks in riddles. Maybe he *is* able to read me as easily as Luka had, but it doesn't mean I have to satisfy him with that knowledge. If he's to ever think of me, he will think of me like an enigma.

"Listen, I know you probably don't spend much time in the Human Lands, but you speak like you're from centuries ago," I say.

His stare presses harder towards me while strolling to my side. On his way over, his face doesn't change once. "Is the way I speak so disconnected from the way those converse now?"

There is a curiosity in his voice, something that tells me that he really *is* unaware of how outdated he speaks. Even though Esme has told me that her brothers speak in such a well-mannered way, I didn't expect it to go so far that they have no experience with the lands outside of the kingdom. The common fae still speak in a decently proper way, but even then, they sound nothing near to how Cassius and Ezra speak.

I shrug, unsure how to answer. "I guess it's not that uncommon if you're from like England, but where I'm from, we don't talk like that."

Trailing at my side, he looks at me like he wants to know everything. Confusing, considering how aloof his attitude is towards Magiks. "And you come from?"

"California."

"Do you know many people from England?"

And that question in itself brings great bittersweetness. I keep trying to avoid questions of my past, but somehow, Cassius knows how to bring it up. No matter how hard I try to disarm, he can trigger the most intense, raw emotions from me.

*Calm down, Arabella. Don't break.*

"Yeah. Some of my friends are actually from around there. At least four of them are. They're pretty rich, so they ended up going to university with me and my friend, Juju." I pause. There are three of them now, not four. "Technically, I should still be at that school right now, but as you know, I'm a bit preoccupied trying to help save your people."

His lips thin. He hesitates before continuing, debating if he should say anything at all. "Do you miss it?" he asks. Stumbling through his words, he elaborates. "Your friends there, I meant."

Reminiscing on my memories with my closest friends, I am overtaken with longing, dragging out a sigh. "I mean, yeah. I've been here for a month, so it's not that uncommon we go this long without hanging out, and I guess technology is nice for messaging, but it's not the same as meeting them for quick coffee and tea runs before classes."

"You could see them if you wished." His words tarry. He seems genuine, but I know better. It's a trap. "If you recall my father's words, you are not to be a prisoner. You have access to roam free, so long as you return at night. Therefore, there is no reason for you to deprive yourself of their company."

He's just openly given me this information. I'm free to leave if I want. I could see my friends. Apologize. I need to leave immediately. "Actually, I *could* probably pick up some of my own clothes while I'm there. But in any case, we really should get back to the missing Fae tomorrow."

We step into the palace, and he goes to his room while I debate where to go.

*Why did I kiss him? And why did he kiss me back with such intensity that I became breathless and dizzy?*

I settle on seeing Reyna and then collecting my clothes from my house after. I okkar inside her apartment, hoping she's home. Luckily, she's in her room on the phone with some man with a low voice I've never heard before.

I knock on the door to get her attention, but she doesn't look up. She doesn't notice me in the doorframe either, apparently. After enough tries, I say her name loudly enough that her head swivels in my direction, dropping her mouth open so wide, someone would think she saw a ghost.

She immediately hangs up the phone and jumps to me. "Bella!" she screams with excitement. "Where the hell have you been? You missed graduation." She pulls me into a hug.

Squeezing her back, I laugh. "Sorry, I've been uh, busy."

We sit on her bed as she grabs some spicy chips from her desk. "Oh yeah. Right. You were in one of your moods." After grabbing some for herself, I take a handful before giving it back. "You really have to start allowing yourself to move on. He wouldn't want you to keep drowning yourself in misery."

"Yeah, you're right. But, I haven't really been honest with you."

Reyna eyes me suspiciously. "Did you commit murder, and now you're on the run?"

Bringing my fingers to my forehead, I pinch it, letting my fingers spread after. *Of course that's the only possible explanation for me randomly disappearing.*

"No," I laugh. "I've just been in this place called Ifaeris and helping the king of Fae. Did you know they actually existed? Like, they're not extinct."

A chip flies into her mouth. "I mean no, but myths have to come from somewhere, right? Most humans wouldn't believe we exist."

She has a point. Despite the fact it's similar to a point Cassius has made.

"Why are you really here?" she asks. "I know it wasn't to tell me that you're alive. You've been messaging me. So what happened?"

I bite my lip, and my toes push into the mattress. "So I kissed this guy there. His name's Cassius." I hesitate. Even saying it out loud feels wrong. Like I've crossed some boundary I set for myself. "He's the prince and the most infuriating person I've ever met, but we have to work together, and I kissed him. I don't know why."

"So you ran?" she says. Nodding my head, she laughs at my indignity. "And you came to me for what? Advice? You know that I'm no good with commitment."

"Actually, I came to get my mind off things," I admit. "Like for example," I lay on my stomach, "who was that guy you were talking to? Non-committal my ass."

Her cheeks turn pink, her wavy, brunette hair closing in on her face over the sides of her eyes. "That was Dylan. We started officially dating like two weeks ago." She speaks of him in a way I've never seen her speak about another man. Like he's from fiction and in disbelief that he is hers. "He works as the lead security at the Cove. He's strong, and built, and gives me a feeling I've never felt before."

At this, I smile. It's sweet being able to see her so happy, seeing her have someone so deserving of her. "So much so that you actually committed to him. Wow, I'm shocked."

"Shut up," she says with annoyance. The blush in her cheeks barely shows through the brown of her skin.

And we talk and talk about what I've missed. About my other friends thinking I was missing. How graduation was drowned out by our friends either being high or drunk, some of them recovering from a hangover. I feel comforted. A brief intermission before I have to return to my duties for the king.

# XIII

## A Dance To Remember

Arabella

Dinner is called by the king, who orders the entire family and me to join. There has to be something important coming because this is the first meal where he's required us all to be in attendance since I got here.

Rather than sitting by Esme and Isa, I sit next to Xavier and Celeste. Cassius sits across from me, but I avoid any eye contact with him, still uncomfortable by our last interaction. I'd avoid conversation with him as best I could, but there's only so much I can do when we have to work together.

The table fills with cheer and laughter until the king walks into the room, him slowly taking steps towards the head of the table. At his arrival, excitement dies down, all happiness from the room turning grave.

Before sitting, the king clears his throat, preparing for an announcement. "My family, and witch," he nods to acknowledge me, "as we have now apprehended someone in the case of our missing Fae, I would like to announce that we will be holding a ball next Friday."

Glances are tossed around the room. While everyone likely has something to wear, I have nothing, meaning I have about a week to find a dress.

The king continues. "This is in celebration. We are that much closer to uncovering who has caused harm among our community." He starts to pace around his mahogany chair, paying no attention to anyone seated. "While there have been some doubts as to how this would be solved, no one had expected Prince Cassius to make headway, I, least of all. So take joy. Make merry this fine eve, and begin your preparations for the coming week."

Excitement rises through the family. Meanwhile, my thoughts are clouding my brain on how I have to prepare for my first ball.

"What bothers you, Arabella?" King Elliot asks from down the table. "Are you not content with a ball being thrown in your honor?"

"Of course not, Your Majesty. I simply have never been to a ball, so I have nothing I can wear." It's the truth well enough, never mind the fact that some dresses, depending on the material, can make me so uncomfortable that I want to scrub my skin until the feeling of it touching me goes away.

He goes over my statement, trying to find a solution for what I've just said. "That is of no issue. You may borrow a dress from Celeste," he says, clapping his hands together.

"I appreciate it, but I don't think I would be able to fit in any of their dresses, since they're likely too small on me," I comment. "I can go into the Human Lands and get a dress. After all, you did say I was free to come and go as I please."

And that's when I see Cassius snort to himself while stuffing a piece of the juicy meat into his mouth. I used his words and played them to my advantage. But this doesn't please the king.

"Nonsense," he objects. "We have tailors at Nexus. The best in the lands. They will have a dress made and ready for you."

With his words, it's clear that this isn't up for debate. The discussion is finished. This also tells me that he doesn't know about my trip to Reyna, meaning Cassius kept my trip to LA a secret.

With the ball being a week away, there's no time to waste with the construction of my dress. I'm to have my measurements done today, giving ample time for the tailors to create it. Considering that I have no experience with dress fittings, I asked the girls and Celeste to join me.

The tailors take my measurements, feeling around different parts of my body, all while my eyes dart around the stuffy room with fabrics of different assortment and colors at every corner. Parts of what they measured make no sense to me, being that the dress won't even touch there. But I figure they need a more accurate sizing since the only other things they've made for me have been casual wear for when I went into town.

The women take note of each measurement number as the others banter. Then, the door barges wide open, and Xavier plops down on the couch next to his sisters. Isa flicks her brother on the head, Dyana running to shut the charcoal door that her brother left open.

Horrified and indecent, I cover my body with the nearest fabric. "Xavier, get out!"

He knows that we're supposed to be in here for my dress, but he doesn't seem to care. He laughs, not taking his eyes off me. "Calm down. You're not the first naked girl I've ever seen."

I frown at him, still covering my body. "I'm not a girl."

Paying no attention to what I just said, he rolls his eyes, putting an arm around the sofa's back. "Well in any case, I'm not exactly interested in you at this moment." I feign offense, clenching a hand to my heart. "Don't give me that bullshit. It's not about you. I'm simply tied up with a boy from the market right now."

All of our interest piques. I raise my brows. "Oh?" I press, wondering if he'll tell us more.

The tailors stand by the beaten-down desk on the opposite side of the room, writing down anything they deem important from my sizing. They call out, asking for any color preferences I have for my dress.

"Uh, I think–"

"Black," Maude finishes for me.

When I shoot her a stunned look, she smiles. "What? You think I don't pay attention to your most worn color?"

"So," Celeste drawls, "what have you and Cassius figured out from the common fae you questioned?"

In all honesty, there isn't much we know that we hadn't already assumed. I have my theories and Cassius has his, both of which we've discussed at length during our shared meals.

"Well I personally think that there's a woman in charge of all this," I share, leaning back on the metal post used for hanging fabrics.

Esme leans forward, her elbows digging into her thighs. "Why?"

"How could you possibly know that?" Dyana asks simultaneously.

I'm not sure how to explain, other than it being a gut feeling and small details that lead to this deduction. "It might be multiple people, but a woman definitely plays a leading role. The only thing we haven't fully figured out is the pattern. Some are high-ranking workers of the lower courts, but then there are some that have no connection at all. Not many Fae have reappeared after their disappearances, and the ones that do, have died in one of two ways. Lords found dead were beaten, whereas the common fae were poisoned. Based on a lot of history, women are more likely the ones to kill and kidnap in cleaner methods than men."

Other than the discussion of the tailors debating over fabrics, silence fills the room.

"Do you think it's a team?" Isa asks.

It isn't something I've really considered. Maybe there *is* another, but two people being in charge isn't something I thought of. With all duos, one always has to be the dominant.

My head shifts downwards. "Maybe. I don't doubt by now whoever's in charge is without a crew. After all, how else would they have tried to kill me? And unless this woman had some power of super strength, she can't be taking all these Fae alone, especially since the victims might not have all been attracted to women. She has to have at least one man helping her."

"Brutal, but good for her," Xavier cheers.

We all stare at him in disbelief. It's such a supportive comment for someone so closely related to the crown. He or anyone in his family could be next.

His hands lift, and his head shakes in defense. "What? I mean, horrendous what they're doing, but you must admit, it's impressive. Am I the only one thinking that?" He scouts around the room to see all our faces judging his statement.

"I guess? But you realize whoever it is has killed people within our circles, right? Meaning, close to killing us?" Maude implies.

Xavier's face goes empty, his head vacant from thought. "Right... Forgot that part," he admits with his head hanging down. "Maybe it's personal against you then. Not the first time we've seen someone kill for personal reasons."

I nod in agreement, a knock at the door right as I do so. From the panicked voice, I realize it's Monty. He sounds alarmed as he calls for his siblings, each knock increasing in sound. Whatever he has to say, it's an emergency.

We tell him to enter, and as he rushes in, he catches sight of my nearly naked body, something I forgot about when talking. His eyes widen, nearly leaving their sockets, and with lightning speed, he shields his eyes with his hands. "Sorry. I needed to talk to my siblings. It's about mother."

Immediately, they all walk out the door and leave to go to their home. Their dad I've met, but they don't talk about their mother.

"What's happening with their mom?" I ask Esme.

"She's been in and out of illness for years. We're upon the eighth month of her coma. I suppose something's changed," she says with worry coating her voice.

"You should all go. She's your family too. I'll be fine. I'm sure there's not much left for them to do! I'll see you later!"

I spend the next hour going over possible fabrics and patterns with the tailors, but all I can really think about is what Xavier had said about a personal vendetta against their family. With other lords in power, killing them off brings them closer to the power themselves. Even if the king tried to help, sometimes there's only the option of choosing one less evil decision over another. I guess you're always a villain to someone, even more so when you have power.

The days leading up to the ball come and go. I have no idea what my dress looks like, or if I'll even like it. All I know is that I plan on getting as much information as I can tonight. The population of Ifaeris is invited, so here lies a perfect opportunity to listen to gossip. Listen to how King Elliot's people truly view him.

Now that my makeup is nearly done, it's time to change into my gown. The tailors bring it in as I blend my dark smokey eye, but I've become too caught up with finishing my makeup to view the dress. One thing after another, I procrastinate viewing it. It's only after I finish braiding the same side strands of my hair that are usually tied into a half ponytail that I get a glimpse of its elegance.

On my bed lies my dress next to the jewelry I am to wear with it. A silver necklace that is covered in black crystals and diamonds lies neatly on the skirt. It shines and droops like a piece designed for royalty. Next to it are black dangling earrings to match, alongside another pair of jewelry for my ears. Something I assume was crafted only for me. The bronze tiara too is made with metals that are shaped like it was created in a pattern of tree twigs. Pearls, diamonds, and black jewels are sporadic across the piece, making it perfect to contrast my neckwear.

With a cape along the sleeves, the cuffs fall to the sides of my arms. Colored as black as empty spaces of the mind, it shines with subtle sparkles that scatter through the mesh layer of the dress. The sweetheart neckline cuts into my chest, bringing an obscene view to the cleavage of my breasts. Somehow, the mesh of the fabric doesn't irritate me as it layers over a soft material pressing against my skin. A slit along the right side of my leg allows for easy access to my recently acquired dagger I plan to have holstered. It's perfect. Everything about the ensemble is something I've dreamt about.

After putting on my lipstick and rings, I strap on my shoes. The black high heels match the shade of my dress while complementing the deep, brown-toned, dark burgundy lipstick. As I mentally prepare myself to join the ball below me, my eyes glance to a ring on my bed. A ring I recognize. With its larger, single laurel leaf-shaped gem, the emerald is unmistakable. It's the ring of the man I despise. My enemy. Cassius.

The ball isn't exactly what I am expecting as I join. Sure there are many Fae in regal dresses, and yes, the lights open like lily flowers blooming, but the energy is much different than I anticipated.

Maybe it's naive, but there's a part of me that hoped that when I entered, it would be grand. That I would pull the attention towards myself, and while I do capture the attention of some, I'm not royal. I don't have the power to stop a whole room.

I decide to use the lack of attention to my advantage. This way I can slip through conversations without people noticing or suspecting me of doing the king's work. If there's one thing that people of lower stature love doing at a big event, it's commenting their true feelings on the hosts through snide remarks and gossip.

The royal family sits along a table that is boosted above us all from the marble stairs onto a platform. The daughters of the king are socializing, while the sons remain with the king and queen.

Cassius' expression looks beyond unamused, but his appearance is something sculpted by the hands of the world's most renowned artists. The black of his clothing mirrors mine, along with similarities in our crowns, though his looks closer to a wreath with rubies woven in. Instead of silver jewelry similar to what I wear, he is drenched in gold. Rather than his shirts that tend to cut into his chest, his top bears a velvet jerkin with golden accents around it, lifting at his shoulders with another black, peasant-puffed shirt beneath it.

I flash him a glimpse of his ring that I now wear on my right index finger, replacing the double-moon ring with a black spinel in the middle that I usually wear. His eyes follow my every direction, the highlight from his cheeks beaming in contrast to his dark eye makeup with round, loose gold glitter rimming the ends of his eyes. Even when I'm not looking at him, I can feel his eyes burning into my skin.

This is heat, and I'm reveling in it.

The two men beside me speak in hushed voices while their laughter booms as loud as the music.

"And you heard of how the prince has been taken with a witch, have you not?" the older Fae with graying hair asks through laughter.

His counterpart, a Powrie with teeth of sharpness, hair shaved nearly down to the skin, responds. "I thought the boy could fall no lower from grace, but he falls for someone as revolting as a Magik." He finishes what is left in his cup, belching as he snorts. "One I would assume is as hideous as the rest of their kind."

Refusing to hear more about how disgusting the Fae find me, I move on.

While continuing through the night, jumping from one

conversation to the next, I find no useful information. All that's clear is that the Fae enjoy fine dining from royalty.

The two women I recognize from the marketplace are by the drinks, except the one with green hair now stands at the same height as Dyana. In the lighting, her wings tint to a blue hue, still transparent enough to somewhat see through. With both here, it's an opportunity to get the answers to questions that I still hold for them.

Casually, I make my way to the beverages and listen to anything they are saying, looking for any window to join in.

"You cannot be surprised they are throwing a ball to distract us," the one named Arlinda says. "The Disaris family is not known for protecting us. Least of all the men."

The other woman, Iris, considers this. Based on her facial reaction, they believe this to be the truth. The common fae don't think the crown capable of protecting them. "I suppose you have a point. What use is paying Zips to them, when it never goes back into our lands."

I drink from my cup so as not to draw suspicion to my stalking around the table. I listen closer, bringing my hand to a pastry near the two women.

"All I am saying, is it's possible that Prince Cassius or the king is behind the missing Fae. After all, the prince is just as wicked as his father. He once sent his shadow to nearly drown another when he hadn't apologized for running into the prince," Arlinda whispers in a hushed tone.

Horror twists inside me. While I know Cassius is capable of such harm, and while I know he would aid in my death by his friend's own hand, I didn't think he would harm someone else for something so minuscule. Regardless of if this happened when he was a child or a teenager, it's such a trivial reason for him to nearly kill.

Iris hums, agreeing with her friend and waving the comment off. "It's not nearly as horrible as the king refusing to take the missing Fae seriously until it affected him. At least Prince Cassius had done that when he himself was younger. Do not forget he has no real authority over his father as prince."

I need to know more. Need to know how else people perceive the family. "Sorry to interrupt, I just wanted to say you both looked lovely," I praise.

Both smile at the flattery. It's the easiest way to make conversation. Especially when you want to get something from them.

"Thank you, dear," Iris reaches out her hand to shake mine. "And who might you be?"

"Arabella. Miss?"

"Iris." She smiles while patting down on her burnt-ginger gown before shaking my hand. Pointing at the Fae next to her, she introduces her friend. "And this is Arlinda."

Arlinda gives a wide smile. Her lilac dress flounces around her legs as she nears me. "Pleased to meet you. Now, what's a witch doing here among us Fae?"

Lie. I need to come up with a lie.

"I was okkaring and had accidentally stumbled across the lands." *True enough.* "And I had met someone who I enjoyed spending my time with. He mentioned this ball, and I decided I had to come."

The two women believe me well enough. "So," I say, "since I don't know much here, what is this ball being thrown for?"

Arlinda is the first to jump at the opportunity to share her theories. "The king says that it was in celebration of their leads as to why Fae have been going missing. Though if you ask me, I think it's a way to cover up the true reasoning. I believe that they need to inspect within their own family."

"Arlinda, don't," Iris cautions.

I keep lying, like an actor putting on a performance. Even more, I hope they don't know me yet as the witch that Cassius takes as a lover. Playing dumb, my brows furrow in confusion. "Whatever do you mean? Why would they cause the missing of their own people?"

Iris lets out a whimsical laugh. "You don't know much, do you?" I shake my head. "They're very cruel rulers. The daughters are wonderful, and Atticus is lovely, but the king is so stuck in his own riches that he never shows compassion to his people. Nearly all who had disappeared were vocal against the crown's treatment of the common fae."

This is news to me. I figured the king may have neglected his duties sometimes, and though I know he is not a kind man, I didn't expect it to be so horrible that nearly all hate his rulership.

"What about the lords who had disappeared and been found dead? Were they against him as well?" I ask.

Arlinda shakes her head. "No, that confuses us as much as it does them, I suppose. The king rarely settles minor disputes, and while the other Elemental rulers govern over us, they hardly send supplies or enough Zips to accommodate our needs."

"Even if it isn't him that's causing the disappearances, to put the prince who is known for nothing other than his callous nature in charge is to doom us all." Iris drops her head in concession.

Xavier stands at the door, his amber-red ensemble complementing his hair that is half-tied. He sends a smile and a wave.

It's time I take my leave and enjoy myself for a bit. "I'm sorry, if you'll excuse me."

Before I can join him, I see Korine at the table with Cassius. Her arms are wrapped around his shoulders while her head rests against his from behind. At the exact second she notices me, she shoots a satisfied smirk in my direction, bringing her lips to the prince's cheek. He pays no attention to her actions, keeping his stare on me, which clearly pisses her off. She throws a fit and starts marching away from him, but it's not sizable enough to cause a scene.

On her way down the steps, I whisk my fingers, causing her to trip and fall flat on her face. She gasps from embarrassment, runs from her place out the door. I swear I see Cassius laugh to himself for a brief moment.

"That wasn't very nice," Xavier murmurs into my ear, jolting me from my place.

"You uh- You weren't supposed to see that." I bite the insides of my cheek sheepishly.

He grabs a glass from behind me, pouring himself a drink. "Hey, I'm not one to judge," he says as he throws up his free hand. "Set the Fae on fire for all I care. She deserves it anyway." He finishes his cup with speed and takes my hand. "Care to dance?"

I nod, Xavier pulling me to the dance floor with his hands around my waist and my arms around his neck. I don't know much when it comes to ballroom dancing, resorting us to swaying back and forth, exchanging jokes between songs.

Cassius is speaking to one of the other lords. He looks almost half a foot taller than me, but not at Cassius' height. His face also looks similar to a bug, with antlers sprouting from his head.

Korine's dad, probably. Even with the noise around us, I can hear their conversation.

Interested in the conversation, Xavier and I spin ourselves closer. In tones that aren't hushed, the pair are speaking about the missing Fae that resided in Enthar.

"Surely you do not suspect me of disregarding the people in my care," the lord argues.

Cassius shoots him a sly smile. "Of course not. There lies no power with shallow accusation. I am merely suggesting that if you were to pay more mind to the common fae, my father's people, they would not disappear on your watch." He turns to his seat. "A decision of carelessness ought to be sought out by fools, such as myself. You may continue doing so if you wish to be relieved of your title."

My eyes widen, and I'm swept away to the middle of the floor. Xavier does what he can to distract from what I just heard, but I can't shake it. It's both confusing and demanding. Cassius holds no commanding power, yet he knows how to wield it as if he does. Sometimes, I think that he knows his role as prince better than he assumes. He could play the game of political manipulation if he put in the slightest effort of understanding.

"So he's just as charming to other people as he is to me, huh?" My head tilts to reach Xavier's gaze, the two of us laughing and spinning as if I know what I'm meant to be doing.

Then I sense it again, Cassius' stare. I feel his presence before I see him. He's standing at our sides, his essence vibrating with irritation.

"If you are done roaming your hands through my partner, I'd like a dance with her." He stares between me and Xavier for a moment, cutting between us during the change of songs.

At once, Xavier rolls his eyes, leaving my side while I beg him not to with a pleading look. But it's too late. He's darting off towards his twin with the other common fae near the back of the room, and my waist is taken by one of Cassius' hands, one of mine held in his other. His thumb presses lightly against my knuckle, the two of us standing in place for a moment too long.

I clear my throat, moving my feet and beginning our dance.

Eyes from all turn in our direction, and I am reminded again that to some, we are a couple. The prince sways me around as he takes the lead with each step. The smirk he wears so smugly whenever he's around me appears, sending a feeling to my brain that I'm about to be embarrassed in front of everyone to see.

"Why don't you just go find Korine?" I sneer.

He rolls his eyes, keeping me from changing partners. Gripping me so that I know I can't leave. "I carry a particular fondness for women who hold me at knifepoint," he hums with an ironic tone.

We dance, and everything in the room disappears. I'm unaware of anything other than us. He spins me, holding me tighter when I swing back in his arms.

"You look intriguing tonight," he says, voice smooth like silk.

I survey him, trying to pick apart his sarcasm. "Is that an insult?"

"Never. I am simply stating that you look different."

With this, I laugh. His hand traces shapes along my lower back, and suddenly, I am alert. I hate myself for knowing the terrible things he's done and is capable of doing but finding him attractive nonetheless. "Because I'm not threatening you?"

His eyes glance down to my dress, then to my eyes, then my lips. "I suppose if that's what you assume I'm trying to convey."

He dips me. And when he does, his free hand drops to my thigh.

Inching its way up. It stops at the touch of my holster. He gives me a look, the corners of his lips quirking upwards. "Is that a dagger?"

"Surprised?"

"I would expect nothing less," he says as he pulls me into his arms.

I look around the room. All eyes are still on us.

"Everyone's looking at us, you know." I hesitate, slowing down our movements.

Cassius slides his hand lower and lower until it settles on the small of my back. He strokes the loose hair from my face, holding it while his thumb brushes my lip. "Let them look."

"We really shouldn't do this," I laugh nervously as he brings his face closer.

Breath heavy near my lips, his forehead presses to mine. "Command me to stop."

When he drags his thumb down my lip and under my chin, I grab him by the top of his trousers, pressing our bodies against each other and crashing our mouths together. While I move against his groin, he whimpers. If I could savor it for the rest of my life, I would make any sacrifice. It's amusing, seeing him break under my touch.

"I think," he purrs, nipping at my ear, "that perhaps I want you."

Returning the same energy of tone and seduction, I whisper back, "Prove it."

The Fae pulls back, eyes filled with lust. He slips his hand through my hair, pulling me close, and without another second, his lips press to mine.

It's hungry. *Desperate.*

"Bad idea," I murmur out as his lips leave their place.

"Horrible," he agrees, pulling our bodies closer and dipping his head low enough to reunite our lips.

Instead of fighting it, I open myself. He tastes like nothing but desire. It's awful. It is everything I could ever want.

As I open my eyes, moonlight shining through the windows is the only source of light I can see. The golden tones from the chandeliers are invisible. Shadows surround us with everyone else in the room disappearing from my vision.

It's us. Just us.

His fingers circle my inner thighs, working their way to my core. He chuckles as his hand pushes my panties to the side. "Based on the wetness of my hand, I assume you want me too."

Lifting my leg, his fingers part my flesh and press into me, his thumb working my clit. We're no longer dancing, but unmoving in place. As I feel myself getting close, he pauses his motions and kisses me, swallowing my moans.

The irony of the situation hits me. We appear as opposites with our color of jewelry but mirror in our clothing simultaneously. While his ears are pointed, mine wear earrings that mimic the Fae. All of that, and we're strung into each other the same way the Fates intertwine the strings of life.

I could stop him. I *should* stop him. Every logical alarm in my body is telling me to stop, but the dominant voice in my brain won't allow it.

I need more.

Against my internal wishes, he removes his fingers from me and wraps his arms around me tight. Then I feel us being pulled into another thinly lit room that I've never seen before.

# XIV

## *Clothing of a Glucose Child*

Cassius

I want her. No. I need to be inside her. Everything about her is what I hate. What I yearn for. I okkar us into Ezra's office. The room in which I will take her.

She props herself onto his desk, looking around the room. "Where are we?"

The lighting in the room is dim, the source coming from a mere candle nearly snuffed. When I do not answer, she gives me an amused face. "Not one for exhibitionism, are we?"

Unwrapping myself from her arms, I part her legs with my knee, snaking my hand through the open slit in her dress. I take no issue if any were to know how horribly I crave her, nor the ways in which I have thought of her nightly. However, I am but a pathetic Fae in need of viewing her for myself and myself alone this night. As my fingers draw near her sex, I can feel the hesitation from her. The tightening of her body.

"Oh princess," I croon, "I am far too selfish to let anyone see what I'm about to do to you."

I trail kisses from the length of her arm to her neck, sucking on her smooth skin to mark her. Her breath hitches, and I feel her, the wetness dripping onto my fingers. Quite the turn of tales from the same who so recently glared at me with hatred.

"Tell me what you want, pretty witch," I purr into her ears, biting down on her shoulder.

Whimpering under me, her body melts at the slightest touch. "I-" Her breathing goes erratic, throwing her head back, shutting her eyes. I circle around her clitoris, kissing her in every exposed area of skin. "I want you," she says, barely above a whisper.

I plunge my fingers into her, curling to reach a spot that elicits a moan. A moan that proves she wants me. I run my fingers through her hair, working from the base up while our tongues rummage each other's mouths. As she tightens around my fingers, I force myself to remove them from her cunt. I would be a fool damned if she came around my fingers the first time I had her.

First, my hand returns from under the dress. Then came the slow insertion of my fingers into my mouth. I take one in at a time, savoring her taste, having her watch me. Even a drop of her is comparable to drinking nectar from the heavens. I have to have more, and if I take any longer, I fear that she would have set my whole body aflame.

My hands tear her dress using the already opened fabric to my advantage. Ripping her panties from her, I expose her flesh to the cool air.

The lower section of her stomach, along with the darker innards of her thighs, are scattered with indents of lightning. As if leading exactly to the mark of her sex. I am absolutely enamored by such beauty. She shudders at the feeling, being at my mercy.

I spread her farther, my tongue dancing circles around her clitoris while my fingers curl into her. "Your cunt tastes as if it were made for the fountain of gods."

A giggle escapes from her. "Are you considering yourself a god now? How cocky."

Speeding and deepening my fingers into her, she shakes from under me. I take my hands and hold her in place, to which she responds by wrapping her legs around my head. A position I am weakened by.

Her fingers tangle through my curls, grabbing a fistful and squeezing them as I bring her closer to the edge. I move my mouth to suck on her as my tongue continues, rougher when she cries my name, begging to come.

As her wetness increases, I drink from her, to get drunk off her alone. She falls to her back. My cock aches for her, desperate to be buried between her core. A tug from my shirt brings me hovering over her. She kisses me, sucking on my tongue and tasting herself. It is so intensifying that it shrinks me to nothing more than a speck in this vast world.

I lift myself, pinning her wrists above her, watching as her breasts raise with her arms. "Tell me again. What do you want?"

"I want you. I want you inside me," she moans, arms struggling to free herself.

"You may want my cock. But we do not always get what we want."

She is desperate. Her eyes fill with hunger. With passion. "I need you. I need more." She hesitates, taking in a sharp breath. "Please."

My eyes narrow, bringing a smirk to my face. "Well if you are begging." I strip myself from my trousers as she watches me, never peeling her eyes from my body. As I free myself, Arabella takes in a deep breath, the bottom of her lip quivering.

"To answer your question, we are in Ezra's personal office." I grab her by the throat, squeezing it lightly, dragging her up so that her chest is pressed against my body. The fabric from the dress scratches against my clothing. I wish to feel her bare.

*Another time perhaps.*

Pushing myself inside her, she lets out a sharp inhale. Filling her cunt with my bare cock, it is divine. I pull out, just enough where my tip is the only thing inside, which only frustrates my body that craves more of her. Going at a rate too agonizingly slow for her, she sends me a look, demanding that I begin moving in her. Taking her. Pleasuring her.

"Tell me," I say. While she looks at me dumbfounded, I continue. "Tell me that I am better than my brother. That you crave my cock far more than you ever desired his."

A light huff leaves her mouth. "You can't really be mad that I–"

Unable to control myself any longer, I push myself in her fully, the warmth of her cunt hugging every vein of my cock. She is desperate, and she will take whatever I give her. I thrust at such a fast pace that we are both at a loss for words. We will give in to pleasure, if only for tonight.

I bring my hand to her clitoris, rubbing in circles, her clenching around me. "Did he touch you like this?" I suck the skin at the top of her breasts. "Did the touch of his filthy hands make you feel this way?" I peer at her, her teeth gritting. She is too proud to say any of it, but it is written all over her face. "Admit it, you will never want something as much as you want this. You want me inside of you, and you hate it."

"Fuck you."

My free hand leaves the desk, pushing through her hair, bringing her close. "Oh but princess, *you already are.*"

I thrust into her faster, but it is not nearly enough. Not from this angle, nor this shallow. I cup my hands under her full ass, lifting her closer to me, tightening any space that lingers between us. Slamming into her, my cock throbs, brushing an area that erupts curses from her.

She uses my shoulders for stability, beginning to meet my thrusts while rolling her hips. "Faster."

"Faster?" I chuckle.

"Faster. Harder. Deeper. All three. I don't care. Just don't stop."

I do as she asks, my abdominal muscles tensing. The sight of her taking me is too heavenly to be reality. She is a daydream, and my biggest nightmare if I am not careful. She's crafted in such a way that even gods would envy. "You do terrible things to me, Arabella. I hate you for it."

Her eyes shoot open, tugging her back to the reality of the situation. She curls her mouth in a devious grin. All too well does she know that this is her chance at taking power from me. Something I could not allow. I thrust into her deeper, forcing her eyes shut and a tear to roll down her face as she lets out a strangled breath.

"Look at me," I command. When she screws her eyes shut tighter, I take my hand from her clitoris and force her chin down, her eyes now wide and gazing into mine. "I told you to look at me."

She whimpers, my thrusts unrelenting. Not losing momentum. Her breasts rise with every thrust. How I wish to shred every piece of this dress until she is standing naked in front of me.

Halting my motions, I feel pride in her desperation that gleams from her for my touch. "Pathetic. So easy to crumble at the feel of my cock."

Her face hardens, refusing to show any vulnerability. I continue pumping at an unstable pace as she tightens around me. The sensation is too much. Placing my fingers back on her clitoris, I rub in circles as she combats moans from releasing. I take my hand from under her and wrap it around her throat, squeezing the moans from her.

"Don't fight it. Allow me to hear your pretty sounds. Let everyone hear who is making you fill with pleasure."

I trace my lips all around her, taking special note of areas that cause her body to spasm around me.

"Cassius, please," she whines for me.

"I want to feel you come around me."

"We do not always get what we want, do we?" she laughs, repeating my words back to me.

Fisting her hair, I yank it down, making her wince in both pleasure and pain.

Noises that come from me sound more desperate than demanding. "I need you to come around me. Allow me to feel you tighten around my cock."

My fingers press deeper around her, rubbing in circles until her body shakes all around me. "Come for me, my violent enemy," I growl into her ear. "Come for the man you claim to loathe."

"Cassius," she cries. And she cries over and over again as I draw out her pleasure.

This is enchanting. The type of occurrence that ancient poets wrote about. I dig my fingers into her waist as the length of my cock pumps in and out of her leaking sex. My body tenses wholly. If I do not stop soon, I will spill inside her, and I have an inkling that would result in something neither of us would want.

I withdraw myself, the sound making a *pop*, and begin thrusting into my hand. "Remind me of your wishes."

She watches me, eyes still full of desire. "Please."

With a tighter grip, I pump into my closed fist. It is less than three thrusts before her hand that holds mine is placed on top of the one around my length. She takes control, fisting me herself. The sight is enough to drive me to completion. She takes tortuous strokes, gliding her hand up and down the length.

Removing her hand, I relace her fingers with mine, the sound of our rings clashing. I take my cock, and she brings her hand to my head, pulling me into a deep kiss, biting down so hard it draws blood.

The mixture of pain and pleasure pushes me until I am undone. I spill onto the innards of her thighs, mixing her cum with my own.

Resting my head against hers, we breathe heavily together as she berates me for tearing her dress, though I am not actually listening. Simply am instead admiring the way she glows enough to overshine any shadow I could cast.

A knock at the door parts our attention from each other. The only to see us depart together before my shadows cleared had been one Fae. This could be no other than Cel.

"Hey, sorry to interrupt, but I think Ezra's coming this way so you might want to leave before he gets here," they caution with sincerity, a giggle suppressed in their voice.

Both Arabella and I laugh at the saved intrusion. Even if he does not catch us, there is no doubt it smelled of sex in this room.

I look at the witch, her demeanor warping to the way she always held herself around me. "Would you like me to walk you back to your room?" I say while reaching for her hand.

"No," is all that she utters before okkaring herself away from my touch.

That's all this had to be. A way to release the tension between the both of us.

Something has shifted between us. Arabella left quickly at the thought of another seeing us together in such a compromising position. Not that I would have particularly liked my brother to see her in such a state.

I wish to check on her, but as I catch myself reaching to knock on her door, I stop. If she wishes to be alone, so be it. There are things far more entertaining for my attention than the aftermath of what has been done.

When the next morning of awkwardness between us turns into days of following up our own theories, I wonder if perhaps there was something I had done wrong. That she thought, just as I, what we did was a mistake. Pleasurable, but a mistake nonetheless. It bears no importance when, after all, she would soon be gone, and I, back to my life before her arrival.

Despite whatever emotion is tied to our actions, we still have matters to attend to. In minutes, I shall meet her at supper, and we will discuss how to proceed with finding who is behind the missing Fae.

I spot the witch as she's leaving from the dining room with a plate half full of food. When she catches me gazing, she takes the plate and attempts to rush past me. Calling out to her, she stops with a sigh, pivoting in my direction.

"I'm assuming this is about the Fae?" Her voice is cold and sharp. She is still attempting to avoid speaking with me, but even she knows we have a duty. If she is to return to her life, she must make such a sacrifice.

I nod, dancing around the idea in my head to ask of her thoughts from our previous night together. "We know it is not singularly men disappearing. Would there not be a struggle if the Fae were taken by force?"

"I guess. I mean if there was, your guards would've found something about it by now. And if they were known to be acting odd before their disappearances, maybe they were drawn to something," she suggests. "I know it's documented that Sirens have lured men to their death, but do you think they can lure women in as well? Or maybe there's some special amulet?"

There are no records of that in our history, but that doesn't mean it is impossible. "Possibly, but it has never been heard of. Do you have knowledge of a Magik that could aid us on that topic?"

"What do you mean?" she asks as she sets the plate down.

"We were told a Magik is involved in this somehow. Do you know any who would know of a creature to answer this?"

Her head lowers with teeth biting her bottom lip. The eyebrows on her face furrow as she glances at different areas in the room. "I might know someone. She's one of my friends." She surveys me as if she is unsure if I will reject her.

"Is she trustworthy?" I cock an eyebrow.

She moves her lips in and out of her mouth, forming the words as best she can. "She knows the ins and outs of the Magik elite. We can ask her." Her tone is both sure of this friend while also being uncertain of something else. As I open my mouth, Arabella stops me by adding to her words. "But I'm gonna warn you, she's a little... intense to handle."

I refrain from questioning what she means, but it's almost as if she thinks me unable to handle who she spoke about. She picks up her phone from the inside of her shirt, and ringing begins.

"Hey, Am!" Arabella greets. "Are you busy right now?"

Another feminine voice responds from the phone, though I do not know how this is possible. "Not really. I'm just in my office. Why?"

Arabella takes me by my arm, and in one blink, we are in an office. It is filled with bright, earthy decor, and plants that surround the walls. Oranges, yellows, and reds paint the room, along with multiple mirrors and crystal artifacts. The sun is brightly shining, contrasting the night that currently befalls Ifaeris.

"You could've warned me you were coming," the same voice from the phone complains.

Arabella shrugs. "Didn't have time. It's important." Exhausted from either the drained energy that comes with okkaring two people such a distance or from not eating her meal, she flops on a sofa.

The friend surveys me, her round, brown eyes glancing between myself and Arabella multiple times. She seems to be unaffected by my presence, as she puts her blonde hair up, refocusing on Arabella. "What's up? Who's this?"

"Prince Cassius of Ifaeris, son of High King Elliot of Ifaeris," I announce, making my presence known. When she does not bow, I am reminded of my unimportance in the world of Magiks.

"Okay, well I'm Amber." Her lips tighten, shooting a look to Arabella. "You got Ara to okkar herself into my office? Impressive." Arabella responds by sticking her hand up, my ring on her index, and gesturing her middle finger at Amber, both of them laughing. "Oh, Ara, I need to tell you about the guy I'm dating right now. You remember Troy? Y'know, the singer? Well some of my people got in touch with his, and long story short, we're together."

Arabella's mouth drops, and she gives a sarcastic laugh. "Are you really dating, or is this some elaborate scenario you meant to send me?"

Impatient with their ramblings, I interrupt before Amber can respond. "Arabella, we came to ask Amber something."

At once, they turn to me, and Arabella recalls what we set out to do. "Am, can Sirens mimic a sound that could draw women in? Or even other creatures in general? You know the same way the winged creatures could with humans?"

Amber's face twists in contortion. "I never heard of it, but it's possible."

"What about an artifact?" I ask. "Would there be a similar device that could draw in a Fae? Something that would cause us to desire something so much, they would leave their family without a word."

Repeating her actions, Amber glances at me, then back at Arabella. "I've heard of a sorcerer. A rich one that's always seen by the most elite of us, and I have it on good authority he's collected many things from every land, both rumored and not." She looks at me and grins. "Things that were taken and considered lost forever by those he would steal from."

Her tone irritates me. It falls far too disrespectful.

"How is it possible that this man stole from our archives without knowledge?" I ask snidely.

She turns back at me, glaring as if everything she does is calculated. There is no question why she and Arabella are friends, despite their opposite personalities and aesthetics. "He wouldn't be a very good thief if you knew, now would he?"

Walking to her desk, she grabs parchment and a writing medium to jot something down. She tears the paper, handing it to Arabella. "He's always spotted at this club. Y'know, Infinite. He owns it. If anyone knows something about a mimicking item, it's him."

We venture into a center that contains multiple shops inside. It's overcrowded and full of mortals, the air stenched with the smell of humans. We stop inside a shop where Arabella purchases hooded outerwear, which she forces me to wear. With the hood atop my head combined with the heat and iron radiating from nearly everything in the land, this is unbearable.

"If you wanted discretion from my Fae appearance, I would have glamoured myself to look mortal," I complain. "Or hidden my appearance from humans."

She does not stop her steps to our destination. "I didn't know all of y'all could change your appearance. But regardless, you can't glamour yourself in public when there are security cameras everywhere to catch the change." Her lips point to a white object hanging on the wall, and I wonder if the object has Faerie Sight. "But keep that glamour in mind when we go to Infinite tonight."

When we finally make it to the intended shop, she walks behind a short, thin, tan woman with long, black hair. She wears a dusty rose dress with sleeves that cut off at her elbows.

Carefully, we sneak behind the witch, and Arabella whispers her name into her ear, causing the woman to jump.

"Bella, what the hell?" she chides. Her dark eyes are similar to Arabella's, though she has a skinnier face and wider eyes than the witch I know. On her dress is a pinned item with the name 'Evie'.

"Evie, this is Cassius. We need you to help find him something for tonight. We're going to Club Infinite."

Evie smiles at me and turns back to Arabella in disbelief. "You? Going to a club? With a hot man that you haven't told me about?" Her jaw drops. "Who are you, and what have you done with Arabella?"

Insulting. As if my clothing is not suitable for a simple mortal area. I ought not to speak, but I do regardless. "Is there something the matter with the clothing I currently reside in?"

"No, no. There's nothing wrong with what you wear, but you need something more casual for the club. Unless you want the attention of some creepy old man offering you money for activities I doubt you'd want to participate in." Arabella laughs, more so when she amuses herself in my unawareness.

While I do not understand the jest of her comment, as this is her world, I will trust her judgment. I am no fool. Already I am out of place with my ears having a different shape.

She drags us around the store, picking multiple clothing options for Arabella to decide on. None of the items are particularly the style

I would choose for myself, but it is all they offer. After deciding between two sets of shirts, we move on to the trousers, which have fewer options than the tops.

Many of what they have for bottoms consist of black or blue rough material that I am told is denim. Hardly have I ever seen this fabric outside of someone I took lessons with once. It was so dreadful, I forced him to strip of it and had it immediately taken to be burned.

"Why must I wear clothing from this section when the choices over there are far superior?" I point to the area on the right.

Evie giggles through her face unmoving. "That's the women's section, which, if you want something from there, go ahead, but I think the point was for you to blend in, Your Highness."

Clothing being categorized in such a way is not something I was aware existed. There are men's and women's sections, but what of those who are neither? We roam the store and continue searching for options, passing through a smaller shop that is inside this one.

Once we finish browsing for clothing dedicated to myself, we stroll through the women's section. Evie hands Arabella a short, velvety, green dress with the halter section containing strings that would wrap around her neck to tie them. She then presses the dress against Arabella's body, taking note where the fitted section to her waist would fall. "I think you should buy this and wear it tonight. Are you still a size twenty?"

"Actually, I'm a size eighteen," Arabella responds casually while taking the dress.

"Oh great," Evie cheers. "This is the last one in that size!" She brings us to the front, where she begins to remove the white attachments from the dress. "Also, you need to go see Vi and

Damien. They have some new design ideas, and she wants you to do the modeling for them."

Arabella smiles at her friend. "Yeah, I'll have to do that another day. I'm a little busy with this whole Fae thing," she mutters while her head bends in my direction.

"You better finish that soon," Evie groans. "I miss talking to you about *that* group and telling you new ways I've been a menace to their friendships."

Whatever this group has done to Evie, it is enough for the two witches to find glee in their misery. I know Arabella to be capable of fighting for herself–she has the tongue of a vicious brat–but it does not make it any less disturbing to know her capabilities match mine.

I put a pair of black, smooth gloves on the chilled counter after Evie finishes with the other two items, Arabella shooting me a look.

"Leather gloves?"

"Simply a precaution."

She figures it unimportant, turning back to her friend. "Evie, we need to use a dressing room. We gotta okkar to my place 'cause I didn't bring my car."

Hurrying to the changing area, Arabella pulls me into one of the boxed stations, Evie joking not to have sex while in there.

"Where are you taking us?" I ask her after she pulls the curtains.

She okkars us into a bedroom. There are portraits of men on her wall, along with paintings of art and a fabric that hangs behind her bed. A desk is at the corner of the room, and on the opposite corner are shelves compiled of books, warping the wood from its weight. She disappears through a door that holds her clothing, similar to the ones we have at Nexus, though this is much smaller.

"If you didn't hear," she walks into a bathroom, heating the water, "we needed to come back to my place. Now take off your shoes."

"Why?" I question her as we both remove our shoes.

Taking my boots and putting them next to the door, she grabs towels from inside her closet and walks towards another door. "We don't wear shoes inside the house."

I scan around the chamber as she closes the bathroom door to bathe. This is her house, a small one at that. I pull the hooded jacket over me and sneak around the floor outside her chamber. The rooms on this second floor seem to be private to others, and I think it best to only lurk through Arabella's.

I descend the stairs into common spaces. There is a flat, black rectangle hanging with sofas surrounding the room to the right of the stairs. To the left is a kitchen area with a tight area to dine. There is a separate walkway that leads into a small alcove with a piano and another room full of art canvases.

There is nothing of interest, so I return to Arabella's room to go through her possessions more thoroughly. Her closet is mainly filled with black clothing, along with a touch of green and white. Other colors are there, but they are in the corner, shoved next to bags.

I move to her bookshelves and note she is one who admires romance novels, based on the short descriptions on them, most of which falling into categories of smutty romances. The covers appear unsuspecting, but the insides are filled with nothing but sex.

*So this is what she is interested in.*

On her desk are colors and powders that I had seen in the shop where her friend works. They are similar to the cosmetics I use on myself. On the floor next to her desk sit multiple pillow-like creatures. I pick one up to inspect the threats it contains.

The sound of the shower disappears, and Arabella partially cracks open the door. "Hey Cassius, I forgot to get clothes. Can you go through the top drawer of the dresser? There's a lot of big shirts in there and I need one."

I grab a large, white shirt and hand it to her through the door. When she comes out, she rushes to the clothing holder and pulls the bottom drawer. She grabs out panties and lounging pants, putting them on before returning to the steamed room. I watch as she unwraps her hair from the towel and combs it, allowing for it to dry.

As she exits the bathroom, the heat from the shower fills this one. With it comes the scent of aloe. A scent that contrasts the lavender one she uses at Nexus. I pick a stuffed dragon from her bed, squishing it for any weapons.

Arabella snatches the toy from me, her face angry. "What are you doing?"

"I was only studying this toy dragon. We have similar things in Ifaeris, though most resemble creatures of our lands and are not kept past childhood," I tease, gesturing to the pile of neatly organized stuffed creatures.

"Fuck off from my plushie collection. And don't touch my stuff," she spits with hostility.

I back away from her. "Why have we come here?"

She lets out a breath, running a hand through her hair. "We needed a place to change and get ready before going to the club. Plus, I have to collect a few things before heading back."

My stomach makes a noise, reminding us both that neither of us has eaten. She laughs, easing all the tension she had just held. "I'll make us food. We should probably eat before we leave anyway, but I don't have any food in the fridge, so I ordered some ingredients to be brought here. The app said they should be here soon, so let's go downstairs."

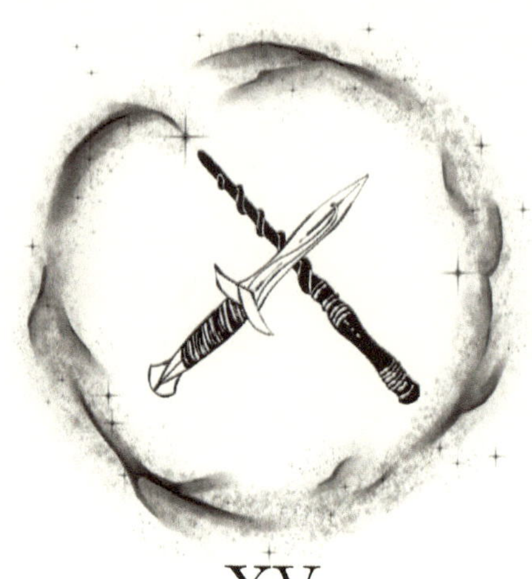

# XV

## *Quick Changes*

Arabella

The doorbell rings, and immediately, I go to grab the groceries from the person delivering them while Cassius sits at the table in the kitchen. Since I won't be staying here long and will be going back to Ifaeris tonight, I only got the essential ingredients for the one meal. Some chicken breasts, dumplings, and potstickers should be more than enough for us. Everything else we already have in the house.

Cassius glances up from the table, watching me drop the plate of uncooked chicken breast onto the counter. "So what is it that you're making?"

"Adobo. It's a Filipino dish. And then I'm gonna make some dumplings. If there's any extra, I'll just leave it for my roommate if she wants it. We share everything anyway." I grab the pots, pans, and the rest of the ingredients from around the pantry, prepping everything to be made. "Can you wash the chicken and rice while I start the marinating?"

He goes to open the chicken from the plastic and looks at me with confusion. "You wish for me to put soap on this chicken?"

I'm taken aback by this question. While I'm not someone who likes to cook, I at least know how to if needed. "Do you not know how to cook?"

"No."

*Of course you don't.* He's a prince. Everything he needs can be made for him. Or at the very least, heated instantly. He's probably never made anything past toast or eggs.

I exhale, but it comes off more as a sigh. I'm going to have to walk through this step by step like a child. "You rinse the chicken a few times to make sure you got any bacteria out. With the rice, you fill it with water and swish it around before pouring it out and making sure the grains don't fall. Repeat it, then add water to the rice till it reaches about the first line of your index finger, then put it in the rice cooker."

"Am I to use my hands for this? That sounds like work."

"Yeah. Believe it or not, I don't use magik when I cook," I remark with a playful tone. "Actually, can you send out your shadow person to help me? It'll make mixing the ingredients easier."

The shadow appears before us and begins to cut the onions as I direct. It finds difficulty handling certain tasks, but it's still more helpful than Cassius, who sits down and watches as we do all the work. When we finish preparing the marination, I sink the chicken into the soup, stick it in the fridge, and set a timer for half an hour. I begin boiling dumplings, waiting for the chicken.

"Does this dish have salt?" he asks, a bit of distress peeking through.

"A little, why? Can Fae not handle salt? Is that why your food has a different taste?"

Leering, he takes offense to this. "Fae try to minimize salt intake due to the iron in it, though we can consume it in small amounts."

When I sit, I see Cassius poking at the buttons of the extra rice cooker.

"What are you doing?" I ask.

He brings the cooker to the table, pressing what would be the button to open it. "How does this contraption work? It cooks the food, yet you do nothing but press mere buttons."

"Honestly? I couldn't really tell you how the mechanics work. I just know it heats the metal pot inside and causes the water to soak into the rice. Whatever water is left evaporates, I guess." I take the object away from him, putting it back in its place.

When the dumplings and potstickers are finished and over half an hour is up, I lay them on two plates. I microwave the dipping sauces and take the chicken from the fridge. Cassius turns on the rice cooker for me, giving about an hour before it finishes, which is just enough time to cook the chicken. Pouring the chicken into a pot, I set the stove on high to let it cook.

"Do you wanna help cook adobo?" I ask while stirring the pot.

He moves from his chair to my side, taking the spoon from my hand. "Not particularly, but I will taste it." He brings the spoon to his mouth, tasting the soup, and his mouth puckers. "Why is this dish sour?"

I laugh at him not being acquainted with foods of this taste. "There's vinegar in it, you big baby. I know it's not something you're used to, but it's a cultural dish." When he wipes his mouth with a paper towel and gapes at me in alarm, I laugh harder. "You'll like it with the rice and chicken, I promise. If not, there's other food."

The food now done, I grab two plates, fill them with rice, pour some of the soup on top, and finish by adding the chicken above. I hand him his plate and grab the utensils from the drawer while he rips paper towels for napkins.

He begins eating, and his body practically becomes one with the plastic chair. "Okay, you were right. I quite enjoy the taste of this. How shall I eat these?" he asks while pointing to the dumplings.

Deciding I want to entertain myself, I grab chopsticks from the drawer and hand them to him. "You take these and grab them with it in the middle. Watch." I take the dumpling with my chopsticks and dip it in the sauce, bringing it to my mouth to bite before setting it down.

He tries and tries, but can't pick up a dumpling for the life of him. I giggle while he glares at me, his nostrils flaring from me finding amusement in his frustration, just as he does in mine. Eventually, he gives up and stabs it with one stick.

He takes more of the chicken into his mouth. "This is far too much food for the two of us alone. Are you taking any with us?"

"Nah, I'm just gonna leave it with a note for my roommate as an apology for being gone so long," I admit while grabbing a glass of water. I begin washing the dishes that were used and put our leftovers in containers with a note.

Leaving the dishes to dry, I don't think before the next words come from my mouth. "We should have a safe word."

He chokes, his head spinning. "Your pardon?"

"Considering I almost killed a man who said something that

pissed me off and threatened to execute another for calling me a whore, I think before I start going too far, you can use a safe word to stop me." Judging by the look on his face, he isn't convinced my suggestion will work. "It might not be that helpful, but it's a thought."

Now that I finished explaining myself, he considers what I said. "If this is what you wish, I ask, what word will be used?"

I go through many words in my head before I settle on one that is subtle enough, but also not so common that it could be mistaken for something else.

After it's decided, we head back upstairs. Cassius goes into my room as I unload the clothing I magiked to be washed while we ate. Then I realize the time. We need to get ready if we want to get inside before they begin charging.

"Where are we?" Cassius asks. "I understand we are at your house, but where is that?"

"California. I told you I'm from here, but I live in Los Angeles, by the school. There's like a five-hour time difference between here and Ifaeris." Shoving his clothes to him, I point to my closet for him to change. "Now, come on. We have to get ready."

I grab my purse from my desk and empty it onto my bed. When the makeup I need falls out, I tear the packaging from the products.

Cassius watches as they come out one by one. "When did you acquire those?"

"When we passed through the makeup section of the store. I stole them," I say in passing.

His eyes widen in shock. "Why would you steal them? I could have purchased it for you. You have no need for these when you magik on your cosmetics. Why? *How?*" His voice raises with each question.

Sometimes I forget that this is normal to me and would be something entirely baffling for a prince. "Okay one, you have money in Ifaeris, but here, it's useless. That means the only money you have here is as much as I do. Two, I do not have money, my friends do. And three, I sometimes do my makeup by hand, and I'm running out. I still need the products themselves when I magik on makeup. It doesn't just appear from nothing."

His face shrivels, scrunching in disgust that he is a nobody in this world, but unaffected at the mention of stealing. He looked more impressed than anything at the mention.

While in the middle of applying my makeup, I hear him groaning in the other room.

"What?" I call out.

"There is a situation. The clothing you chose for me is dreadfully dull."

"Yeah, well better that than sticking out more than you already do," I remind him as I put on my earrings.

Walking from the bathroom, I peer from the frame, seeing a round-eared Cassius in one of my faux coats. "Are- Are you in my coat?"

He pats the sides of the sleeves, feeling the soft material of the fabric. The silky, silver shirt is halfway unbuttoned and tucked into his black pants. Chains from my jewelry collection are layered on his neck, his hair combed with my golden leaf clips on the sides, the little bit of hair falling over his brow as it always does. "It complements the clothing, does it not?"

I want to smash my head against a wall. "Yes, but-" I pause, thinking of an excuse only to come up with nothing. "You're not wearing that."

He groans, saying something under his breath while begrudgingly handing me my coat back. It actually goes well with my outfit, so I throw the black coat onto my chair while Cassius wanders into my bathroom, picking up my razor. "What is this bladed device?"

"A razor. Which reminds me, I need to pack that." I take the object from his hand.

"Why?"

Enchanting the inside of my small purse to enlarge what can be held in it, I throw my shower products in with the razor before I button it. "In case I need it. I haven't shaved in like three months."

His eyes shift and his brows furrow, doing the math. "But you have been with us for only nearly two months? And we have waxers at your disposal."

I stare at him with a deadpan expression. "Your point? I barely grow hair, and shaving is faster than waxing, so..." I go back into the bathroom to change into my dress, tying up the back and making a mental note to meet with the waxers.

"An interest in smutty books, I take it?" he teases.

The mascara drops from my hand, smearing onto my under eye, and my mouth widens.

*FUCK*. My body can't move from its place. *If there is a god out there, please say he didn't go through my books*. "What?" I put on an innocent voice like I have no idea what he's talking about.

"He pounded his long, hard co–"

*NO*. I fling open the door and hurl myself at him, slapping the book from his hand. He gives me a suggestive look, finding humor in my disorientation. He laughs, putting on his gloves while I put the book back, refusing to look at him.

"If you desired, we could always play out your little fantasies. After all," his voice drops an octave lower, lowering himself to my ear, "I am but a room away."

Heat rises to my face, and there's a part of me tempted to take him up on that offer right now, but I refuse to let him have the upper hand. I turn and push my hand against his chest. "Don't think just 'cause you did the bare minimum of making me come that it was anything more than hormones." I give a slight smile, dragging my finger down his body and lingering over his abdomen while magiking the smeared makeup from my face.

"Now let's go. Our ride to take us to Infinite is here," I say, bending down to pick something from the floor, giving him a full view of my thong from the short dress.

# XVI

## Unexpected Appearances

Cassius

As the sun begins to set, we arrive in a building with colorful lights flashing through the windows. When we leave what is called a car, Arabella thanks the man who is controlling our transportation and takes me behind a long line of mortals around our age.

"Okay, here's the plan," she says while grabbing my arm, "you're gonna act like my boyfriend to draw attention away from the fake ID I made you. We go in, sneak around to the top floor, and go into his office. Got it?"

I nod, irritated with the length of time we are spending in this line.

She pulls me down as we make our way closer to the front, hissing into my ear sarcastically, "And don't try tricking any humans into killing themselves for your sick pleasure."

There is no seriousness in her tone, though I know this may not be entirely a false narrative involving my past.

With one couple in front of us, she takes out two rectangular-shaped items from her bag with our faces, handing me the one with my face. When the guard collects them to inspect, shining a light on mine, she twists her fingers, speaking with him.

"Aw babe, aren't you excited to go to your first club?" She ganders at me, kissing my cheek. She twirls her fingers in the direction of what is called a bouncer, speaking to the man. "You know, this is my boyfriend's first time at a club. Isn't he so cute?" When the human ignores her, rolling his eyes to the side, she takes in a deep breath, concentrating on manipulating his mind, muttering, "I think you should let us in so we can enjoy our time and see the boss, don't you?"

The man's face is beginning to detect there is something amiss.

"Good sir, it is quite riveting for a man of your stature to have such a job, when you are built for far more," I say. His eyes shoot up, and a grin starts forming. Flattery is what he craves. "My Dragon and I are so excited to participate in the festivities that your boss has curated. Considering the strong guarding he has chosen, I am sure you are the reason behind why Infinite is so renowned."

He hands back the rectangles to us, appearing confused by my wording but smiling from the praise. He whispers for the man next to him to take us to a 'VIP lounge' on the second floor. While walking through the dancing bodies and boisterous music, the other guard leads us up the stairs to a private room.

"Dragon?" Arabella says loudly, raising her eyebrows.

"I had to add to your story somehow. Pet names work, and so

does flattery. Besides," I whisper into her ear after scanning her body, "you are as hot-headed as a dragon, princess."

She elbows my side at the comment, attempting to not drop our romantic act. Once the guard leaves, she untwists herself from my arm, offering me a far better view of her attire. She is so beautiful, it troubles me. "I can't understand why my magik didn't work, but I guess this was an easier way to the second floor. I think we passed the owner's office on the way here." She points through the glass at the closed door by the stairs. "It's the only office that didn't have a name. I say we go in."

Following her lead, we go towards the door, opening it to find a man with long, blond hair in a rotating chair. She closes the door to hide the violence that may ensue, or so that we may hear better.

"Ah," the man says. "A witch in my office. To what do I owe the pleasure?"

Arabella takes a seat on the blue, suede chair that sits across from him. "Cut the shit, Jefferson. We know you steal from creatures."

The polite mannerisms drop, his face turning serious. "So, I see this is business?"

"*Wow*, a true genius of a thief," Arabella remarks. "We have a few questions if you'd be so generous to answer them."

Jefferson observes her, calculating every move she makes to be one step ahead. "Depends on what you have to offer me, wouldn't you say, sir?" he asks while looking at me.

"If the witch says we have questions, I would think it best to answer her, lest you want to cause yourself harm." I take a seat next to Arabella, removing my gloves to summon my shadow to guard the door.

His face lights with delight. "So you have brought not only a Fae but an Elemental one. Interesting." He rises from his chair towards my shadow. It would seem that there are some Magiks that are aware of our existence. "So what questions do you have, Miss...?"

"Huǒ."

The look on his face turns sinister. Nearly as unsettling as the guards must feel in my presence. "Well Miss Huǒ, I'm glad to be of help."

She glances to me, subtly shaking her head. I know it best to let her handle the situation, since in the eyes of other Magiks, it is her threats that are far more deadly than a Fae's.

"Your bouncers are human, but I couldn't use magik on them. Are they charmed?" she asks sternly.

His eyes lower at her, disregarding my place in the room. "Yes. I assume you were attempting to sneak in your Fae boyfriend here?"

At those words, she falls aback slightly. "Cassius he- Uh- He isn't my boyfriend. We were just saying that to distract them."

There is nothing more between us than contempt and built-up tension, but her words still stir in an uneasy manner within me. I assume it to be normal when the line between hatred and desire is so thin, their only commonality being passion. It is foolish to harbor any emotions for her when my thoughts simply stem from the time we are forced to spend together.

"You seem to show more interest in our relationship than what we came here for," I comment in her support. "I'll wager he is but a *common thief* with no ability to aid us." Standing, I move my legs, strutting to the door.

His face hardens with determination to prove himself. "I'm no common thief, boy. Get that through your head."

"What do you know about the missing Fae?" Arabella questions.

He joins his hands together, acting as though he is clueless of any of the Creaturelands. "I'm afraid I don't know what you mean. I myself am barely knowledgeable of creatures beyond our own kind."

They exchange questions back and forth, Arabella struggling to extract information from him. Their interaction becomes repetitive, no more than him denying all that he knows. I study the room, attempting to find a book, artifact, anything that will clue in a way to hold something over him. His shelves are decorated with historical documents that can be found in our libraries. A wooden floor, covered by a rug that likely leads to a passageway out, or at the very least hides something. A small vault stands behind his desk with numbers to press.

On a statue, I spot it. A medallion that has the Disaris heirloom. One that is foretold by our history to carry the original crest from the first Elementals. It sits on a portrait bust, clear for any person to see.

I take the necklace from its place, tangling it between my fingers. "You play us for fools, sir." I turn to him. "You speak on knowing little of the Fae, yet you hold a Disaris family heirloom." I slam it on the desk. "This had gone missing years ago."

Arabella peers at the necklace, then at me, quirking a sinister smile. "So Jefferson, care to speak on that?"

He begins darting his eyes around the room. A tell if I have ever seen one. "I have people that attain things for me constantly. If this belongs to your family, it was not guarded well," he insults, reaching for the necklace.

Snatching the necklace from its place, I chuckle. "You speak of not knowing about Fae, and yet you are all too eager to take what is rightfully ours. Thief."

"I told you, boy, I am not a thief," he grits through his teeth.

I pocket the medallion, outsmarting him. "Ah, but you said you are not a common thief. My darling, Arabella here has already made clear that you omit information from us. So I will ask again, what do you know about the missing Fae?"

This time, he hesitates. He's running out of options. Out of lies or deceit. "I will tell you for a price." He grabs my hand, eyeing the garnet thorn ring that sits in the middle of my left finger, replacing the emerald one.

With a flick of Arabella's hand, the man flings to his seat, unable to move. "Now, kind sir, we mustn't put our hands on what isn't ours."

Lurking around the room of artifacts, she grabs a bust that sits upon his books. "It would be a real shame if someone were to lose this, wouldn't you say?" With a blink, she appears at his knees. "A bigger shame if you were to lose something you view of more value." Her knife hovers over the zipper of his trousers. When she cuts the button, his eyes widen with terror.

"Okay, okay," he concedes, pleading for his life. "Take what you want."

Arabella holds the tip of the knife to his throat, sweat beating down his forehead. "We don't care about your stolen shit. Now we're gonna ask you some questions, and you're going to answer them honestly this time. Got it?" Shaking, the man nods, hair clinging together from sweat. "Good boy." She draws the knife back from his nethers and sits back in place. "Now, does any creature exist that can mimic the sounds to draw in other creatures? Similar to how Sirens call on humans?"

He gulps, still terrified of Arabella. "No, Sirens themselves only have the ability to lure humans. No other creature has a similar ability."

"Pity," I sigh, sending the shadow behind him, constraining his arms and cutting the circulation from his hands.

"Wait, wait," he yells. I hold my hands, commanding the shadow to stop. "There's a stone."

Stabbing the desk, Arabella circles to his side. "Go on."

Panting and tears leave him hyperventilating before us. He may be a thief, but he has as little courage as a child being caught with sweets. "Sirens' powers don't extend beyond humans, but there is an existing stone that causes someone near to hear their greatest desires."

Both Arabella and I stare at him. This information is of little use to us. He is running in circles to escape from his own demise. One which will come sooner if he does not elaborate on his vague statements.

"Why would this stone be of importance to the missing Fae?" I ask.

He laughs hysterically. A man delirious and coming to terms that no matter what he says, he is doomed. "If you heard all your greatest desires could come true, wouldn't you follow where it led?"

"And where is this stone?" Arabella demands while bending to meet Jefferson's face, the back of the dress exposing her dimpled ass.

Jefferson huffs, both in humility and anger. "Funny enough, it was stolen from me not a few months ago. Ironic isn't it? To steal from a fellow collector?"

"I guess they're returning the favor," Arabella mutters.

I take the weapon from the desk, handing it to Arabella. It is a true wonder how she snuck that past those guarding the door. "What else can you tell us of the missing Fae?"

Multiple and sporadic twitches come from his eyes. "Nothing, I swear. You can use the witch to use a truthing spell on me. I'll even take down my shield."

Arabella stands behind the man, placing her fingers on both sides of his temples. Her eyes roll back and she mouths something before returning to reality. "He's telling the truth."

She gives him his freedom back, and we turn to take our leave. On our way out, he murmurs, "If the Stone of Elestial is truly being used for the disappearances of the Fae, you're in for a bigger battle than you think."

We shut the door, ready to exit, but are stopped by someone with short hair similar to Arabella's. Only, this Magik is without hair that falls along her forehead. Her features are similar, though this woman has a flatter nose and rounder eyes, as well as being thinner and shorter.

"Arabella?" she calls. She looks deeply into Arabella's eyes before embracing. The thinly-strapped, mauve top that is worn cuts off above her navel, and her loose black trousers end above the heels of her boots. It's apparent they are friends, being that Arabella is willing to stay in her arms.

"Vi, this is Cassius. Cassius, this is Violette," she yells, attempting to be heard above the roaring music.

When Violette reaches for my hand, I am pulled down. "Do you two want to join us?"

Arabella tenses at the thought. "No, we actually have to go."

I smile at the friend in kind. "If you desire to join us, we have a VIP room," I say, pointing to the room we were given earlier.

Violette's mouth drops with excitement. "I'll get the rest of the group and meet you inside."

Before Arabella can object, Violette is dashing down the stairs as fast as possible while gripping the railing, clearly nearing high intoxication.

When we get into our room that is gracious enough to somewhat drown out the music, Arabella takes a sharp inhale, her energy turning hostile and cold. "Why the fuck would you invite my friends here?"

"You are the one that said you missed your friends, did you not? I thought this would make you less unpleasant."

She throws her coat onto a sofa, prepared to yell at me in a way she believes I deserve, but at once, the door opens, and four other Magiks have joined us. They bring mortal, alcoholic drinks and pass one to both Arabella and myself. Each greets Arabella with a hug, spreading themselves on the seats surrounding the room, the dim lighting from the glass windows that overlook the downstairs floor passing through. All but one have accents that are different from Arabella's, though it differs very little to hers. These must be the English friends that she has spoken of.

One has dark skin, similar to Helena's, his hair shaven and a wide nose with full lips. He reaches his hand out to me. "Hey mate, I'm Damien."

I shake his hand, appreciating the gold and black buttoned shirt that is worn with black trousers and held together by a belt.

Another, with shorter, wavy, chestnut hair and hazel eyes, shakes my hand. The Magik wears a white cotton shirt with a plaid, open-buttoned shirt over it. The breeches of his ensemble are a taupe color, nearly the same shade as his slightly tan skin, with pockets by his knees. "I'm Grayson. Nice to meet you," he drags out as if asking for my name.

"Cassius. Prince Cassius of Ifaeris," I clarify.

The final Magik smiles at me. She is bigger than Arabella, though also taller. With long, curly, red hair similar to my cousins, though hers brighter, she wears a floral dress and a blue denim jacket. "Well, Prince Cassius, you must be important as hell to be taking Bells from us this long." She giggles, winking at Arabella.

"Yeah," Violette says. "She must really like you if she barely answers the Wands group chat anymore."

Arabella is wounded by these words. "That's not true! I answer as much as I can. I told you I was busy helping the king of Ifaeris."

"Yeah, but it's not like you've been hanging with us much since Luka anyway," Grayson says.

Arabella takes the shot from Grayson's hand and swallows it whole. "I'm gonna order drinks." On the way out so no one may hear, she mutters, "Maybe take a few more shots before I'm back."

When she leaves, I am alone in a room of her friends whom I do not know. They seem to feel just as uncomfortable in this situation as I am. I drink the glass that was given to me in hopes it will distract my thoughts. From speaking amongst themselves, I gather that Damien and Violette are a couple, along with Grayson and the other friend.

"So are you all men and women? Or is there something else you are? My sister does not identify by either, though they still ask to be called sister," I say to make conversation.

Violette speaks for them. "Juliette and I are women, and Damien and Grayson are men. Do you like being called a man or?"

"Yes. Though I would think it best to refer to me as a prince."

Juliette laughs as if she assumes I jest. "Yeah, well, you're not a prince here. And we sure as fuck won't be calling our friend's boy toy by prince."

My cheeks burn with displeasure. In response to the alcohol or the comment, my mind reels. "Arabella and I are not romantically lovers."

The room falls into awkward silence. I draw back, not expecting them to have assumed such a thing. I had thought if Arabella did speak of me, it was in anger. In hatred. In disgust. Her friends are not aware of her true stay in Ifaeris. Or perhaps she has rarely spoken of me at all and they think us arriving together implies our relationship.

"What is this Wands group chat?" I ask, open to anyone in the room to answer.

Damien pulls Violette onto his lap. "It's our text group chat name. 'Five of Wands'. You know, like tarot."

"It *used to be* 'Six of Wands' but Gray over here thought it would be funny to change it to 'Five of Wands' not a month after Luka," Juliette says while eyeing Grayson from the side.

Luka. It is the second time his name has been mentioned. The first time had caused Arabella such visceral tightness, she left the room. Whoever Luka is, he's someone of importance to this group.

"Is Luka another acquaintance of yours?"

The energy in the room plummets. Violette removes herself from Damien to speak. "Ara hasn't told you, has she?"

"I am afraid she does not tell me much of anything. She does not deem it important to what we are trying to accomplish," I confess to them.

Violette sucks in her cheeks, biting down and turns to all her friends. "Luka's our friend. And Ara's boyfriend."

Every muscle in my body stiffens, my breath stifled. She has a lover and never uttered a word of his existence? Not once had he been brought up after she bedded my brother. While I was inside her. I do not care if I was what she had wanted, but to lie and use me.

"I can see you're not taking this the way I meant it," Violette says, bringing a cup to her mouth. "Luka *was* Ara's boyfriend. He died." She takes in a breath, all of them sitting with the utmost sincerity. "He was stabbed, and Arabella took it really hard. She barely talked to us at all. Avoided eating. She was broken. To this day, she blames herself."

I observe all their faces, suddenly filled with grief. "Did *she* murder him? That is the only reasoning for her to be blamed."

Juliette speaks instead. "That's the thing. She didn't, but Bells isn't really one to forgive herself. She struggled enough as it was before Luka's death. And when he died, she drowned herself in self-blame."

"Especially didn't help when that bitch Delphi made her feel like shit," Grayson barks. "Harping on Ara with her little group of friends whenever they could."

Arabella returns, partially intoxicated and hardly able to move without wobbling. As I sit her down, she snickers, resting her head on my shoulder.

"Ordered drinks for us! They're coming up in a little!" She smiles wide. I can feel her cheeks grow on my shoulder.

Grayson takes food from his pocket, taking a bite and handing the rest to Arabella. "How much did you drink?"

She takes the cookie, giggling after every bite. "Three... Five... Nine shots." She laughs, coated in childlike harmlessness.

"Oh gods," Violette says.

"What?" Arabella looks at her friend. "I've drank more. And I ate this time! I'll be fine."

A servant comes in with a glass bottle of alcohol and multiple glasses. The one behind her brings in water and glasses.

More humans.

We manage to trick Arabella into drinking water, to which she strongly fulminates. When another man with a button that writes out 'Mike' enters, he takes Arabella's hand, kissing it and asking if she needs anything more.

She gives a polite smile, giggling. "Thank you, but we're good."

"Oh, but I can take really good care of you." He pulls her closer.

Rage fuses through me. Arabella is far too intoxicated to fight him, though I do not doubt she would attempt it. She shakes herself from his grasp but carries on her infatuation with him.

"I do like a man who knows what he wants," she says, pouting doe eyes at him.

He brings a hand to her waist, wrapping her in his embrace. "Then let me show you how I get exactly what I want."

"I think it best you leave her in the care of an equal," I insist, removing his hand from my witch. While I take enjoyment in watching Arabella squirm, I refuse to allow a human to touch her as he does. Nor take advantage of her.

A whistle from the other side echoes in the nearly soundproof room. "You really thought to pull rank to a waiter?" Grayson says.

"You and cocky, arrogant men, Bells," Juliette teases, pulling her with them to dance.

Through the night they all are moving around the room, partaking in games and singing horribly off-key. Regardless of whether I know how the song goes, it's obvious they are drunk. Arabella is laughing with her friends and smiling. She is also the only one that seems to be holding the tune. It is a state I have never seen her in. While there are moments of her enjoying herself among us, she is never unguarded fully. She holds her walls up so that no one may see her truly. Seeing her with Xavier is the closest she has ever been to dropping her guard.

All of that is nothing in comparison to how she is behaving at this moment. She is smiling and wheezing, trading stories about what she had missed in her time away from them. She supplies them in turn with stories of Ifaeris. I laugh alongside them, finding humor within the tale of her threatening a man for hurling insults and a plate at us.

"That's our Arabella, violent and always ready to jump a bloke," Grayson says.

Arabella makes a gesture with her middle finger towards the sorcerer. When I laugh along, she watches me with a smile that shines as brightly as the sun handed down from gods.

"Get me water," she demands.

As I hand her a glass, she drinks it all in one gulp.

"You enjoy taking orders from me, don't you, Your Highness," she mocks, giving a shallow bow and falling into my arms.

I push back the hair from her face, the sweat coating my fingers while I send a lazy grin. "At times."

She gives me a smile with her eyes closed, and I take her to one of the black sofas, where she lays her head on my lap. A glimmer of trust. She is trusting me to hold her, and it does not matter if this is due to her drunkenness. She trusts me enough in her most raw state to let me touch her. I smile to myself, placing her coat over her and running my fingers along her arm as she sleeps.

Grayson puts his arm around Juliette after passing a drink to me. "Our friend has a thing for rich men, doesn't she?"

Juliette elbows him, her eyebrows mixing. "Don't say that when you can't even get a girlfriend yourself."

"I can get a girlfriend," he defends. "I bet if I wanted you, I could get you." His eyebrows jump.

She slowly presses her lips to his cheek, his eyes growing wide. He stammers through words, though none forming a complete sentence, causing everyone in the room to howl.

Violette takes another shot, tossing me a slim, fried potato. "At least she's consistent," she teases, pursing her lips and cocking her head in my direction.

A groan escapes from Arabella. It would seem that she is conscious enough to raise her arm and gesture the same middle finger to her friends. One considerably crude, but normal within their relationship.

Unsure of what Violette had meant by that, I pay no mind to her comment. "If any of you share a house with Arabella, we made food and left the excess in the kitchen."

Juliette bites on her lip, excitement growing through her. "Oh that was you? Can't believe she's cooking again."

I lift my head to the group, who are all at a loss for words. "How do you mean?"

"Ara never cooks. It's rare. As rare as seeing a supposed extinct

Fae species, I guess," Violette quips. "If you're ever someone who gets to eat Ara's cooking... you're a lucky motherfucker." She watches Arabella sleep as she shuffles her body to the other side. "To going from a uni student to joining a prince."

"Oh please," Grayson laughs. "She's known she was destined for some royalty-ass life forever. That's why Luka would buy her the jewelry he did."

All their eyebrows lift at Grayson's comment.

"And yet she could kick all our asses like a warrior if she wanted to," Damien retorts.

They all raise their glasses to his statement.

*So this must be what it is to have friends.* I enjoy the company of Korine and Harrison, but never does it feel like this. Our dynamic consists of villainous torture. To demonstrate our superiority over anyone and everyone. But here, they are equals. There are no titles nor hierarchy. Simply a group of people who, in earnest, love and care for one another.

It's not as if I doubt my family cares for me, but they would never attempt to know me the way they would each other. I am the one that they would mention when using the phrase, "You cannot choose family". Ezra and my father aside, I am tolerated, never loved.

Violette, Grayson, and Juliette are on the other side of the room, dancing to the music that they play from their phones. Not a single one of them is on the beat, but not a care in the world can be found in their movements. They motion for me to join them, but I cannot leave Arabella. Beyond that, she is asleep on my lap.

"You really did something to her," Damien says, taking a seat next to me.

"Might you repeat that?"

He laughs, shooting his arms up. "Relax. I just meant that none of us have seen her this social in a long time. She was happy tonight, even if she's passed out now."

Arabella wakes from her nap, clearly beginning to sober. She combs through her hair, taking a moment to recollect her surroundings. After checking the time on her phone, she panics. It would be nearly an hour before dawn at Ifaeris. "We should probably go," she says to me.

We exchange our goodbyes as her friends proceed to berate her for not seeing them as often. When she promises she will spend more time with them after she finishes her business in Ifaeris, they look at her with suspicion.

"You better not keep her forever, princeling," Grayson says.

"I, Cassius Disaris, hereby give my word to return Arabella Huǒ to you when the time of bringing justice to the persons causing the Fae disappearance comes."

"Okay Princey," Violette mocks. "You could come around too if you want."

This is very strange. I'm not accustomed to others asking for my company, outside of a revel or something intimate. Arabella takes me down the stairs and into a bathroom filled with multiple toilets and blockings between each.

"We are in a toilet," I mention loudly over the blaring music.

She holds my arm. "Yeah. We needa okkar to Ifaeris and needed to do it someplace private."

I look at her with uncertainty. "So you chose a toilet?"

"People will just assume we're fucking. It's not that uncommon at clubs." She smiles, attempting to wink in my direction, but in her partially drunk state, both her eyes close instead.

It is as if she knows I want her again. It is selfish and cruel, but I need her. How could I learn of her mourning tonight and still be mindless enough to want her in every way she would be generous enough to allow?

We okkar to Nexus, and when we arrive on the grounds, we are laughing about the night, Arabella skipping through the grass. As we approach the front entrance, there is not a guard in sight. Something is amiss. We run inside, voices coming from the throne room. They are so loud they reverberate through the foyer.

Inside the throne room, my siblings step aside to show us what has occurred. It is my father.

King Elliot, the High King of the Fae, the descendent of the Spiritus bloodline, sits on his throne, dead.

# XVII

## *Winged Pleasure*

Arabella

King Elliot is dead. This fact alone is enough to sober me. I don't belong in this room. It's too personal. It isn't my family, but yet I'm staying. Here, next to Cassius, to the Fae family I have gotten to know. Nothing I say to comfort him would change his death.

The guards found him too late. He had been dead for over an hour when they had gotten to him. There were no signs of forced entry, no footprints, and no hidden passages into the room. It was as if a ghost had come in and out. Maybe someone had okkared in here, but the guards said there were no signs that the king had struggled.

If someone fought the king, wouldn't there have been a scream? There should have been a warning. Something to indicate he was not alone. And why were there no guards in here to protect him? Were they in on this?

I have so many questions, but none of them have an answer.

It isn't my place to say anything. All that's known is that there was no trace of magik anywhere around the grounds until Cassius and I returned.

The Disaris family is arguing. Over what to do with the body, when to plan the funeral, who will rule next. Queen Helena is having none of it. It is, after all, considered still the middle of the night, so she orders for everyone to return to bed, having the knights take Elliot's body to be preserved until she decides how to best honor him.

Everyone walks to their prospective rooms, and I follow Cassius into his. There's no hint of sadness on his face. He tends to hold one of two faces around me. It's either a glare of contempt and disgust or an arrogant grin. Both represent his hatred towards me. But still, he's lost his father. The news was sprung on him after a long day of doing the king's bidding in the Human Lands. He deserves to have someone check on him.

I sit on his bed next to him. "Are you okay?"

"My father has just been murdered, and you ask if I am okay," he hisses. When he turns to me, his face lessens in hostility. "He has never held love for me. Why should I care if he is dead?"

I say nothing. He is allowed to grieve in whatever way he feels like. It isn't my dad, and it's not my business to dictate how someone else comes to terms with death. I inch farther from him and twirl my fingers around each other, giving him the space he needs. "Regardless, if you need anything right now, you can ask."

Something has to be wrong with me. Why am I empathizing with someone who helped his father entrap me to solve their people's disappearances? He is not mine to care for, neither am I his. He is cruel, horrible, and everything I shouldn't like, and yet I find myself sometimes enjoying his company.

It's idiotic, irrational even, to feel such panic whenever he is around me. He's wanted me dead since the moment he set eyes on me and made it clear even further when he told Korine that my kind deserves to die. He doesn't want me. He may have wanted to be with me sexually, but he doesn't want to be *with me*.

"If I asked you for a small token of your favor, would you grant it?" His voice is longing. He doesn't want me out, and he isn't ignoring me. This whole time he was processing what I said. Maybe even willing to take me up on my offer. He scoots himself closer to me, the knuckle on his hand nearly brushing against mine.

It still isn't grief in his voice. He wants something completely different.

"Depends."

His two hands cup my face, pulling me into him. At that moment, I surrender everything to his touch. I let him shove me into the bed, pushing me farther up the mattress. The feeling of heat lowers below my stomach, likely soaking the panties I have on. I wrap my legs around him, my dress riding up as he grinds himself into me.

There are too many clothes. Too many pieces of fabric between us. I want him in me, raw and instantly. I push him off, taking off my jacket, dress, and underwear before unhooking my bra. I'm not about to let him wreck another dress, especially not one I just bought less than twenty-four hours ago.

This time it's me who's tearing through his clothes. With half his shirt already unbuttoned, I undo what's left, reaching my hand into his underwear to stroke his hard cock. It would appear he was anticipating this a lot longer than a few moments. He lays on his bed, and I straddle him, grinding my naked core onto his length that's still covered by the fabric of his underwear. He's moaning, completely consumed by my every move.

"I want you to sit on my face," he murmurs.

Pushing myself from his bare chest, I stare at him in disbelief. He can't be serious. "What?"

He wears a smirk. Pulling me down onto him, pressing his lips into mine, and exchanging soft kisses. "Sit. Make me your personal throne, princess."

"I- I don't want to crush you," I hesitate between each kiss.

But he sucks my neck. Cupping my breast. Squeezing it. Making it hard to say no to anything he asks of me. When his hands reach my clit, teasing me with slow, light circles, I know I'll give in.

I probably decided I would the moment he asked.

His hands lift me a bit to move himself under my body. He's sucking on my nipples, his hand working my other breast. My legs shift for any kind of friction. A line traces around my chest with his tongue at every place he kisses.

I arch my back against him, the feeling of our bodies so raw against each other. It isn't like before, this is primal. This is animalistic.

It's obsession.

He chuckles at my body's responsiveness to him. "If I were to die while you rode my face, I will have died an honorable death. Now sit. You cannot feel my mouth on your cunt if you refuse to come near it." He bites on my nipple, a cry of pleasure ripping from me.

With that, I move, crawling on my hands and knees, hovering myself above his face. I'm still not sure if this is the best idea, but there isn't any time for me to have second thoughts. In the next moment, Cassius grabs me by my hips, forcing me down.

His tongue explores the inside of my core, my clit, everywhere. He feasts on me like a starving man who hasn't eaten in days. It's euphoria and almost brings tears to my eyes.

The grip he has around me loosens, pushing me up.

*Oh shit. I did hurt him, didn't I?*

Instantaneously, I'm proven wrong. He works two fingers inside me, dragging his mouth to work on my clit. His tongue is a pen, and the poetry he's writing upon my flesh are hymns of religion. When he curls his fingers into me at a rapid pace, I feel the twist in my stomach tighten. I'm about to come on his face, and all I can do is grip the pillows below me.

His tongue strokes in waves, making me whimper above him. I come with his mouth continuing to suck on me, his fingers still pushing through me. I'm screaming. I need him to slow down, so I bend my body, lowering myself against his torso, reaching my hand towards his hardened length. He pauses his movements, pushing me away from his face.

"Impatient. Cannot be content with me taking only part of you?"

Even without seeing his face, I can feel the corner of his mouth lifting.

Smug asshole.

He takes me under him, stripping off his underwear and freeing himself fully. "Are you always this wet for me, princess?" I refuse to answer. He can't know just how right he is. "You never fail to taste so delicious," he purrs, pushing inside me.

His hands clench the sheets around us, thrusting in me at a

speed I don't think should be possible. He dips his face into mine, pressing himself against me. Muttering a string of curses as his head rests around my neck.

The whole world could fall from beneath us into nothingness and it wouldn't drag out nearly as much emotion from me as this moment is. He continues to mark me, the bruises from his previous bites still fading.

I arch my back the moment Cassius reaches a different angle inside of me. He takes it a step further, wrapping his arms under my waist, hitting so deep, it's almost painful. I grasp onto anything I can, utterly crumbling around him.

"Hold me tight," he commands.

When I do what he says, he draws his wings from his back. I've never gotten a good look at them, despite the fact he's carried me while flying. In those instances, I was asleep or unable to focus from being stabbed.

They're huge, black as his shadows, feathered like an angel who fell from the heavens.

"Wrap your legs around me, princess."

The moment I do, we're in the air. He's gripping my waist, pumping himself into me while we're high above the ground. With every flap of his wings, the momentum pushes him into me more intensely. It's terrifying that he could drop me at any second, but I still kiss him with everything I have.

"Look at you, taking my cock," he taunts.

While sucking his neck, I dig my fingers into his wings, causing him to wince. I smile. "It's only fair I return the favor, since you wanted to mark me."

His eyes blacken with pure craving. I would never be satisfied, no matter how many times he looks at me this way.

I begin meeting his movements, rocking my hips, pushing him in me as much as he will fit while the sound of the room fills with our bodies slapping together.

"I'm going to ruin you," he goads, voice guttural but weak.

I challenge him. "You can try."

He thrusts into me deeper, making me mewl in pain.

"Good girl," he moans. "*My good girl.*"

"*Fuck*," I cry. He snakes one hand between our bodies, his thumb rubbing circles around me. I'm a mess, whereas he looks at me with pure, unbridled devotion.

Bringing myself up to him, I feather kisses against his jaw, trailing my way to his lips. My arms hold his neck, hands rummaging through the curls of his hair. "Gonna come."

"Who's making you feel like this, princess?"

The skin that covers my eyes squeezes. This is too much.

"You," I whisper.

"Care to repeat yourself? I do not think I could hear you." He takes his hand from my clit, slapping my ass so hard, I'm sure it's red.

"You, Cassius!" I scream. "Gods. It's you."

Pleased with my response, he wraps me tighter in his arms. "You're mine, darling."

His thumb presses into me harder, and I come around him, my flesh gripping his cock as he begins lowering us to the bed.

"Finish in me," I blurt stupidly.

The world stops. He is stunned in place. I don't even realize for a second what I've said.

"Pardon?"

"I have a spell that works as a contraceptive. Come in me. I need to feel you. All of you."

It's no time before he finishes lowering us, resuming his thrusts into me. "You love this, don't you?" he croons into my ear. "Taking a prince's cock." He thrusts. "Begging for me to come inside your little cunt. To fill you."

He pushes into me, driving with desire. I take him into my mouth, swallowing all the words he spews from his mouth.

"You feel so good in me," I cry, throwing my head back.

The warmth of his cum fills inside me. One pump after another, he chokes out my name.

Cum starts to spill from me, the excess falling onto the inside of my thighs. Thoughts of still wanting him swirl into my mind as he lifts his body, slowly taking his cock from me, a sharp gasp at the lack of presence that was once there leaving me.

Now coming down from our highs, I stand to reach for my dress but am pulled by his arm into Cassius, on my side. He wraps his arm around me, pressing his still-naked body into my back, cradling me.

It is suffocating. Worse when he presses a gentle kiss onto my back, his sharp cheekbones cutting into my skin. I have to get out of here.

"What have I said about grabbing me?" I reprimand.

At once, he removes his arm from around me, pushing himself to sit up against his headboard. "Tell me," he snaps. When I stare at him, his face is grim. "Tell me all the hateful words your venomous tongue has been holding back. How you cannot bear the thought of me. But be honest when you speak on how you hold nothing but contempt for me."

"It's sex. If you feel something after two sessions of it, that's your own problem."

This is self-destruction in its purest form, and I can't stop myself. I want to stop, I do, but I can't. I just keep going, and I know I'm going to hurt him.

"Very well," he says. "You are free to leave if you wish. Just remember that if I was not so preoccupied with taking care of you in your drunkard state, perhaps my father would still be alive. Perhaps I could have done something to stop it." His hands go up, dismissing me from his room. "I will see to it that you are released from your obligations at once."

He enrages me. I want to tear him from where he lies. "Correct me if I misunderstood, but are you implying that your father died 'cause we were out tonight? Getting information that *he* asked of us. When even your guards weren't able to save him?"

"That is exactly what I am stating. You were foolish enough to get yourself drunk and fall asleep, whereas I was forced into socializing with your kind. You ought to be free come tomorrow if it is decided."

If I thought there was anything between us, it's gone. He truly hates me just as much as I suspected. I take my clothes from his room, slamming the door on my way out. My throat tightens and stings, but none of that matters.

I hate him. I hate this place. I want to go home.

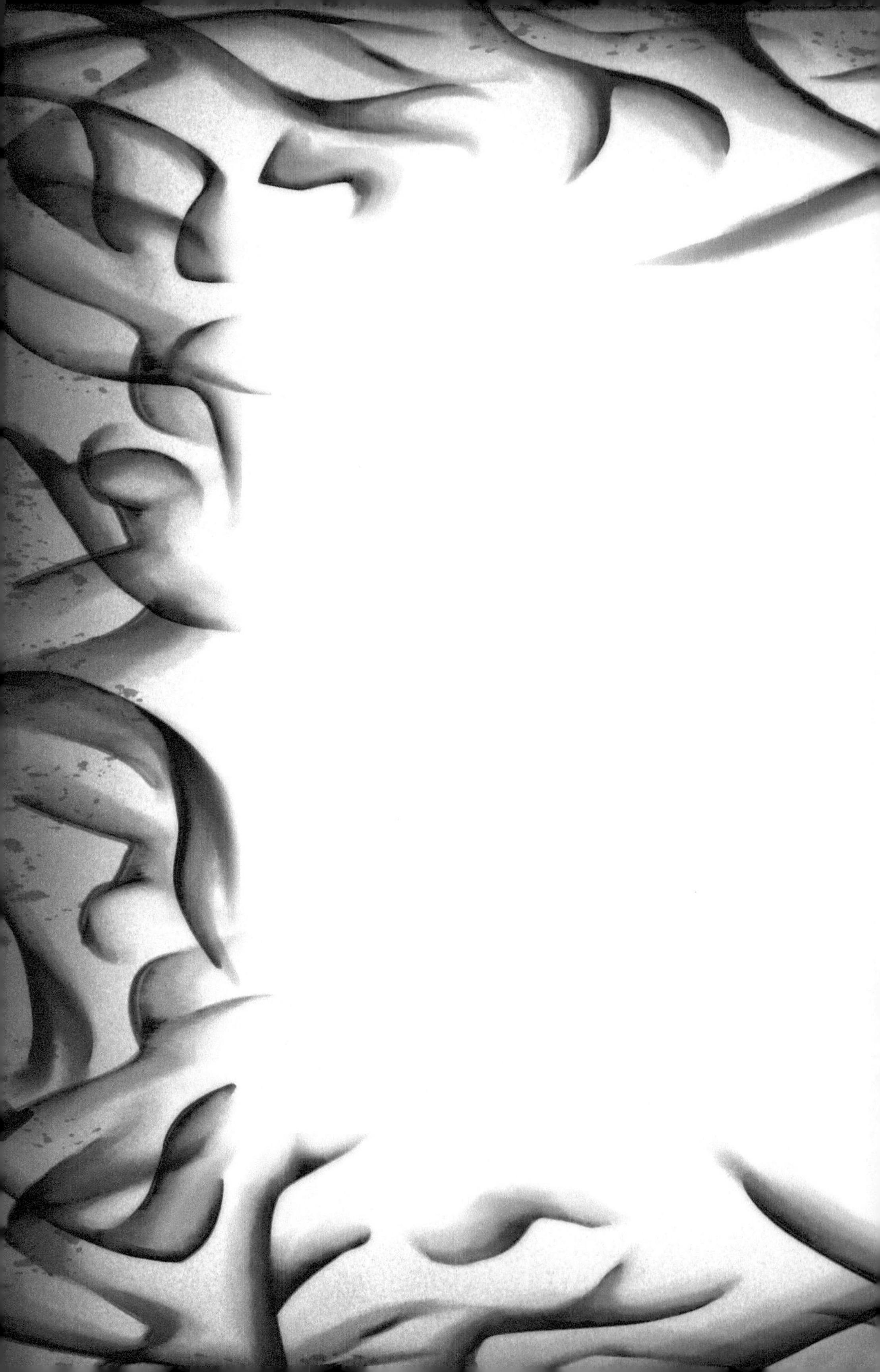

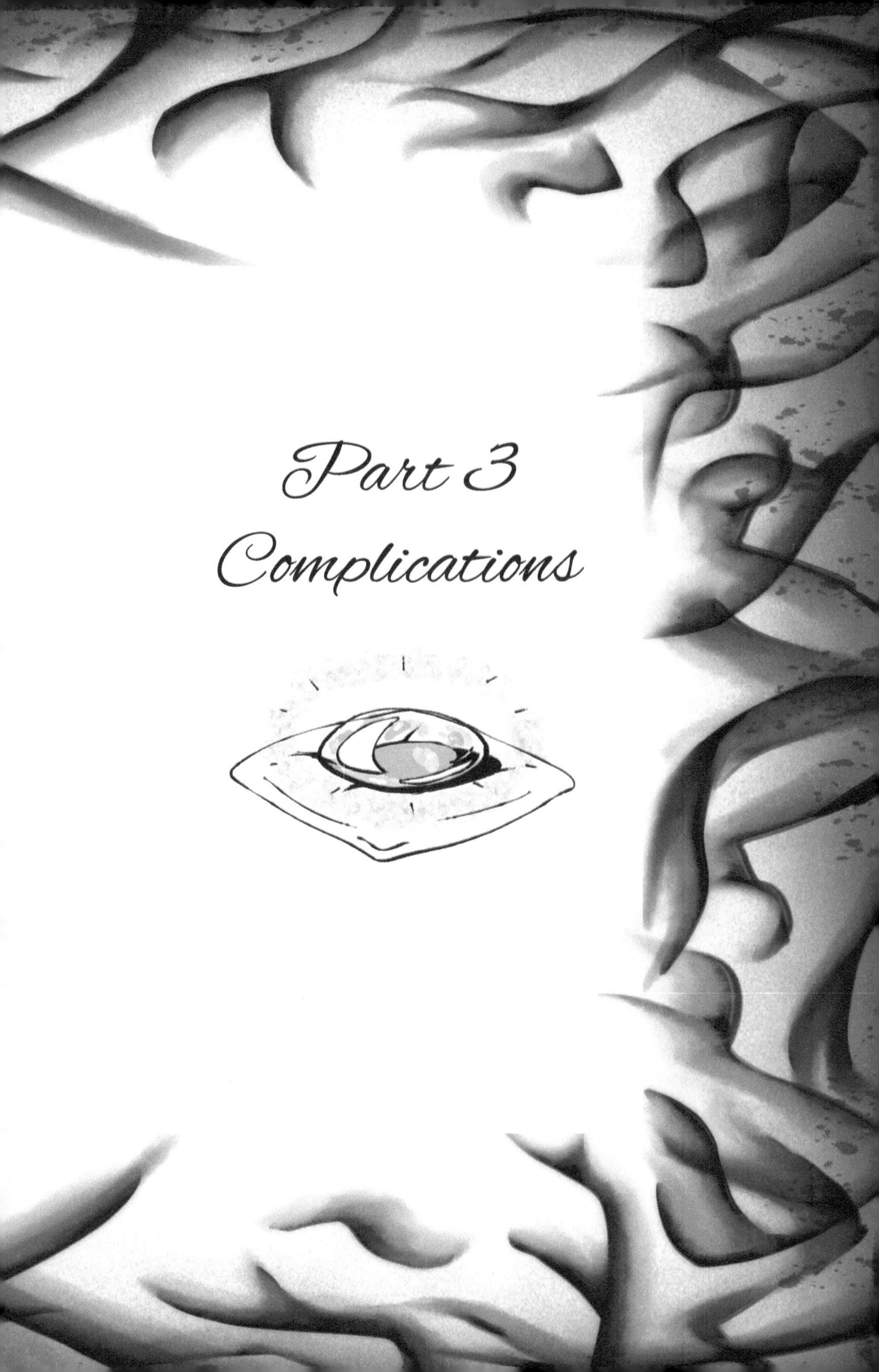

# Part 3
# Complications

# XVIII
## Royal Deliberations

Cassius

Sleep is the furthest thing from my mind. Not after my father's death, nor after what Arabella said to me. It does not matter that my father is dead, at least not entirely. He was hardly a father, and for the first seven years of my life, I did not exist to him. His death should be a relief, yet it makes me recall that now both my parents are no longer alive.

While I adore Helena as a mother and how she is likely the only one in our family who shows any true care for me, despite not being her own, my true mother loved me every bit as much as my father did, if not less. But I was her opportunity towards ladyship. What she did not account for is that my father cared very little for any of the women he would have affairs with. His death reminds me of every way he had failed as a father. And the atrocity he had made me witness as a child.

*This was odd. Father never sent for me to be retrieved from the prisons. Gavin, being the big brute that he is, had grabbed my arms, informing me of my father's requests.*

*"Will mother be coming with us?" I looked at him with wide eyes.*

*Gavin looked at me, shaking his head and putting me upon his shoulders. "She will not have to. She will be present in the throne room."*

*We trotted to the waiting room from the prisons, Gavin joking to ease my fear. I think he was aware of how hard it was being alone in the private cells, but he treated me kindly. He always brought toys and food, and sometimes, he took me into town. I think that he did this because he felt bad since mother had gotten me sent to prison for talking back to father.*

*I liked to think of him like in the stories. The ones I would take from the libraries in the times I was allowed in Nexus.*

*Patting the top of Gavin's head, he paused, looking up in my direction. "Yes, princeling?"*

*"Why did father call for me? Do you know?"*

*He just let me down from his shoulders, his eyes widening from his head when I looked at him. He seemed upset. "What are the marks on your skin?"*

*I felt around the raised, scarred skin on my lower back, and my face burned with shame. "Sometimes when I visit mother's chamber, she gets upset with me. When I disobey her, she gets out the whip and strikes me."*

*Gavin looked at me with sadness in his eyes.*

*"It's not that bad. She says I deserve it, and I am lucky that father does not see the disappointment I am since he is capable of far worse." When I saw the concern on his face grow, I added, "At least in the*

prison cells, you feed me. Mother won't allow me food when I stay with her in the servants' quarters."

Before he had a chance to say something, another guard called us into the throne room, where my brother Ezra stood next to my father, who sat on the throne. Ezra was already much older, and his voice was changing since the last time we spoke.

My father watched me enter, his eyes narrowing until I bowed. "Hello, my son."

"Hello, father," I said, barely above a whisper. It was the first time I had been allowed into the room. It was huge with gold and whites everywhere.

When my father motioned for me to join his side, I ran up the stairs, stumbling on the rug, so I could stand on the other side of his throne as Ezra did.

"Where's mother?" I asked. "Gavin said she'd be here."

Ezra watched my father before snapping at me. "Father didn't call you here for your questions."

Our father chuckled, holding his hand up to silence us both. "As you likely know, your mother has not been keen on your presence since your birth. She has become more insolent ever since." He observed me.

"Why are you telling me this?" I demanded. I wasn't dumb. I knew mother was mean.

He rose from his throne, circling the back to meet me at the side before pulling my arm, forcing me to follow him to the front before the stairs. Kneeling to meet my eyes, he took a big inhale before speaking. "While I acknowledge I have been a bit unfair in your treatment and punishing you for your mother's disobedience, it is she who will pay the ultimate price today."

I scanned his face, unsure of what he meant. "I don't get it."

*"Guards," he called, sitting back on his throne.*

*Then came my mother, chained like the other prisoners in the common dungeons at the base of the tower. Upon seeing me, she snarled, fire burned into her eyes. She was fighting to free herself, flailing her body around as the guards attempted to constrain her.*

*She focused in on the throne, her eyes darting between me and my father. "You bastard!" she shouted. "You mock me by bringing the boy into this. You really believe his being here will force an apology? For demanding a title when I bore a future heir to you? Kill him for all I care."*

*My father looked at me, then Ezra, then back to me. "Now, sons, you will see what becomes of someone who speaks against a king."*

*A cruel smile grew on his face, and he appeared like a villain.*

*"Knight," he called. My father motioned his hands, and within a split second, Gavin chopped my mother's head from her body. A loud thump echoed as her head fell to the floor, followed by her body spilling blood from the blow. I could see the bone from her spine. Her head rolled towards us, and her eyes remained open.*

*Tears filled my eyes as my father's face grew satisfied, while my brother's was in shock. I was scared and angry and not sure what had actually just occurred. My anger then somehow manifested into shadows.*

*Darkness filled the room while I felt the stare of my father. My mother was never kind or nice, but I didn't want her to die, not actually. No matter how much I wished it when she would hit me. Then, a shadow man came from my hands and jumped at Gavin, bringing him to the ground. It held him down and ripped his eyeball out. His screams of pain roared through the palace.*

*I wanted to make him pay. To make everyone answer. But I wasn't aware I could do this.*

*My father clapped his hands, and I turned to him. Then light filtered through when I saw him smiling at me.*

*"Prince Cassius, your abilities are impressive. I will have a room prepared for you in the west wing among your siblings. You are, however, to remain in Phantom Tower for a week, being that you nearly blinded my knight." He smiled at me. "My congratulations, prince."*

*On my way out, I heard Ezra ask why our father would suddenly offer up such a kindness.*

*The king said loudly enough so that all may hear, "He may be the damnation of the crown with his impulses. Best to keep him under better watch."*

I walk into a council room where Helena has asked us all to meet. My siblings are all present, bickering over who would take over for my father. Helena had already stated that she's made peace with giving up her crown if it means she can peacefully remain at Nexus, free to do her own bidding and stay with her family. She is considerably content with her life and has realized she has a distaste for ruling.

My presence is trivial here, as everyone knows I do not care to be king. It is only a matter of time before Ezra claims the title. We all know very well that father was eager to name him as the heir to the crown when the time came. None of my sisters possess the ability nor drive to lead. While I suppose they would win favor with the support of the lands, they are happy with lending aid to them while not having to be the face of terrible decisions.

This leaves Atticus. Taking into account the amount of good he has done for the common fae and his love for them, he would be a great leader. Certainly better than Ezra. With Atticus in charge, he would take the concerns seriously, but he is too invested in his family's domestic life to give it up for power.

"What say you, brother?" Ezra says, calling for my attention over the simmering voices.

Esme nudges my side, signaling to answer. When I do nothing, she speaks to me. "Cassius, while we all know you don't ever care to give your input, now is not the time to be silent. Whoever's in charge rules all of the lands."

I ponder my response. If I am to have a say, I will weigh in on my opinions, though this could easily be chosen by Helena, and myself, without responsibility.

"It may be best to eliminate who is and is not fit to rule," I respond. "Those who do not wish to rule shall move to the right to make this easier."

Everyone but Ezra has gone to the opposite side of the table, leaving him the unanimous vote to make him king. The room is uneasy. Mother too is unsure of this, judging by the way her lips pucker then immediately thin.

Helena, the only one of us to have experience, speaks up. "I would think it best to put it to a vote. While your father attempted to shelter his daughters from any insight on ruling, if any of you so chose, I, of course, will guide you."

All three of my sisters shake their heads.

Cel breaks their silence by suggesting something none expect. "I think Cassius should be king."

I snort, assuming this to be a joke. I had long given up any strong feelings to rule years ago, especially when it seemed as though Ezra would be the chosen ruler. Being king means responsibilities and work that I have no interest in doing.

"Now, why would you suggest something so foolish, sister?" Ezra laughs, disregarding their suggestion.

They glare at him. "Well if you think about it, Cassius is impartial. He'd be willing to make actual change, and considering how many already fear what he will do or say, with his reputation, it could instill fear to both enemies and those who disobey."

Maude shifts her head from one side to another. "That's true. Plus, if seeking counsel, he can depend on us. The lower courts' rulers have been easily charmed by his words before. Cassius would be the face of the king, and we can all serve as his court."

"This is unwise," Ezra retorts. "He has no training to be a king. No war leadership. No experience."

His words may be truthful, though I scoff nonetheless. "Need I remind you, brother, that I had attended many of the same meetings that you had? While I have no formal training, I am able to face the people. Or do you forget how I have spent the past months conversing with common fae? Learning the issues they have due to our disconnect to them."

Perhaps what I am saying is an exaggeration of the truth. I rarely paid attention in the meetings, but it changes nothing of what I say when my brother only knows of the political logistics and nothing of the overall common fae.

Esme smiles at this. "On top of that, he has Arabella. Should she choose to stay after bringing the person responsible for the disappearances to justice, she could aid him."

"Think of it, the feared shadow prince and the witch who put an end to the disappearances being the rulers. It would bring respect from everywhere once every creature hears of it, possibly reaching the Magiks themselves." Cel speaks this all with such sureness, I'd believe they had the utmost confidence in my abilities to lead.

All but Ezra shout in agreement. They are unaware of how Arabella is waiting in her room for her dismissal. How, now that she has an opportunity to be free, she is rushing to take it. She will be leaving us all.

"Speaking of," Atticus chimes, "where is Arabella?"

Their attention turns back to me.

My lips tighten, preparing my next words. "She is a bit peeved with me. We had an argument last night, and I told her I would see to it that she is freed today."

"Ha," Ezra shouts. "You think him worthy of being king, yet he was willing to free the witch with no power to do so. He is not a king. He is weak."

If she wishes to leave, holding power as king would likely give me the ability to do so.

Maude yells across the table, looking as if she is getting ready to push it into our brother. "He may be giving freedom when he has yet to hold power, but at least he's attempting to help her. When has he ever shown generosity otherwise?"

My sister is quick to jump to my aid, but even quicker to make jokes at my own expense.

"Tell me Maude, what purpose do you serve besides fucking a common fae?" I ask.

Her face immediately rages. In a furious calm, she fires back, "At least he knows how to make someone stay with him."

"If you believe that, sister, then you agree that he is not fit to rule," Ezra says.

Maude frowns, her head snapping to Ezra. "Do not get it twisted in your brain that I'm agreeing with you. Or that I'm on your side. You'd be a horrible leader, Ezra."

When he opens his mouth to object, Atticus speaks. "You've never viewed our sisters as equals, and just because you were handed the Leader of the Guards' title, the most you ever did was train with them. You possess no real skills and will never learn unless you start from the bottom up. Perhaps train with our army under General Callian if you want to learn discipline."

The room goes quiet. Cel is snickering. Atticus finally spoke what we had been thinking for ages, and for once, Ezra holds no retort.

"So is it decided then?" Helena asks. "Cassius will take over as the king?"

"Arabella will likely be the one making decisions, since she's the one coming up with theories and getting information from people anyway," Esme laughs.

"At least she's willing to take action and nearly die for this cause," Maude agrees.

They continue making jokes and take pleasure in deliberating her successes in comparison to my failures, laughing at the reminder I have yet to do anything productive.

"Your inability to act on your own will be your downfall." Ezra's mouth lifts, his arrogance showing. "Tell me, brother, do you grow tired of taking my scraps from the women you so desperately want?"

My jaw tightens. I bite down, resisting the urge to rip him apart in front of all our family. To take revenge for the years of cruel remarks and beatings he has thrust upon me.

"Or do you remember how I had the pleasure of lovely Arabella long before you ever could," Ezra goes on.

Locking eyes with him across the table and taking slow strides towards him, holding myself with a deadly calm. "I recall her words calling you decent, while she cried my name out like a prayer."

When we are face to face, moments from tearing each other apart, Cel barks, "Shut up, both of you! Neither of you should be speaking of Arabella like an object."

"Even with the witch, neither of you would be as great a ruler as I. The two of you will bring the Elemental rule to its ruins," Ezra says before pushing me to the ground. From his side, he pulls a whip used to train the horses, ready to unleash it onto me.

Just then, the doors open with a furious Arabella marching towards Ezra, burning the whip from his hand. "Maybe you and all the other Fae think Magiks weaker or less superior to rule, but believe me when I say you have no idea what I'm capable of. Or the things I'll do to achieve what I want."

She grabs my hand, pulling me up. The room's attention is fixated on every muscle change on Arabella. She has asserted her power in front of them and is unapologetic in every calculative move she makes.

"Long live the king," she challenges Ezra, waiting for him to defy her words. With no return, a wicked smile appears on her colored lips. "And just so you're aware, you pale in comparison to *King* Cassius. Might wanna work on that if you ever wanna truly satisfy someone."

Stunned, I am with an enormous smile. Unlike Maude's previous defense, Arabella's words do not falter with mockery.

Arabella struggles out the door, her legs slightly wobbling from the events of long hours ago. She is undoubtedly still infuriated. After the exchange that had just transpired between Ezra and myself, I know her words determined she is speaking in earnest.

# XIX

## *A Royal Bind*

Arabella

Outside Nexus sits Xavier on the steps next to a large, woven basket. Over his shoulder, he yells my name, telling me to join him.

I guess he heard me approaching.

"Come on," he says, grabbing my wrist. "You clearly need someone to talk to." His brows raise, face teasing me. "I'll even let you talk on forever about your emotions."

We walk to the fountain that parallels the garden, Xavier pulling out a blanket from the basket and sets it down for us to sit. I help him unload the food, the two of us sitting in comfortable silence for a moment while the sounds of nature whistle around us.

Xavier opens the champagne and pours it into the glasses, a lot getting on his pants.

I giggle, watching as the bubbles continue to splash onto his clothing, soaking it completely. "So what's all this about anyway?"

"What do you mean?" he asks while wiping the liquid from himself.

"This." I wave my hand towards all the setup he did.

He smiles, patting my head like a dog before handing me a glass. "The girls told me what happened in the council room." He takes an exasperated exhale before taking a sip from the glass. "I know you've endured a lot since you came here, but you shouldn't let Ezra's words upset you. He's just mad because no one wanted him as king."

Sighing, I down the champagne before fully refilling it. "I know, but it wasn't just Ezra. It was Cassius. There was too much happening that led up to it, and I'm just so tired of it all. I should be with my friends right now, but I got trapped here."

"So what happened? You're not doing yourself a favor by keeping silent."

And so I tell Xavier everything as we eat. From the first time we went into Enthar acting like a couple, to Korine trying to kill me, to the sex after meeting my friends. I tell him about how much I loved seeing them and how I felt weirdly comfortable with Cassius meeting them, which confused me all the more. Even if no one here knows it, it was the happiest I had been in months.

I explain my fear of intimacy and aversion to touch, which caused our fight the night his father died. Eventually, I finally tell him about the council room and everything I heard. I walked into that room for my freedom but ended up eavesdropping on the things they said about me ruling alongside Cassius. And after hearing how Ezra spoke about Cassius and me being weak, I snapped.

Cassius may be an asshole, but I refuse to let Ezra speak to him that way, especially not about me. I know they don't get along with each other, but knowing he would beat his brother makes me feel guilty for the times I've made ridiculing jokes towards Cassius about Ezra. He is a coward for thinking to use a horse's whip on his brother just because he didn't get what he wanted. It made me question the scars on Cassius' skin and if Ezra's the one who gave them to him.

Unfortunately, after leaving that room, the earrings were still connected to me, and I'd have to wait to speak to Cassius again to remove them.

*At least now that he's king, he has the ability to take them off and leave me alone.*

When I return home, there would be no way in hell I'd allow for any of them to find me. Sure I'd miss the friends I've made, but I wouldn't be able to handle remaining in contact with any of them. Not when they all would remind me of my trauma here.

Other than inserting jokes every now and again, Xavier listens thoughtfully, calling Cassius an ass for putting the blame of the king's death on me.

"I guess he's the king now," I laugh.

He shakes his head towards the grass. "Gods help us all."

"Do you even believe in them?" I ask while taking water from the basket.

His legs cross, brows knitting while his eyes glance at the sky. "I don't know. I don't think any in our family do, but that ignorance might stem from the notion that we as Fae are almost immortal, even more so when you're an Elemental."

"*Hmm.*"

I dig through the basket in hopes of finding some sort of blade, and to my surprise, he has scissors. Parting my hair and gathering the grown-out bangs, I begin trimming them, trying to give them back their shape.

Xavier laughs. "What are you doing?"

"I need to cut my hair. It's grown out too much, and the bangs swooping to my side are irritating me," I state, paying close attention to my actions.

He takes the scissors from my hand, beginning to trim it himself. "Here. Let me."

"So you can tattoo *and* do hair?" My brows rise, and I giggle. "What can't you do?"

While tucking the longer strands behind my ears, he holds the bangs, surprisingly cutting them the same way I like. "Get someone to date me, apparently."

I put the rest of my hair up, giving him a clearer view to shape the bangs to my front.

"He's staring," Xavier points out.

My eyes shift towards the back entrance of the palace to find Cassius watching us intensely.

"Let him. He has no reason to be angry with me after what he said," I say in a biting tone. "Now pay attention." I shove his shoulder. "I don't need you fucking up my hair."

"Okay, okay." He leans himself closer to my face, the cold of the scissors brushing my skin. "You know, this isn't really fair what you're doing."

I rub my eyes, trying to remove the piece of hair that fell in, making them twitch. "What do you mean?"

"Have you really not noticed?"

He takes the scissors away from my face and I stare, cocking my head and blinking a few times, waiting for him to go on. Xavier rolls his eyes, smiling as he shakes his head. I wonder if he is irritated with me.

"You and your inability to take a hint," Xavier teases. As I flip him off, he does it back, laughing at our twinned reactions. "He isn't a big supporter of how close you and I are."

I tilt my head a bit in Cassius' direction and see him trying to burn his gaze into my bones.

*What right does he have to be pissed at me after blaming me for his father's death?* After all the terrible things he said to me prior to that? I let out a huff and turn back to Xavier. "If he's that upset, I think I'll enjoy my time with you even longer."

While wiping up the last strands of hair from my face, he smiles. "And I'll be happy to be at your disposal," he insinuates while pumping his brows twice.

"You're insufferable, you know that?"

"Says the Magik whose personality is just a mirrored image of myself."

My face scrunches, involuntarily reacting. "Gross. Don't talk like him. You and I both know you have the capability to talk like you're from this century."

"True," he surrenders. "He cares about you, you know."

I lay on the blanket, covering my eyes with my arm. "That's nice in theory, but if he's not willing to put in any effort, then I have no incentive to do the same."

He throws his head back, grunting in frustration. "You're both so stubborn. This goes both ways."

"Okay, but he said it himself. It would be easier for him if Magiks died. I'm still pretty sure he hates me."

"No he doesn't," Xavier cuts off. "He doesn't hate you. You

think he would pay such close attention to you if he did? How he notices the clothing you prefer and has the tailors create shirts that closely match your favor. Or how he takes note when fabric makes you uncomfortable before requesting new clothing be sent to your room? When he personally picked the dress with materials he knew would make everyone stare at you like you were descending from the heavens for the ball?"

I had no idea he did all that. I assumed the tailors just caught wind of the clothes I commonly wore.

"I think I looked more like I rose from hell," I joke to avoid dealing with what was just said. If I think too much into it, I would only imagine something that isn't there.

Throwing his head back, he groans in exasperation. He pushes me forward, closer to the doors, as I stand. "Talk to him."

"Cassius," I call out, looping up the stairs to his place.

His face remains still, completely unreadable to me. "Have you grown bored of my cousin's romantic affection and seek another's attention, or have you come for another reason?"

My lips part in uncertainty. *How are you jealous of Xavier and me, but so hard-headed when I try talking?*

When I don't speak, he tramples over my thoughts. "Just so you are aware, I have chosen to honor my father's command. You will not have the tracker removed, nor are you exonerated from your trespassing until we find whoever is the cause of the missing Fae. You are still bound to the grounds."

"But you said–"

"As the appointed High King of Ifaeris, I hold the power of your freedom and my word is final. As prince, I sought your release, but as king, I deny it forthwith. Though I do hope you find better ways to entertain yourself outside isolating to the point that you are left with no one."

There are no words in the world that could explain the amount of rage I feel. I slap him, turning and storming up to my room. On my way up, I yell, "You're just a good-for-nothing bastard whose only purpose consists of being a burden onto everyone's lives."

I hear Esme stomping to him. "What the *fuck* is wrong with you?"

The peaceful sound of the winds blowing through the tree accompanied by the sounds of the water and tiny water Sprites flying around make for good ambiance as I read. Of course, I would rather be in bed, but a building with Cassius is the last place I'd want to be right now.

The calming noises are cut short by Esme joining me, grabbing my book to view it for herself. I hate that everyone knows the lake is my source of comfort away from them all, but I can't find it in me to care.

"Ah, information on my family, I see." She giggles, keeping the book out of my reach. I would stand to grab it, but that would expose me too much. "Did you borrow this from the library? I must assume you've done some *very* specific research on us if *this* still holds your interest so far in."

"Listen. I can explain."

When she looks at me, silently waiting for an explanation, I let my head fall in defeat.

"I can't explain," I say, laughing.

"I'm sorry about Cassius and what he said." She looks at me

with sincerity in her eyes, apologizing for something that she isn't the cause of.

I meet her stare, sharing a light smile. "You know, you were my first friend here. I never thanked you for visiting me in the cells those days. Or how you vouching for me is probably what saved me from being killed by your dad."

"Don't mention it!" she says while patting my thigh.

She's so beautiful. I knew from the moment I saw her that I could have a crush on her, but our friendship only solidified that.

We gaze into each other's eyes before mine falls to her lips, reaching behind her neck to pull her in. She opens her mouth, allowing me to deepen our kiss before she retreats and sits up straight, while her breathy moans imprint into my brain.

Immediately, I get off her, sitting back at her side. I can't bear to look at her from being so embarrassed. Instead, I stare at the lake, my body frozen.

"I'm so sorry," I blurt in panic. "I shouldn't have assumed."

Esme takes a moment to collect herself, and I let her while an immediate pit falls heavy in my stomach. My pulse is pounding in my throat with the scolding thoughts I overstepped in some way or that she didn't want me to kiss her.

"No," she finally says. "It's not you, don't worry. I figured that at some point, something was going to happen between us. I find you attractive, you made it clear just now that you found me attractive, but we know it would not work."

"What do you mean? Cassius and I aren't together."

She slowly lets out, "Yes, but I think we are both using each other to avoid our true feelings. I harbor feelings for my friend in the Human Lands. She's the one I always sneak off to."

As disappointed as I am by her reveal, I respect it. She's likely right. We both mixed platonic for romantic, and we know deep down neither of us truly want to date the other.

"He didn't mean what he said before. I know what he feels for you. I see it in how he treats you. I don't want to be the person who hurts him more. Not after everything we did. We neglected him while idly watching how our father and brother treated him through the years. Saying nothing and taunting him due to assuming he was terrible in nature."

I have no words. Nothing to respond to this. He's still selfish and hard to communicate with, but so am I. The knowledge keeps me stunned in my silence.

"But I think you changed that. Or at least brought out the side of him that wasn't completely villainous." She smiles at me, reassuring that I don't have to respond. "You know, our father was always a brutal man, but he seemed to take it out on Cassius most of all. The whole tracking down the missing Fae task was punishment for him in order to return to his good graces."

My brows knit, and my mouth opens to speak. "How can someone return to good graces when it seems like he never had it in the first place?"

Laughing at my comment, Esme turns towards the water. "Our father is the definition of what mortals call a snake. Or I guess, *was*. He would play kind to everyone, but he was horrible, especially to Cassius. His mother demanded too much of the king, and after she was killed, he took out the rage he had remaining from her on him. He always viewed Cassius as too dangerous, so I think breaking him down was better than a possible defiance. Ezra just followed suit."

"His mother was killed?" I ask, aghast as my face stills.

She nods her head a few times. "The day after his birthday, when he was eight."

I look at the soil. That's a terrible way to grow up. Losing your mom so young the day after your birthday and having your father and brother abuse you for years.

"Which is almost ironic, since our father was killed on his birthday this year," she chimes at the coincidence.

My eyes grow wide, moving from side to side. "Wait. His birthday? As in a few days ago?"

"Yeah. Some people would assume he was cursed, but I doubt it. Just heavy coincidence."

He spent his birthday with me. In the heat, searching for evidence. And he took care of me while I was drunk, spending time with *my* friends, only to come home to his father having been murdered.

If I'm being forced to stay here, I'm going to find answers by myself. I'm still pissed at Cassius for what he said to me, for what he blamed me for, and for how he treated me when I spent time with Xavier.

I asked Kabir to take me into Hearthis, since I can't ride a horse on my own yet. The ride is bumpy, bricks creating many of the buildings that contrast to Mindae's flatter greenery and wooden structures. I laugh as he recalls our days when I was his annoying prisoner. Our friendship may still be a guard and guarded one, but it is nice to have him around.

"So you finally pulled your hair back so we can see your face? To whom do we owe that pleasure?" I jeer.

He blushes as he redoes his hair into a half bun, letting the rest flow down to his neck, his uniform different than usual. It's only been a day since I saw him last, but he looks completely different to me. The guard uniform he wears for purposes outside of the palace holds more armor for protection. He now resembles more of a general, though he has said there is a difference between the knights, army men, and our guards.

"Oh my gods," I gasp in shock. "You have a crush on someone, don't you?"

"No."

"Oh, you so do," I utter to myself, watching him walk far from me. Even if it isn't a crush, it's something like it.

We leave the horse at a stable before striding into town to gather information. There's nothing more than whispers and gossip about the king's death. How he died, if it was a conspiracy, how he probably had it coming. It isn't surprising to me to hear of their hatred towards him, especially after knowing the treatment he had towards his own children.

As we sit down to eat, we listen in on the talk of those around us. At the table next to us sits a couple, cheering at the king's death but also concerned about who will take over.

"I just worry that with the king now gone, one of his wretched other sons will take over," the Fae man with purple hair says.

His partner grabs his hand, kissing his knuckles. "Who knows, perhaps one of the daughters will take over. They've treated us far kinder than the princes, save Prince Atticus."

The violet-haired Fae takes bites from his soup. "Maybe you're right, Lance," he agrees with the bald man. "At least Prince Atticus bothered enough to meet with the common fae regarding our issues."

"He and the princesses are also the only ones who bothered to listen and attempt fighting for us. And when they couldn't, they'd bring in materials and money to supply us."

"For all the Zips we supply to the crown, you would think it would protect us from the disappearances," Lance mutters. "Delcan, losing you is one of the worst fears I could imagine. Good riddance to the king, and may our next ruler give a damn about us."

Delcan clinks his glass against Lance's. "Hopefully the next one will build more schooling for healers and find better ways to house and feed those of us who cannot provide enough for ourselves."

"Personally, I believe he had it coming. Maybe the Fae haven't gone missing but instead banded together to start another colony, free of the monster," Lance suggests.

His partner shakes his head, releasing his hand from Lance's. "Oh please. Most had no money. Besides, how would you explain the deaths?"

I study their conversations, taking note of how much the crown has disappointed them. No matter how many of them had come to King Elliot, things never changed. All were let down and were forced to barely scrape by when they needed aid. They weren't protected when they needed it most from the crown. In every way, the crown served more as a punishment to them than leadership. If the High King and Queen could not protect those who governed others, what hope could the common fae have for themselves?

"Is that Prince Cassius' lover?" Delcan asks his partner.

I'm really hoping he isn't referring to me, but per usual, my instincts are right when I see both turn to me.

Lance's face shrinks in disgust at the sight of me. "If she weren't accompanied by the royal guard, I'd think not, but their appearances suggest otherwise. Let us leave."

Trots from their hooved feet sound around the area. I'm laughing so hard my sides cramp.

"Why is this so humorous to you?" Kabir asks.

"I think that your uniform gave us away." I shake my head, lifting my shoulders. "Real discrete," I remark sarcastically, putting my index finger to my thumb and lifting my three remaining fingers.

His face remains still as usual. "Was I meant to wear common clothes? What if we were attacked?"

Eyes shifting from one corner to the other at his comment, I take a sip from my tea. "You don't even have army men patrolling Ifaeris' borders. I'm sure we would've been fine. Besides, it's called dressing casually, and you told me half the reason people wouldn't speak to Cassius and me was 'cause they didn't trust the crown. Your uniform represents it in its entirety."

He frowns, his eyes narrowing at me. "They would've assumed something was wrong regardless. I can smell the witch on you."

My mouth drops while holding a smile, letting out a breathy laugh. "Oh so you're saying I smell now? Watch your words before I remind you of your uneven haircut, Curly."

"Shut your mouth, Creature. Or maybe I'll throw you back in the chains."

I grin at him. "Try it and see where it lands us both. In a bed perhaps." I wink at him.

Freezing, he is at a loss for words. I thought that by now he was used to the way I joke and banter, but he finds me just as crude as the day I annoyed him into talking to me.

"Haven't heard you this quiet since you refused to talk to me in the dungeons," I tease. He still says nothing, hiding his face from mine. "Anyway, we should get back to the palace before it gets late."

He regains his head, rejoining the conversation. "We have yet to gather any information."

"That's not true. We learned that the king was so useless to his people that even the common fae would believe others to disappear and start another colony."

"How is that useful?" Kabir questions.

I leave Gold Zips on the table with extra tip. *It won't hurt Cassius if we spend more money on his people.* "Easy. It gives a reason as to why people would rebel and kidnap other Fae. It rules out Magiks and adds to the theory the Stone of Elestial was used to lure people into a cause against the crown. And that gives motive to kill the king. It's why they said his reign was coming to an end. If we focus on the common fae who needed help from the crown and were turned away, we'll likely find the Fae who the rebels target for disappearances."

Once we reach Nexus, I write all the findings down onto paper, as well as my theories on how to proceed with the information. I slip it under Cassius' door on the third floor, where he has now taken over the king's chamber. Maybe it's petty of me to do so in order to avoid speaking to him, but I know if I do, it'll result in us screaming at each other again. Being alone means I can get information without any royal assumptions getting in the way. And once word gets out he's the king now, coronated or not, fewer people would be willing to speak to him.

# XX

## A Broken Fae

Cassius

Asking for information proves much more difficult without Arabella at my side. The common fae are reveling in my father's death, which I cannot fault them for. He was a horrible ruler to his people. He refused to send aid when they needed it, brushed past the disappearances until it was a possibility of harming him, and overall hoarded the riches of the lands for his own gain. All things I now have the responsibility to fix.

While I could very easily rely on a court, I have no one I trust enough to appoint. My siblings hold their own opinions, but if Ezra had any say in counseling, it would be just as risky as if he did hold the power of king. There is Arabella, who does care about the needs of the common fae, but she will soon be gone.

Though the people of the lands will heed my orders, they certainly do not like me. Enjoy my riches and indulge in my held revels, yes, but to assume they like me is unreasonable. I can hear their whispers as I pass and feel the anger in their glances and bows when I speak with them. Things would be much simpler with Arabella. She holds a better rapport than I when we are around them. Knows how to use their thought processes against them.

That aside, she is still hurt by what I said to her, and in honest, I am still angry with myself for saying such things. She refuses to meet with me. Instead, for days she has come home nightly, slipping her findings under my door without so much a knock. If we simply traveled together, there would be no need for her written reports.

The sky shifting to twilight as I return to Nexus, I spot two Fae at the edge of the Darkened Forest, sneaking between the openings. The wiser decision would be to call for a guard to join me, but there is no time, so I follow behind them, not to be seen.

I recognize one of these men. He is called Cato. He met with my father months prior to the disappearances, asking for food to be sent to Aquatius last winter after the tiff between him and Lord Theodore. My father, being the petty man he was, thought it fair to punish all of Aquatius after their lord had called him selfish. It was a fair insult, being that the king cut protection on the land when Merfolk near the area had gone hungry and decided to feast upon the hearts of Fae.

Cato is speaking to another man, one that I have seen before as well. He is the villain who threw a plate in mine and Arabella's direction. The man who she threatened to have publicly executed. He looks changed, decrepit even. His back now hunches, and all the muscle is beginning to lose its tone from his body.

*What are they doing here?*

"I'm not sure if I am ready to commit to another meeting," the tall Fae whispers.

Cato frowns. "If you wish to serve another one of the corrupt Disaris family members, go ahead, but the meeting begins soon, so act quickly."

The broken Fae's eyes fall to the dirt, the under of his eyes weighed down by sorrow, whether from following the orders of Cato or the loss of sanity.

"You have the opportunity to see your family again. What keeps you from taking it?" Cato holds a hand to the man's shoulder in obvious hopes of persuading him.

The man nods with hesitation. "I serve the one true ruler of Ifaeris."

The corner of Cato's mouth twitches. "Good. Now do you remember the schedule when we hold our meetings?"

He shakes his head. Both men are off guard. I have the opportunity to take one for information. However, being that I am one Fae against two, with my little abilities in combat, I am at a disadvantage.

I hide behind a tree, slowly attempting to get closer and hear their murmured conversation.

"Now the meeting times may vary from week to week, though we tend to hold them at night post supper. Will you take the honor of attending tonight?"

Cato pulls a tiny stone from his pockets, barely larger than a pinky's nail. It reflects with rainbow iridescence through the white shine of the rock itself. With how the man becomes lost in a trance from it, I can only assume this is the object that Jefferson mentioned.

As the man reaches his hand towards the stone, I crouch through different hidden areas to view it. I begin to send out my shadow to grab hold of one of the men, guaranteeing there is one way to retrieve answers.

*Snap.*

I had been paying so little attention to my surroundings, I stepped on a branch. With the silence of nothing else in the forest, Cato twists his head in my direction, cursing when he sees another figure. There lies no use in continuing to hide myself. Rising, I step from my place.

"Well, well," Cato remarks with sarcasm. "If it isn't Prince Cassius."

The other Fae remains still. He is at a loss for words, petrified in his spot.

Cato *tsks* at the cowardice from the other man. "To what pleasure do we owe the presence of the shadow prince?"

"Actually," I smirk, "it's your shadow *king* now. Befitting, is it not?" I laugh. "And I *suggest* you tell me about your meeting times."

Shadows engulf our surroundings, creating a border and entrapping us. They slowly close in, to which Cato responds with a sarcastic laugh. "Not going to happen, princeling."

With that, they disappear, okkaring to their meeting, the location of which I'm clueless.

No matter how much disdain Arabella feels for me, the information I have come across requires her attention. We work better when we are together, and it is high time we move past our petty squabbles.

I knock on her door to find that she is still sound asleep, based on the snores I hear at the opening of her door. Her room is neat, other than the unfolded clothes pile in a basket and her cosmetics that spread in a disorganized manner on the vanity in her bathroom.

"Arabella," I whisper, her body moving slightly, moaning at the sound of her name.

Repeating her name, I put my hand on her arm, gently moving it. She wakes with a start, a short breath taken in as her eyes shoot open and her body thrashes in all directions. Her leg that was raised close to her chest kicks my groin area, and I fall to the ground with a yelp.

"Shit, sorry," she shrieks, ripping the covers off her and kneeling to my side.

She tries amending for her reaction in any way she can, while I have a hard time breathing. The pain stretches for eternity. I recoil inward as she places her hand over where she kicked.

Suddenly, the pain subsides, and I am able to feel the other parts of my body. "What did you do?" I ask, sitting up on her bed.

"You know, magik isn't just for torture," she points out, handing me a glass filled with water from her nightstand.

I drink it all, taking time to rekindle my breathing pattern. When I see that she has moved next to me, I notice she is in nothing but her sleeping brassiere and thinly lined underwear. My heartbeat pounds viciously, speeding at a pace that would warrant death.

A death by any other would be torture, but by her, it ought to be considered a rebirth.

Arabella takes the glass from me, setting it back down and studying my face. "What? Disappointed it was water instead of vodka or something?"

"No, I just... Never mind."

Her eyes keep themselves on me for a few moments before her eyebrows lift and she walks towards the door and shuts it.

"Okay. Did you need something, or were you here to point out how lonely I am again?" she says with wrath in her tone.

Biting my lip for my loss of dignity, I keep my words to myself. "No. I came to discuss what I've discovered in the Darkened Forest and how it pertained to your findings."

While I sit close to her pillows, she takes a seat towards the foot of her bed, crossing her arms. "Go on."

"Do you recall the man you threatened to execute for calling you my whore?"

She slightly nods to her side, a smile rising to her face.

"Well, he and another man I had seen several months ago had met in the forest, speaking of meetings and who they serve as their king."

Her arms fall to her sides, putting her weight onto them. "Okay, so they have meetings. I thought we figured as much. Was the meeting with others in the forest or were they heading to one? And why didn't you call for someone to go in with you? Why would you go alone? You could've been killed."

"The same man you threatened is weakened. Cato had promised the Fae meeting his family once more and took out the stone Jefferson spoke of." I lean, resting my head on the hand atop my leg that sits on the bed.

She crosses her legs together, now fully facing my direction. "So what happened? Did you get either of them?"

"They okkared somewhere before I had the chance."

"Oh."

Arabella rises from her bed, towards the wardrobe at the near corner of the room that sits in line at the foot of her bed. She pulls out a large, vibrant, canary-colored paper bag with parchment stuffed inside and hands it to me.

I take it, staring at her, nonplussed. "What is this?"

"Just open it," she orders with a smile.

When I begin removing the paper, I peek at the coat that I once put on, alongside different cosmetics.

"I heard it was your birthday, and I remembered how much you liked my jacket, and I mean you wear makeup too, so I wanted to give this to you," she jabbers, rolling through her words. She walks to the desk that sits past the foot of her bed and opens a small box full of jewelry.

Hesitating back towards me, she puts something in my hand. It is my ring that I had delivered to her the night of the ball. "I thought that maybe I should return this, since it's yours," she says awkwardly.

"Keep it." I hand back the ring, slipping it onto the finger she has consistently worn it on. "It is yours."

Her cheeks stain with rose, and her eyes flutter. "I can't keep this."

"Either you keep it, or it will be tossed into the waste," I promise while shrugging. "Follow me. I have one thing more for you."

# XXI
## *Half Apologies*

Arabella

Cassius takes me into a vaulted room under Nexus after I change. The palace is already huge above the ground, so I'm not sure why I'm surprised they keep an armory under it. If anything, it's smart to do that.

The room is full of different types of weapons, ranging from medieval morning stars, to axes, and dagger fans too. I marvel at each of them. The walls are covered in sharp swords that hang on display and flails that are mounted securely.

In comparison to the rest of the palace, this vault remains untouched from the newly renovated areas. The floors still remain stone, and there is easy access to grab the weapons if needed.

I grab a crossbow from a table, closing one eye and aiming. The sound of the bolt shooting to the wall plunges through the air, frightening me enough to drop the weapon onto my foot.

"You really should not touch that," Cassius warns, picking up the crossbow from below me.

Bending to rub my foot from the impact, I tense my body in hopes it will lessen the pain. "Thanks for telling me now," I bark with sarcasm.

On cue, his cocky smile appears. It's less annoying to me than it should be. "I fail to see how it is my fault you do not know how to wield the weapon."

"Why did you bring me into a vaulted armory, knowing I'm still mad at you?" I touch the sides of a sword, feeling the cold touch and smoothness from the metal, careful not to cut myself.

He strides to a table, grabbing something with a chain. "There was something in here I thought you ought to have. This armory is usually only opened during wars, but as king, I made an exception."

The chained weapon from his hand wraps around my neck, a hollow, outlined moon on one end, a shuriken on the other. Cassius inserts the star through the opening of the moon, turning it into a necklace.

"You and I have been at odds for far too long when there is no longer a reason to. What I said was unfair. You are far from being alone and are more exquisite than any bottle of wine." He releases the hold from the chain but continues locking his eyes in mine.

I part my eyes from his, taking in a breath when I realize I've stopped breathing. It isn't an apology, but it's likely the best I'll ever get from him.

"I better be." Smiling, I look back at him. "After all, you did spend six hundred of your father's Zips on me."

He lets out a snort, shooting his brows up in agreement. "The necklace doubles as a weapon. Unlatch the star from the moon, and you can send the blade to hook into your target. You can also use it as a lasso to aim and tie the target down, slicing them in the process."

"Why are you trusting it to me? Considering I just shot an arrow into stone."

"If there is anyone who could turn a small weapon into a statement, princess, it would be you."

My heart skips a beat, all while my body shivers. There's just something about the way his words make my soul flutter.

"Weapons wouldn't need to make a statement if hidden correctly," I say, fighting a smile.

He brushes the hair away from my face, using his hand to tilt my head up. Then he's lowering himself, kissing lines along my neck. "Are you still upset with me?" he breathes into my neck.

"Yes," I breathe.

He chuckles, knowing the lie in my one word, moves his face to watch me before pulling me into a kiss. I allow this, missing his taste, his presence. He holds me, cradling me in his arms as I deepen the kiss, not pulling away for air.

But it's him who detaches himself from me. "I don't think I believe you," he purrs roughly. "Will you accompany me to Aquatius?"

# XXII

## *Return of the Dragon*

Cassius

I okkar us outside the gates of the House of Chauvet in Aquatius before we go into the town. Unlike the other areas in Ifaeris, Aquatius cannot be traveled to by land, and we do not have time to travel by ship. Okkaring or flying are the fastest methods, though both are grueling.

"You okay?" Arabella asks.

"Give me a moment." I take a rest, holding my hand against a wall while eating the baked pastry she hands me. It has been far too long since I have okkared myself to such a land I could hardly visualize, let alone with another.

The land of Aquatius is much different than that of Mindae, or the other lands for that matter. They are secluded from the rest of us, and father rarely bothered taking us here. There is hardly an area where bodies of water don't run through. Greens and waterfalls surround the areas of the ruler's manor, the winds causing the leaves of trees to fall into the water. It smells of fresh water and florals, but not so strong that it overpowers the senses.

Arabella leans against the wall, her eyes darting in every direction while taking in the scenery. "This place is beautiful."

"I should have assumed you'd admire this land the most. You already spend much of your time along Lake Mindae."

She holds from arguing, instead, smiling to herself, walking in the direction of the town. This is the one area we have yet to explore. Neither of us has ventured to this side of the lands, which means we lack information from the Fae that reside within. Common fae peer in our direction, some bowing, some fawning over our presence.

"You know," Arabella speaks, linking her arms with mine, "a lot of the common fae have valid concerns."

My eyebrows furrow, pausing my steps. "In regard to?"

"Just that they make points about how the crown failed them when they needed it most. I'm not saying I agree with their methods and kidnapping others to prove a point, I just think that with all the riches you have, it could go back into its people." She looks at me, shrugging. "Redistribute the wealth and maybe listen to them, Your Majesty."

I hold out a smile as we resume walking. "You seem to care an awful lot about the future of the Fae, considering you carry no desire to remain here."

"Yeah well, I'm not heartless." She tilts her head. "Your father treated his people so poorly and took out his petty feuds on them. He caused an uprising that literally resulted in his death. I'd say if you value your own life, you should start taking their concerns seriously."

I sigh with a heavy exhale. "Unfortunately, when I am officially crowned king, it will result in carrying on the abomination of a legacy my father had left."

We resume roaming through the town, taking stops at a few sellers when Arabella gets distracted and wanders off. Today is honoring the birth of deceased Lord Theodore's daughter, Theodosia. She turns eighteen on this day, and after the recent passing of her father, her mother made it a priority that today would bring nothing but joy.

When we enter a shop that creates jeweled pieces and other accessories, Arabella walks off, following a worker, then returning from the back room with a purchased bag. Once we step outside into the open area, she takes a crown that had been wrapped inside and hands it to me.

Taking the piece, I hold it in my hands, examining the details. "What is this?"

"Your last birthday gift," she says, beaming while placing the crown on my head. "I had it commissioned from the store owner days ago after sending a letter, making sure it would look like the tiara you had sent for me the night of the ball."

*So she is aware it was I who had done that.*

I take the crown with patterns that rise up similarly to elk horns and crosses of fire from my head, placing it back in the bag. "I appreciate the gift you likely spent with my Zips, but I refuse to wear it when it represents such evils."

"Why do you feel the need to carry the weight of your father's doing? We aren't the sins of our parents." Her lips are nearly closed, mouth partially parted and her front teeth appearing through the small opening, unsure to continue. "You aren't a terrible person just because they were. It's not your fault how he raised you."

Long moments pass before either of us says anything. Her voice lowers to a murmur. "You're not a monster."

The sound of the common fae bustling through in excitement for the parade overpowers the moment shared. Arabella laughs and takes my arm, pulling me in her direction.

"What do you suppose we do to extract information today?" she asks into my ear, loud enough so I can hear above the commotion.

I lead us into an alley, ensuring no one can hear us. "We are aware that the Stone of Elestial is the cause behind putting the Fae in a trance, and we know the one possessing it is someone with a personal vendetta against the crown for refusing to send supplies to Aquatius. Considering the man who had hurled insults at us is the one he was targeting, I'd say it produces a commonality."

"So anyone who met with the crown and was turned away is a potential suspect." Her face goes blank, thinking of how to proceed further. "Let's walk around, and if you recall someone from the throne room, we start there."

The witch always thinks everything in detail. Going through every scenario in her head for the best outcome while playing it off as if she is only making simple guesses. Whether she is aware of it or not, every move she makes for our cause has reasoning.

After moving through the stoned marketplace, I have come up with nothing. There is not a soul that I recognize. None will speak with us. Not with the news I am king now reaching them. When Arabella and I separate, I find myself missing the cool of her touch, envying the eyes of those who gawk at her with desire as she speaks with them. Eyes I would sooner rip out than allow to strip her from where she stands. Something all too easy to read while they drop their gaze down the bustier of her top.

When Arabella returns to me, she mentions a man by the name of Eden who once met with the king. She says that he can be found running his restaurant, Wallflower, at the edge of a waterfall that hangs above a cliff on the seaside.

We travel to the establishment, one that is surrounded by multiple shops and areas for regal gowns. The walk is not dreadfully far, though it would be faster if I just fly us there. Arabella is persistent that we walk, so I scoop her into my arms and arrive us there in short minutes, rather than what would have been half of an hour.

I land us in a nearby crevice between two shops across from the restaurant. The area is busy with Fae crowding around every surface, making it difficult to dispatch us with no eyes to witness. Around Wallflower is a line stretching far, indicating its popularity among the people of Aquatius. Those that stand have been watching us since far before our landing.

"I have an idea," she says as I set her down. One hand grips my arm, rebalancing herself, while the other is tightened into a fist, her face appearing as if she is about to hurl bile.

My eyebrows go up in anticipation. "Very well, let's hear it."

Her face hardens for a moment, unable to tell if I am being true or not. When my face lifts, signaling for her to proceed, her lips tighten before she goes on. "I'm sure you've noticed, just like me, that people tend to share more information with me in public, rather than you. Probably more so with you being the king now, so I think if I ask Eden alone about his activities, he'd be more likely to tell me, rather than the pair of us."

I debate her ploy, curious how she will approach him. "And how shall you get him to speak if he refuses to flat-out tell you what he knows?"

"*Hmm.*" She pauses. "I guess I'll just assess the situation, and if he's interested, flirt with him."

This is not the scenario which I was hoping or prepared for.

She snarls at me. "*Ugh*, are you gonna try stopping me from getting the information I want from him?"

"By all means, don't let me deter you from taking what you want." I pause. "For you will never stop me from taking mine," I coo before pressing my lips against her ear. "In fact, if I recall correctly, you were all but begging for me hours ago."

Her throat clears, shaking herself and straightening her posture, stepping a few paces away from me. "I think that's him. The one with silver hair."

She points to a man through the glass, who wears a mint tunic and royal blue trousers. He is moving around his restaurant, checking on the guests, greeting them, and sipping through a brass cup.

"How can you be sure?"

"You really doubt me?" Her eyebrows rise, immediately ignoring the look I shoot her. "The girl from the town said that he had gone to the king months ago about his daughter, who disappeared."

When we get a better view of his face, she blinks as her jaw drops. "Gods it's hard to tell how old Fae are. He has a grown daughter, but the man looks like he's thirty-five at most."

The man exits through the left side of the building, holding a bag of waste and dumping it into a compartment. He takes a glass that is nearby and tosses it in with the rest of the waste before peering around and wiping his hands on his bottoms.

"Well go on, Dragon," I whisper. "You had proposed speaking to him yourself. Now is the time."

She turns to me slowly with a contorted face, sticking her tongue out. "*Blegh*. Are you gonna keep calling me that? I thought we were done with that nickname."

"I think I quite like the way the name makes you discomforted," I say, smirking.

"You know I could still stab you," she challenges, reaching for her dagger.

Putting my hand over hers, I lean closer, holding her stare. "You seem to enjoy threatening me with your knives. If I did not know better, I would assume you'd use it on me for other forms."

"And if I didn't know any better, I bet you'd enjoy it."

Arabella takes off and does not look back, but if she had, she would have seen that in that moment, I would have fallen to my knees before her. My breathing has stopped while my heartbeat is erratic. She is unlike anything I have ever come across, and I hate how powerless I am around her.

Eden spots her before she can get to him, whereas I watch them from a shrub. He is all too eager to speak to Arabella, his eyes bewitched by her presence. There is no way for me to overhear their conversation in its entirety, though his body conveys he will break for her.

I stalk as closely as I can so as not to be seen by both Arabella and Eden. A bookshop sits adjacent to where they stand, clearing a view to the restaurant's side and making the two visible from the corner of my eye. He smiles at her, brushing her hand with his thumb, taking her hand into his.

She giggles. She actually giggles at whatever it is he has to say and makes no attempt to stop him from pressing his lips against her cheek. Even from the distance, I see her eyes study his body up and down. She has a habit of moving her tongue along the crowns of her teeth, sticking to the bottom of her top tooth while she flashes a cocky smile. It is something I have caught her doing when she flirted with others previously.

Fury builds inside of me, though I have no reasoning to feel such a way. She spoke of her plan to seduce the man if it came down to it. Knowing this information and witnessing it though are two separate things.

It is when he grabs her wrist that I find myself acting. When he puts his hands around her waist, she removes him, attempting to free herself from his grasp. I see the alarm on her face when his hand twists her wrist so hard, it holds her in place, turning her hand white.

I grab him by the shoulder, causing his head to turn towards me. "I have found that it is not wise to advance continuously on those who reject you. Especially when your unwelcome touch is on your king's new High Reeve."

Arabella's eyes fire with ambition, unsheathing her dagger from its place. I had unintentionally just appointed her with a high-ranking position.

She kicks the man from behind his knee, throwing his balance off and shoving him into the wall as she holds the blade to his throat. "Now, what were you telling me about taking me to your little meeting?"

Eden attempts to shake himself from the enclosed space. "I don't have to tell you anything. You think I wasn't aware of who you are, witch?" He lets out a howl as she presses into him further. "Everyone knows of your existence. The king's lackey. The one he sent because he couldn't be bothered to save his own people."

Her fists clench and he grows weaker, dropping to the ground. I send a shadow to hold him, stepping on the back of his calves. He screams in agony, others beginning to take notice of our presence.

As tears drop down his face, he cracks. "Okay, fine, I'll tell you what you want to know. I'll tell you of the meetings and everything. Just give me your word you'll spare me."

I turn to Arabella, suspicious of how quickly he is willing to give up what he knows. She watches him, shifting her weight from her right to left as he rises to his feet, shaking from her magik.

"You were supposed to have died," he mutters, glaring at her.

She huffs, letting out a breath before grinning. "Yeah, well maybe you should try harder next time. Though I guess you held true to your word about the king's reign coming to an end. Now what do you know about the missing Fae? You seemed so ready to part with the information at the slightest chance to lay in my bed."

"I would have rather rid you while in it so the true king could take power easier."

Dragging her fingers down the skin of his arms, her eyes spark. "You can fake a lot of things, but you can't undo the fact you were begging to run your hands along my body in exchange for your knowledge on your 'true king'. And you definitely can't fake the stiff of your dick that was pressed into my stomach as you said it."

"Tell us all you know and I will consider the possibility of sparing you from life in chains, living among the harshest of guards," I vow.

His eyes shoot between the two of us. "They hold meetings to discuss the crown."

"And my father's death?"

He lets out a low chuckle before pushing between us and sprinting towards the street of other common fae. Before I have the chance to react, Arabella chases after him. I follow her through the crowd as I attempt to run behind, losing her and my breath at the same time.

When I reach her, the man has fallen to the ground, his legs held together by the weapon I recently gifted her.

# XXIII

## *Desecrating the Throne*

Arabella

Eden is fast, but he lacks endurance. I chase him through crowds of people, profusely apologizing to those who I push and stammering through "excuse me" at least a dozen times. I sprint down the street, the heels from my shoes likely causing blisters, but that's an issue for a later time.

I zip through an alleyway and finally spot him on the other side. There's practically no one around, so I take the weapon from my neck, unhook the shuriken from the moon, and hold the base. I spin the necklace above my head three times, launching it underhandedly right under his kneecaps.

The chain spins around him, blade latching itself deep into the skin of his calf and knocking him to the ground. I run, keeping my foot on his back while the weapon stops him from okkaring to a different location. As I unclench my fists, I take in deep breaths, controlling my speedy heart rate.

Minutes later, I hear the sounds of heavy panting behind me. I turn my body and see it's Cassius, bending to his knees and using them as support for rest. I watch him, not uttering a word while he slides himself into a sitting position against the wall.

In between heaves, he speaks. "How did you get to him so fast?"

"You're about to vomit. You can't really tell me that you're this tired?"

Based on his glare, I can tell he is. I am too, but not so much that I'd be this dramatic. I shake my head, letting out a light laugh between my own breaths. "We ran like maybe three blocks."

He rises, walking to my side. "I had to run farther to find you."

The man's still grunting in pain, attempting to pry the weapon from his flesh. When he touches the edge, he cries, bellowing curses as the drops of his dark blood leak down his calf.

I observe him in puzzlement. "The blade isn't even that deep. How can you weaken from something so small."

"The iron," Cassius says. "I have told you that pure iron is lethal to Fae. It is why it burns him upon contact and why he cannot remove the weapon without incredible pain."

He turns to both openings of the alleyway, tapping for me to pay attention. "We should take the Fae from the view of the public eye. I do not suspect an audience would encourage our cause."

Reaching into my bag, I pull out the suppression cuffs I prepared in case we found someone to take back. Convenient that I remembered to pack this but forgot water. I bring the man to his feet while Cassius leans on the wall, watching me.

"If iron is so debilitating to the Fae, why were you able to put the necklace on me without gloves?"

"Had I said it hadn't pained me to touch it?" Cassius holds the chain by Eden's legs, ripping the weapon from his skin and handing it back to me without touching the iron from the star. "Come then, let us leave the presence of any onlookers."

"Masochist," I mutter under my breath.

The Fae king's mouth twitches before we share the energy of okkaring us back to Nexus.

Upon our arrival, Kabir is waiting for us. He stands at the door of the throne room, his face stoic, per usual. While he has always been attractive, his newfound style makes him all the more enticing. The bronze of his skin truly complements the length of his curly hair.

"Hey, Kabir!" I exclaim. "How's my favorite guard?"

A smile creeps onto his face and his face lights. "Significantly better, now that I see the both of you safe." He looks at the man between us in shackles, bringing himself closer and eyeing the Fae before returning to his professional self. "And who is this?"

"Another who we will be questioning," Cassius states, pushing Eden towards Kabir. "This fine specimen was another who had partaken in the attempted murder of Arabella."

Kabir's eyes burn, giving a glowering nod before taking the man out to Phantom Tower.

I wash the makeup from my face and shower before changing into a set of pajamas and meeting Cassius in the throne room. Closing the door behind me as I ascend up the stairs, I take a seat next to him on a step.

"Do other Fae have powers like the Elementals?" I ask. The question bothered me since I got out of the shower. "I know you said they live longer and can okkar, but I'd have to assume that they have more power beyond okkaring, beauty, and a longer lifespan."

He moves to his throne, crossing one leg onto his knee and leaning the weight of both his head and arm on it. "All Fae outside of the Elemental bloodline have two abilities outside of their longevity of life. One, as you know, is okkaring. The other is the ability to manipulate the minds of mortals, forcing them to obey our command or believe reality to be different than it is. It's how we can alter appearances, both our own and others. Fae have similar magik, though ours are called glamour."

A memory pops into my head. The bouncer from Infinite. "Then why weren't you able to manipulate the bouncer outside the club? Or command Jefferson to give us information."

"I knew upon your failure to convince the guard, attempting to glamour him myself would render useless. My abilities, while powerful, are not as strong outside of Ifaeris, though that can be discussed at length when it is not the late hours of night. With Jefferson, only humans are able to be controlled by the Fae, similar to how you can persuade well with your magik, but cannot take full control over another. Your kind can be fooled by our glamoured appearances, but not manipulated to do our bidding." He pauses for a second, arrogantly curling a smile to himself. "And was I not just as convincing with my words?"

There's no point in asking why he didn't try with the bouncer, not when we can't change the past. I let my leg stretch to the step below, bringing my left knee to my chest as I tilt my head slightly to view him from the side.

"That man today," I pause, "thanks for intervening, but I could've handled myself."

He rolls his eyes, smirking at me. "Is that why you hadn't noticed he was planning his escape since the moment you showed him mercy?"

His constant need to belittle me is irritating. It's like he finds pleasure when I'm worked up. He rises from his place, taking a glass of wine from the corner and drinking it. "Perhaps if you had realized sooner that he was in no mood to give up the information he knew, you would not have shown him such kindness."

"Am I supposed to read his mind?" I ask casually, not giving in to what he wants. I hate the way he scrutinizes me. How he always thinks of me as a toy for his pleasure.

Cassius lurks towards me and curves his hands around the widths of my cheeks. "Oh Ari darling, you would have stopped him much sooner."

That name. That fucking name. No one has ever called me that other than Luka. With that, every buildup, every moment between Cassius and myself leading up to now, crumbles like the foundation of a mountain during a landslide. It's bad enough that he reminds me of my dead boyfriend with their similar features, but the way we interact, the way he gets under my skin, I can feel my whole world splitting and burning with fire.

It's too late. I can feel the indignant words forming before I can stop myself. There's no way for me to bite my tongue and keep from saying something I know will ultimately hurt him.

"That's rich. Coming from the Fae who never lifted a finger in his life," I spit, standing from where I'm sitting and marching up the remaining steps to face him. The words keep coming. One wrong move and he could easily throw me down the steps. "For months, I've done all the hard work. The theories. The plans. I even got fucking stabbed, but all you've done was throw petty fits, insulting me at every chance you get and scowling at all the common fae."

He snaps as violently as I do. The sharpness of his bone structure, contoured by the shadow from the chandeliers above, cuts into him from his tensed jaw. The same way it does when we bicker. "Because you refuse the help of others when anyone attempts to do so. I am the king and you will respect me as such." His voice is firm with authority. He finally sounds like the king who holds the power that he has.

I step closer to him, refusing to back down. "If you had forgotten, you're still not *my* king. And I'm only here 'cause you'd track me down if I left." I can faintly feel his breath from how close we are. "Why don't you tell me why you *really* kept me here. Or why you still keep Korine around. And how you still love her enough to keep her at your side." My voice is shouting, shaking through my last statement.

Any dignity I have left just drained from my body. A plethora of things I could have said, and I still feel a tinge of hatred for the Fae who once tried to harm me for her own joy. It isn't from jealousy, but even as that argument occurs in my mind, I know I'm only trying to fool myself.

"I do not love her," he says absently.

It's all he says, and for a moment, as everything stills, neither of us moves from our place. I look up at him, his eyes as black as obsidian and as hot as the lava that's used to form the rock.

I scoff at the comment. "Yeah? Then tell me, what *do* you love?"

He offers no answer. Just another question to twist it back

to me. "Why do you expect me to offer up all my thoughts while you provide me so much as an angry snarl at the question of your interests?"

"You still have a power imbalance over me as the person in charge of my location. I don't owe you an explanation," I bark. "And besides, you know things about me."

Cassius moves past me towards the left window, walking away. "I know nothing of your past, save your dead lover."

My eyes shoot up to him. How could he possibly know about Luka? I've never once mentioned him. The only time his name's been brought up was at Infinite before I left for drinks. I can feel my skin chilling, my heart rate slowing down to nothing.

"Come now, have you no words to speak?"

He steps closer to me, running a hand through my hair as I tense, still wondering how he came across this knowledge. "It was your friends who had informed me." His voice is sharp and sardonic. "Your friends who had spoken of your relationship after knowing me for mere minutes. One that you have yet to ever mention to me."

I can't be upset, can't even blame him for his curiosity. I'm just as interested in his life as he is mine, and I literally just berated him about Korine. If I heard a stranger's name, I'd also probably ask about who they were. Despite this logical reasoning, I remain heated in rage. It wasn't their place to tell before I was ready.

Nothing about Cassius' words makes any sense. At least not the purpose behind them. He deflects all I ask, but it's nothing short of what I would have done, which is what makes it all the more irritating.

I push him away. "You're the most confusing person I have ever met. I never know what you want from me. You want my whole life's story, but I'm sorry to tell you that it's just one trauma after another, and if you really want to hear it, we'd be stuck in this throne room for weeks."

Then, I start laughing.

"For once in our time together, stop making a facetious jest of everything and tell me what bothers you." His voice is angry. Raw and broken. He is just as worn as I am. "I want you to tell me everything about you. Tell me why you have yet to speak about your family, but will offer me stories about your friends."

There's a brooding silence. With every breath between us, the room fills with more tension. I want to lie, and lie, and lie. To continue convincing myself that I feel nothing for him and all that's between us is sexual desire. But I can't. I sit on the edge of the queen's throne, pushing my fingers on the skin of my lids to my temples.

Against everything in my brain trying to tell me not to, I break through the quiet. "I think they love my brother more than me. They'll deny it of course, but it's evident to anyone with eyes who my parents favor." I take a hesitant breath, terrified of the vulnerable state admitting this puts me in. "They say they wanted me to be independent, but the second I so much as stepped away from the direction they envisioned for me, it's like I wasn't even their daughter. Like I'm some outcast they were cursed to deal with."

He glances down to the floor with a tilt of his head in astonishment that I have revealed this part of myself, or perhaps understanding that he is able to relate to it.

"Arabella..." he trails off, "I had not meant to–"

"You say I never ask for help, that I'm too stubborn for my own good. It's because my mom made me so hyper-dependent on her that I couldn't trust anyone else to care about me. With her, growing up, the way I looked, my shape, everything about me, she acted like it would be undesirable to anyone. My dad wasn't much help either when he'd shame me for anything I wore. So I stopped caring about what anyone thought about my appearance. I shouldn't have to apologize for simply being alive."

My throat burns. Like each vocal chord is being cut with razor blades. "My parents though, they hated what I wore. They acted like I was asking for it, and when it happened-" I'm trembling, swallowing the lump in my throat and fighting off the urge to cry. "*When he happened*, I couldn't tell them."

A tear falls from my right eye. I calm myself, taking a breath and counting my pattern along my thigh to ground myself into reality. I shouldn't be crying.

"I couldn't tell them and prove that they were right. So I started looking to fuck everything. To show that I was desirable. To feel good about myself. 'Cause maybe I could feel wanted. Maybe it would wash away the disgusting pain that *he* didn't want me even after what he did. I don't care how others perceive me 'cause that's their own issue to reflect on, but I refuse to ever feel that way again."

I stop speaking. It's something I never expected to admit out loud to another person again. Even my last statement is somewhat of a coated lie. Realistically, what others think of me has shaped me into who I am.

His eyes observe me, not with disgust, but with pity. And I don't know which I'd rather him view me with. He stands there, unable to say anything. Maybe he's afraid that what he could say might set me off again. I'm too angry, too tired to fight right now.

"Arabella, I should not have forced this out of you."

My lips thin, and my eyes fall to the ground. "It's almost pathetic, isn't it? To crave love so badly after the abuse someone put you through?" I don't dare to look at him after my confession. Not when it means confessing this is true for more than just my family.

The Fae puts his hand under my chin, lifting my head to meet his gaze. I blink, registering how he towers over me while I sit. Taking my hand, he raises his arm, me standing so that we're in front of each other. "It's not pathetic. You cannot help the way you react in such a mental state. And your family—"

"Don't. I still love them."

Facing each other, he traces his fingers along my cheeks, across the bottom of my lip, down my neck. "If I knew who he..." He takes a moment. "If he so much as looked in your direction, I would make him suffer," he says lowly, kissing my neck.

"Painfully." His lips reach my jaw.

His breath is hot on my neck. Lips brushing by my ear, voice dropping low, primal, and predatory. "Until he was begging for mercy."

He nips my ear, and I realize too quickly how much I want him right now, regardless of who could walk in. His hands wrap around my waist as I pull him down from his neck, locking our lips together and gasping between each kiss.

"Just say the word and we will stop," he breathes.

We have unfinished business from this morning, and I would rather curse myself than end this.

"Please."

His mouth curves into a grin. "Use your words, princess. My hot-headed dragon."

That horrid nickname. It's disgusting, but his continuous chuckle after he uses it makes me hate it less each time it's used.

I use his cocky attitude to my advantage, knocking him into the king's throne and gripping the crest rail while pushing his legs to the front as I cage him. I straighten my back, let my breasts fall in perfect lining with his eyes, visible through the deep cut of the shirt. He glances at them then back at me, helpless.

Smirking, I bend down and take his lips for my own, grinding on him and taking power over him.

It's exhilarating.

He reaches along my back, running his fingers up and down my skin, tugging along the shirt's hem to signal to remove the fabric. Our mouths slide together, only parting when I remove my top, ripping through his as payback for my dress. We still have our pants on, and I can't help but find amusement when he bucks his hips under me, whimpering at the constraint that the fabric holds against his cock.

Now, it's he who begs. Moans fill the room with every circle of my hips. No banter or snide remarks are exchanged. Something about this is softer than any time we've ever been together.

While kissing along his neck, I bite down. He brings his fingers into my shorts, moving my panties aside as he circles around my clit. "This is what you wanted, was it not?" he hums into my ear as he brings his other hand to my breast, pinching my nipple and forcing my head to throw back in reaction. "For my reverence. Veneration."

I grind onto his fingers, swiveling my hips against his thumb to pick up the rhythm. He leans up, lips close to my breast. "Well now that you have it, what will you do, witchling?"

As the High King, he has power. Under me, the power is mine.

And I have no intention of forswearing it.

This is far too good for me to pass up. Stopping all my motions, the look of fear strikes into Cassius. "Have I done something to–"

I kneel before him, pulling his pants and underwear to his feet. He kicks the clothing to the side, and I take the tip of his cock into my mouth, circling my tongue around his head before bobbing my head down the length as far as I could.

His head rolls back. All I can see are the whites of his eyes. With force, he grabs the back of my head, thrusting into my mouth.

It's almost funny he thinks he can take back power so easily from me. I bat his hand away, and at once he releases me. I slowly hollow my cheeks, sucking on the length twitching inside and releasing it with a pop.

"You try that again and you're not coming. Understand?" I look into his eyes with sternness. Being so utterly weakened, he nods furiously.

I take off anything that covers my bottom half, climbing on top of him, my knees on both sides of his. His legs spread, putting me into the splits as I hold myself up on the remaining cushion, the velvet grazing the cheeks of my ass. His cock is hard against his stomach, his eyes begging me to do something.

And do something I shall. I bring my thumb to the tip, brushing the slit as he whimpers out. My hands wrap around him, making eye contact as I pump his cock.

He puts his hands over mine, stopping me from finishing him, and in a swift movement, kisses me deeply.

Lifting my body, I push myself higher. I bring a hand between our bodies, lining us up and slowly sinking onto him until the two of us inhale a satisfied breath.

I bounce. Roll my hips and drag him deeper. He reaches to my clit, moving in slow circles that match my hip movements.

"That's right, princess," he croons as I moan. "Defile the place you were once sentenced to death."

With that, I remove his hand from its place, rocking faster. His lips part, mouth quivering, barely able to form a sentence outside his pleas.

But instead of my own body being the only to move, his arm wraps around my waist, steadying me as he attempts to thrust himself in tandem.

I can only smile, gripping his shoulders while the sound of our skin slapping hits the walls. "Now, my king," I slow, fully pressed against his body, "do you think you deserve to come?"

"Yes," he strangles out.

"You haven't been very good for me."

The top of his lip quivers. "Please, Arabella."

My eyes narrow. I press my lips against his, dragging my nails along his torso. "How long I've waited to hear you beg."

He sucks on my nipples, mirroring his tongue with circles as I did to his cock. He's trying everything he can to waver my decision to allow him to come.

If only his kingdom could see him now. Their High King at the mercy of the witch he once hated. It delights me to drown myself in this thought.

"Princess, I–"

I clamp my hand over his mouth. "*Shh*. Take it, my dear Cassius. I don't want to hear another sound from your mouth unless you are screaming."

He gulps as I ride him faster, speeding up my hips while his hands fall to his side.

"That's it," I whisper against his ear. "You're enjoying this, aren't you?" I kiss him, biting his lip hard enough to draw blood. "Me having full control over you."

The king screams, guttural as I feel him gripping me and squeezing the apex of my thighs, forming a bruise. All while he pumps in and out, his cum releasing inside me.

Sounds of our moans are probably heard outside the room. We aren't exactly trying to be quiet.

Curses and cries leave his mouth. It drops open as he shuts his eyes from the sensitivity of me riding him past his orgasm. I bring my hand to my core, parting my legs more as I reach to my clit and rub in fast circles.

I fall apart, my body clenching around his as I moan in pleasure.

He presses his lips gingerly against mine, the softest he's ever kissed me. I sit there in his arms for a fleeting moment with his cock still inside me, tarrying my leave.

After a long enough time, I get up from my place, putting on my clothing one by one. His hand grazes my arm, a silent plea. I bend to the side of his throne, resting my forehead against his for a moment, closing my eyes and letting out a small breath before removing myself from his hold. I don't want to hurt him with everything I refuse to deal with.

"You don't understand what it's like to lose your first love. To have them ripped from you after years of thinking you weren't enough. How I see a glimpse of him whenever you and I speak to each other." I descend down the stairs, putting on my shirt and walking towards the door. "I'm really trying, but please understand, it's not fair to do this if I could hurt you with the thought of him."

# XXIV
## *Slices of the Truth*

Cassius

The guards have set an extra room within the heavily guarded top floors of Phantom Tower with a table and chairs. While escorting us to meet with Eden, Kabir spares no detail on the conditions our prisoner has been met with the past three days.

Prior to today, Arabella and I reached the decision to allow Eden to rot in his cell for a bit, accustoming him to his future, should he choose not to continuously step out of line. With what Kabir exposed, the man has reached such a low, he refuses the few bathing privileges that are given and hardly eats at mealtimes.

The three of us walk towards where we will be interrogating, Kabir leading, Arabella and I standing side by side.

"I will be right outside," Kabir assures. "Should you need anything, have Arabella knock on the door."

With his gloved hand, Kabir opens the iron door, allowing us into the small area. Aside from the table in the middle, there sits three chairs. One on one side, two on its opposite. Eden's head rests on the table, his hands and feet chained together. He is beaten down, lifeless, his breathing sparse.

The clinging of his chains clashes together as he lifts his head, a faint grin appearing on his face towards me.

"Your Majesty," he mutters slyly while holding his hand out to gesture.

Arabella takes a seat, putting her arms on the table and smiling back at the man. She is dressed in a corseted, long-sleeved shirt that comes off the shoulder, her bottom wearing a handkerchief skirt that falls around the top of her tattoo, cutting at different sections. Such clothing differs greatly to our end goal of today.

"Hello, Eden. How quickly you've forgotten about me."

He scowls at her. "I haven't forgotten about you, witch."

"Ah." She lets out a small chuckle. "So acknowledging people's presence only extends to royalty, I assume?"

I sit next to her, crossing a leg over my knee and leaning my body towards the table. "I have heard stories about you, Eden."

"Have you?" His head quirks. It has become apparent that he loves hearing about himself. "What tales have you heard? Are they as horrible as those I have heard about you?" He scoots his chair back, leaning on the backrest. "You have heard them, have you not, witch? How the king once watched as his own flesh and blood was murdered in front of him, doing nothing."

She slams her hand on the table, the lace on her sleeve caught on the wood. "Enough with your tricks. You're stalling for time. If it's pain you want to cause... Cassius?"

With the look in her eyes, I am aware of what she is signaling. I spread my palms, summoning the shadowed figure to leave me as Arabella pulls her dagger from her thigh, handing it to my personal double.

"Now," I say softly as the figure grabs Eden's left arm, tracing the tip of the weapon along his wrists, "will you decide to answer us, or will we have to extract information with my own methods?"

The Fae refuses to splinter, holding the same smugness he has carried since the day we met him.

"Perhaps there is reward in what it is you can tell us," I offer.

He remains silent. I toss my hand and my shadow digs the knife into Eden's skin, slicing it horizontally, deep enough to see blood vessels.

Tears roll down his eyes as his screams pierce the room. Sounds of chains rattle as his feet kick into the underside of the table.

"You're just as heartless as your father," he spits, saliva and sweat flying.

Arabella puts her hand up, telling me to stop my shadow.

At once, I do as she says.

She walks around the table, standing behind the Fae and gripping both sides of the chair. "We know you have information about the missing Fae." Her fingers dig into his shoulder. "But first, tell me how it felt knowing you attempted to kill someone you know had done you no wrong?"

When he says nothing, she shrugs, nodding to me with her head angled. On her command, I allow the shadow to cut into him once more.

"I find that murder hasn't quite helped your cause." I laugh. "For you see, King Elliot was killed, yes, but as it stands, I am king, and the person you follow is not."

For a slight second, I see from the corner of my eyes, Arabella's mouth forms a slight smile. She is amazed by my tone.

"Tell us about who's in control," Arabella demands while gripping his arm across the chair, causing more blood to flow. "If there's someone poisoning the Fae, or if there's a team–"

He scoffs at her words, cutting her off. His silver hair drips sweat into his wounds, a few strands reaching the openings itself.

My shadow cuts into him, this time cutting vertically. Blood pours from his arm, unstopping. No matter how much pressure Eden attempts to hold it with, it proves futile while he begins to bleed out.

"I know not of any woman," he shouts. "Heal me, and I'll tell you what I know."

The witch knocks on the door, and a healer is sent in. She mends his wounds, closing the entry points and stitching his skin back together, leaving multiple scars. Pleasure floods my senses as he winces when Arabella holds his arm, aiding in recirculating the blood in his body.

At the healer's leave, we take our seats, Eden watching us with dismay through each process.

"Do we have to repeat the ordeal of ripping through your skin, or will you tell us what you know this time?" Arabella says with a threatening voice.

He rolls his eyes. "Yes, yes. I have already tried playing you twice now. Both of which resulting in consequences that nearly ended me. I would be foolish to attempt it a third."

"Have you decided that *now*?" I laugh. "I would have thought it foolish to attempt it the first time against such a powerful witch."

His tongue clicks, shifting his eyes between Arabella and myself while he licks his lips, rubbing them together. "I have never heard of the woman you guess at. But I have heard of a man."

"Go on," I allow.

"I've been alive for over two centuries. And in my life, your father was the worst thing to happen to the Fae in Ifaeris," he bites.

Arabella crosses her arms, rolling her eyes at the statement and setting her feet on the table, crossing them. "Yeah, yeah. We know he was a terrible king. You're not the only ones who had an issue with him."

It is but truth. My father had been long hated before I or my siblings had been born.

I add to her statement. "It was well known that he was not a good man, nor was he a kind father, but it does not explain why abducting neighboring common fae would bring any justice to him."

"You believe we had just been taking them from their homes?" he laughs. "We held meetings. Constant ones. We were given orders, and those, such as I, who had proven our loyalty were regarded with higher trust. From that trust, we were then able to occasionally meet with our leader."

"And he gave you the orders on who to target?" Arabella questions.

Eden's posture fills with pride. Boastful that he was given the responsibility after years of being denied a position in the royal guards. His hatred must have only fueled greater when my father had disregarded Eden's daughter. "We were given the tasks of seeking out those who were loyal to the crown and those who were willing to rebel."

Recalling Cato and the man from Windwyrd, I figure that was

his purpose in the forest. "Am I to assume that Cato Locksynd is also tasked with such a position?"

He smiles. An indication that I am indeed correct.

There is no reason to believe what he is saying is not honest. Not when it is impossible for Fae to lie. However, while we cannot lie, there is the possibility of twisting our words, bending them in such a way it can keep from relaying the truth.

He has not given enough information that would invoke suspicion, other than his smile to my previous question.

"What of the many missing Fae who had been found dead?" I ask.

His eyebrows rise. It is likely he is unaware of just how many Fae have been murdered and simply assumes himself to hold more importance than he truly does.

The bottom of his foot drags across the ground, his face only directed at his legs. "Their deaths were not harmful."

"Liar!" Arabella accuses, voice roared.

"I cannot lie, witch," he grits through his teeth. "Or have you still not learned anything of our kind?"

She bites her lip, surrendering to his words, recalling what I once told her. "So you *think* it was harmless. Doesn't mean it wasn't planned."

"Then what use is it to ask me these questions if you will focus on minutiae?" he remarks, his voice harsh.

I have grown bored of his responses. His existence matters very little to me, and all this talk brings us no closer to discovering who is their leader. Nothing he has said exposes who their 'true king' is nor what he wishes to do with ruling. At the rate we have been going, it bodes more useful to find another Fae who is associated with whatever they have planned, though I realize each Fae has also answered in riddles. Refusing to speak at worst, ambiguous at best.

"If you are done exaggerating your position and disrespecting my reeve, I would advise you to hurry along with what you know. Your execution is still up for debate, as you assaulted the High King."

Now he grows nervous, eyes bulging. He trembles from the lack of nutrients he has consumed in the prior days, but when I turn to Arabella, I realize he is shaking from her twirling her knife between each finger. The one I have not seen since I had a dagger and garter to be sent up to her room. Her knife too, I have had bladed with iron.

"I did not assault the king," his voice cracks.

Arabella laughs maliciously. "You say that, yet your entire rebellion feeds around revenge against the crown. If not physically, your participation is just as guilty."

"Everything I have done was for the good of the people," he claims.

"No, everything you have done is treacherous against the people you claim to fight for," I remind him.

My reeve strides to him, holding the weapon to his throat as she stands behind him. "You have yet to give us important information. Do so, and I'll consider sparing you."

Eden hesitates, unsure of whether to believe her or not.

"I make a High King's vow that should you provide us with useful information, I will not send for you to be killed." It is my word, an unbreakable promise that I may be giving too lightly.

Satisfied well enough with my answer, he speaks. "As I said, I know not of a woman in charge. But the man, I have only seen his face but once." He gulps. "He never revealed his name, just that he claimed to be the rightful king of Ifaeris and would lead us into a better age."

"His claim is of little importance," I say.

He licks his lips, smiling at what he has to say next. "It may be." His head looks up at me. "For my king looked exactly as your father had at such a youthful age."

My body goes rigid, my blood stilling. Everything races through my mind instantly. Questions of what this could mean and who it would be charge through. He reveals something of such importance to spare himself, yet all I can think of is exactly who this may be.

"There we go." Arabella pats his cheek. "See what happens when you listen and do what you're asked?"

She then rushes to my side, grabbing my hand and dragging us out. Knocking on the door, Kabir opens it, allowing for our leave. I cannot see it, but I can hear as guards take Eden from where he sits, forcing him back to his actual holding place.

As we walk through the exit, into the grass and towards the back of Nexus, Arabella breaks the silence. "Why don't you ever fight others yourself?" She pauses, attempting to rescind her words. "I mean, why is it you always send your shadow to handle carrying out your physical threats?"

"I am not well acquainted with a sword. Neither have I ever been talented with it."

She laughs at my statement, stopping her steps in disbelief. "The High King is terrible with weapons? Are you serious?"

"As grave as my father's death." I walk past her, my head turning in her direction. "Now come. We have a sibling of mine we must speak with."

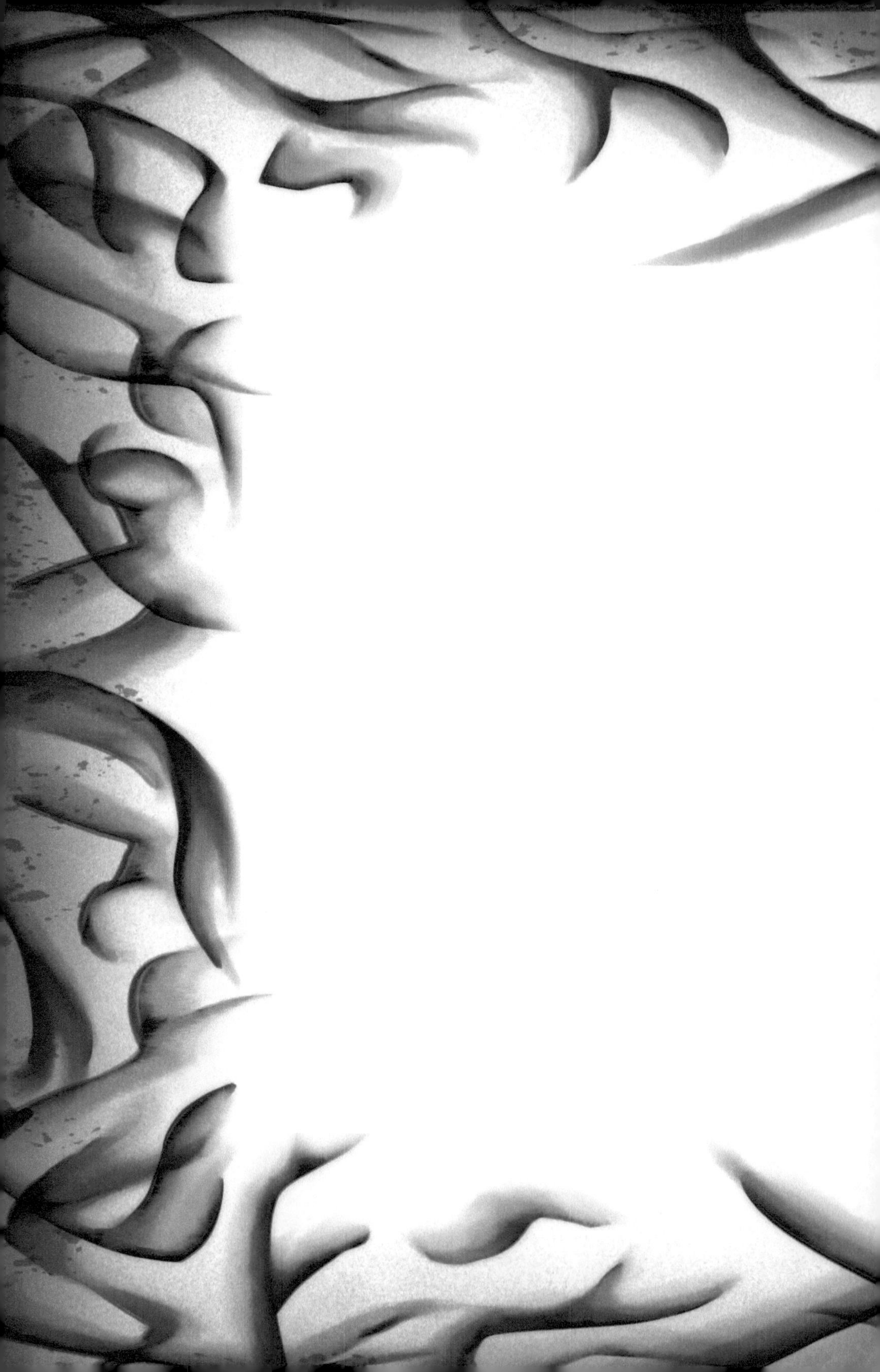

Part 4
Revelations

# XXV

## *Abandoned Kids*

Cassius

If I thought there was any good in my brother's morality, it had dissipated when Eden confessed. While it is obvious he said so assuming it would secure a mishap on our part, he was not aware that we'd previously theorized their leader had to have some connection to the crown. We thought there was a personal agenda, but for Ezra to concoct an uprising against our father made little sense.

Arabella and I speed closer towards the training guards with Kabir, his face unaware of anything that occurred in that room. The three of us search for Ezra, with myself walking paces ahead of the other two.

Kabir whispers to Arabella. "What are we in search for? What had you learned?"

"Turns out Prince Elliot Junior is the king of the missing Fae," Arabella says.

"You're sure?" Kabir asks with a tone of surprise.

"We were well aware of his ambition towards becoming the king. It comes as no shock he was prepared to take the crown by any means necessary." I pick up my speed, striding towards Nexus with haste.

"Cas. Slow down. We don't even have all the facts." Arabella grabs my shoulder, pulling my attention towards her.

My steps falter at the name she just called me. It's one I have not been called for a very long time, yet coming out of her mouth, it sounds of an angelic call. "What did you just say?"

She looks at me, assuming I likely hadn't heard her when she all but screamed. "I said we don't have all the facts."

"And what would you suppose we were possibly missing?"

Her demeanor stills. She thinks something amiss but is unable to name what it is.

"My king," Kabir says, "when has Prince Ezra been seen without a guard to account for his whereabouts? He has always, and I mean no disrespect by this, but he has been handed privileges his whole life. What would he to gain by leading a revolt against your father and murdering him when he could have simply waited?"

Against my impulsive desire to defame my brother's title publicly, Kabir makes a fair point. Our father was thrilled to have a version of him take the throne, and had Ezra had simply waited, it would have been his to collect. But there is no other likeliness within our family to whom Eden had spoken of. Atticus, Ezra, and I are our father's only sons, and Atticus shows no facial nor body similarity to our father.

No matter. I will carry on with the sinful brother of mine.

"Regardless of what we have seen, it does not discredit what we have been told. We must locate Ezra at once and question him."

We find Isaak, the knight behest of my father's choosing, training among the other guards. When he spots the three of us alongside Kabir, he gives a command for the rest of them to continue in his absence before jogging to us.

"Your Majesty, Lady Arabella, Kabir, is something troubling the three of you? You walk with such determination," Isaak says, breathing heavily when he finishes.

Kabir speaks for us. "Isaak, have you seen Prince Ezra today?"

His posture straightens slightly. "He was not here to direct the afternoon training. I had assumed he was with you in the cells. Is there something wrong?"

"There carries a possibility that the man in charge of the missing Fae looks precisely as my father had in his youth," I answer.

He nods with a speck of surprise on his face. "I spotted him last in the foyer this morning, leaving with his breakfast."

At the end of his statement, Arbella nudges my side. "I think I just found him." She cocks her head in the direction of the opened doors. A glimpse of his body passing towards the throne room can be seen through a window.

"Thank you, Isaak," Kabir says as we speed inside the palace and into the throne room.

Following Ezra, we hide behind art busts while he makes his way up the steps, rambling on a tirade about the unfair treatment of losing the crown.

Arabella holds an open palm to her mouth, stifling a snort. She clears her throat, causing my brother to startle. In surprise, he curses at the audience he had unknowingly given a performance to.

"I see you've been taking losing kingship well," she laughs sarcastically.

Kabir, the serious man that he is, chuckles at her comment. It would seem the two of them have bonded through their spent time together. I would much prefer this, rather than a guard who cares not for her safety, though to admit so would be far too revealing.

"Have you come to goad in my misery, or do you have a purpose for interrupting me?" Ezra remarks snidely.

I smirk at him. "Brother, I am the *king*. The throne room is mine to enter freely, not yours."

He sneers at me with a locked jaw, anger evident in his eyes. "I am aware."

"We've come here," Arabella says, glancing at me for a moment, "because we have some questions regarding your dad's death."

Ezra studies the three of us, releasing a huff when he realizes the lack of jest in her tone. Then, with wide eyes, he reaches the conclusion that there lies no humor in our coming. "You cannot honestly think I have anything to do with–"

My shadow shoots from under me, sliding its way to my brother through the floor and rising in front of him, pushing his body onto the king's throne. He struggles, attempting to free himself, while my shadow transforms into a constraint that hugs around his torso.

"I believe you to know more than you let on," I hiss, leaning close to his confined body. "In fact," I laugh, pacing around him as our father would have done had our roles been reversed, "if questioned thoroughly enough, you would be found guilty of high treason against the crown."

"This is ludicrous," he spits, a pause after every word. He wiggles his shoulders, attempting to free himself of my shadow's grasp, but it is of no use when he is only restricted further.

Arabella takes a seat on the queen's throne, facing the side of Ezra. "Is it?" she challenges, pulling the throne he sits on closer. "Because if I recall correctly, you were the one who pushed your brother to the ground, ready to whip him when your siblings didn't vote you king. I'd say it isn't outrageous to assume you'd start an uprising due to impatience."

"Where had you even come across this information?" he demands, still refusing to admit his part in this.

"Eden," I say. When the name does not register, I elaborate. "Though, you might be more familiar with Cato Locksynd. The man you and father had met."

His face hardens in vexation. "I do not recall knowing well of anyone by the name of Cato."

Arabella stands above him, her fingers going towards his temples, the magik from her fills the air.

Ezra goes still, legs slightly trembling, unsure of what her magik would do to him. On his face, his eyes widen with a memory clearly snapping into place.

"Please," he beseeches, "I swear I know nothing of Eden, nor what the uprising against father is about. The only time I had ever come across that name was a common fae who had come to me, begging to join the armed guards. I rejected him since father said to do so. I met him years ago and had not been bothered with his existence since. If he had fed you this information, it could not be me he spoke of."

"For someone whose ability can decipher liars and word twisting, you sure became a master of words yourself," Arabella mutters.

I take his chin in my hand, squeezing it, a sharp breath leaving his nose. "While you may not recall Eden, he informed us his leader had resembled father in his youth. Now, Atticus looks nothing like father, and I know I am not behind this, which leaves none but you."

There was never a point in our years together where I was in power. I have obtained control over Ezra, and it is taking all the restraint I have not to strike retribution for his years of treatment, rather than obtaining answers.

He must see the built-up rage in my eyes. I have never seen him cower before me, let alone petrified beyond words. "I- I barely have father's features," he stutters. "Other than my eye shape, nose, and hair, I resemble my mother. You can ask anyone. Ask Helena! I am more tan than he, and I have a wider jaw and–"

"Enough with your ramblings," I command.

The room fills with silence. Arabella backs from my side and stands next to Kabir. At the look of her, she gapes at me with wide eyes, blinking in tandem with the guard.

"Cassius," she calls, "he doesn't know anything. I told you earlier it made no sense for him to take the common fae. What purpose does it serve to kill other Fae, especially lords beneath him?"

"Listen to my pet. She obviously has more sense than you," Ezra barks.

She takes one slow blink while turning to my brother with the smile I know her to have only when enraged. Her eyes are full of darkness, her mouth terrifying. "You shut up. You don't get to speak to him like that, considering he's showing you mercy after years of what you did to him."

I smile to myself at her words. After all the many things I have done to her, she shows compassion to me.

"As king, I have settled on a new Leader of the Guards." I release my shadow's hold on my brother, returning them to me. "You, Ezra Disaris, are hereby stripped of your duties as Leader of the Guards, and they will henceforth be surrendered to Arabella."

His face drops, offense overtaking him. The single power he held left is now nothing. "What?"

Arabella too looks at me in disbelief. "You can't be serious. I have no knowledge about being a guard and barely have any formal fighting abilities."

"She will also serve as coordinator between the guards and General Callian of the Ifaeris army," I add, disregarding her words.

She pulls me aside. "Cassius, I know you're trying to make a point, but I can't be Leader of the Guards."

"What would you suggest? I must appoint someone."

Her eyes glance around the room before finally landing on the guard in the room. "How about Kabir?" At the sound of his name, he joins our private conversation, assuming he was called. "He's the one with enough patience to guard me. And considering how loyal he is to your family, despite what others throw at him, he's willing to protect you with his life," she goes on, singing his praises. "Plus, I can't be a coordinator, Leader of the Guards, *and* your reeve."

Kabir stares at her with confusion. "What am I meant to be doing?"

I answer before Arabella is able to. "Would you like the honor of taking Ezra's place as Leader of the Guards?"

His face turns vacuous with a flicker of excitement. Few occasions have I seen emotion on him, other than his worry for Arabella engaging in mischief. "Your Majesty, I am not equipped for such a role."

"Semantics," I stop him. "You have proven nothing but a noble protector to our household. Father had appointed you to protect my sisters, and I have never seen you lack in your duties."

My reeve glances at him. The look in her eyes she gets when she is preparing to bargain with others. "If it helps, I can always be your associate. The one you come to talk to when they're getting too overwhelming and you needa gossip about them."

He smiles with pride, fully prepared to take on his higher role within the guards. "You're sure, Your Majesty? This is quite an honor."

"If you are someone Arabella entrusts to lead, I assure you that you are qualified."

Kabir bows to me. "Thank you, my king."

Arabella snorts at him. "Never gonna get past court mannerisms being taken seriously instead of a joke."

Just as she says that, the door bursts open with a very frantic Helena. Her violet eyes glow with alertness. "King Cassius, you and Arabella must speak with me immediately. Ezra is innocent."

We wait for her to join us by the thrones, Ezra brisking past us. He glances back, and Arabella shoots her head forward at him, causing him to stumble to the ground. When he leaves, my reeve and I take a seat on the thrones while Helena sits on the steps. Along with my brother, Kabir exits, guarding the outside of the door.

Helena turns to me once the door shuts. "King Cassius, I implore you to hear my words before moving forward with the missing Fae."

"Mother, I am still your son, am I not? In the privacy of our family, there is no need for you to address me with such formalities."

Despite me not being of her blood, she raised me as her own, just as she had Esme and my other siblings. What I say brings comfort to her face. We are the family she has left, after her family was killed in the war nearly sixty years ago, and her sister went comatose for months.

"Ezra may think himself pompous and did whatever it took for your father to favor him as his heir, but he lacks the backbone needed to lead a rebellion against your father." Her head peers around the room before moving towards us, Arabella offering the throne.

When Arabella sits on the floor, my mother takes a brief moment before explaining further. "You may wonder why I know for certain it was not Ezra who is the man that looks like Elliot."

"Who informed you this was why we had needed to speak with him?" I ask.

"Isaak had asked me while I was returning from the gardens if I knew where your brother was. When I had asked why, he informed me of what you had told him."

"You're so sure that it isn't Ezra," Arabella says. "How?"

My mother pauses, ensuring we are alone. "I was not Elliot's first wife. Nor is Ezra his first born."

"We have always been told Ezra is the eldest since father's reign as king. How could we have a sibling that no one, not even the other rulers or common fae have heard of?" I ask.

"Prior to our marriage, he was married to another Fae, named Aurora. She was a common fae, and your grandfather despised her once hearing of her plans to leave Ifaeris. She desired to build a family among humans." She pauses, standing to pour herself water from the corner.

While she is doing so, Arabella continuously glances at me, silent in just as much perplexity as I.

"You are aware of the battle we had fought against the Gigantia, correct?" Helena asks.

I nod.

My mother takes this and Arabella's silence as enough of a confirmation to continue. "During the twenty-three-year battle, the woman your father had come to love had bore him a son. They married in secret, and as she was someone of no importance, none thought her more than another one of his lovers."

Honestly, how much had father been keeping secret from us all? *How many things has Helena kept quiet for his sake?*

"What all do not know, is that during the final battle, while your grandfather had died, another had been killed while your father sought peace with the other creatures. He drew treaties, and on the final night before he was coronated, a witch had come into his chamber, taking Aurora's life as she slept while he was out. A banished Cyclops had contacted the witch in hopes of continuing the bloodshed."

Her eyes fall to the floor in sorrow. Evident enough that this was a woman my father had loved, my mother lets out a sigh. She always has shown such empathy. It is something that made me question why she had wed my father throughout my entire adolescence.

She collects herself enough to neutralize her face. "Your father had kept the son a secret from the rest of the kingdom. He did not want to put the child or his wife in harm's way, and had he not been visiting me that night to see his son, the young prince may have been killed himself."

"And that's how you two met and married?" Arabella asks.

"We married soon after he was crowned," she says, confirming through a nod. "The witch was put to death, and with her, the only other person who knew of their marriage. Elliot and I kept his son's identity a secret, but what started as protection, quickly twisted into resentment and hatred towards the boy. At age six, your father could no longer bear a reminder of Aurora, so he demanded that I dispose of the boy."

I am at a loss for words. If father had just taken proper care of the boy and faced his grief, things would be vastly different.

Arabella seems less shocked but rather enraged by this reveal. "You knew of this helpless six-year-old and just left him to fend for himself?"

"Don't be naive," my mother returns sharply. "I found Aurora's brother and his wife. They made plans to leave Hearthis, but were waiting until they would be able to financially provide for themselves outside of Ifaeris. I gave them extra supplies to aid them for survival in the Human Lands, and they left."

"You just allowed them to take him while knowing they could easily tell him of his parentage?" I berate.

She glares at me. Though I am grown, I still fear her punishing words. "I had assumed once they moved to the Human Lands that they wouldn't speak of his parentage. It was ignorant on my behalf to assume so."

The only word to describe my state of mind is flabbergasted. I am sitting as a king with not one, but two brothers who desire the throne, one of which, willing to murder for it.

"Had I known that becoming king would set a price on my death, I would have sooner let Ezra take the crown."

Arabella is unsure what to do. She stands, scowling at me for my comment firstly, then glancing around before taking my hand while she leans on the side of my throne, rubbing circles between my thumb and index finger. "What was the kid's name?"

My mother looks at us, my eyes refusing to meet hers. "Adonis."

"He has to be fifty by now. And you married the king to keep his secret?" Arabella asks.

Helena nods. "It was the best scenario. I gained power as queen, while he was able to ensure I never said a word about his life." She takes in a deep breath and speaks calmly. "You likely assumed that Elliot and I did not marry for love, but we did, just not in the romantic sense. He never moved on from Aurora, and I desired a better life for myself and my sister. Through the years, the torment ate at him. He became someone the other Elementals had not recognized. No one knew of his greatest pain but me, which was why he put all his work onto his court and the other rulers."

"And Adonis? What became of him?" I ask.

"I never contacted the family once they left. I should have, but I lacked the courage to communicate with his family after what your father did to him."

I stare at her. "What did he do?"

"You may think your father cruel with his upbringing of you, but with Adonis, he was far worse. He stayed as far away from the boy as possible, but when he was with him, he was in a constant, drunken state, bellowing curses and shaming the boy. Adonis had appeared exactly as your father did, but the knowledge of knowing his mother birthed him was enough." She stands between the now too-close thrones that sit next to each other. "If I am admitting things, the reason he likely treated you with such animosity is because you resembled a lot of Adonis, both through your personalities and looks in youth, though his eyes carried the Disaris blue."

Too many thoughts race through my mind. I have just discovered my father's hatred towards me was not only my birth mother's doing, but his inability to move on from his past.

While my mother attempts to comfort me, Arabella sits in the small space left on the throne, resting her head on my shoulder. While I learned she is not comfortable with touch, she offers me this. I rest my head on hers, squeezing her hand tighter, holding her as long as I am able while she grants me the privilege.

"My son, your father took to Ezra because he carried out orders without question. Adonis may be just as power-hungry. What our kingdom needs is someone who is willing to do right by the Fae and refuses to be so easily influenced," Helena says, exiting the room.

Arabella releases a breath at the close of the door. "That was a lot. How are you feeling?"

The witch holds true concern for my well-being. After everything she confessed to me about her family, I understand why she cares about my emotions from this reveal. There are many things I am experiencing, all of which are difficult to focus on.

"I had prepared myself that in my father's death, we would receive stories thrust upon us. Discovering he willingly threw out his son for simply being alive is a burden I hadn't expected."

Sorrow briefly floods my mind, both for Adonis and myself. Regardless, no matter what treatment he had as a child, my brother has now chosen the path of destruction. He's chosen to murder all in his way of the crown, which includes myself.

While taking a seat in place of where my mother was sitting, Arabella runs her hand up and down her arm. "He's a grown adult, and while what your dad did was horrible, no one can change that.

And through killing, Adonis now seeks the throne to avenge what he believes is his birthright."

"I never thought he could reach any lower than how he treated me, but now I am aware he held such disdain for the two of us, due to our mothers but in vastly different ways." I shake my head, angry with my father.

Her fingers run through her hair. "What do you need right now?"

Truly, I have not thought of what I need. Instead, I wish to forget everything. "I would find it helpful to scream at the top of my lungs."

"So scream."

My eyebrows lift at the suggestion of her words.

Unfazed, she says nothing to change her words. "Screaming can be a good release. Sometimes we just need to do it."

Spreading her legs and putting her hands between her knees onto the cushion, she trills her lips to fill the tensed silence. "So do you want to go back and continue questioning Eden?"

I rise above her, cradling her cheeks in my hands. Kissing her forehead. "I cannot step foot near that man for the foreseeable future. If I did, we can both assume he would not leave that room alive."

She nods, following me out the door and leaving me to my own indignation after I ask her for privacy.

The previous day is something I cannot recall properly. I find myself buried in liquors and iceheart dust. My room is trashed, a desk broken. As I glance down, my top has been singed and my pants removed.

I am dizzy, my head is aching, and I am most certainly not properly sober.

Stay. I only wanted the witch to stay. If she would only grant me the honor just once. Have I blacked out for so long that not a single member of the house has noticed? I am in desperate need of food. I feel starved.

Arabella would likely jeer at me, find merriment at my lack of sobriety. Or worse. Stop me from doing this altogether, forcing water into my body and keeping me hydrated. It would be hypocritical of her to do so, being that she copes so similarly.

*Where is my witch? What have I done?*

There is but one solution, to carry on. I will continue indulging myself with such fine treatment until she returns to me.

Before I am to resume my consumption, I take Arabella's suggestion. I grab a pillow from my bed and bury my head into it, screaming with all the energy and anger I have raging inside of me.

It feels vindicating. Perhaps an idiotic idea to do so now as my headache worsens.

Pounding knocks hit my door. It's likely those I have spent the last day with. I laugh so violently that tears fall from my eyes.

# XXVI
## *New Perspectives*

Arabella

It's obvious that Cassius needs time to process things, and I would be overly attached if I refused him his space.

After Helena told us about Adonis, Cassius disappeared into the king's chamber and told me to take the next day for myself. Honestly, I have been so overwhelmed, and a fresh set of ears might help bring us closer to finding Adonis. We've run enough theories past each other, and talking to Eden again without Cassius would be pointless since he has made it perfectly clear he seeks entertainment in revealing information that will further hurt the Disaris family.

That thought in mind brought me to my house yesterday. I spent the remaining hours of last night sleeping and most of today catching up on reading. As I finish my book, I message the Wands group chat and ask if they want dinner.

The five of us pick up Mexican food from the taquería down

the street. Three of them order enchiladas and tacos while Damien and I order carne asada fries to share with the group. For the two of us, I make a special side order to have one be spicy.

We all begin devouring the food in my living room as I tell them everything. I explain what we're dealing with and the details I've withheld from them out of fear of their reactions. Though I confessed my true reasoning in Ifaeris before, I never explained the actual dangers or my stabbing. I would've updated them regularly on new information we come across, but that's too much detail for random messages. In person, I'm able to explain about Eden and what Helena told us about King Elliot's first son.

"He promised to let you go, then forced you to stay after saying you push everyone away?" Damien's face contorts angrily.

"Yeah but–"

"I'll kill him," Gray cuts me off.

"So let me see if I understand this correctly," Juju says as she finishes her bite into another taco. "Dead king has an old son that he exiled as a child 'cause he couldn't get over his wife that also died?"

I nod my head. "Well, when you put it like that–"

"And the son is now so hellbent on becoming king, he killed his father?" Damien asks, a brow raising.

"Wouldn't any of you?" Vi says, taking a sip of the horchata. "Imagine if you could live for centuries, and for the past about five decades, you're raised by your aunt and uncle who told you that the only reason they're raising you is because your dad wanted nothing to do with you."

We all go quiet, and it's clear we all understand why Adonis did what he did. I never thought his reasoning wasn't valid, but I think he may have taken things a little too far. Killing Elliot and the other Elemental rulers would have been enough.

"Not to mention," Gray adds, "if the king treated Adonis so poorly that all he received were curses and yelling, it makes sense he'd resent the guy."

This is one of the infrequent times that Grayson is making logical sense. Sometimes, these moments scare me.

I stab a mouthful of the carne asada, stuffing it into my mouth before speaking. "The only issue is that I don't get why he'd go through all that trouble of causing an uprising if he was going to kill them anyway. It makes no sense."

Reclining the chair, Vi takes the remote from the table, muting the show we have playing in the background as she unbuttons her pants. "Does it have to make sense?"

"I guess not. But wouldn't it've been easier to wait longer to kill the king if he wanted more supporters to follow him?" I ask.

"Maybe he couldn't wait," Juju suggests. She uses a napkin, wiping the salsa that has fallen onto her chin. "Maybe someone had pushed for him to kill the king sooner."

Damien laughs. "Or he wasn't the one to kill the king. You did say that no one could be found around the grounds and that it was impossible for someone to sneak past the guards. Maybe it was someone on the inside or someone okkared."

My head turns to his. "There was no trace of magik when the guards had checked. His body was still heated when the guards found him, so it couldn't have been someone who okkared. We all know our magik stays remnant in the air to other creatures hours after a spell."

"So you really don't think it could be a Magik?" Juju asks as she struggles to put her hair into a bun, fighting with the auburn curls. "You *did* say that the Fae have issues with us, and the king executed a witch for killing Aurora."

I shake my head, affirming my previous beliefs. "I don't think there was a Magik there. At least not that night."

With a mouth full of taco, Gray speaks while chewing. "Not like we can blame those Fae for hating us if what they said is true." He swallows. "That means some of our ancestors slaughtered a majority of their population. They *should* hate us."

"Still don't understand why we were never taught about this war during lessons," Juju comments.

Vi stares at her, deadpan. "Oh we all know why they didn't."

"Hey, can you get more fries?" Gray asks, flicking his wrist towards me.

Getting up from my seat, I walk to the counter we set the food on. "Spicy or regular?"

"Regular. Are you insane?" Gray shouts.

I gather the rest of the fries, deciding to take the container back to the group. There's about half a box left, but with the way Grayson eats, he'll just consume it all.

Handing the box to him, he begins devouring the food.

"Still don't understand why y'all refuse to eat spicy food," I laugh.

Damien flashes his head in my direction. "Hey!"

"Other than Damien."

Gray goes back to filling himself with food, moaning at the taste. "Because you two are the only ones insane enough to not care about how it will affect your stomachs."

"Or," I say, dragging out the 'r', "you're just a baby who can't handle spice."

He sticks his tongue out at me, all of us laughing. It makes it funnier when Gray knows how to cook but uses me and Damien as his tasters whenever the dish is spicy.

"He's right about you not caring about how it'll affect your stomach though," Vi teases. It's aimed at me and only me.

*Fair.*

When we finish our food, we clean the kitchen, throwing away the paper plates and digging into the freezer for ice cream.

Passing the rolled valskull around in the circle, we alternate between inhales and taking a scoop from the tub of dessert. It may not be the most sanitary thing to do, but we've all shared drinks before, so this isn't too different.

Vi inhales the drug, passing the joint from her lips to Damien. "So let's talk about the real reason you're deciding to hide from Cassius."

Heat rushes to my face. "I'm not hiding."

"*Sure*," Damien says, handing the joint to Gray, "and Grayson and Juliette haven't been in love with each other for the past couple years."

Juju's mouth drops, Vi lightly shoving Damien's shoulder for admitting that.

We all know, considering how much the two of them act like a couple, but both oblivious and unaware. They've never said anything. It's unspoken.

"You like me?" Gray asks Juju in shock.

My eyes keep shifting to everyone in the room. I'm pretty sure my mouth is still open from Damien dropping that.

"Uh, yeah," Juju replies, averting her eyes from her crush.

"Oh thank the gods," Gray says, his body relaxing and breathing with relief. "I never knew if you were serious or not when you flirted with me."

"Yeah, yeah," Juju brushes off. "Bells over there isn't saying anything. We all know it's 'cause she's trying to distract us from answering Vi."

*Shit. She caught on.* I guess that's the consequence of staying with your best friend since fourteen. She knows me in every way.

Gray diverts his attention back on me, the whole group staring. Waiting for me to answer.

"What?" I ask.

Vi looks around the room and back at me, her face turning soft. "You know it's okay to have feelings for him."

"Luka's been gone for half a year, Ara," Damien chimes in, offering comfort.

Chipping at the paint on my nails, my body begins slightly rocking.

"You can't keep denying yourself happiness because you still feel guilty over something you had no control over," Gray lectures.

I hate that they're all right, explaining to me about my own feelings. But it doesn't change how guilty I feel. Like I'm somehow having an affair and cheating on Luka. I'm still angry that he was taken from life so early and I never got to say goodbye. Angry that I let something so small cause us to separate in the first place. It's irrational and makes no sense, but if even Luka's childhood friends are telling me to move on, deep down, I know I should.

I just miss him.

Juju gets up from where she's sitting and moves next to me,

turning towards the side, sitting cross-legged. "We all saw how you looked at each other at Infinite." She grabs my hand, holding it. "You told us that he managed to help you harness your power. That's special."

I inhale the rest of the second rolled valskull, hoping it'll drown out my guilt-ridden thoughts.

"Plus," Damien says, "you haven't looked as happy and energetic as you were at Infinite in months. You were dancing and laughing with us. Luka would want you to be happy."

"The man may have been just as hard-headed as you, but he wouldn't want you alone forever just because he can't have you as a ghost," Vi adds, somewhat joking to make me comfortable.

Gray finishes the rest of the ice cream, setting the tub onto the table. "Oh I don't know, Vi. Man could very well be haunting us right now, cursing us for suggesting she move on."

We all burst out into laughter, Damien telling Luka to move something or throw an object across the room if he is angry about Cassius. An ice cube falls from the fridge, but other than that, nothing happens.

"You know, I probably don't even have to work for him anymore," I confess.

*Oh I'm definitely high.*

Their faces turn to me, pressing for an elaboration.

"I mean, I know he said he was honoring his dad's commands, but realistically, I probably don't have to stay if I don't want to."

Juju walks to the kitchen, grabbing some water for herself. "What's stopping you from leaving then? Y'know, since you're in denial about your feelings for the new king."

I point to the earrings the guards pierced into me, reminding them of their purpose. "Tracker. If I leave and don't come back, they'll hunt me down and kill me."

"You really think that he would do that? Have you killed when he was cradling your drunk ass when you passed out on him?" Damien questions, aware we both know the answer to this.

For a moment, I wonder if he would. Cassius definitely doesn't show the same signs of contempt towards me as he once did, but considering how quickly he was willing to cast me out in anger makes me question if he still holds resentment towards being bound to me.

Thinking back to the ball, I remember the women who said he had someone nearly drowned for bumping into him without apologizing. He's admitted to never killing another, but now that he's king, it's bound to happen. At the very least, it's likely he'll send someone to death. But then, I doubt I'll be the first.

"I don't know," I admit. "I would like to assume he wouldn't, but with his history, he has done things just as cruel for far less."

"Oh come off it," Grayson groans, exasperated. "We know he wouldn't. *You* know he wouldn't. Just admit you're staying there because of your annoying need to finish something you started."

Vi's face opens, impressed. "He has a point. You *are* at a point where you seem determined to see this through."

Gray gestures towards her comment, the action begging me to see that he's not alone in his statement. He stares at me for a moment, rolling his eyes. "You're just as bad as I am. How do you not clearly see you both want each other?"

"No offense Gray, but you're not exactly one to talk about love, considering the fact all Cas and I have done is fuck."

As soon as I say that, his head shakes. His eyes shut before popping out, with his mouth gaping.

"You two *fucked*?" he screams in horror.

"Did you just completely miss where I said that in the group chat?" I ask.

His eyes dart towards the rest of our friends in the room. None of which are surprised by my comment. Actually, we're all laughing, wheezing from trying to catch our breath and making jokes about what just happened.

"I started getting bored of you talking about him, so I got off my phone when you would." Gray rolls his eyes, snorting to himself.

Flipping him off, I chuckle softly.

"You can't act like you weren't just as tired of Juli and I being completely oblivious," he defends.

"Fair point. But how did you miss me talking about us having sex *multiple* times?" I berate. That, and sex versus feelings are very different things for me.

He shrugs.

Juju pats his shoulder in an attempt to stroke his weakened pride. "If anything, you being just as bad at picking up on his feelings for you, knowing how bad Gray and I were, makes it worse."

*Do I actually have romantic feelings for Cassius?*

I toss and turn at night thinking about our interactions. Oftentimes, I replay them in my head, but usually for the purpose of attempting to figure him out. I find myself enjoying his company more and more, even craving his presence outside of our obligation. Most of all, I hate thinking of him with others intimately. They're emotions I've avoided, shutting down the thought when it clouds my mind.

"For two people who *just* found out they were hopelessly in love an hour ago, you sure are taking the piss out of Ara," Vi says in my defense.

Grabbing my purse from the floor, I stand, pocketing some rolled valskull. "I should probably get back. The king's been alone for over a day, and who knows what he's gotten himself into."

As we're saying my goodbyes, Damien taps the back of my shoulder. I turn to him, waiting for what he has to say.

"One more thing," he says. "You two should probably interview that Eden guy again."

My brows furrow, brain wondering what has prompted him to say that.

He scratches the back of his head. "I was just thinking, considering the bloke was willing to take a deal, maybe you could strike another one? Say you'll offer him freedom if he gives more information about what he knows."

"That's smart, but Fae can't lie," I tell him.

Violette pinches her nose. "Then *you* lie, and Cassius just has to say nothing. Even if Fae can't lie, they can twist their words, right? So not saying anything would be similar to those lines."

She has a point. It's not like I haven't seen it done before. This is still something I'd have to go over with Cassius, but it's worth a shot.

"He doesn't seem smart," Juju says. She immediately clarifies. "Eden. I meant Eden doesn't seem clever enough to figure it out. Based on what you said before, he likes the idea of feeling important. Say you'll spare him and assign him a role in the royal council or something." Hugging me tightly, she whispers into my ear, "Do what you have to, to get the information you need. But promise that you'll come back and visit us."

I pull away from her embrace and see the freckles on her face rising, her cheeks dimpling with hope.

"I promise."

About to okkar, I hear a voice calling. "Don't get yourself killed, Ara," Vi announces. "I'd hate for Grayson to change the group name to 'Four of Wands' a week after your death."

"Hey," Gray whines defensively. "I wouldn't do that."

While adjusting the beanie on his head, we all stare at him. And when he finally pays attention to our faces, he shoots his hands up. "Okay, maybe I would."

I roll my eyes, grinning at my friends and okkaring home to Nexus.

# XXVII

*Selfish Decisions*

Cassius

Opening my door, I find Xavier and Montgomery, their attitudes bubbling with glee.

"I was expecting someone else," I sigh with disappointment. The only thing I am able to accurately remember is inviting Harrison and Korine for wine and entertainment. After that, my mind is slated with absolute nothingness.

Montgomery shakes his head, shoving a glass of water at me while Xavier pushes past and flops himself onto my bed.

"Surprised you're alive after all you consumed yesterday," Xavier teases, dropping crumbs onto the mattress with the breakfast he eats.

I survey the two, waiting for either to inform me of what occurred. When neither of them goes on, I ask for myself. "Had yesterday gone so horribly dull that I invited the two of you?"

Xavier laughs, his back falling onto the sheets.

"Oh wow," Montgomery says. "You truly have no idea what happened yesterday, do you?"

Rolling my eyes, I have no time for their prolonged explanations. "Care to enlighten me?"

Montgomery takes a pastry wrapped in a napkin from his pocket, tossing it to me so that I may eat. I may feel irritation, but my hunger far outweighs the annoyance. He sits on the chest at the end of my bed as I sit on a chair that had been tucked into a table in the corner of my room.

"You blacked out," Xavier states.

*Does he think me an idiot?*

I cross a leg over another, leaning back into the cushioned seat. "I am aware of that. Would you care to tell me what happened while I was inebriated, or am I to continue guessing?"

"You had too much iceheart dust and drank practically anything with alcohol. From what you told us, but more importantly what we were able to understand, you invited Korine and Harrison," Montgomery explains. He runs his hands through his hair, hesitating with his next sentence. "After you told them about Adonis, Harrison suggested inviting others over and drinking until you were able to forget. He pulled out iceheart, and you were pouring wine into your mouth like a fountain."

*That sounds very much like me.*

"And you were aware of this, how? I am sure I had not invited the two of you to join us." The pounding in my head throbs. Nausea takes over, and I require more food.

Running into the bathroom, I stick my head into the toilet, hurling bile that has been creeping its way up since I woke. Sweat beads drip down my forehead, forcing me to rest my head on my arm, putting the weight on the toilet seat.

I am miserable.

The twins join me in the bathroom, sitting on the sink's counter. Xavier taunts my suffering. "That's what you get for refusing water when we demanded you drink it last night."

"And the food," Montgomery adds.

"Anyway, Harrison pretty much took advantage of your state, invited some common fae, and wrecked the palace," Xavier says.

Montgomery hands me my glass full of water, and I take it graciously, swallowing every last drop.

He sits back on the counter, observing my movements. "We don't know everything you did, but when Celeste okkared over to us and explained how annoyed they were with your noise, we came to Nexus and sent everyone home."

"Your two friends were the hardest to force out. Harrison and Korine were finding too much pleasure in their actions. The three of you were keeping entertainment by making one of the servants play until she cried," Xavier says.

"No, *they* were making the servants uncomfortable while *you* were nearly passed out on a table, laughing at them," Montgomery clarifies.

Xavier chuckles at his brother's comment, realizing his ignorance to that detail. "After we finally sent everyone out, we found you asleep."

"And that's when we brought you up to your room as you yammered about the night," Montgomery continues.

It is horrifically degrading to receive this information. Not only was I not aware of what occurred, but my cousins had carried me to my bedchamber. Though, I continue to find it quite amusing that for a land that fears me, all are eager to be in my company for such revels.

I flush the remains of the bile down the toilet before starting the water to wash my hands and brush my teeth.

"I'm assuming you don't want us to tell Arabella about this," Montgomery says, but he poses it as a question.

Wiping my hands on a towel, I pay no mind to the implication. "What would be the difference whether or not she is aware of what occurred?"

"Well for one, it's humiliating," Xavier mocks while drumming his fingers. "And for another, I hardly think Arabella would be too thrilled to know you still spend time with the Fae who tried to kill her."

In honest, I have been avoiding Korine as best I can since that incident. Being friends with Harrison means she is indirectly invited to any outings that he and I hold.

Originally, I meant for only Harrison and myself to have a drink, but he insisted on Korine joining us. Saying that, "we find the most enjoyment when the three of us are together", though more often than not, Korine finds bliss in the displeasure of others, whether it be unhappiness or awkwardness.

"Why would Arabella care one way or another with my time spent with Korine?" I ask.

Montgomery scoffs. "Why are you so dense?"

"Whatever I feel for her is no business of yours," I rebuke sharply. Taking an inhale, I feel my mind whirling. "If I do feel something for her, she will never return those same feelings. She refuses to let me get close enough. Not while she thinks me her nemesis."

"Sure. If that's what you've convinced yourself of." Xavier sits on the floor, his back against the obsidian bathtub. "She's someone who struggles with intimacy, and I've never seen her more cautious about her feelings than when she talks about you. Why do you think that is?"

*How can you say this when you are the one she is the most herself around?*

After seeing Arabella with her friends in the Human Lands, I immediately understood that she is as relaxed with them as she is around Xavier. He is someone she trusts completely. She may find something about me attractive, but I am one she yells at until she breaks. After what Violette told me, and after Arabella delved into her past, I understood why she kept that hidden.

"Were you aware she still wears the earrings that locate her?" I say, redirecting the subject.

They shake their heads, suspiciously eyeing me on what will come from my mouth next.

"I had told her she was not exonerated for her crimes, but in truth, I had forced her to continue wearing it out of anger."

While that confession holds part of the truth, it is not the entirety of it. I refused to take the jewelry off, for if I had, I knew she would leave and never return to Ifaeris. She would never stay for me.

Both stare at me in repugnance. They utter nothing, though I can feel their judgment through the glares they throw as knives.

A fist slams into the side of my face before I had taken awareness. "You're a stupid, fucking prick," Montgomery berates.

Agreeing with his brother, Xavier holds strong, scolding me. "You're so selfish that you would hold her here against her will?

How does that make you any better than your father who punished the Fae?"

I'm in no position to argue. I deserve every bit of what they throw at me. As defensive as I am at their words, they are correct. I am keeping her here out of pure fear and selfishness. She deserves more, but the thought of her absent from Nexus, nothing but a wraith in a fleeting moment in life, it is something I cannot bear.

"If you don't release Arabella from her bind to you and let her decide for herself if she wants to stay," Xavier grabs me by the opening of my shirt, "king or not, I will crush you until you cannot move again."

Exceedingly aware of how Xavier has come to care for Arabella, I guarantee that this is less a threat and more a promise.

I am finding myself exhausted from this conversation. "Must we deliberate over the proceedings of my romantic life? Arabella will eventually be released from the earrings, but should she choose to stay, far be it for me to stop her."

"Well, then let's discuss the whole abandoned cousin intel you were fed," Montgomery suggests.

"What is there to be discussed?" I ask.

While cracking his fingers, Xavier stares at the ceiling. "Perhaps you should question him again." He looks at me. "You two *are* planning on questioning him again, right?"

My eyebrows furrow, arms crossing as I lean back on the counter. "What do you suppose makes him any more important than seeking another Fae willing to give information?"

"Family spite," Montgomery says. He jumps down from where he was sitting, though it is a one-foot drop from where his feet were hanging prior. "Common fae had already believed the disappearances to be caused within the circle of the crown. Considering the revelation of your father's death, I'm sure that adds to the theories."

"Technically, they *were* caused by the crown," Xavier says, referencing Adonis. "If the common fae were made aware the Disaris bloodline had been responsible for the disappearances and deaths, especially those who are completely unaware of the revolt against the crown, they may riot and make things worse."

They are both with excellent points. While Arabella and I have made no definite plans to question Eden again, it is not something we have discarded as a possibility.

# XXVIII
## *Blown Minds*

Arabella

We have to requession Eden.

After coming back late last night, I decided to wait until the morning to talk to Cassius about how to approach the situation. He consented to setting up a false position for Eden and letting me do most of the speaking. He also informed me of the threat that would impose if the common fae were to find out about Adonis' true parentage, and I agreed that while people suspect him of being from the Disaris bloodline, the knowledge would be far more endangering towards the safety of the family.

We eat breakfast in mostly silence since he's still suffering from the consequences of his consumption and the black eye Monty gave him. According to Xavier, Cassius threw a party in my absence and blacked out, chucking up his guts the next day. I shouldn't find it funny, but it is.

"You may find my suffering comical, but had we not forced water into you when your friends joined us, you too would understand my fatigue," Cassius says through gritted teeth. I can't tell if this is from embarrassment or annoyance with me.

"I don't think me falling asleep from exhaustion after our conversation with Jefferson is nearly as bad as passing out on a table and being carried to my room by my cousins."

His brow quirks. "Were I you, I would keep from calling what we did with Jefferson a conversation."

"Why?"

"Most conversations don't consist of threatening the other parties involved." The side of his mouth forming a smirk, he brings the cup of juice to his lips. "But I suppose there is no fun in normality with you."

Glass raised to his comment, I let out a small snicker. "So we both had interesting days."

He glances at me, completely unaware of where I'd left to. "What had you done in your free day away from me?"

"I slept at the house and spent the next day reading. Then I had dinner with my friends and came back."

Our plates are taken by one of the servants, who then cleans the table.

The king and I begin walking up the stairs of Phantom Tower, him reminding me that flattery works best with Eden, rather than threats. I'm not great with words, so I'll cover any needs of lying, and Cassius will be the persuading charm when needed.

Kabir once again meets us outside the same enclosed cell as before, the setup remaining the same. He's barely been on prisoner watch since he was appointed the head of the guards, but he insisted on being here when we came.

"Should I have a healer ready to rush in?" Kabir taunts.

Glaring at him, I can't help but let a small smirk slip from my lips. "That won't be necessary."

Cassius stops behind me before entering, lowly muttering to Kabir, "Have one prepared, regardless."

The door shuts, leaving Cassius, Eden, and me alone. It smells like sweat, body odor, and wet dog. I try not to, but I gag anyway from the unexpected mixture. Eden doesn't show weakness or emotion at our entrance. His silver hair has turned greasy and ratty, his eyes haunted and hollow. It's also clear, based on his smell and appearance, that he still hasn't taken a shower since his arrival.

Eden watches us, a sadistic grin on his face. "How lovely it is to see the king once more with his witchling executioner."

"I would tread carefully on how I spoke of Lady Arabella," Cassius warns. Then, his charming smile appears. "You of course may do so, if you desire another deadly encounter."

He gulps, a shaky breath coming from him. "What do you wish to know?"

"We are willing to strike a compromise with you," Cassius offers. "A barter, if you prefer."

Glowering at us, he weighs the comment. "What type of compromise? I'd prefer to refrain from saying another word unless I am guaranteed my freedom."

Stalking towards the chair, I take my time sitting, resting a leg on my knee as he watches us, trying to predict our next move. I look at Cassius, feigning confirmation as he gives a curt nod. Impatience grows on the king's face, which is ideal, considering it gives the illusion that what we have to offer is legitimate. Eden will assume us to be hesitant to offer the bargain, posing it to be all the more true.

"I can give something better than freedom," I say. "If you tell us all you know, give up meeting times, your 'true king's' intentions, everything, we're willing to offer you a high position for the king."

He considers this, leaning closer to the table with the top half of his body hovering and pressed against the edges. "What position might that be?"

Again, I answer for the two of us. "You will be given a top rank in the army, working alongside General Callian."

His eyes widen slightly with his body loosening. Though I'm no mind reader, it's easy to tell that this would give him the position that he wants. "And this is binding? Will it hold true after I tell all that I know?"

"Yes. Would I lie?"

I am, but he doesn't have to know that.

Suspicion rises to his face. He still doesn't trust me, not that I can hold that against him.

"I want to hear from the king," he demands.

"What?" I hiss out. I'm almost insulted that he wouldn't believe me.

Cassius looks to me with skepticism. We both know that Fae can't lie, and this is Eden's way to ensure that we will hold our word.

Subtly shaking my head at him, I mouth a "no" to him as he finally takes a seat.

"The king's word, or I say nothing, and you're back to searching for another Fae," Eden says with all the power that he has over us at this moment.

"Very well," Cassius obliges. "You have my word that upon the information you provide, should it prove useful to Lady Arabella, you will be given the position of high rank within the general's army."

I bite down, doing my best to not reveal my anger at his decision. We agreed to let me lie, and by doing this, he has to keep his word.

Eden smiles with ambition written in his eyes. "Well then, let me begin with the Fae disappearances."

"You said that weirdly," I note, needing to find a way to push past my contempt for Cassius' agreement with the Fae. "Are you suggesting it's more than luring Fae into a revolt?"

His eyes narrow, lowering with enthusiasm at our lack of knowledge. "It has always been more than that. You see, while you might assume that we used the Stone of Elestial to brainwash the Fae, many of whom we targeted were those who took issue with the rulership."

That much we already know.

"However, what you may not know, is that the stone was mainly used on those who were considering leaving the group," Eden adds. He coughs roughly, spitting onto the floor. "Word would go around about our meetings to discuss our issues with the rulership, and as we continued to discuss our means of taking the throne, many disagreed with our methods. With that set of individuals, we would use the stone on them, which promised to grant their wildest dreams and essentially convince them to stay."

My foot drops to the ground, and my hands fold into my lap. "And that's what made them disappear."

"Not quite. You see, once under the influence of the stone, you lose your sense of control over yourself. You become mindless until the one in possession of the stone says otherwise."

"You have the ability to control the minds of the Fae, yet you kill them anyway. That seems counterproductive if your intention was to create a revolution," Cassius points out.

Eden bites his lip, the top one raised to his nose as he scrunches his face. "We had learned there were few minds who were able to break free of the stone's hold. Long enough to consider leaving and informing the crown." He hangs his head down in shame. "I was not aware of the deaths past the first two until you informed me, but I assure you that the others were to have their deaths as painless as possible."

This explains why the common fae women spoke about their loved ones attending meetings before their disappearances. And those who attended the gatherings must have known that if they said something when noticing a missing Fae, it would result in the same outcome.

These poor families don't know where their loved ones are, and even worse, those gone have become an empty shell, losing all their sense of self.

"What about the lords that had been killed?" I ask. "Were they part of the rise against the crown as well?"

"Gods no," Eden laughs. "They had just gotten too close to those of us who were leading towards a meeting spot. Our king had decided their fate."

"You had mentioned regular meetings," I remind him. "Where and when were those held?"

"We held them every other week on Thursdays. Occasionally, we had a meeting the week after, but it was sparse."

"Has it occurred to you that you are ripping families apart?

People assume their family dead, while you hold them against their will."

"It's the sacrifice you must be willing to take," Eden seethes.

"Not when they are being taken and their minds stripped of free will," Cassius counters.

Eden gives a mocking half bow of his head. "Oh, Your Majesty," he sings monotonically, "was there such a thing of free will under the rule of your father?"

I am fed up with his stalling. Though Eden's tendency to rile up Cassius provided the reveal of Adonis, I have a feeling that now, Eden is doing this out of malice and self-pleasure. "Are you going to tell us where these meetings were held, or will you keep flirting with the king like a kid trying to get their crush's attention?"

"So impatient," Eden fires. "The meetings were held on the edge of Enthar, near the ocean. There are ruins left of the old Oris manor that had been abandoned for nearly a century. Each land of Ifaeris has an assigned Fae to meet with the members before okkaring to the meeting spot. I, of course, was in charge of Aquatius."

Looking at Cassius, I scoff. "So they're meeting at Korine's family's old house?"

"It would appear so," Cassius responds.

"And your 'true king's' real intentions?" I ask Eden.

Smiling, his eyes light maliciously. "To bring Ifaeris to its true power. To care once more for all its people and rid us of your rule. Killing every last one of you until we are free."

Cassius laughs, but I can see in the way he tenses that he's worried.

"It's never gonna work. You killed one king, but another rose to the throne," I dismiss. "And even if you kill Cassius, how much more Elemental blood will you spill until you finally realize your king is no better than them?"

Eden cackles. "It's amusing that you believe we are convinced the two of you are lovers when all have witnessed you threaten your... ally."

"They're no different than the ones I gave to the last I loved. Besides," I glide towards the Fae, whispering into his ear, "what's a royal romance without a few threats?"

"Your tone is always coated in delight, yet you are constantly covered in colors for a funeral's mourning. Why is that?" he asks with amusement in his tone.

I smile, head angled at him. "Oh, you didn't hear? They scheduled yours early. I was simply preparing."

His face of levity drops. "And did poor Luka die due to your tongue?"

My body becomes rigid as I feel a frozen ice rushing to my throat. "What the fuck did you just say?"

"Poor, young Luka. Dying while attempting to save you from yourself," he taunts, unaware of the meaning of his words.

Everything is closing in on me. My chest tightens, and the floors feel like they're caving from the ground beneath.

"We have been paying closer attention than you think. Now you endanger another due to your alleged care," he says playfully while reaching to stroke my cheek.

I dodge from his touch, backing away from him. All I see is his blood, so dark it nearly passes as a shade of raven. I hear Cassius' voice, but it just sounds like muffled noise. My fists clench as I stare intensely into Eden's eyes. So much that I can see the light leave from him.

His eyes begin popping from his head, and his skull explodes, blood and bits of his brain hitting me. It's at the sound of his body hitting the floor that I realize what I've done. The initial adrenaline from more powerful magik wears off, my energy partially drained the same way as if I had stood in the sun too long. Bearable to continue on, though there is the initial feeling of needing hydration. I wipe the pink chunks from my cheeks and turn to see Cassius staring at me.

It's hard for me to gauge his reaction to this. His face isn't flushing with horror, but neither does it show absolute satisfaction. I assumed he would find entertainment in my actions, considering the stories I have heard about him, but he says nothing.

"You promised not to have him killed. I didn't."

His lips crack into a smile, taking a cloth from a pocket and handing it to me. "Just so you are aware, I had never intended on giving him the position in the army."

I look at him in doubt. There's no reason to change his answer now that the Fae is dead. "You said Fae can't lie."

"My exact words were, 'should it prove useful to Lady Arabella'. You could have just as easily found it useless, and he would have stayed down here for the rest of his days."

We walk towards the cell door and Kabir opens it, face unchanged when he sees what's inside.

"Sorry. You might wanna get someone to clean that up," I say sarcastically, scratching the back of my head.

Kabir calls for the guards to dispose of the body, but I get the feeling he doesn't mind that I killed Eden. He looks almost proud to the point that I think he contemplated doing it himself.

# XXIX

## *His Weakness*

Cassius

I wait for Arabella at the bottom of the stairs. Upon deliberation, we had given ourselves another day of rest before traveling to Enthar and locating the meeting area held by Adonis.

After nearly an hour of waiting, I march up the steps to find what is keeping my reeve. I lightly knock twice on her door to ensure she is awake, but at the fourth knock, I open it.

She jolts from her place at my sight, ripping what she calls earphones from her ear and setting them on her bed. Muttered curses leave her mouth, though all are jumbled together and incoherent. "Ever heard of knocking?"

Her eyes then drop to the healed contusion on my cheek. For a moment, her eyebrows cross with the slight tilt of her head, forgetting that creatures outside of Magik also heal at a rate faster than humans.

The witch dresses so similar yet different from those in the lands, with a black skirt that drops down to her ankles and slits on both sides of her legs. The fabric of her cream-colored top stops above her navel, while sleeves hang from the sides of her arms. It mirrors the top half of dresses many of the common fae wear.

Eyeing how high the openings in her skirt rise, I cannot keep myself from asking, "Will that not be difficult to maneuver in?"

"Not really. If I have to run, I'll tie the back and front together like shorts," she dismisses casually. Grabbing the crow-colored boned bodice that hangs on her wardrobe, she stretches her arms through the straps, zipping and tying the front, then swiftly striding towards me to tighten the strings in the back.

I tighten each section, a bit of air releasing from her when I tie the strings together, spinning and backing her into her desk. We stare at each other for passing moments, neither of us touching the other. Instead, she turns her body back towards the scatter on her desk.

After putting on the last of her jewelry, we leave her room, stopping at the stairs. She turns to me, expressionless. "So are we okkaring there, flying, or walking?"

It is late afternoon, and the warmth of the approaching summer season is evident, though our heat does not nearly reach the temperatures of what she is accustomed to for this time of the year.

"If you wish, I could fly us there."

She runs her nails against each other. "If we're trying not to draw attention, it might be smarter to okkar." She titters softly to herself. "But you do know the exact location, so we don't end up in some strange forest and imprisoned by a Fae king, right?"

Her jest, while funny, only makes me want to put my mouth

on hers. But instead, I say, "I know the edges of Enthar. When we arrive there, it should not be difficult to find the remains of the Oris grounds."

She takes my arm as I visualize the oceanside of Enthar and the land that borders the sea. As we are pulled to a new location, we arrive outside the marketplace that touches a section near the border.

We peer around, searching for onlookers. The only Fae that has spotted us is a young Goblin, who, upon seeing me, slaps his hands over his eyes and runs off.

"Have you ever been to this place?" Arabella asks, walking as if she is aware of where she is going.

I take her by the arm, turning her south, her scent of pear blossoms and water lilies whisking into my nose. "I have not personally been there, no. However, Korine used to speak of the residence, claiming it was haunted when we were children."

She lets out a breathy giggle. "If everyone believed that, it makes sense why no one would assume revolution meetings are held there."

Arabella is precise in her statement. My father had long forgotten about the manor, being that it was the last to be destroyed during the war of Gigantia. Though he had sent guards to search for the missing Fae, none had bothered to venture past the populated marketplaces. This is a territory forgotten by most.

As we walk, we move through twists of branches that curl from tree stumps, some coming below Arabella's hips with thorns and leaves. They're similar to those in the Darkened Forest, though the trees there are far more varied and full of life.

Pushing past a final low-hanging branch, we find the

cobblestone building. It is demolished, flooring and rubble from the upper stories now tumbled and cracked on the ground.

We venture through the first floor, separating and popping in and out of chambers. It is completely empty. A breeze can be felt on the second floor, and for a moment I wonder if Korine was correct in saying that these grounds are haunted.

When checking the last room that isn't completely torn apart, Arabella and I conclude that the missing Fae do not reside here. We walk through the entrance, accepting the failure of today.

At the bottom of the stairs, I hear the faint sound of a door creaking inside.

"Arabella," I whisper, "do you hear that?"

She climbs back up the stairs, standing at my side. "We don't all have Fae super hearing."

Ignoring her remark, I keep myself from a counter. "I heard a door creak and light footsteps."

We both crouch down, hiding ourselves out of eyesight.

At the sight of footsteps, Arabella pushes herself up and ties her skirt, chasing the Fae inside. I follow behind, sending my shadow after him. It tackles him to the ground, Arabella keeping her foot on the Fae and her heel digging into the creature's back.

"It's the common fae who tried to hit us with a plate," she pants.

He twists his head to hers. "I have a name." His back arches, wiggling under her but falls to no success when she applies more weight onto the foot, the pressure more intense on his back.

"And your name shall be of importance," I acknowledge, "once we need it for your death sentence."

Arabella takes chains from the bag strapped to her back, placing them on his wrists and keeping him from standing. "You can't even deny that you aided in the assassination of King Elliot. King Cassius saw you with Cato."

She brings him to his feet, and I now once again see the Fae that was fueled with such hatred in our first interaction. No longer is he the man in the forest with Cato, but a muscular Fae, with determination to burn the crown to ashes.

Bringing her hands to her waist, Arabella stares him in the eyes. "You were cursing the crown for their little care of the common fae, and yet you, another common fae, knew the disappearances had not truly been caused by the crown."

He steps towards her. "The name's Adrik. And at least I was correct in calling you the prince's whore."

She assaults him with an open palm, the impact of her upward motion cracking his nose and fracturing the bones. Blood drips from his nostrils as he roars in pain, holding his nose with his chained hand.

"I've been wanting to do that forever," she beams, smiling. The adrenaline in her contentment subsides, hand shaking up and down.

Standing between Adrik and myself, she okkars us back to Nexus, handing him to Kabir, who is in the servant's dining area plating his supper.

As the Fae is being taken away, Arabella and I stride to the family dining area, where our food has been prepared for us.

"Oh thank fuck." She exhales once she undoes her bodice, throwing it onto a chair. "Let's eat outside." Picking up both our plates, she walks out the back doors, descending to the grass. "The sun's going down, and it's nice out. That is, unless you don't wanna get your cape-looking mantle or pirate-ass shirt dirty."

After removing the mantle from its chain, I meet her at the

grass by the fountain. We sit next to each other with our plates on our laps, making jests and conversing. She tells me of her day with her friends, and how Grayson and Juliette are now lovers. It is a wonder how they did not know their love was there prior to Damien commenting.

Towards the end of the meal, she reaches into her bag, pulling out a bottle of lasialic and pouring it into two golden chalices. It would have been much more enjoyable, had she taken this out from the start. I stare at her, my thoughts fazed.

Handing me the cup, she takes a sip. "I got the chalices while we were handing off Adrik."

"The chalices are not why I look to you in such a way."

Her eyes shift, processing what I mean. At the moment she understands, her head nods. "*Oh*. I've kept lasialic with me since I took it from your room."

Rummaging through her bag once more, this time with fervor, she pulls out a rolled object, lighting it with the tip of her finger. She inhales, breathing out smoke and repeating it twice over. At her silent offer, holding the object out to me, I decline.

"You don't like valskull?" she questions.

"The herb is similar to how your alcohols do not affect Fae as heavily as our own will."

Shrugging, she takes in another inhale. "Honestly, it barely affected me until I started mixing it with mugwort."

"Perhaps I will try," I say, taking it from her and inhaling it myself. Mugwort gives quite the relaxing high.

Breathing becomes difficult after exhaling. I cough until my flesh feels hot and my skin clammy. Arabella is watching me, laughing as I accept I am nearing my death.

"If this is your first time smoking with valskull *and* mugwort, maybe don't try inhaling a quarter of the joint." She takes another sip of the wine, and upon finishing it, she begins drinking from the glass. As she realizes my staring, she holds the bottle farther from her mouth. "What? I figured we were gonna finish this anyway, and you've seen me naked, so this shouldn't matter."

I attempt to inhale the valskull with redemption in mind, this round, coughing significantly less. While taking a sip from the lasialic, the honey seems more potent with the mixture of the mugwort. She looks at me with pride, giggling at my reaction, while remaining speechless.

She lays herself on the grass, staring at the stars that are slowly coming into view with the night sky. "So, will you ever tell me why you hated me?" Her face turns to mine. "I mean, *why you really hated me.* You took one look at me in the throne room and seemed like you were ready to watch my execution with a front-row seat and popcorn in your hand." She pauses, glancing down to my legs and back at the sky. "Considering I know you didn't like your dad, I can't imagine you were supporting his command."

This is a conversation I have feared. I never anticipated confessing my original aversion. Not when I planned to part ways long ago, or how I hadn't expected to feel so strongly towards her. For so long, I did not know why I resented her so.

Both of us are beyond coherent intoxication. She goes silent, finishing the valskull and watching the stars in contentment. I'm unsure if she wants an honest answer, or if she wants one at all.

I set myself down beside her, joining her gaze at the burning suns. There is nothing but absolute silence between us, which only scares me. "You're everything I hate. Or everything I was meant to."

Her head turns to mine, looking at me with a face that seems to be disappointed.

Unable to look her in the eyes, I turn back towards the incoming glowing moon. "I thought you an abomination the first I saw you, due to your kind being the murder of the Fae. But then I hated you for far worse. You live a life without fear, and for a long while, I had not understood why I couldn't stand the sight of you." I pause. "I know now it stems not from antipathy, but a feeling of captivation."

I hesitate. If I continue, if I tell her everything, I risk her leaving.

Instead, I grab the small device from my pocket and release the jewelry from her ears. The small brush of the earrings can barely be heard as it falls to the grass. She touches her ears, feeling nothing but the hole pierced through her skin.

"You hadn't been afraid of my father. You were frightened, but not of him. You weren't intimidated by me, and that terrified me. Wanting you terrified me." I am too far gone. This rushes out of me, similar to water flowing down a stream. "I had been so afraid, for I want you far more than I have ever craved another."

Arabella shivers, and I brush the side of her cheek with the back of my hand. She shifts her body closer to mine, leaning her head on my shoulder. "If we're confessing things, you should probably know I'm not as violent as I act like I am."

I move my body a bit to look down at her with a lack of credence. Every move takes strenuous effort, and my movements feel slowed.

Rolling her eyes at me, she scoffs. "I know I make threats, but it wasn't until I got here that I would follow through on them." Her arm wraps through mine, intertwining our fingers. "Your father didn't take me seriously when I begged him to let me leave. I wanted you all dead when I was stuck in that cell with nothing but my thoughts to keep me company. But I promised myself when the guards held me down and shoved the earrings into my skin that if you wouldn't let me leave while pleading, I'd become so vicious, so wretched to anyone that tried to harm me, they'd regret it."

This plan, I'm afraid, became effective to the highest degree.

She chuckles a bit, shifting her head and returning it to my shoulder. "I thought you'd pick up on that when I told you different ways to manipulate the common fae. Fear can present itself through things other than violence. You of all people should know that since you twist your words to walk the line between truth and lies."

Her body rises as I study her movements. She pulls grass from the soil, transforming it with her magik into a leather cord before removing the rose ring she often wears and weaving it into the thread.

"Why are you giving me this?" I ask as she wraps the pendant around my neck, allowing it to dangle.

"I have your ring. It's only fair you have mine." She falls to her previous place, mingling our fingers and taking a soothing breath. "But honestly, I didn't think my ring fit the same style as yours, so I made it a necklace." Unsure of my reaction, she adds, "The ring's rose gold mixed with silver, so it shouldn't clash with your jewelry."

Unlatching my hand from hers, I climb on top of her, leaning into her lips, my knees around her body. She grabs me from the back of my head, forcing my weight down on her, and as she rolls her hips, the cloth that restricts my cock feels tighter. This, I can feel.

Both of our bodies slam into the mattress as she okkars us to her room. I kiss her neck as she moans, wrapping her legs around me. This is everything I could have possibly asked for. The two of us with hatred no longer present.

She is breathless, whimpering in curses as my hand pushes the opening of her skirt aside, fingers reaching her clothed cunt. I rip her panties, circling with pressure around her clitoris.

"Gods. *Fuck,*" she moans, digging her nails into my back.

My lips trail uneven kisses up her neck, leading to her ear. "Oh darling, the gods will not answer your prayers, but I guarantee being on your knees for me will grant you what you desire."

Pushing me up, she crawls off the bed, dragging me to the edge. She attempts to pull down my trousers, but when she is unsuccessful on her own, I stand, sliding them off in one swift motion, along with my underwear. The bottoms are thrown to the door, her eyes looking up at me, similar to a Siren luring a man to his death.

I think, perhaps, I would very much like that.

"I recall you once telling me you dream of me." She kisses my inner thighs, halting before the base. "Tell me, my king, what fantasies have you had of me?"

She slides her tongue down my cock, her hand pumping what is unable to fit. I'm allowed no time to respond, only given pleasure while lost from her wicked mouth alone. I take her hand from the length, thrusting into her mouth and holding the back of her head, throbbing at the sensation.

"I've fantasized of you on your knees in front of me. Begging for my cock." I thrust deeper. She gags while tears fall down her face, shooting gratification to my actions. "Telling me you are just as depraved as I am for you. That I am all you desire."

Ripping her from her place, I carry her, dropping her on her bed as I feather my lips down her stomach. My hands grip the fabric that keeps me from her, pulling them down with greed. I kiss her cunt, whirling my tongue around her while curling two fingers into her flesh.

I hitch a leg over my shoulder, gaining more access into her, while she strings curses from her mouth and grips the silk sheets. She stretches her body up slightly to touch my shoulder. My free hand presses her onto the mattress, interlocking our fingers together with hers squeezing tightly.

She whimpers, her breath unsteady as she tightens around my fingers. Nearing her orgasm, I slow. This is much too soon to end our actions. I pull my mouth from her flesh, her hips lifting in response.

"So needy," I chuckle.

"I hate you," she spits in a half-moan.

I flick my tongue while crawling up to her. "You hate your king?" I laugh into her neck. "How blasphemous."

Our skin is bare, her leg lifted in the air, leaving enough space as I push into her.

Arabella's back arches as one arm holds around my neck, another hand in my hair, pulling me closer to her body. She spreads herself, inviting me in. Her hips move upwards, my skin grinding along her clitoris as I make slow, deliberate strokes inside her.

"Hey Bella, I heard you were back and–"

A door opens, and without looking, I know the voice belongs to Esme. At the turn of my head, I see her eyes go wide for a moment before she covers her open mouth and immediately brings the hand to her eyes.

Meanwhile, Arabella's body goes still, attempting to break contact with me.

It does not stop me. My thrusting persists, fucking her mercilessly to where her eyes roll back. To my own disappointment, her hand covers her lips to keep from moaning.

My hand brushes down the side of her body towards her clitoris, appreciating every extra curve of her on its way there. Her fingers grip the strands of my hair, erupting a wince in pleasure.

"Get out!" I yell, unyielding from my returned gaze upon Arabella, who is all too ethereal for me.

"I'm so sorry," my sister apologizes. "I'll talk to you tomorrow." She backs away, eyes still shut and locking the door at her exit.

My lover slaps my arm in frustration as I am undeterred from pushing in and out of her, my fingers now circling her once more. I suck on her breasts harshly, taking her hand from her mouth so that I may hear her. "You were so eager to take me at the ball while all eyes were on us. Why now are you so timid?"

Her fingers return to my hair, pulling me to her lips.

I am hers in every way that matters.

And any way that doesn't.

I still as I feel her nearing her release, placing both hands in hers and lifting them above her head. She opens her mouth for me, my tongue tracing the inside of her lips.

"Please," she whines into me, moving her body to create friction. "Let me come."

Flipping our bodies, now it is she who is over me with her knees pushing into the bed. I pull her onto me, smacking my hand onto her ass, continuing to pump myself deeper into her. "Use me to make yourself come undone." I run my hand through her hair, nipping at her ear. "Take what is yours."

Her lips twitch upwards, eyes as dark as her hair. She holds my shoulders, pushing my length as deep inside her as she can take.

Then, she kisses slowly from my cheekbone to meet my lips, moving down the center of my chest.

A goddess, my demise, whatever one would call her, I would be a fool to let her leave my hold. She holds my hand as she takes me in, rocking up and down, her breasts moving with her actions.

My cock begs for a release. I feel as it twitches inside, hips jerking into her.

She brings her hand lower, twirling in harsh circles until she is coming around my cock. She screams in pleasure, throwing her head back as my hands fly to her waist, thrusting violently as she draws out her high as long as she is able.

As her breathing controls, she collapses her weight onto me, her body fully pressed into my skin. The side of her face falls to the crook of my neck, lightly touching her lips against it.

I continue my actions, pushing hard and fast into her.

"Can't do it," she groans with a strangled breath between the last two words. Her arms push herself up to face me. "Too much."

"You know the agreed-upon word that will cease all actions." Holding her, I halt all motions. "Now, are you going to say it?"

Her eyes narrow, a suggestive smile creeping on her face, sinking her body, molding it with mine. It's a face that forces my body to cling to her so that we may never part.

My hold on her waist tightens, forming a future bruise. I roll us, putting her on her back, her legs wrapping tightly around me.

My hand reaches for the headboard, giving stability to pump myself inside her. "If you recall," I croon, stroking myself deep into her, "this is what you begged for." My hips are nearing the parting of her flesh, my cock buried deep in her. Tears form in the corner of her eyes. "Now you can and will take me, for I am nowhere near finished with you."

"Fuck," she quivers, her breath hot against my neck.

Selfishness be damned.

I bring my hand to her throat, the top of her head rocking into the cushions of the pillows along the headboard.

"You have freedom at your fingertips and yet you stay," I hum. With one hand, I pin her arms up, my other gripping her throat tighter as I suck her hardened nipples, tugging the jewelry towards one side. "You stay for me." I kiss my way back to her parted lips, inviting me in.

Her eyes shut at my words. Freeing her hands, she scratches her nails down my back. I feel as her stomach flexes through the softness, and with the strength of her arms, she drags me into her, arching her back and lifting herself until her lips meet mine. The moans she releases are distracting me just as her cunt takes me in, clamping tightly around my cock while she unravels beneath me.

"Princess, you feel so good around my cock. You were made for me," I profess, moans befalling my lips as I spill my cum into her.

This is not enough. It will never be enough. Being a witch means she lacks the lifespan of a Fae, but I am determined to mark her for as long as she lives.

Grabbing her dagger from the nightstand, I unsheathe it, marveling at the blade. My princess lowers her legs onto the bed and her eyes turn in the other direction. After a moment of silence, she redirects to me, her arms propping up half of her body, arching her eyebrows at me.

"What are you planning on doing with that?" she asks with a nervous laugh in her voice.

She is absolutely breathtaking, laying back while I remain inside her. A smile so light, I scorn myself for every day that I have broken it from her.

I cannot control myself, for within seconds, I crash into her lips, dropping the dagger to cradle her body and head when her arms give out from support. Lowering her into the bed, she giggles as I take the tip of her blade and draw the cold edge down the center of her body.

"Cas?" she whispers. Her hand reaches to mine. "Seriously, what are you planning on doing with that?"

Both my hands hold hers down on each side of her torso. Her hand is so close to the hilt that if she so desired, she could take it from me.

"Say that again," I demand, my voice dropping, mouth twitching.

Her head tilts to the side, lips parting in perplexity. "Huh?"

My body, now impatient, urges me to move inside her. I suck from her neck to her collarbone, assuring all will see. My hips move up, plunging far within her, hitting a spot that causes Arabella to keep tensing her muscles around me. Her body relaxes, legs raised and bent.

I use this in my favor, tracing her own weapon from one arm, along her body, and down the other. She trembles at the touch, eyes wide at me while her breath shakes. It is difficult distinguishing if this is from fear or lust, but as she gazes into my eyes, her teeth biting onto her lip, I find she feels the latter.

Bringing the dagger to her neck, I press the blade against her throat. "Do you get the same disarming feeling as I do when you hold the sharp blade to my throat?" I push into her faster, my head dropping from the arousal. The edge of the weapon drags down her neck, closer to the top of her body. "How humiliated you must feel knowing the roles are reversed."

Her hands shoot to my shoulders, pushing me up from her. "Shut up before I take the dagger and use it on you."

"Oh I'm counting on it, princess," I counter, putting our foreheads together and kissing her hungrily. "Now be my good little whore and take it."

I pull my cock from her, cupping her breast in one hand, licking her nipple with my tongue. The feeling of having her in my arms, vulnerable after so long of denying ourselves, is stronger than any power I have.

"Get on your hands and knees," I command, lifting her body and tossing her onto her stomach.

Abiding, her arms push the pillows aside as she switches positions. I run the weapon down her spine, pausing at the small of her back and lightly pressing the edge into it. She winces, whimpers and curses uttering as she begs for more.

"It's obvious you find as much pleasure in this perverse act as I." Circling the edge along her ass, I sink my teeth into her. "You may not want to admit that you are mine, but this?" I smack my hand brutally onto her ass, the skin turning red. "This is mine."

I dig the dagger into her, carving my initials onto the cheek of the same side that inks her thigh. Blood dripping from the opening, I move my tongue along the drops, licking to where we are one.

"And now I am yours." My cock rams into her. Slick with the mix of our cum, I slide into her with ease. If I were able to spend eternity inside her cunt, I would consider the validity of the gods. But right now, in this moment, she is my god. Blessing me with every prayer I cast into the night.

"Fuck," she cries. "Gonna." She holds back. "Come."

I throw the dagger off the bed, taking her and putting myself on top as she lays on her back.

"Not again," she groans. "What are you doing?"

Chuckling, I push myself into her, rocking my hips at a rhythmic, fast pace. My fingers go to her clitoris, rubbing with pressure. "I would hate to deprive myself of seeing your pretty face as you come."

The taste of her tongue consumes me. It is as besotting as any alcohol or hallucinogen.

She pulls me down, her mouth breathing ruggedly into me. "If you keep me from coming one more time, I will okkar so fast out of this bed, you won't ever have a chance of touching me again." She kisses the tip of my ear, gnawing down onto my shoulder as my thrusts stutter in response.

My hand presses to her lower stomach, deepening the sensation while she tightly convulses around me.

"I think you enjoy this. The unrepentant pain I cause you."

A laugh manages to produce from her as she holds herself from moaning. "That's presumptuous of you."

Rocking deeper, she lets out a sharp gasp, shrieking to any power that be as her orgasm approaches. My hand palms her breasts while my mouth juxtaposes my actions, sucking bruises harshly to every surface area of skin it touches.

I watch as her eyes squeeze, mouth parting as pleasure rips through her. Her whimpers go silent, biting her lip. An attempt to punish me for keeping her from her pleasure.

Gripping her neck tightly, I move my mouth to the peak of her breast, biting softly on her nipple. My fingers reach to her cunt, my lover screaming in overstimulation. "That's it, witchling. Take my cock like the good whore you are."

She surrenders from fighting at last, singing my name in gospel. I kiss her lips, biting the bottom and raising my face to gaze into her eyes.

"Mine," I croon with absolute admiration.

"Yours," she confirms in a light murmur as her eyes behold mine, her face softening.

It is one word I have longed to hear. A sound like air.

"You will destroy me to nothing." I come inside her, our hands locking as she sucks my tongue with her mouth, sending out her heavenly laughs that could grind me to nothing but ash.

She is glowing. The adoration I feel for her aside, she burns with the same fire that runs through the tips of her fingers.

My cum spills from her cunt as I pull my cock from her, readying my departure from her side.

"Wait," she rasps. Her hand reaches for my arm as I am rolling off the right of her bed. I turn back to see her breath staggering, her face filling with fear.

"Stay."

We bathe, washing ourselves from the day and the acts that occurred within her room, allowing the cool breeze of night to enter while we relax in the calming waters.

Crawling back into bed after shutting the windows to keep the rain out, she wraps herself around me, pushing me towards the wall. Our naked bodies press against each other as she lies on her stomach. Her head rests on my chest, and the weight of her leg raises on my thigh while I remain euphoric.

"You have always had control over me, but with what I say next, it can bring me to your feet, doing your every bidding," I speak sweetly into her hair.

She remains unmoved, and for a moment, I believe her to have fallen asleep. Instead, she flattens her hand along my skin. "What do you mean by that?"

After a long breath, I tell her my name in its entirety. Something that gives her so much power over me, I would obey her at once.

"Cas?" she asks when pushing herself to look up at me.

I smile, gazing into her gleaming eyes that once held nothing but hatred for me. "Yes, my violent nemesis?"

She grins at me, her eyes squinting as she lets out a laugh from her nose. "Why are you looking at me like that?"

"I savor your voice when you call me that."

"Has no one called you Cas?"

My face drops from its state. "Not anyone I am particularly fond of, no."

Her eyebrows raise as a gentle giggle escapes her. "Now you're fond of me?"

*Did my confession hours ago mean nothing?* Is she so blindly unaware of what I feel for her?

"Does this come as news when I was unable to distinguish between your vexed feelings about me and soft-spoken clues that suggested otherwise?" I ask as my fingers brush through her hair.

She lays her head back on my chest, drawing shapes onto my skin. I can feel her arm snaking under the pillow above her. "I guess I've been guarded, but you've been hard to understand my entire stay here. Was I supposed to telepathically read your mind to find out you didn't hate me?"

"Gloat if you must, but I would much rather play the fool than grovel at the feet of someone who cannot return the love I hold for them."

Nuzzling her head along me, she presses a kiss onto my chest before drifting off to sleep.

# XXX

## Abrupt Reunions



We wake to frantic banging on my door. I turn behind me, looking at Cassius, who is pulling me tighter into his arms, now covering me in kisses. A silent bargain offering me something if I don't answer. I shake him awake, throwing him his underwear and one of my oversized sweatpants as I wrap a robe around myself.

Answering the door, Kabir stands waiting, a solemn expression clouding his face.

"Kabir? What's going on?" I ask.

His eyes widen, presumably spotting Cassius and offering a suggestive look when his eyes dart back down to me.

I shake my head, whispering, "Not now."

"There's a Magik at the door," he says. "Claims to know Lady Arabella."

Rushing towards the stairs that peer into the foyer, I see someone sitting on the small bench that's pressed against the wall. They're wet and covered in mud. It's entirely possible they've been walking around in the rain the entire night, based on their disheveled posture. The hunch of the Magik's shoulders seems entirely foreign to their body.

It's then that I recognize his clothes. His hands with slight veins that are visible. The unmistakable blond with light waves that fall from his head, which nearly mirrors the shine of the sun.

*Holy shit.*

"Luka?"

"Hi, love."

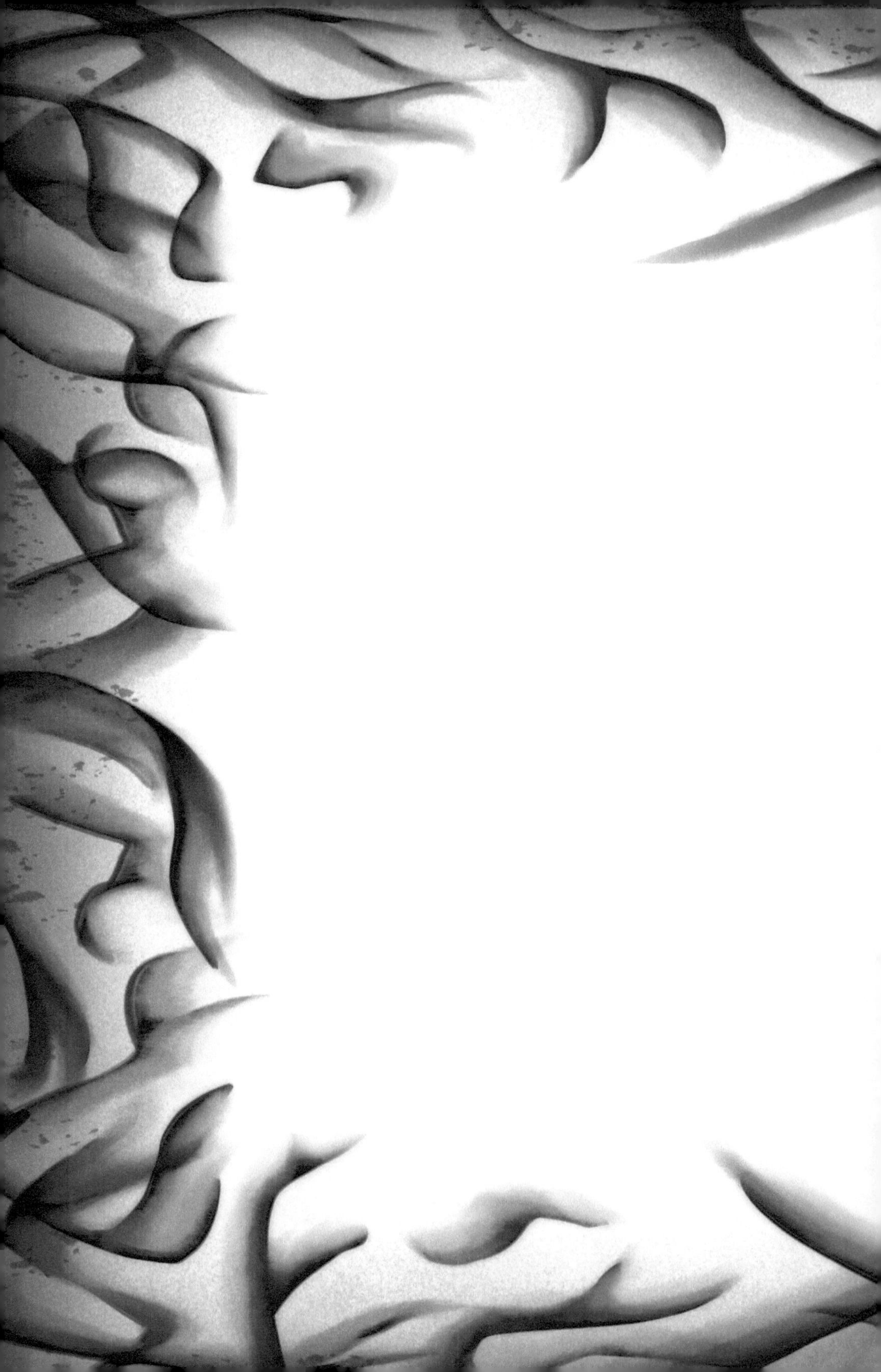

# Part 5
## The Return

# XXXI

## *Broken Hearts and Torn Limbs*

Luka

*Cold air and silver peered into my eyesight when I woke. Everything was hazy, and there was only a small trace of light from the stairs that looked to be fifteen paces from me. Someone I couldn't see stroked my cheek, telling me to sit up. My body was in immense pain. I couldn't remember anything other than a sharp sting running through me.*

*The room was clearly meant to be hidden from the public. There was nothing in it, at least as far as I could tell, other than the stiff table I was placed on, a silver platter that my hand hit when I sat, and a wooden chair that my foot grazed. Everything seemed to slip my mind but one detail.*

*Arabella.*

*I needed to go to her.*

There she is, my girlfriend. The witch I'm so desperate to hold again. I hear her voice before seeing her. She stands at the top of the two-sided curved staircases in a pink robe, her hair completely different.

*How long have I been gone?*

Behind her stands a man with black hair in her gray sweatpants and a bare chest. His ears are pointed, and I take rampant notice when he wraps his arm around her waist. I wonder how quickly it would take to run to her.

"Luka?" Her body goes into shock, shoulders dropping.

I didn't realize how long I missed my name passing through her lips, especially now while another's hands are on her. I shoot her a faint smile. Run my hand through my hair as I gaze at the woman I love. "Hi, love."

Both descend the stairs with the guard who let me into this palace. Wherever I am, *whenever I am*, things have changed beyond my comprehension.

The three of us congregate in an area with couches. It builds next to what the guard said is the throne room. With the urgency the guards have when it comes to escorting both Ari and that man, I can only assume he is their ruler.

The room appears less of a living room area and more a waiting room. I sit on the couch, my girlfriend sitting to my left, as the man who stood behind her prior takes a seat on the couch adjacent to us.

"Who are you and what do you know of Arabella?" the royalty sneers.

Ari says nothing, continuing to stare at me in awe.

"Luka," I respond.

He gives an unamused frown, like my existence is bothersome to him. "Ah yes, you were the lover of Lady Arabella."

*Were? Lady Arabella?* Too many thoughts revolve around in my brain. Urges fester within me to brashly reply to the man, though I keep from doing so.

"You were said to be dead," he remarks in passing, crossing a foot to rest on his knee.

I look at him in perplexity. "Dead? I've been conscious. An absurd dream perhaps, but not dead, I assure you."

My hand is grabbed by Ari. She rubs circles on my palm, and it's enough of a reaction to tell me that he isn't lying. She doesn't think I'm real. I've been dead. Meaning everything I experienced on my way here was not my vivid imagination.

The man watches me, his head pointed askew towards my direction, curling into a suspicious smug look. "If you are truly the Luka of Lady Arabella, surely you would not find trouble in presenting your name."

Ari grips my arm, silently pleading not to speak it. Her worry is odd when a name holds nothing to us. Regardless, I refuse to give it in full.

"Luka Caedos. And what should I call you?"

"King Cassius, though Your Majesty will do." He throws his head back in frustration, following by holding his hands together and leaning forward. "How is it that you are with us?"

Still, Ari hasn't spoken a word.

"I don't know," I admit. He's unsatisfied with my answer, beckoning a guard to him and whispering something into his ear. I'm convinced this is all another long nightmare that I haven't woken up from. But everything is too real, too physical for it to be something in my head. "The last thing I remember was talking to someone on my way to Arabella, and then I woke up with insurmountable pain throughout my body. I was being cared for by someone I presume was Magik."

Suddenly intrigued by my story, the king turns his attention to me, drinking from the chalice given to him. It smells of wine. It's concerning that someone would be drinking so early in the day. His hand waves in the air, and golden, glitter-like magik circles towards me. Ari raises her hand in retaliation, tightening it into a fist. From then, the magik disintegrates into nothing.

I understand too late that these creatures are not Magik, but possibly Fae. We learned of their existence once in my childhood, but any documents of their presence have told me they were supposed to be extinct. They look similar enough to humans, or enough to pass as Magik, if not for the ears that give it away.

"Not that I can recall much from that room, but I was held in an area with no strong lighting, and it's not likely I was held there longer than a day, two at most." I try to recall what I can, but it all feels like a blur. Things are blending together, and now it's impossible for me to distinguish what was a dream and what had been reality. "The next thing I know, someone okkared me into the woods around dawn and told me to continue walking until I found Nexus Palace."

I huff out a breath of displeasure, focused at the mud that now seeps into my clothes. It's filthy. Unprofessional of myself. "I walked through rain and mud, not having a clue where I was going. It wasn't until I saw an open land that I asked a gentleman to direct me towards here. He warned me of the king, which, I suppose, is you, and his witch lover."

Ari releases my hand. Turns away in shame.

The king eyes me. With my low alertness from exhaustion and

how he seems to take nothing with seriousness, I can't predict what he will do next. "Perchance, was there a woman who had sent you here? Possibly speaking of a 'true king'?"

"I'm not sure what brought me back," I reply plainly. My eyes drift to Ari, whose eyes are wandering everywhere, trying to understand the events unfolding. "I would like to have two minutes with my girlfriend before I'm hounded with questions regarding my death that I wasn't aware happened until minutes ago."

Right as the king is about to say something, the guard from before rushes through the doors, panic plastered on his face. "My king, Lady Arabella, there's been an attack at the front of Nexus. I urge you to seek safety."

Ignoring his request, the three of us run to the door, watching as multiple creatures battle, blood spattering everywhere. Ari disappears, and within minutes, she is back, fully clothed in spandex leggings, boots, and a shirt.

*She okkared. But how?* She okkared with ease, but the last I saw her, I would take the two of us. A monumental accomplishment, when I realize it doesn't seem to tire her as it once did.

"Kabir," she yells to the guard. "Need another dagger."

Pulling up garters to her thighs, she catches the sheathed dagger from the guard, tucking it into the empty holster that wraps around her other leg. Her neck carries a weapon of sorts, along with the necklace I gave her on her last birthday.

She and the guard dash outside. In seconds, I lose track of him, watching as Ari drives the knife through the chest of a blue creature with razor-sharp teeth.

Another creature charges towards the palace. Towards me. Ari spots him, blue flames radiating from her fingers. She launches a ball of fire towards it, striking the creature down from its place.

Farther and farther from me she goes, battling with the guards, like a fighter from the stories she reads. She's not using conventional combat skills but instead combines a mixture of her magikal abilities and eagerness to wield a weapon in the way she assumes it is to be held. Some of which I know are incorrect, though it is doing the job of executing them.

Flashes of warriors slaughtering Fae are in every view of my perception. Killing each other with weapons that I've only seen in scholarly books or museums.

A larger Fae nears Ari, but she doesn't notice. I take all the energy I have, focusing in on the creature and stopping her blood circulation until her heart stops beating. She falls to the ground with a large thump, causing Ari to whip around, smiling at me in thanks.

Despite all that is happening, it warms me to view a smile gracing her lips.

I watch in awe as she dodges from a Fae plunging his sword towards her. She sweeps her foot from under him and pushes him into the ground with the other, standing atop him. Stealing the sword from him, she smites it through his throat, keeping him pinned to the ground.

Kabir barrels through multiple Fae, protecting her from the four that approach. He skewers them similarly to meat on a stick.

This, I plan on thanking him for later.

Ari races through the Fae, big and tiny, her hair flowing through the wind as she moves, sliding under those with wings and throwing a necklace around one that flies above her. She brings the short Fae down to the ground, constricting his legs with the necklace and burying his head into the dirt. In the next second, she magiks the separation of his torso from his head, spine ripped apart completely.

Careless and inattentive to my surroundings, I'm pushed to the ground by Ari, an arrow narrowly missing me. She glances at the direction the arrow flew from, locking in with the Fae holding the crossbow. Her skin heats, burning me, jolting me back from her touch.

She straps a dagger to the arrow, tying it together with the string from a Fae's tunic. Her hands twirl from her wrist–the arrow now floating–and sends it back to the assailant. It goes straight through his heart in a clean shot, the point of the blade edged into the tree.

I'm smiling, watching her as she uses her abilities. She's gained so much control over her fire. Over things she's struggled with.

We run towards a fountain, a safe area from others fighting. Many of the smaller Fae, whether Pixies or others I'm unaware the name of, appear less injured than the larger Fae. She stops at the one she stabbed a sword through, grabbing the weapon as we jump behind the fountain, shielded.

Removing the sword from her grip, she hands it to me. "No real time to explain, but Fae are real, and pure iron harms them the most. Go for the heart or for vulnerable areas." She catches her breath, nearly hyperventilating. "Stay here, and stay hidden. I'm assuming you don't have enough in you to fight after being gone so long."

I stare at her, attempting to understand how she picked up on her ability to control her powers so quickly. I'm unsurprised by this, but curious nonetheless.

"What?" she breathes heavily while putting her hair up.

"How?"

Rolling her eyes, she kisses my cheek, preparing to leave and disfigure whatever remains. "I told you, no time to explain."

She takes off towards the last three aggressors, saying something to Kabir before the two fight. They parry from every move against them. Ari holds them in their place as Kabir lunges at them, ending their lives. Guards run to the entrance of the palace towards another with a javelin-like weapon.

They bring him down, ripping his legs from his body. Only, I notice, unlike the others fighting, the being doesn't seem to hold any magikal abilities.

He's a human.

A distraction.

Another Fae pops from the bushes, circling around the palace, and I notice the tower which nears the forest I saw in the morning has an opened door.

I chase after him, sprinting and slicing the sword in the direction of his ankles. He falls to the ground with a yelp. Ready to end his life, something touches my shoulder, and the projection of my name can be heard.

Turning my head, I see Kabir's hand on me as Arabella runs, shouting my name in defiance of what I'm about to do.

When she reaches me, she kneels, heaving in oxygen. I peep to her in curiosity, astonished by her mercy when she has just killed so many.

The Fae tousles, grabbing Arabella's wrist as she attempts to stand from her place. "Gavin, take Adrik back to his cell and see if you can find out how he escaped in the first place."

He nods. We walk back up the steps, her arm around my waist, using me as a crutch from the pain in her leg.

Once inside, I sit again in the foyer with columns that are backlit from the windows behind, halls on both sides just as decorated as the open space, with perfectly picked decor to balance the room. I do my best to grasp everything that's occurring while moans from those still alive can be heard. I let out an empty breath, Ari looking at me, sitting and linking our arms together.

"You hardly fought in that battle," the king fumes, stomping in my direction.

I rise from my position, prepared for another altercation with the short-tempered king. Based on the untouched look of his clothes, he himself did not join in arms. "Pardon me for not being prepared to participate in a war only *days* after being resurrected from the dead. You will have to excuse me for being a bit disheveled."

He draws nearer to me, challenging me where I stand. He looks unsuited to fight.

Easy enough to kill.

It's aggravating to see someone so arrogant, yet throwing blame. "And where were you?" I demand. "I didn't see you on the field protecting your supposed kingdom."

"I am *king*." He smirks, returning to a charming demeanor. "The guards serve to protect me and Lady Arabella."

"Will you two shut the fuck up?" Ari reprimands while remaining seated. Her hands spread from her eyes outward, continuing her movement, wiping down her face. "Fighting among ourselves won't get us anywhere."

The king angles his head to her. "She speaks."

"What did you just say to her?"

"Luka, not now." She gets up from her seat, pulling my arm back as I lean my body towards his.

Something rages inside me. The urge escalates to knock him from where he stands. "No, I would like to know what he could possibly have against you." I shake my arm from Ari's hold, shoving the Fae king into the wall. My forearm against his throat keeps him locked, struggling breaths barely coming through. His balance is off. I should kill him for speaking to Ari like that.

Someone like him does not deserve to be alive.

"Luka!" she shouts. "Let him go. Now."

The command in her voice is unlike anything I have heard her use before. Sure, she has shouted and demanded things of me, but this is for fear of safety.

Fear for *his* safety.

*Why is she protecting him?* I think back to not long ago, when he stood behind her, holding her close. Just as I would have from anything that threatened her. While I was gone, did she fall for another?

It is irrational to expect her to remain loyal to only me in my death. More so unreasonable to hold it against her, being that I wasn't aware of how long I was gone. The thought still freezes me in place.

And I feel like someone has ripped my heart from my body.

I shift my weight away, him clearing his throat and adjusting a sleeping shirt that he now wears.

Ari glares at both of us, eyes wide open. A sharp inhale from her nose carries through the area, lips sucking into her mouth as her eyelids squeeze shut, likely rolling them back. "My boyfriend comes back from the dead, and there's a surprise attack at the entrance of Nexus. We lost two of our own guards, and this is the petty shit you two are gonna focus on?" Stepping in front of me, she stares down the king. "You know as well as I do that this isn't a coincidence. Don't be an idiot. You're smarter than that."

The king ponders this as she backs into me. Upon reflex, my arms go around her body, wrapping her tight. She's right. However, my priorities lie elsewhere at this moment.

He looks between the two of us. "I can see you two have much to discuss." His index finger grazes from under her, raising her chin to meet his gaze. "Very well, Arabella. I have duties I must attend to before the coronation. Your belongings will be brought to the queen's suite on the third floor, and Luka may take the bedchamber's left adjacent." By the end of his sentence, he strolls away with three uniformed guards.

"Are you well?" Kabir asks her.

She sighs, refusing to put on a show of feigned cheeriness. "No, but I'll be fine. Go take care of Cassius. And let me know if you find out how Adrik got out."

The guard walks briskly, speeding towards the direction of the king and fellow guards.

Ari's eyes lay upon me, hollow and exhausted with what's bothering her. "Luka, we needa talk."

"An understatement, to say the least. What is the king's issue with you? I still don't know where we are."

She stops me from going on. "I'll tell you everything. It's a long story, but in summary, Cassius is the High King of Ifaeris, Magiks are entitled assholes who never bothered to tell us our true history, and other creatures beyond Merfolk, Centaurs, and Giants exist." Pausing as if she is done, she quickly adds on. "Oh, and Fae have been kidnapped, so it's up to the king and me to solve it."

"How long have I been gone?"

Her lips thin for several seconds before clicking the roof of her mouth and speaking. "Nearly seven months."

"And how long have you been here?"

"Almost three months."

We take a seat in the waiting room, her bloody clothes dirtying the couches. I sit where the king had previously, facing the witch I love, her face hanging in her hands. I take a hand from her, hold it in mine.

"How did you wind up here? And why were you so keen on protecting the king?"

Truthfully, I hope to hear she is under obligation. I fear her honesty. That she has replaced me, and my return now puts her in a position she is not ready to be in. Call it overprotective, but the king would be wildly off-base if he assumes he will keep her, especially now that I have returned. We've worked too hard on our relationship just for it to be ripped to shreds by my death. I have been given a second chance, and I refuse to waste it.

But in the back of my mind, I know I would let her go if it meant her happiness. I hate myself for that.

Saying nothing is all the same. She can't bring herself to admit it. To utter the words saying that she has grown to care for another.

I kiss the back of her hand, assuring her that I am okay. That I've returned. It's difficult when she often finds herself torn between hatred of herself and insecurity of my love for her.

She takes in a deep breath. She holds herself like air that's been stuck in her lungs for too long and is trying to escape. Stiff. Alert. Too afraid to make a sound if it means causing me discomfort. "You're not going to like it, but I accidentally okkared here and was taken to the king on grounds of trespassing. My options were to be killed on the spot or help them find who was taking the Fae."

The detest I hold for the king now returns, tripling in size. "The king tried to have you killed? Give me a moment, and he will be dead." I shoot up from where I sat, stepping towards the door. "Where is his room, love?"

Laughing, she grabs my arm, pulling me back to her as she hugs me tightly, pressing her head on my chest. With her show of affection, I rest my chin on her head, comforted in her touch.

"No, Cassius didn't try to have me killed." She pushes herself from me, looking up into my eyes. "Well okay, his friend tried, and he didn't do anything to stop her, and honestly, he kinda had his shadow thing hold me down, but I planned on killing him too a few times, so it's fair."

I gaze down at her, staring into her eyes and smirking.

"Also, it's not his fault I got roped into this. It was his dad, who was the king at the time, that demanded my punishment. You know I'm terrible at okkaring." She takes my arm and wraps it around herself as we make our way towards the stairs. "I was late for class and accidentally ended up here. I don't really know how it happened. It just did."

I burst out in laughter, holding onto the wall to keep me stable. Ari's face contorts, both in confusion and defensiveness. "Of course, love. If anyone were to mistakenly loiter onto royal lands, resulting in this outcome, it would be you."

She huffs at me, fighting my arms as I struggle to embrace her in apology.

"I missed you," she surrenders, melting into me.

Kissing her forehead, we ascend the stairs. She leads me up

another floor, this staircase different from the last, with a dark rug covering the steps, marble handrails, and thicker balusters. Though not long has passed, any time apart from her is agony.

"I missed you too."

Once we enter the queen's chamber, I gape at the size of it all. While I own multiple large estates, this is beyond riches even my family has acquired. A chandelier hangs from the ceiling, the bed sitting in the middle of its opposite wall. The wall itself from behind the bed holds a cushion, while fabric drapes highly from all four bedposts.

Along the wall of the entrance sits a fern-shaded sofa with gold rims and a desk with two dark armchairs along the side of the window. There's a large room for clothing alone and an onyx bathtub outside the marbled shower. Though elegant from royalty, much of the decor inside the palace has elements of the earthly nature outside.

"Cassius was being really generous to give me the queen's chamber." Her face quickly grimaces in annoyance. "Even if it's across the whole wing from him."

"I still don't understand why you befriend him."

"He grows on you." She begins stripping and discarding her bloodied clothes in a barrel at the corner of the bathroom while heating up the shower. "Honestly, he reminds me a lot of you. He made adjusting here familiar."

"If I remind you of that paper bag you'd call a personality of his, I'm deeply insulted, love."

She watches me as I remove my muddy garments, motioning for me to throw them into the same barrel before she steps inside the shower.

I observe her every movement as she washes her body. Every instinct in me begs to take her right here. Caress her slowly while the water pours on us. Though, through past experience, we learned that it is not our best idea. Even more, I doubt either of us has the energy it would take to satiate my craving. If I were to have her after months of separation, I want her for hours. Days. In long, hard strokes, only parting my lips from every crevice of her body when I am nearing an unconscious state.

Looking at me with eyes of innocence, she asks, "What are you thinking about?"

"You." I kiss her lips, our bodies pressing together. "Always you."

At the end of our shower, we change into sleepwear, food having been left outside our door by one of the servants. It's then that I recognize that hours have passed, and it is well past midday.

Ari steps from the bathroom in nothing but boxer briefs and a sports bra. She throws me one of my shirts that she kept at her house, alongside underwear a servant sent to me.

"Cassius hasn't been crowned king yet?" I wonder, shoving a piece of meat into my mouth as we eat at one of the tables in the room.

She shakes her head. "I mean he's king and all, but the official coronation has to happen on the day of a full moon." Taking pasta from my plate, she bites, eating it after she swallows a portion of her salad. "Something about cycle endings and new beginnings."

"Would it not be more logical to crown him on the new moon then?"

"Not my place to question their ancient traditions."

Silence passes between us for minutes. We have long finished our meal, leaving it on the cart outside the door to be brought down by the servants later.

"So you're dating a king now," I say in hopes she'll shut down the implication.

Her face turns to me, eyebrows knitted in an attempt to observe my true feelings on the matter. "I'm dating you." I smile at her, and she realizes even if this is the answer I wanted, it's not all. "But do you want the honest answer?"

"Well I would prefer not to be lied to, but I fear the truth may be just as painful." I prepare myself for what's to come. To hear her explicitly tell me that she wants him, possibly loves him.

She sighs out, breathing in before saying, "I don't exactly know what we are. We've had sex, and I like him, but you being here complicates things... a lot."

I should appreciate her honesty. After all, it's I who asked for it. She's free to do as she chooses, and I'd never want to attempt controlling her. But right now, I can only think of marking her.

"For you, it was half a year of my absence, but for me, it's been as if no time has passed. If I were able, I would have broken anything in your eyesight to feel my presence."

Her lips press to mine, and I savor her taste, captivated by every second we were apart.

"Well you're here now, and I can make up for every day I missed you," she hums, grinning.

"You missed me? That's adorable," I taunt, brushing the hair from her face and cupping her cheeks.

Both of her eyebrows raise, prompting a way to bait me. "Yeah, 'cause I totally wasn't gonna miss the love of my life who died coming to see me."

We lie together, talking for hours. She brings me up to speed on the things I've missed with our friends, as well as everything she and the king have learned in terms of the disappearances of Fae.

"I missed you." I kiss her lightly at her temple, down her neck. "Tell me again that you missed me."

She pulls herself up to my lips, kissing me and stealing all the air from my lungs. "I never wanted to lose you in the first place."

"I would understand if you still want to be with him, intimately or romantically. My presence is a shock to you, and I know you may need time."

Laying her head on the pillow, she waits for me to lean my body against hers. "I love you, mahal."

*Mahal.* The word in Tagalog she uses to mean "my beloved".

A long time passes before I realize she's fallen asleep in my arms. I smile to no one else but myself, pulling her in closer and feeling at peace for the first time in what's now been months. I would slaughter every last living creature that roamed the universe if it meant we would remain together. Happy. Considering the events of today, it's entirely possible that this is what would have to be done.

# XXXII

## *Desperation*

Cassius

I hadn't told an untruth. There are indeed preparations that need to be done before my coronation. Whether or not I am the sole one to carry them out is a different subject of importance.

Esme and Cel asked to plan the ceremony, only coming to me for pertinent questions, such as color schemes and a guest list. Though the whole of Ifaeris is invited to join in the revel after the crowning, it had been decided the coronation itself to be more intimate. With the last king killed in the very throne room I am to be crowned in, we deem it best to make the coronation exclusive to family and those I invite.

The tailors go through endless questions about what I will wear, ultimately deciding on leaving that talk to my sisters. This is not the best way to fill my time, though I'd sooner choose this over the rampant thoughts of Arabella leaving Ifaeris with Luka.

Why would she choose to remain here with me while fate has granted her another chance with the sorcerer she longs for?

*She was never mine to keep. Not truly.*

Laying on my bed, I fill myself with wine and Etherfruite, awaiting an answer. Perhaps the silence of my chamber will communicate with me if the alcohol does not put me to sleep first.

Without knocking, my family enters my room, spreading themselves out as if this is their room to roam freely.

"Out," I grumble. "Away with you all."

Protesting is useless. Not one Fae in this house understands privacy. Montgomery shuts the door before dropping himself on the floor next to his twin.

"Why have you all gathered in my room?" I question with the intention that they will leave at my words. "Has Adonis killed another member of our family in my absence?"

Cel smacks me from behind my head. "No, you insensitive ass. Can't we check if you're okay?"

Unintentionally grinning, I take another swig from the bottle. "You have never shown concern for my problems before."

"That was before you were king," Maude points out.

Atticus takes the lasialic from me, and I hear him emptying it into the sink from the other room. A waste of fine wine, truly. "We heard about the return of Arabella's lover. The one she fell for in the Human Lands. How are you handling it? Should we be concerned that you said something so terrible to her?"

I let out a chuckling breath. My brother is in a rightful position to ask that, my past being taken into consideration. "I did no such thing." My voice is hoarse. "I fear I may have done something worse."

"Oh spirits, Cassius," Esme groans. "What worse could you have done that hurts her more than before?"

My chest caves in on itself at the thought of Arabella now with Luka. Perhaps right now she is planning on packing her belongings, readying her leave back to the mortals she is so fond of. "I left her alone with him. It is but a matter of time before they leave the lands."

My siblings' faces all soften, ridding their taunting and mockery they must have prepared.

"Don't be so melodramatic," Xavier berates. "Just because you left her alone with him, doesn't mean she's going to leave. Stop feeling sorry for yourself and get up."

Before I have a chance to argue, Montgomery too joins in. "You trust her. Have some faith she'll do the same."

Their efforts are valiant, yet I find myself strangely uncomfortable. "Your attempt at empathizing aside, why would you all come to my support, save the content for ridiculing me in the future?"

The air in the room shifts.

Maude sits next to me, throwing her arm around me and giving me a hug at my side. "Despite us not being kinder to you before, you deserve love." She looks at me and sends a consoling grin. "Besides, you were absolutely unbearable prior to Arabella's presence in our lives."

"Don't distance yourself because you're too cowardly to tell her you want her to stay," Cel says.

Esme tousles my hair. "No one has ever seen you this way. Do not remain idle and hope that she will choose you for your expert ability to avert her at all costs."

I roam around the fictional library, not entirely sure of what I am looking for. In the furthest depths of my mind, I know Arabella has often found herself in this room specifically. It's filled with romance novels and books that transport her into different worlds. Very often I have watched as she became encapsulated by a book. Many times, she lost herself when her attention was required most.

Footsteps creep from behind me. Arabella is never one to make light of herself if she wants to be acknowledged.

Turning around, I find my witch leaning along a bookcase.

"You," I mutter.

"Yes, me," she voices in a light manner, stepping towards me. "Or were you expecting another one of your lovers?"

Perhaps I have fooled myself into believing she would be here. Even without searching for her directly, I know her essence fills this room. This is the place she loves most when inside the palace.

We sit silently at one of the tables as I continue drinking the contraceptive tea I take monthly. It tastes of lychee and pomegranate.

"I will never understand your all-consumed fascination for these mortal tales," I mock, tossing one she recently returned. Fae tales are far superior in terms of epics. Most mortal stories base themselves after us.

She laughs, half rolling her eyes. "Don't act like I haven't caught you reading some human works. Besides, what do you have against those authors anyway?"

"I despise humans. Nearly all Fae do."

"You know, I was joking before about not tricking a human into their death." She watches me as if waiting for me to speak, and when

I do not, her eyebrows twist. "So that isn't just some piece of lore they had made up to scare children?"

"Humans would be blindingly overjoyed to take advantage of their abilities, if they had the power that we do."

Her mouth opens, nothing coming out as she formulates a response. "You just described any living being ever who misuses their power. Just because humans have their faults, is it any different from Fae, Magiks, or any other creature?"

When I say nothing, she crosses her leg over the other, creating a beat with her fists. "I get why you reacted the way you did."

Surely she does not. If she were aware I was selfish and praying for the downfall of Luka's return, she'd think me as appalling as her pretenses from our first meeting.

"Do you now?"

"You wanted me to clear things up with Luka," she admits. "I came here to tell you that we should focus on why he was brought back. It's probably tied to Adonis."

"My father's spawn, ever the devil."

"And you're included in that bracket," she quips out in a small chuckle.

I stick my middle finger at her, mimicking a distasteful gesture I have seen her do many times with her friends.

She laughs harder, surprised and responsive. "Did you just flip me off?"

"An unkind thing I have learned from you," I answer with a smirk.

Moved towards her seat, I bend down, holding her face in my hand. Her cheeks warm brightly with a blush. Pressing my lips to hers, she lets out a gasp, wrapping her arms around me, bringing me closer.

"Don't leave," I say, but it is more of a plea. "Stay with me until you tire of my presence. Even then, remain with me."

She sighs out of her nose, her breath shaky. "I care about both of you, but this is something I need to sort out on my own. Our first priority is finding Adonis."

Slipping from my hands, she leaves the room. In the thoughts of my own, I am troubled by the fact that perhaps she is correct in her priorities.

# XXXIII
## *All for One*

Arabella

Why is Luka so understanding? More important things are happening, but I'm worried about my feelings for the king and my boyfriend who's been dead. How much more self-involved could I be? Even now, Luka sleeps beside me, patient and willing to do what it takes to help solve the missing Fae.

While I'm sure he has his own motives, it terrifies me to know that he's willing to stick with me through this. He sees the care I have for the Fae and expressed that I could split my time between here and with him if I choose. I really don't know how someone like him exists.

Spending days with him, telling him of everything we learned, and him chiming in with his own ideas, made me think over the role I play for the rebellion. I'm now a pawn in their sick little chess game to sacrifice if it means the end of the Disaris ruling.

I slip from the bed, throwing on shorts and grabbing breakfast to bring back to the room. As Luka tosses and turns in bed, murmuring something about where he is and why he's in pain, I eat discreetly. The explanation, I assume, is his subconscious bringing him back to when he was reanimated into life. It's something I've asked about, but whenever he's awake, he can't remember anything. We tried using magik to go through his memories, but that's resulted in nothing as well.

Unable to calm my nerves, I pace back and forth around the room, thinking through every conversation, questioning, and word I've heard from the common fae. I can only wonder how they learned so much about me without owning technology.

*Have they gone into the Human Lands? Followed me when I traveled back to meet with my friends?* All are likely options, though if any came across my Magik friends, I know they would have told me. Nothing adds up, and I'll need to understand it all as soon as I can. If it's possible to bring back Luka, how soon will it be before he's taken from the world again?

That question is what haunts me more than anything.

Luka wakes. Frantic. Moving his arm around the bed in search of me. His eyes bolt open, darting his eyes around the room and only stilling once he sees my face.

As I walk to the bed to sit with him, I see beads of sweat on his forehead. He's breathing, smiling widely as he takes me into his arms. I hold his hand, and he brings the back of mine to brush against his cheek, kissing it as he lowers it to his lips.

"Morning," I giggle.

He rubs his eyes, lips pressing into my cheek. "Is it morning?"

"The sun blazing through when I opened the curtains was the

first sign, yeah. But I didn't expect you to continue sleeping this long, considering you've been asleep for months."

Looking at me in suggestion, his brows shoot up. "And by asleep, you mean dead."

I shrug with a grin, walking to my closet to change into clothes for today. "Is death not just the last sleep we have?"

While putting a shirt over my head, one that makes my wide frame look smaller, I feel Luka's arms wrap around me, holding me tight, his breath warm against my neck. He spins me around, leaning into me. His kiss lingers, lips peppering all over my face, to my neck, and finally my chest as I giggle through each one.

"What do you have planned for us today?" he asks.

"Well, not much can be done since Cassius has meetings with the lower courts' rulers. Still not sure why I'm not invited to that, but too late now, I guess. You've had enough time confined in this room, so I'm having Kabir give you a more thorough tour of the lands."

As I magik on makeup and finish clothing myself, I can tell from Luka's face that he's uncomfortable. He sits on the edge of the bathtub, arms crossed and frowning. "Do you have responsibilities that require your undivided attention? I can easily be of assistance if this is time-sensitive."

I search my closet for clothing he can wear, but all I can find are his washed clothes from days ago. "I have to talk to the family." It's not a lie, but it's not the full truth. And I hate lying to him. I throw him his clothes, which he reluctantly puts on. "Ask Kabir to take you into Mindae to the marketplace. They have nice clothing there, and I'm sure you'll find something."

Begrudgingly accepting, he kisses me one more time before he exits. "If you're going to kiss him again, just know I will kiss you harder. You may be free to experiment, but know my heart is yours."

Shivers continuously run through my body until I meet Xavier, Monty, and Celeste by Lake Mindae. It eats me from the inside out that I sent Luka off because I need time away from both him and Cassius. My mind is so unclear, and I have to refocus on finding Adonis.

"You're being more pensive than usual. It's concerning," Celeste says while nudging me.

Their words shake me from my thoughts. I take another bite into the cracker from the charcuterie board. "Sorry, a lot on my mind, I guess."

"I think she's distracted from two men throwing themselves at her," Xavier jokes.

"Like you would know what that's like, Xay," his brother taunts.

They wrestle in the grass, pushing and shoving each other deeper into the ground, towards the water. Those two are dumb as hell sometimes. I don't understand how they can be so grown but act no different than two children fighting over petty squabbles.

At this point, Celeste rolls their eyes, now facing me. They hand me a small piece of bread with honey and cheese on it. "You're feeling guilty about something. I can feel your energy. If you want me to eradicate it, you know I have the ability to manipulate emotions."

"No, it's fine." I smile. "Thank you though. I just feel guilty about all of this."

"What is there to feel guilty about? You have no control over another's actions, let alone being forced here or your lover returning."

Though they have a point, it doesn't do much to ease my conscience. So many things are out of my control, but it doesn't ever stop me from being in a constant state of anxiousness. "There's just so much going on. Luka's back. And while I'm ecstatic about that, I feel ashamed I'm worrying about what to do with him and Cas, when my first priority should be helping find Adonis. We're no closer to finding him now than we were before."

Waiting for them to respond, I feel the knot in my chest slowly untangle. Celeste offers me an apologetic look, indicating they've toned down my emotions with their Elemental ability. "You shouldn't feel responsible for things beyond your power. And while you have multiple worries, it doesn't mean you aren't allowed to fret over one thing while also having sympathy for others who have it worse. The world isn't so black and white."

Their words are a sense of comfort to me. Every waking moment of my existence is thinking in extremities, and even though I know that logically my thoughts are irrational, hearing other people reassure me always helps. The brothers stop fighting, joining us again but still throwing food at the other. What falls into the grass is now being eaten by small creatures that take fast as they go.

"Still worried about the whole Cassius versus Luka thing?" Monty questions.

I nod. "What do you think I should do?"

All of their faces contain different expressions. Celeste's face pales sheepishly, Xavier has a look of insinuation, wiggling his eyebrows, and Monty's lips thin.

Monty is the first to speak, starting when no one else does. "It would be wrong to tell you to stay with Cassius without admitting our bias. Regardless if he was callous to you, I'd much rather you stay here than have him revert to the Fae he once was."

Xavier groans. "Let her have both. Fuck it and have a three-way."

I snort, choking on the liquid, getting some on my skirt. The water that's in my mouth suddenly dribbles out a bit at his comment. "That's not what a three-way is, Xavier."

"Fine. Who cares?" He throws his arms up. "Why force yourself to take on this pressure when you know they both want you?"

After dinner, I enter the queen's chamber and find a focused Luka reading a historical book of the lands. It's one that mainly divulges the history against Magiks, the war, and how we had gone into isolation from the other creatures in existence.

"Interesting read?" I say, pulling his focus to me.

He closes the book, moving to the bags of clothes he got today and begins folding them on the bed. "You weren't making light when you said Magiks had not taught this."

There are about three other books pulled from the Fae archives on the desk. Sometimes I worry that he'll never allow himself to do things for his own fun or self-pleasure, rather than assuming all his time must go towards a more academic or professional goal.

"You do anything with Kabir today besides shop and tour Mindae?"

His face hardens, scowling at me. "He spoke of your stay in Phantom Tower and the tracker you were forced to wear. Why did you keep this from me?"

"It wasn't important," I brush away, knowing it would end in an argument. I steal the clothes from his hands, taking his outlet, which keeps him from asking what he wants to know. "What's actually on your mind?"

"The Fae you told me to spare, why was he important?"

Shaken by the question, I think on how to best explain it without

Luka jumping to anger. It wouldn't be with me, but it would stir up more questions of the things I've left out in detail. "Cassius and I encountered him months ago, and recently, we found him again when searching through their meeting place. He somehow escaped the cells, and we haven't questioned him yet."

"Then we do it together," he says. "The three of us. I was brought back the same day that he escaped. I'd be an idiot to think that you and Cassius hadn't discussed them being linked already. You asked that I stay and help you. I'd like to know just how this man relates to me being at your side right now, love."

His request is fair. Maybe having him with us can be beneficial. I weigh out the options, mulling it over in my head, settling on nodding at him as confirmation.

"Can we tell anyone I'm back? Or at least my mother?" he asks immediately after my nod.

The fabric drops from my hold. I sit with him on the bed, leaning my head on his shoulder. "I don't wanna tell anyone yet. If something happens, and you..." I choke on my words, at the sting in my throat. "If you don't get to live very long, I don't wanna give them hope and have it taken from them."

The confession is a harsh truth that I also have trouble facing. I've suppressed the thought whenever it's appeared in my head. It pains me to think of it, but it's harder saying the words aloud.

Luka gives a light smile of understanding before going into the shower, beckoning for me to join him.

It hits like a punch that's knocking clouds of air out of me. I realize now just how much Luka's return holds an effect on me, or at least now I'm finally willing to admit this to myself. He's my weakness, and I would've dropped anything to be with him again.

It's too bad whoever brought him back didn't account for my ambition holding more power over my emotions. Especially when my decisions are now fueled by the determination to keep Luka alive.

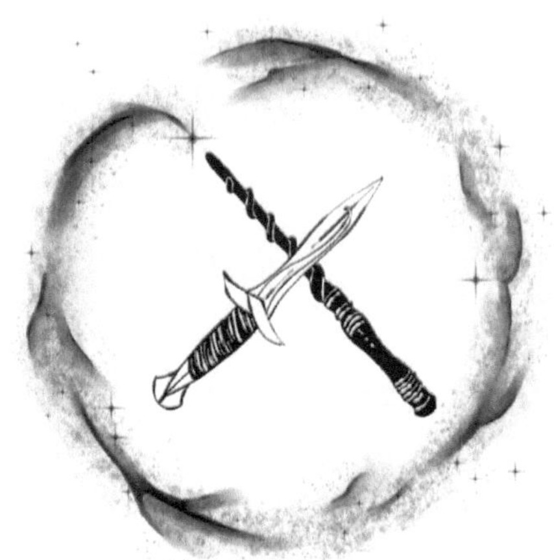

# XXXIV

## Two for Justice, Four for Fair

Luka

Being twenty-two, resurrected from the dead, and working with my girlfriend's interest of a Fae king is not something I ever planned on for my life, but neither, I suppose, was being killed. The prisons, though not excruciatingly filthy, are still no place fit to walk through. The knowledge that Arabella was forced to occupy a space here burns through me.

She holds my hand as Kabir leads the four of us into a confined cell room, the door built from iron.

"Remember, there's two main pieces of information we need to extract from him." Ari opens the door, letting the High King in. Whispering to herself, she walks in after me. "We'll get three if we're lucky."

There is nothing in the room other than a table and four chairs.

Three are sat together on one side, the Fae strapped to the one on the other.

"Hello, Adrik," Cassius greets pleasantly.

The creature only grimaces at him, remaining still in the chair. "Your Majesty." He looks at Ari, myself, then back to the king. "Have you come to take my life today?"

I look to Ari, who is sarcastically smiling, basking in the wry comment. "Not if you feel like answering our questions."

He scoffs. Grumbles out, "You already have me in iron chains. It is not as if I have the capability to escape."

Something leaves the palm of the king's hands. In two seconds, a shadowed silhouette figure stands over Adrik, behind him and ready to strike. "But you have already escaped, have you not? Or am I to believe Luka nearly killed a figment of collected imagination?"

Cassius' apathetic nature is warranted. Rather than the previous attitude I saw him in, now he holds the posture of a leader. I stew silently, wondering over which is his real form.

Ari gives a subtle nod, telling me to trust him. "Tell us how you escaped, and maybe we'll be a bit more generous with your punishment."

Her words are just as hardened as the king's. I have grown accustomed to her angry threats, her quick tongue and untamed anger, but her level-headed composure grows more stilling than anything she's ever said.

Adrik goes stiff, finding the truth in her words. "I escaped when my king had sired me to do so."

"How did he do that?" I demand.

Attention from all turns to me. Neither the king nor Ari expected me to speak.

"You claim to know the intentions behind our cause, yet know nothing of the power our king holds." Adrik's posture turns vain, offering a lazy grin with his teeth browning. "He cannot be killed. Nor will he be."

His hand reaches towards Ari's, nails dragging in lazy circles, attempting to close the grip on her. She winces away, quickly pounding a fist on his, a fever radiating from her body.

The king looks at him in curiosity, fixing a look of amusement. "You speak of him not being able to be killed. Was it he who murdered our father?"

"Our?" Adrik's face drops, mouth gaping.

"It seems you were unaware," Cassius muses. "Let me be the first to present you with the information that your 'true king' is a member of the Disaris family. Any power that he has comes strictly from the Spiritus bloodline."

Ari heeds his words, carefully formulating how to use the Fae's surprise against him. "I'll ask again, now that you're aware of who you serve. How did you escape?"

"I cannot explain how he did it, but he could move through walls, blending in with the shadows and appearing in my cell before okkaring us out the other side of the iron door." Adrik cowers, swallowing down a gulp of uncertainty.

The king and Ari look at each other, Ari whispering, "That must've been how he killed your father. He snuck through the shadows. It's why there was no trace of magik in or out of the room."

We turn ourselves back towards the Fae, angry with all that is going on.

"I propose that you speak on all you know, now that you have been made aware of the parentage of your leader." Cassius struts to Adrik's side.

He sneers at the comment, reluctant to reveal more, despite what he has been told. "What more do you need to know?"

"You seem to have escaped from the hold of the Stone of Elestial. How?" Arabella separates her legs, leaning towards the table. She flicks her fingers, and in an instant, Adrik's chains tighten.

His face weakens, contorts inward. Nothing but mindless thoughts written in his expression. "I don't understand."

The Fae's answers are an equivocation for something deeper. A partial truth, but not a total lie.

"The stone Cato held towards you. How did you free yourself from its power?" Ari asks, repeating herself.

He looks at her, slipping his hand on hers. "I heard a voice guaranteeing I would unite with my family. That was all the stone had said."

Tired of his non-detailed responses, I take the dagger strapped to Ari's thigh and stab it through Adrik's left hand. He howls in pain as I slowly cut four fingers from his right. Bleeds heavily until Ari holds her hand up, pausing the flow and keeping him from death.

*Losing a few fingers won't kill him.*

Adrik looks at me in rage, but more importantly, fear. I smile, keeping the blade etched through his flesh. I don't want to stop. Instead, I want to continue until he's dead. Beat him bloody for the things he and others have done to Arabella. If I could kill him and anyone involved, there would be no next opportunity to harm her.

"One finger for every time you have touched Arabella without her consent. And an extra two for calling her a whore after throwing a plate at her."

The king peers at me, wide-eyed for a moment, revealing his silent thoughts before returning to his disposition.

Adrik pleads with them, fully aware that his cause will end in nothing more than bloodshed.

"Shall we debase your ego further? How you watched innocent families be torn apart," Cassius gibes, striking silence into the Fae. "Blaming us for disappearances while attending meetings and seeing the people you claimed to care for."

"When is your next meeting?" Ari demands.

He spits on the ground next to her. "I'd rather die than surrender myself to your corrupt ruling. I see now that you're just as immoral as any. Let these lands burn to the ground."

His laughter sounds maniacal. Hysterical.

"We were already made aware you meet on Thursdays," I comment. "When is your next meeting?"

Continuing to groan in agony, he watches me as if he has the upper hand. "You're just a puppet. Dooming your own fate by trusting your life in the hands of destruction. Leave while you remain alive."

A foot flies into the air. Knocks Adrik to the ground, the seat that holds him going too. Ari stands, picking him up by his shirt and lifting him back upright with magik. She holds him close, her face close to his. "When was your last meeting, you piece of shit?"

"Kill me, witchling."

She releases him, looking at the two of us. "Let's go. We can find someone else to help us."

"I told you that your mercy was too kind," I say.

Arabella turns to exit, but halfway through her movement,

Adrik grabs her by her waist, spinning her in his direction. "Careful of him witc–"

In a flash, blood spurts from his throat, the king holding Ari's dagger in his hands without remorse for his actions. She blinks a few times, stunned at what he just committed.

The Fae's lips quirk, wiping the blood on Adrik's tunic, blending with the clothes he already wears. "You detest touch, and Luka had already cut off fingers as a warning." He hands the dagger back to her as she stares at him in aghast. "Come, Dragon. Let us three return to the meeting spot of the rebellion."

"Dragon?" I look at her in amusement.

Shaking her head, she sighs with defeat. "Don't ask."

As her steps part her from my side, I stand in place, laughing to myself.

I definitely intend on asking.

After changing from his clothing, the king okkars the three of us towards the edge of land. We stand outside a broken-down ruin. It's torn apart, stone and rubble everywhere, while a stained window is shattered. Plants are growing from the cracks, and a half-standing statue is on the verge of crumbling completely.

Before our departure, Ari had explained this is the meeting point of those against the crown and where they found Adrik prior. She told me of the missing Fae, though none reside within these ruins, with only meetings being held here.

"Why have we returned here when it is neither Thursday nor night?" I question the two of them.

Ari turns over rocks on the ground, searching for something. "We needa see if there's anything at all that was left behind from the last gathering. A paper, personal item, something that could clue us in."

I begin searching–nothing of importance being found–when from the corner of my eye, I spot a young boy, skin the same shade as clovers, observing us. He has to be no older than five, possibly eight. I have no idea on the correct sizing a child should be. When he sees me looking back at him, he runs from behind the tree. I speed down the steps, following him with Ari and the Fae king behind.

Catching up to the boy, I hold him, picking him up as he kicks and flails his body in my arms, forcing me to set him down. A child of his size should not be as strong as he is, but he should also be smarter than to attempt fighting someone much larger than him.

The king narrows his eyes, holding the Goblin's face between a hand. "You watched us from the last time we were here. Who do you serve?"

"Cas, he's just a kid," Ari berates. She turns to the boy, rubbing his back while he sniffles and wails. "Hey, it's okay. What's going on? Were you spying on us?"

The child shakes his head, reaching his arms up for Ari to carry him. She looks at him hesitantly for a moment before carrying him in her arms and rocking to calm him.

At the stop of his crying, she sets him down on the steps while he grips her finger in his hand. "You're the king," he says, pointing at Cassius.

"Yes faeling, I am."

The child attempts to breathe through his nose, only for it to be blocked and sounding like an animal. "I'm not spying. Promise."

Then, do I remember that not all children are raised the same that I had been. I've never grown up around families that have children much younger than myself. I'm reminded just how innocent a child is. They know nothing of the harsh ways of the world.

Cassius bends down to the boy, attempting to make eye contact. "Who ordered you to watch us?"

He hides his face behind Ari's arm, tears starting to well. I sit beside him, patting his head, his lips quivering.

"King Cassius won't hurt you," I assure him. "He will protect you with whatever you have to say."

I'm blatantly lying to the child. I don't know the Fae well enough to confirm what I've said, and being that he sliced the throat of a Fae not one hour ago, I may be manipulating the child towards disaster.

Eventually, he relaxes enough to put his head on my arm, looking at the king. "I saw you here last time. I wanted to ask if you knew where my mother was, but I was scared."

He shies away from all but Ari, giggling when she goes to tickle him.

"Your mother?" I ask.

Nodding his head, he jumps from where he sat. "She was being weird, and I followed her here at night after father had put me to bed. He never knew I was gone."

Ari smiles at him. "You're so clever, aren't you..." she draws out to get his name.

"Arwan," he says confidently, standing with a grin on his face.

"Well Arwan, why don't you tell the king what you saw when you followed her," I say. I try to be gentle with the child, but within the past year, the only young children I have been around for longer than twenty minutes have been Ari's family.

Arwan looks to Ari for guidance. As she nods her head, encouraging him to speak, he speaks of what he knows.

"Mother would always leave Thursdays. I followed her here and hid until she came out, but it was past bedtime." He looks at us as if we'll reprimand him for staying out after his father put him to bed. "One time, a few weeks after my uncle disappeared, I fell asleep, and when I woke up, it was bright and the sun was out. When I ran home, father yelled."

"He was probably worried about you," Ari says in a nurturing tone.

He shakes his head. "No, he said mother had gone missing. I think it was my fault for falling asleep."

"Do you recall a stone when you followed your mother?" Cassius asks.

"I don't think so. But I memorized when everyone would come here. One day I want to ask if they know where my mother is."

Ari looks up from Arwan to the Fae king. "Do you think you could tell us when the next meeting is?"

Smiling, he runs to a rock behind the tree he hid behind. "I write it down whenever they meet! They'll be here tomorrow night. After dinner."

"Thank you, Arwan. I will make sure to find your mother," Cassius says, looking at him with a promise.

There is a possibility my original judgment on him was flawed. Skewed towards hatred, albeit from jealousy. It's my emotions that drove me here.

"She's not a Goblin like me though!" the child says urgently. "Can you remember that when you find her?"

The king nods, and Arwan skips away, happiness beaming through.

As he leaves, I think about what was said. His mother was

attending meetings until his uncle had disappeared. Ari said that the Fae who had the stone used on them only happened when they threatened to leave and expose the truth to the crown. Another reasoning the stone had been used was if a Fae needed extra convincing.

Those attending meetings may have had different reasons for attending, but their continuation to show up is rooted in the same issue. This means that the boy's mother also took issue with the crown and wished to dismantle the monarchy. The mother must have been exposed to the child's uncle's appearance and realized that the same people who are holding the missing Fae are the same ones that tempted angry common fae to join their cause. People's desires and wants often change. With the stone's lure of control, I realize that the object is what keeps them stagnant and remaining with Adonis. It's also what will cause their death in the end.

"Luka. What did you figure out?" Ari asks, tapping the sides of my arm.

"I may have uncovered what broke the Fae from the hold of the Stone of Elestial."

The king arches an eyebrow at me, waiting for a response.

"Many of the Fae joined the rebellion because they wanted to rebel against the king who had taken their family, right?"

"*Mm-hmm*," Ari confirms.

I proceed forward on my rant. "Some had the stone used on them because they threatened to inform the crown as well, right?"

"Yes," Cassius answers. "Get on with it."

"Well for some, the stone may have been used to hypnotize them after seeing the missing loved ones, but for others, it could mean breaking free from the hold."

Ari's eyes roam different areas around our view while standing in place. "What do you mean?"

"Think about it." I grab her arm, gripping it firmly with strength. "What do you want right now?"

She shakes her arms, attempting to loosen her wrist from my hand. "I want you to let go of me."

When I do, I draw myself closer to her, holding my fingers to her cheek.

I want her.

Here. In her bed. Anywhere I can.

"What do you want now, Blossom?"

"I want you to stop being confusing and tell me where you're going with this," she barks with irritation.

"That there is my point, love. While the stone promises to grant our greatest desires, many of the Fae who had the stone used on them had the wish to see their family again. Wants change. Desires change. Meaning, if the life that was promised is no longer of issue with the Fae, it makes breaking free from its power easier."

Both are taken aback by my discovery. A breath leaves Ari, impressed and smiling at what I just said. What is not spoken from the king earns a glimmering grin.

"You ought to have been here sooner," he praises.

"So now what?" Ari asks. "I'll go to the meeting tomorrow and report back what I find?"

Simultaneously, the king and I both shout at her in response.

"NO."

"You're not going," the Fae tells her.

An eyebrow shoots up, provoked. "'You're not going' as in, you won't let me? What kinda bullshit is that? Did you suddenly forget that I've killed multiple Fae by now?"

"Do not believe for a second I forget your ability to protect yourself," he laughs.

I find myself siding with him in full agreement. "I agree with the king." Both look to me in surprise. "Knowing you are able to fight and letting you walk into the meeting place of the enemy without protection is different. Your safety must be prioritized."

Her mouth opens to argue, but the Fae stops her.

"Spare us your arguments."

His ivory shirt hangs open as the golden chains that are attached catch to the ruffles.

With the way Ari glowers at us, there is nothing we can say, no point raised that will keep her from attending this meeting.

Ari's hands reach to the chains, yanking them down towards her forest green blouse. Her anger is as abrupt as thunder breaking a calm silence. "Either you recognize I'm going, or you'll find yourself with me missing and no way to track my whereabouts."

In my short time here, I have admired how he is so protective over her. Someone who is able to match my concern for her recklessness.

"You are to bring Maude with you," he concedes. As he fixes his shirt, the crown he wears tilts to a sharp angle. "Though any Fae glamour on you can alter your appearance, Maude's ability can change you so that even other Fae find your true appearance undetectable. You abandon if she says so."

He turns to me, and I nod to him in agreement. Though neither of us fancy the idea of sending her to Adonis, endangering her life, there is a mutual understanding that she would go regardless. At least this way, safety will be in numbers.

She reluctantly agrees, planning on how she will get there.

The king tells her of a man that his sister is seeing. One that will possibly be able to find the exact location of the meeting points. This means additional protection, which I much prefer.

Her being away from the palace means spending time alone with the king. Time I'm sure she would enjoy watching as a spectator. Though I find myself slightly disliking him less, I still know nothing of him.

While I can see that Arabella found herself with her time in Ifaeris, I wonder if what I offer is enough for her. I ponder this constantly since I've returned. That aside, it brings joy to see her so sure of herself. Decisive in every move she makes. She allows me to remain at her bedside nightly, reassuring me with every kiss that she loves me, but I question my place with her regardless.

At my expression, she kisses my hand, thanking me for pointing out my theory before linking between the two of us and okkaring back to Nexus.

# XXXV
## Arrogant Fae

Arabella

Finding myself in the same abandoned area at night brings a numbing sensation to both my stomach and throat. Gideon, Maude's boyfriend, let us know about a friend that was delighted to hear of Gideon's interest in the cause. Unbeknownst to him, the Fae shares a bed with a member of the family the friend detested.

So far, Gideon has been cordial towards me, considering I'm the reason the woman he loves is currently in great peril of being exposed at the center of the rebellion meeting spots. Before okkaring here, I asked, out of curiosity, why half of his hair was shaved, to which he vacantly responded by explaining it was in honor of his brother. No follow-up. No elaboration. Just a blunt statement that just barely answered me.

Now the three of us stand among other Fae, Maude with violet curls and a different form completely. I, on the other hand, am glamoured to have hair, golden as the sun, ears as pointed as a sword, and eyes green as moss. As an added precaution, Maude had glamoured me to have horns coming from my head, curling in like a ram's.

The common fae wait patiently for the meeting to begin, chatting amongst themselves.

It's torturously boring to just stand here alone, unable to take my phone out and distract myself. Instead, I turn to Gideon. "So you said your hair is in honor of your brother. What happened?"

"Half his skull was split during the war against Gigantia. I shaved the other half of my head to mirror his." He laughs, lost in thought of the memory. "Against what you'd think, it was caused due to one of our own Fae. My brother attempted to aid one of the Giants in shelter, and that was his penance."

My mouth opens to speak, but for a brief period, no words find their way to be voiced. "You fought in that war? How old are you?"

"A hundred and two."

Far be it from me to judge age gaps in a species where they're practically immortal. At least we all look similar in age, and Maude's well into her twenties.

Silence reigns through the crowd as someone appears at the top of the stairs. There stands a shadowed figure with a silhouette that seems familiar. When they step into the light, a Fae that looks exactly as we were told reveals himself.

It's Adonis. He has pale freckles that cover his face, dark pink lips, and messy, curly hair. He's handsome, of course, looking as ethereal as most Fae, but he has the excess of beauty that the rest of his siblings exude. If I were one of his followers, I would be absolutely starstruck.

Helena was correct in saying that he resembles something like Cassius, but this Fae has the bright blue eyes of his father. If what Eden said is true, the king was an attractive specimen in his youth.

This is weird to me. Didn't all the other Fae say that it was improbable for Adonis to make an appearance? What about today is so special?

He clears his throat, grabbing the attention of those of us standing around. His hair is black like tar, with a length that's longer than Cassius'. It reflects from the light of the torches held by others around him. "My glorious Fae, who have joined me, as many of you know, we have been working under the true king of the Fae. I am pleased to inform you that there is now a face to back the loyalty to whom you stand behind. For it is I, Adonis, who leads you."

The crowd begins to cheer. I turn to Maude, holding two fingers to my mouth and faking a gagging sound.

His voice rings throughout the area, the only other sound being the rustling of the trees from the night winds. The only thing louder than him might be the lime clothing he has on. "Now you may be curious as to why we fight against the current Disaris rule. Why we fight against the Elementals who currently hold power. Let me tell you a tale." He moves from the center, pacing around like this is a stage, and he's giving a performance. "Long ago, during our fight against Gigantia, King Elliot sired a son, one exiled after years of cruelty. You may ask yourself how it is that no one had heard of him. I am here to explain that he was kept in hiding until he was sent to die by his own father."

Some Fae break out into "boos", while others talk amongst themselves in conspiracy.

"Groundbreaking," Maude whispers into my ear.

I snort at her comment. "Riveting acting of a lifetime."

Attempting to quiet the audience, Adonis continues his story. "He grew bitter after losing those who raised him. Not only had he been abandoned by his father, but not once had his siblings gone searching for him. Nor had they saved him from his life of anguish when he so desperately needed the love of family."

Everyone in the crowd glances around, voices raised in anger. At this, he feigns a rueful attitude, acting heartbroken at what he has to say next. "I had discovered this Fae's background early on in my youth. When he attempted to use something deadly against me, I buried his mentality where he stood."

"Did he just metaphorically kill himself from his story?" I ask, leaning in towards Maude.

"It's a better ending than whatever is happening right now," she replies.

While his story isn't a lie, I wonder how he's able to twist his words into explaining he killed off his past self, only to reemerge into the fraud he presents himself as now. I can't really tell if he means he tried to kill himself, or if his outlook on life changed. Maybe it was both.

Adonis recenters himself. "For too long have we been ruled by the cruelty of the current Elementals. Those in power thought themselves more powerful, due to the fact their bloodline carries abilities others do not."

"He realizes he speaks about himself too, right?" Gideon asks.

My shoulders raise, mouthing an "I don't know" back to him.

"What good has their rulership done when they themselves were not able to save the Fae from the slaughter of Magiks so long ago?" His voice is now projected and raised with valor. "I propose to end those of them raised in Ifaeris. Killing all until there is no one but us, fairly ruling over the other. I promise that honey and sweets will always be ready for all Fae, regardless of status. Aid and Zips shall be distributed where needed. Allow me to lead Faeries into a new age of light."

Roaring with cheers and praise, the common fae blindly support his false promises. Regardless if it's unobtainable in a realistic sense, he wholeheartedly believes he can lead the Fae into a utopia. It's narcissism at its peak.

He thanks the Fae for their dedication and support in him, continuing his speech about why he would make a better ruler than those in the past. Part of me wants to drown out his words completely, but the other part of me knows there is too much that could prove important for the future. His body language, the blind confidence, the hatred he carries for his family.

A vicious, quirked side of his mouth presents itself into the crowd. This makes him look so much like Cassius that it's scary. "Accept me as the true king and rightful heir to Ifaeris."

I bite my cheeks to keep myself from saying anything that could draw attention. Never in my life have I known someone to be so full of themself. Initially, I felt sympathy for this Fae, but evil has shaped and corrupted him.

"We begin our quest and attack Hearthis in three days, come midday. Make your preparations. And may we enter this new era with the love and support of those we hold most dear." He okkars from his place along with the hooded figures behind him, who I assume are the missing common fae.

The others who remain disband from the premises, whether through okkaring or walking on their own. For a second, I remain there, thinking of the abundance of information I'll have to explain to Cassius and Luka.

# XXXVI
## Never Have I Ever

Cassius

I suppose there was nothing I could do to keep Arabella from attending that meeting. While I am assured she will be kept safe by my sister's lover, I know better than to think he would protect the witch before Maude.

Esme's meaningless banter spewed the plan to the rest of our family, which is how I came entrapped in the room I'm currently in. I am surrounded by my family without the company of my mother and Ezra. The lot of us make merry in my father's old consort room, which, after many deep cleanings, has been retired and made into a common space.

Luka stands in the corner, keeping to himself, acquainted with none but Kabir and myself. Out of offering, I bring a wine to him, assuring firstly it is not lasialic to keep from repeating Arabella's first experience.

He takes it graciously, thanking me with a lazy gesture, his foot tapping on the floor. He, just as I, is impatiently awaiting the return of Arabella. I cannot think of any time I have lived through where something felt as excruciating as this.

While the sorcerer stands beside me, we pass inconsequential pleasantries, avoiding speaking of what either of us feels for Arabella.

"Ari must have threatened you by now," Luka says with a crispness in his voice. "Has she tortured you as of late?"

I snort at his comment, appreciating he too understands what it is to be on the receiving end of her lashings. "She's been preparing my castration since the day we met. It would appear that she finds entertainment in terrifying others."

Agreeing with me, he lifts his glass in cheers. "I would think the sex counterbalances her empty threats. At least she was only a menace to me. You witnessed her bring others to their knees."

"In a way, yes."

Extended time in silence and multiple refills of wine later, Luka says tentatively, "You've met our friends."

"They were kind. Spoke highly of you."

"Then you're aware that they are practically family."

Nodding, I find my words inserting themselves where they do not belong. "They are much more kind to her than how she spoke of her blood, though I know as well as the next that families have their complications."

He stops me from rambling in my own idiocy. "Things are different for her. Families all have their issues, but in many cultures, they believe poor treatment by parents is acceptable. They feel obligated to love them for providing the basic necessities since their parents had it worse."

"How is it that children do not speak up in their own defense, at the very least?"

"I highly doubt you stood up for yourself when your father made you feel unworthy, King Cassius."

I stay silent, fully understanding why Arabella kept me from speaking ill of her family.

"Cassius," I respond simply.

As I begin to ask more about their other Magik friends, Xavier pulls us both into a circle of my siblings, all of whom are drunker than I.

Laughter is welcoming me when we join the circle, wine being poured into my cup by Cel. It's odd to enjoy myself in their presence. Perhaps if father had been killed sooner, we would have found ourselves pleasantly in each other's company.

"We should play a game," Isa suggests.

I look at her in question. "You brought me here to play a game?"

"But what would we play?" Dyana giggles.

Esme lightly jabs Luka with her elbow in laughter. "Any suggestions, lover boy?"

Name after name, Luka lists a handful of mortal drinking games. Some of them have found their way to Ifaeris, some none of us have heard of.

"Card games exist," Luka suggests with irritation.

They shake their heads.

"No cards," says Cel. "None that any of us would bother to look for anyway."

Luka holds his hand under his chin, lightly tapping his fingers along his cheek. "There's also 'Never Have I Ever'. It's a drinking game where those participating go around in the circle saying something we have never done, but if you have, you drink."

"The whole glass?" Monty asks curiously.

"No," Luka says in a monotone voice, "just a sip. Unless your goal is to black out."

Atticus sits between Cel and Xavier, hunched over and eyes half open. "Shall I go first?" When no one volunteers, he goes on. "Never have I ever been stabbed."

None but Luka takes a drink.

My brother realizes what he said at Luka's action, puffing his cheeks in guilt. "Sorry."

We go around the circle multiple times, all of us now inebriated and incoherent.

Monty takes another sip of the wine, emptying his glass. "Never have I ever fallen for someone I knew I could not have."

Nearly all of us drink, his brother smacking his head. I entertain myself with my cousins' argument, distracted from the things around me.

Xavier grins at me as though he has thought of something clever. "Never have I ever kissed Arabella." He speaks with such clarity, I've forgotten who is in the room.

All eyes turn to Luka and myself, the two of us tensing awkwardly. To my side, I see Esme shrug, taking in the alcohol while others fixate on us.

My cousin must think it funny to remind us of this.

As Luka and I drink, moving past this, Arabella returns. Her blonde hair is now returned to its original color, the sleeves from her deep red dress rolled.

The others pay her no mind while Luka and I stand, walking to her.

"Before you say anything, Maude is safe. Nothing happened. She just wanted to stay the night with Gideon."

Isadora runs, embracing Arabella before handing her a shot and returning to her seat.

Arabella pulls us aside, telling all she learned from their meeting. She speaks of how Adonis spun the tale of his story in a way of encouragement to lead the uprising and the attack on Hearthis that will come in the nearing days.

Placing the undrunken shot on a table, she exhales deeply. "I won't lie, your brother is really attractive. If he wasn't set on murdering all the Elementals aside from himself, I'd find him all the more pleasing."

"Ari, love, you'd fuck a tree branch if it degraded you," Luka mocks, throwing his arm around her shoulders.

The words offend her in part. "I would not!"

"You had sex with me," I quip.

Her lips clamp together, offering no rebuttal.

"Case and point," Luka says, extending his free arm in my direction. Despite the small of alcohol he has had, he holds his face straight, only smiling when turning to Arabella.

My siblings depart to their room for the night, my cousins to an empty chamber on the second floor, I'm sure. As Arabella and Luka take their leave to their rooms, I call to Arabella, halting both in their place. "I would like a moment alone with my reeve."

She thinks nothing of it, unraveling her fingers from his. "I'll be up later."

He kisses her head, waving before leaving.

Taking a seat on the deep blue couch, she crosses her legs over each other, waiting for me to join.

"You know, I don't know if I'm ready to go into an all-out civil war," she admits, dread in her voice.

"I would think you'd enjoy a bit of violence with the sharp words you lay out."

Grunting, she throws her face into her hands.

Eyebrow raised at the silence instead of rebuttal, I become concerned. "I must admit, seeing you this way is discouraging when you are the strong one of us two." Grabbing the last of the open bottle, I drink until there is no more. "What troubles you?"

Her fingers stop from picking at the paint on her nails, slapping her thighs lightly. "I don't know. Nothing." She breathes. "Everything."

"What do you feel?"

"I'm exhausted, I'm tired, and I feel selfish for wanting everything, but considering what I've dealt with, I feel like I deserve it." She admits this all with tightness in her expression.

I bring myself closer to her, breathing her in. My lips go to her neck, my hand lightly pressing around its side. "And what is it you deserve?"

She tilts her head, exposing more of her skin to me. "Y- You," she stammers, taking a sharp breath. "Luka. Both."

Pushing me away from her, a wary look takes residence in her eyes. "If we survive all this, the three of us needa have a talk."

"You mean *when* we survive this, Dragon."

# XXXVII

## *Climactic Reassurance*

Luka

Two days have been spent deliberating and conversing how we would fight against Adonis and his followers. Those who had fought the day I arrived had poor combat skills. Had I been less blinded by surprise from the news of my death, I would have been more alert. I could have killed more than I did. Ultimately, we've agreed to keep the general and a few dozen soldiers stationed at House of Smoldris, protecting the Elemental Fae from the Flameling bloodline.

Tomorrow we will fight, battling together. I had hoped that Ari would keep herself from harm's way, but being as stubborn as she is, she's insisted on joining. The closest to a compromise we agreed on is for her to remain behind a protected window, only using her powers to kill from a distance.

As she joins me in bed, her anxiety bounces through the room. I hold her tight, hoping to mollify her through it, but her body tosses around.

Sitting up, she props her back against the headboard. Turns to me. "I've given some thought about you and Cassius."

Nerves jump from my body. Judging by the way she's hesitating, I can only imagine that this isn't news that will work favorably for me.

"What have you concluded?" I prepare myself for the blow, though it will hurt no less.

Kissing me, she grabs my hand, holding it between both of hers. She bats her lashes twice before slowly moving the hand to her lips.

The unspoken is tortuous.

"I love you, but I also can't deny my feelings for him." She laughs airily, shutting her eyes. "Xavier told me to keep you both. I thought the suggestion was insane when he said it, but the more I think about it, the more I figured that he could have a point." Her body shifts away from mine, gauging my reaction. "I won't do anything you're not okay with, but if you'd be comfortable, I'd want to have you both."

I'm unable to think. The softness on her face washes any anger or apprehension I have away. "For years, I have been selfish and unkind. For months, I was dead and away from you. I was forced to deal with the knowledge that if you chose him, if he was who you truly desired, I'd find a way to live with it."

Ari's body has become still. Marble as a sculpture and elegant enough to be admired by all. She hasn't smiled, nor has she rejected me. A response worse than her denying me. She says nothing.

I wait for something from her mouth. A loving word. A harsh

truth. But still, nothing leaves her. At this moment, I fear that what I said will change her mind.

At last she breaks from her state, air stuttering from an exhale. And suddenly, I am able to breathe again.

"I missed you," I confess, holding her against my body, my fingers gliding up her shirt.

She takes her shirt from the hem, lifting it above her head and throwing it in the direction of the bathroom. "What about me did you miss?"

Grinding my body against hers, I'm grateful neither of us is wearing many items of clothing. She shimmies herself from her panties, bucking her hips against my underwear that creates a barrier between our bodies.

"I missed your lips." Pressing my lips to hers, then down to her round stomach. "Your tongue." I reach towards her thighs. A beautiful parting into the warmth my cock craves. "Your thighs."

Her legs squeeze together, the plump of her skin tightening around my head. My tongue reaches her clit, spelling words to describe my love for her. Fingers move from my side, thrusting into her cunt in the rhythm of sonnets.

"Need more," she whines, gripping me deeper into her.

I part my mouth, leveling my head so that I can look into her eyes. "Tell me you want me."

"I want you," she whimpers, eager to come. "Please. Touch me."

My eyes narrow, taunting her. "I am touching you." I kiss the skin by her tattoo. "Or do you mean touch you like this?" My mouth returns to her clit, sucking while she tightens around my fingers.

"That's it, love." My right arm reaches to her full breasts, pinching her rosy-brown nipple while my palms massage her from under.

She tastes just as mouth-watering as the last time I had her shaking from under me.

If I thought myself weak beside her before, I am now a man possessed.

My tongue flattens, vertically stroking as she tenses, myself relishing her cries of pleasure. I feel her come undone beneath me, trembling as I continue to curl my fingers into her. My eyes gaze at hers, sucking each finger.

Her body lifts, snaking an arm around my neck and pulling my weight onto hers, roughly kissing me. She bites my lip, running her fingers down my torso and past the waistband of my underwear, towards my cock.

"Off, now," she demands.

"I hardly think you are in any position to be commanding orders, love."

Snickers leaving her lips, I sense the mockery that is about to release in her voice. "Please, oh please, you powerful creature. I beg you to take your underwear off so you can mark me as yours."

Against my desire to keep her edged, I rip off the cloth from the elastic, kicking it to the foot of the bed. My cock stiffens, painfully hard, tip leaking from pre-cum.

I debate on teasing her more, toying with the idea of making her wait. But when she looks at me with those damn eyes, her cunt leaking, I would kill anyone who keeps me from being inside her for another moment.

Her back arches as I push myself into her, pumping in multiple times, holding her wrists at her side. Parting her swollen lips, her head throws back against the pillows in pleasure, breath stammering.

"*Luka.*"

At the sound of my name leaving her mouth, I release my grip on her, staring into her eyes and forcefully kissing her. I allow my tongue to explore every part of her, from the inside of her mouth, to her neck, and around each nipple. Sucking each until the skin around it purples with bruises, the pressing of the jewelry indenting her skin.

"Have you waited for this?" I chuckle into her ear. "To be taken by me? Filled by my cock?"

"No," she moans out.

A lie.

I thrust into her deeper, speeding up my movements as her heels dig into my arse. "While Fae do not carry the ability to lie, may I remind you that I have tasted every one of yours since the day you denied your true feelings for me?"

She shutters at my words, her cunt squeezing tighter around me when she brings her hand down to her soaking core.

"You will always be mine," I say, continuing to thrust into her.

As if unsure, she pulls her hands from my back, wiping sweat from my forehead and stroking my cheek. "Do you still want me?"

I don't understand why she's so uncertain when it's her that can bring me back from any tranced state. "My love, your cunt was blessed by the gods enough to bring me back from the dead. Rest assured when I say I want you, I mean all of you. Every curve, every thought. I want access to every part of you, as long as you'll have me."

She smiles, holding me down while she marks my throat, gliding her lips on my skin until she reaches the lobe of my ear. "If I am yours, then you are mine."

The vibration of her hummed words repeats in chorus in my mind, bringing me closer to filling her with myself.

"I'm a desperate man, love. But only for you."

Pulling out of her until only the tip remains inside, I watch as her face glowers at me, hand trailing to pleasure herself as compensation. I can't have this, not for one second. Leave the woman I love to take care of her own needs when it should be me. Screaming until there is nothing in her voice but hoarse whispers.

I pull her from her back. Lifting her while she wraps her legs around me as I sit on my knees, driving my cock into her. "I want you to make me a promise."

Her face locks in confusion, keeping her arms tightly around my neck. "You know I don't make promises during sex."

"And yet I hold the power while my cock remains buried in you." I grin at her with arrogance, stopping my motions until she listens. Her eyes squeeze shut in exasperation, rolling her hips. I put a hand over her mouth, keeping her from arguing. She is a weakness that I would undoubtedly fight for. "I want to be clear that if you want us both, you have us equally. You will not value one over the other."

She groans, continuing to move herself while the warmth of her body strokes me, timing in rhythm with her desperate desire.

Honestly, I need her far too much to wait for an answer.

My cock pulses, demanding I claim her soon and hard. The deeper I thrust, the tighter her hold on me is, lowering us both back onto the sheets with her under me. I can't stop. Even if it is what I wanted, the look of pleasure on her face is enough to keep me inside her for ten lifetimes.

Slaps of our skin fill the room, pressing me with the burning desire to keep her from all that would harm her.

I slow my thrusts, filling her slowly and deeply, forcing as much of my length into her that will physically allow. Brushing the rolls of her side as my hand travels down. "No matter what happens on the battlefield tomorrow, I will ensure that nothing harms you. I protect what I treasure."

"Luka," she whimpers. "Please. Please. *Fuck*."

It drives me mad how easily I fall under her spell. I drive into her with a ferocity that can only be described as barbaric.

"Does my love need to come?"

She bites her lip, a single tear rolling from the corner of her eye. Nodding, her panting grows choppy. Small, high-pitched sounds escape her as I rub circles around her clit.

"Come, Blossom. Allow me to feel the one thing I've thought about for days."

Her body rocks against mine, her cunt squeezing my cock as she comes beneath me, chanting invocation after invocation.

"If you want to prove how much you missed me, spill into me until I am nothing but yours." Her sincere smile curls into a devilish smirk, crashing our lips together and weakening my knees.

My movements falter at seeing her squeeze her breasts. She is a being, divine. A celestial trap that I would gladly sacrifice myself for at her call.

I delve my cock into her with such finality, it pushes her head deep into the pillow, ripping my orgasm from me and spurting my cum into her one pump at a time.

"You are mine. Forever," she whispers into my ear, grabbing my neck while I moan her name until she pulls my lips onto hers.

After showering, she nuzzles herself into my chest, mindlessly scraping her nails across the ferns that tattoo both sides above my hips.

"What's wrong?" I lace our fingers together in an attempt to soothe her worries.

Sighing, she moves closer, the warmth of her cheek resting on my shoulder. "I'm just worried about my abilities. What if they just stop working? What if I fuck up and get more people killed tomorrow? "

"My love, what if you don't? You've managed to grasp control over your magik already. Don't doubt yourself into letting your insecurities overtake your progress." I brush my free hand through her hair, parting the strays that cover her face. "You have always had violence and rage inside you. Now you can put it to use."

"And you're sure you're okay with this?" she asks with hesitance in her voice, raspy from fatigue. "Staying here with the Fae *and* Cassius? I can find a way to split my time."

Rubbing her soft arms, I hold her tighter, physically solidifying to her this is what I want. "I would not agree if I weren't fully ready to accept this. Besides, the king and I have come to an understanding with each other."

She is unworldly. Spun from tales of ancient legend, and all that I could ever want.

When she drifts off into sleep, I ready myself, mind and body, for the battle that is to come tomorrow. I can only hope that the three of us make it out alive and unharmed. Knowing how my girlfriend likes to approach things, I suspect she is planning something.

All I can do is wait and hope it won't get her killed.

# XXXVIII
## Cutting Loose

Arabella

It's time.

I change into Faerie leather that protects my legs, my upper body covered fully in silver metal to protect my chest. Along the armor are knives, easily ready to be unsheathed. Multiple straps wrap around my thighs with enough areas to hold the blades I need. Though I promised to fight from the manor, using my magik from a distance, it doesn't hurt to keep weapons at my side for safety.

I shove on my boots, made also from Faerie leather, tying half my hair with a hair tie. Their shoes are much more comfortable and supportive than any I have ever worn.

Luka wears pants similar to mine and a long, dark gray tunic that cuts into his chest. I'm caught gawking, but still unable to pry my eyes from him. I don't really care when he looks like that.

As I'm about to leave the room and meet Cassius at his, when opening the door, he's already standing at the frame, staring at me, dumbstruck. His frock coat reaches above his ankles, pants tight, but not to the skin, fitted the same as Luka's.

"Why are you looking at me like that?" I ask. He looks at me like it's the first time he's ever seen me.

"You're in trousers."

Discounting the lounging pants I use as pajamas or leggings I wear casually around Nexus, I guess this *is* the first time he's seen me ready to leave the palace in pants. Especially when the times I wore suede bottoms were when I was sparring with Kabir or when I went into town alone.

"Did you actually think I was going into a full-on battle in a miniskirt?" The end of my question raises, the humor from my thoughts shining through.

He observes my every move, eyes fixed on my body in lust.

I shake him. "Hello?" Shoving him again, I try for his attention.

At my side, Luka appears from my room. "Knowing the weapons you conceal under your clothing, I wouldn't put it past you."

The three of us walk down into the armory under the palace. Many of the weapons were taken yesterday, along with guards and army men, to protect those who reside within the manor in Hearthis.

Most of the Disaris family agreed to stay at Nexus, making sure there is protection and someone to rule in the case of possible death. Knights too stay to keep them safe. The only ones who will join us are Xavier, Ezra, and Dyana. Atticus insisted on going, but I wouldn't let him. Not when his wife is due to give birth any day now.

Dyana is at the seas, listening and watching in the chance the rebellion will attack from water.

Leather straps are wrapped around Luka. There are blades, chains, and throwing knives along the line that connects to the chest plate he now wears.

Cassius puts on gloves, carefully protecting himself from the iron that molds most weapons.

I grab my dagger from its place, checking to make sure the edges on the double-curved blade are sharp. In the other holsters, I've secured a fan that shoots out blades and four knives. In my pocket is a spiked knuckle ring of iron. Of course, I also have the necklace with the shuriken.

"Don't die," Kabir calls to me.

"Don't cower," I respond to him as a joke before he okkars away. Looking back to Cassius and Luka, I cock my head. "That goes for you too."

Okkaring to Hearthis, we walk through the gate, greeted by a ruby-haired Fae. Her sage eyes are kind, though filled with sorrow, anticipating the destruction of her home after losing her father to Adonis.

"Greetings, King Cassius, Lady Arabella, and..." she trails off when she gets to Luka. "I do not believe I've been acquainted with your name yet."

"Luka," he replies. "And how are you important to today?"

I don't think he meant it to come out as rude as it did.

"Lady Fatima," she responds coldly. Her face holds a sneer, while her flatter nose lifts in irritation. Those of Hearthis typically act pleasant towards others' disrespect if it allows them to save face, though I can't imagine today being one they would uphold traditions for. "Daughter of deceased Lord Marlon, now Lady of Hearthis. My husband, Pyrros, will be here momentarily. He will fight alongside you today."

Taking her aside, we stand together, knowing the two of us are to fight from behind the windows of the hall, while her husband joins.

Pyrros is just as beautiful as all the Fae. His brown skin is covered in special Fae armor that looks similar to leaves, a sword strapped to his back. When he turns to me, his eyes are the color of honey.

"So what's your power?" I ask Fatima.

She smiles, her eyes shifting to match the tone of her hair. Luka begins fanning himself with his hand, falling to his knees as his skin ripens like a tomato.

"I can boil people from the inside out."

Glaring at her, I kick her softly from behind her knee, breaking her attention from my boyfriend. He's given a chair, Pyrros looking back at his wife.

*Note to self: don't make her mad.*

Dyana rushes in, wet from the sea. "They're coming. They moved between the borders of Aquatius and Hearthis."

General Callian orders everyone to get into position on the grounds while tying up his long, white hair and joining them. Fatima and I rush to the second story, stationing ourselves at windows across the same wall.

There's a brief moment of silence before screams of the common fae run through the grounds. The sounds of metal clashing and bodies falling to the dirt pierce the air, signifying the start of the battle.

I watch as Fae move from place to place, my magik just barely hexing them. A flash of light hits the ground, flames from my fingers trying to target them.

Fatima grins in satisfaction, heating a body that approaches her husband. The body steams, the boils large enough to be visible from our distance.

It's honestly disgusting.

Another body explodes, flesh popping from his biceps. Some Fae fall back at the sight, shielding themselves behind trees and firing arrows towards the front. There aren't a lot in the battle, most of those fighting spread widely through the grounds. Still, there's blood being spilled all around.

Out of the corner of my eye, I see Cassius' shadow slaughtering Fae with ease while the king keeps himself out of sight and harm's way. He is not well acquainted with a sword, but what he can't do himself, his shadow does.

Weapons are slung everywhere, blood covering the dirt.

"How are they doing this?" Fatima shouts. "They should not be able to hold themselves in such a battle, let alone wield the weapons they do. They are being punctured with iron, yet some have not died."

That's when I have the realization. If Adonis was able to slip in and out of the palace unnoticed by hiding in the shadows, he would be able to attain weapons from the armory without a problem.

I take the crossbow from the table behind me, aiming it at the Fae nearing Xavier. As the Fae falls, Xavier lunges a sword into another who is running from behind.

Harrison, Cassius' friend, chills the air, forming icicle spikes from the little moisture there is. He throws them in any direction he can to strike a target.

When I was told Harrison would show up at all, I was surprised, since both his mothers refused to join in aid. That and I've heard he heavily finds amusement in the displeasure of common fae and their lives. His body is shaped with spikes on his shoulders, weapons hooked to them. But there's no time to distract myself with observing him.

None but he of the Elemental blood joins us. Aquatius sent guards, as did Enthar and Windwyrd, but no Elementals come to stand in arms.

We're losing. Multiple Elementals, two Magiks, skilled warriors at our side, and we're still somehow losing.

Fae drop one by one, iron embedded into their flesh. It's a complete bloodbath.

Snatching the knuckle ring from my pocket, I put it on, handing the crossbow to Fatima. "Bolts are in the bag next to you. Fire where you see trouble, boil where you can."

"Where are you going?" She looks at me with thunder in her voice.

I run towards the door of the room. I can do more on the field if my focus is at a precise distance. "Joining in on the fun."

"If you go, I shall too. I'm not being left alone up here while you fight."

Smiling, I hand her one of the knives I have concealed. "You know how?"

"No." She shakes her head. "But I know how to stab and where to burn someone at the exact place of impalement."

That's all I need to hear as we leave the room.

We run into the field, Cassius' voice yelling at me in outrage from behind protection.

Fatima and I split, brawling against Fae that attack.

They're strong. Agile. Not well skilled compared to those of us fighting against them but still just as dangerous.

Sprinting to Kabir's side, I bring down a blade into the furry Fae that's mounted him. He pushes the dead to the side, gripping the small blade that is pushing through the Pooka's throat.

The guard smiles at me, wiping the strands of hair that came loose from his bun with the front of his palm. "I knew you'd fail to stay up there much longer."

"Nice to know you believe in my plan."

"You have a plan?" he asks disbelievingly, now standing back to back with me.

Fae circle us, pointing their weapons and closing in.

"Trust me?"

"Not particularly," he laughs.

I lock arms with him, tracing a circle on the back of his hand. He stiffens himself as I prepare to push myself off the ground.

"Now," I shout.

The guard lifts me onto his back, spinning around as I shoot fire from my hand, burning every Fae around us, both larger and smaller than me, to the ground.

Their bodies are cut from their legs, nearly the same way as they would have been if sliced through with a blade.

The tang of their blood permeates my nose.

I throw the sword to Kabir, who moves to join Gavin in battling four Fae.

Another approaches me. One who had stood by me at the meeting I attended. I duck from her punch, magiking her to levitate above me before slamming her into the ground.

Tears cloud in her eyes. I know I shouldn't, but I hesitate. Just enough for her blood to reflow. A moment later, I see a crooked smile form on her face.

Wind is knocked from my chest, pushing me to the ground as another tall Fae with wings of ginormous bay leaves appears above me.

*Gods I wish I had more combat training.*

My feet spin me as I hold onto his boot between my arms, tipping him, unbalanced. I use my left arm to knock him to his back, taking my left leg around his body and holding him to the ground. The knife attached to my armor comes loose, just in time for me to stab his chest, dragging it from there to his belly button.

I hear tramples of footsteps coming towards me, and I ready myself for the impact. When nothing comes, my eyes shoot up and see Luka and Cassius holding a Fae.

Cassius has his wings spread while he's holding the man by his neck, his right leg keeping the Fae in place. Luka roars out, plunging firstly a blade down the body, then his hand through the Fae's chest, ripping out his heart and disemboweling him.

The bloody weapon drops from Luka along with the Fae who has a sliced open torso.

Any thought that develops is devoured by the dying.

Many of these Fae simply wanted fair treatment from the crown. But this has resulted in death or the disappearances of their loved ones.

The two men focus on me, nodding to tell me they are okay.

I pick my fan from my side, launching the knives at the Fae about twenty feet away from me. One strikes the back of her head.

Another pierces through armor, though I'm not able to tell if it's fatal. One hinges into a leg, whipping their head in my direction.

The Fae takes her gloved hand, pulling the weapon from her head and charging herself at me. The adrenaline of pain is burning through, stumbling her steps towards my body.

I sweep from under her, landing a punch into her gut.

Her mouth, bloody and gurgling, begins choking. I take my dagger from my thigh, stabbing it into the Fae while she attempts to strangle me until her very last breath.

Turning around, the guards I have become friendly with from Nexus tear others from their bodies. The common fae are ready to die by any means for Adonis. Their loyalty is sad when he's not willing to do the same. He didn't even bother to be here for them in battle.

I hear a laugh. One I recognize from my stabbing.

"Come to finish me off?" I challenge.

A Fae, hidden behind another, pushes her body to the ground. This one is barely taller than me. "Why finish you off when you can join us?"

He launches himself at me, slicing a sword deep enough through the opening between the metal and my pants, deep into my skin. I'm not nearly quick enough. He okkars. Immediately, he is behind me, holding the sword to my chest. "You would make a good consort to His Majesty."

"You think I crave companionship over power? That's your first mistake." I throw my head back, knocking him backwards and grabbing the weapon by its hilt after it drops to the ground.

His face wets with tears from the force, a hand covering over the bloody nose.

I clench my fist tight and concentrate until he's frozen in place, me stabbing the sword through his groin.

Running faster and harder towards Cassius and Luka, arrows fly at me. I move everywhere, zagging my movement so they don't get a clear shot, but some still graze my armor. Never in my life have I exerted this much energy.

Everyone is trying to survive this.

Some of the common fae are being impaled by iron, though no plunge holds through their skin. It's like they're all solidified vapor, similar to one version of Cassius' shadows.

*How is that possible?*

A cry is heard from the distance.

"King Adonis," a Fae yells.

I jerk my head back, seeing Adonis appear from the edge.

He makes his way towards the battle, some of his fighters going still. About thirty more Fae are behind Adonis, all marching or flying.

"*FALL BACK!*" General Callian screams with a strained voice.

His son backs, leading men into the manor.

Some take that as an opportunity to shoot at them. Axes, arrows, javelins, and other weapons I have no idea the name of are thrown. Many are struck, killing them on the spot.

A shadow seeps through the grounds, sliding from one area to another until Adonis reaches us with speed.

"A call for backup so far into the battle when one side is losing shows the little faith you have in your followers," Luka says, diverting Adonis' attention from the Fae retreating.

Adonis purses his lips, looking at the Fae that lay dead on the ground. "By the looks of it, it is your king who is losing the fight."

He clicks his tongue. "Pathetic. A small pick of Elemental Fae against a battalion of common fae and you still lose. How pitiful to watch the fall."

Ezra rushes, a two-headed sword in his hand, thinking himself able to overpower Adonis.

Once he nears the eldest Disaris, Ezra moves right through Adonis' figure. In the quick movement, Adonis grabs Ezra's weapon as he moves through him, turning to jab it right through his brother's stomach.

"Are you still twisting your words to avoid revealing that you are one of us, brother?" Cassius says with a merry tune. He's completely ignoring the fact his brother's dead ten feet from him.

Looks are thrown around, murmurs not able to be heard over those still bothering to fight.

Luka looks at me, mouthing something I cannot understand.

"What?" I mouth back.

"Hide," he mouths again.

Staring at him, I shake my head subtly, refusing to move.

His face softens from the tension. "Please?"

Trying to blend in with the others who are running, I sprint, diving to a dead Fae, smearing her blood on me and throwing her body that smells of ammonia and rust over mine.

My heart is beating fast, pounding hard in my eardrums.

By the time I'm covered, I've missed something from the three's conversation.

"Or have you not heard, the so-called 'true king' you serve is just another Disaris son," berates Luka to one of Adonis' followers, gripping the sword at his side. "He feels scorned and cheated from rulership. Your efforts mean nothing if he is crowned."

Adonis' face pushes past red and appears as dark as the Fae blood spilled.

"Pay no mind to the two. Their word means nothing."

Cassius lets out a low chuckle, smiling at the common fae as if they are on friendly terms and this is a meeting of truce. "Deny it then. Deny that King Elliot was your father."

He verbally says nothing, but his face says everything.

Some Fae retreat to a place unknown, some remaining still. Both actions make it unclear if this means defeat or something bigger yet to come.

Instead of speaking, Adonis takes a sword, swinging it in the direction of Luka and Cassius. He misses, rage increasing.

Cassius' shadow returns by his person, leaping to the rebellion leader, only to go through him like a ghost.

"My abilities extend to others, if you were curious why you were unable to land many deaths," Adonis taunts, cutting through the fabric on Luka's leg and slicing his skin.

They try, but neither can strike him. Neither of them can draw blood. With every hit, Adonis simply turns his body incorporeal.

Kabir shields them from behind, watching their backs as others rush to kill Cassius.

While many have gone into hiding, Fae now crowd the three of them. It's apparent that the reveal of Adonis' true parentage changes nothing on their allegiance.

I hate doing nothing. Watching as this goes down while all I can do is stop the hearts of one assaulter at a time.

It's lucky that there's too much happening for anyone to notice where I am. Another stroke of luck that none notice when Luka turns back to me multiple times.

Adonis has a choice. He can either shield his warriors to keep them from being wounded, or he can protect himself.

He chooses himself, leaving the Fae he rules over to die. Now the battle is even. Now we have equal footing, if not better.

The trained army marches back into battle, attacking all who charge toward the King of Ifaeris.

Weapons are clinging, bodies falling by iron.

It's obvious there will be no prisoners taken by Adonis. Mercy will not be shown to those who do not bend to his will. He's a man filled with vengeance.

There are two battles occurring at once. One is the fight for what the common fae believe is right, the other is with a brother seeking retribution for the actions of his father.

I whirl back to the battlefield, joining those who fight with us, stabbing a dagger through the back calf of a Fae attacking Xavier.

"I thought you were going to stay in the building," he questions, humor coating his voice.

My roundhouse kick to the ribs lands on another Fae near us. "And miss out on saving your ass? Guess again," I yell, going after another Fae.

There are bodies. So many that I jump through while whipping around a sword I took from another.

The Fae named Cato hovers over another Fae. One I assume to be his lover.

I stop the airflow from his lungs, choking him as I behead him from where he kneels.

This gets Adonis to snap his neck at me, smiling as he slithers through the shadows.

There's only seconds for me to think of a plan while he and

Cassius' shadow wrestle. Before an idea can come to my mind, Luka splits the ground, collapsing a small area of dirt around Adonis' solid body.

Many wounded fall into the cracks. If the iron hasn't killed them, the fall into the earth's harsh waters will.

Adonis becomes distracted, vulnerable from his focused attention.

I sprint at him, a flame engulfing the sword I hold. In a singular sweep, I cut Adonis' right arm down from his shoulder. The bone is now visible, blood and limb gushing from the detachment.

Adonis screams in anguish, his body collapsing to the ground. Putting a foot over him, he stares at me, his eyes full of fury. "YOU BITCH!"

A huff of laughter leaves my mouth with a small sound, my face hardening as I stare directly into his eyes, matching his cold rage.

"Yeah."

# XXXIX

## *Bargaining, Bargaining*

Luka

I have hoped that taking Adonis would be the end of this, but with so many that had retreated from the field, I know better than to place belief in something so idiotic.

No one's slept. There are no celebratory gatherings, no amusement in the palace. Only the grave mourning of death.

Still, the three of us stayed in the king's office last night, speaking about Adonis and what to do with the common fae we *have* managed to capture. Many we assume to be innocent, forced into this by the power of the Stone of Elestial.

Now, our trio enters Adonis' heavily guarded cell. It's similar to the one we questioned Adrik in. Private, though this cell contains iron enclosing every wall with a clamped-shut door to match.

"If it isn't the sorcerer back from the dead with his lover and hers," Adonis throws with sarcasm in his voice.

Three chairs are on the opposite corner, wooden and new.

Ari twists her fingers, summoning the chairs to our side and sitting. Putting her arms at her knees, her legs spread with her hands held together in the open space. "Sure have a punch in your attitude after losing your supporters." She pauses, pursing her lips and smiling. "And, I suppose your arm."

"I've lost nothing," he hisses, turning to Cassius. "But you, can you say the same, young brother?"

Cassius takes in a breath, bored and unenthusiastic. "What is it you demand from me?"

Adonis smiles at Cassius. "You tell me. It is not I who has come into *your* cell with an agenda."

"No, but we thought that you'd have more to say," I respond.

"Such disrespect for someone who we have granted a second life to."

"Stop stalling, Adonis," hisses Ari. She, just as I, is not willing to listen to his poor attempt at engaging. "You wanted to rule. Now tell us why."

She needs direct answers, not the pettiness of familial past being unleashed. If that were the case, the two of us would have remained behind the closed door, letting the brothers have it out on their own.

"Was I not clear? I wanted to give a better life to my fellow Fae," Adonis spits back.

"You wanted a better life for yourself," Ari remarks with correction.

The Fae is too calm, remaining too collected in his answers. This is either a trap we stupidly fell into, or Adonis has accepted his loss far too easily.

"If gaining a better life for the Fae includes a better life for myself, who am I to oppose?" he voices, silvery with arrogance.

Cassius steps to his brother. "I have to confess, I find it quite enthralling how you claim to be a better ruler, and yet you are just as capricious as father."

I stay quiet.

To comment and agree with Cassius on this would be a baseless accusation. I have not known the Fae long enough to accurately judge his statement. However, with what Ari has explained, I find myself internally siding with the king anyway.

"Don't try to convince me you cared for the old man," Adonis rebukes with light-heartedness. "From what I have learned, he mistreated you far longer than he with me. So, don't fool yourself into believing you care for him now. Our father was a waste to this kingdom."

His brother laughs lightly. "That we can agree on."

My thoughts were miscalculated. Adonis is far more skilled in the art of manipulation than I expected.

"You want a better life? Fine. But what makes you fit to rule when you had to force Fae minds into obedience? When all they did was think to question your authority," Ari says, straightening herself in the chair. A posture she rarely holds.

Adonis' eyes go to her, delight leaving his face and turning into intrigue. "I am the rightful heir. It would do you a service to speak kindly to the king, once I am free. Perhaps then I will be most generous with your punishment. And other things amongst that realm."

It would be wise to inform Adonis not to look at Arabella the way he is. For Cassius' and my sake, but more pressingly, his. I could warn him that he should fear the way I'm running through multiple scenarios in which I kill him for speaking to her in such a way. If he thinks Arabella ruthless for amputating his arm, he knows nothing of what I would do to him.

"I would think you more savvy than to side with the king, who knows nothing of being a ruler. He's the same Fae who indulges himself only in the selfish pleasures of his desires, unless I am mistaken," Adonis disrespects. His eyes scan Ari's full body, lingering over the bruises that color her skin. "I may offer a bargain yet."

The anger residing on Cassius' face remains firm. He's prepared to strike Adonis where he stands. Possibly send shadows and end his life.

Ari's hand goes towards Cassius, mine fisted and ready to act.

"What bargain could you possibly offer that would excuse your actions?" I ask, distracting Cassius from proceeding.

"Grant me one thing. Let me have an audience with Helena. If you do so, I will tell all I know about the whereabouts with complete honesty."

Stopping the both of them before they speak, I answer. "Bargain for you to give ambiguous answers and mislead us so that you can take the crown for your own and kill Helena? No."

Mine and Cassius' arms are pulled to the door by Ari. She knocks, and Kabir opens it, leaving so the three of us may speak.

At his exit, both Cassius and I look at Ari. It's evident she is considering Adonis' offer, though I know she would never take it.

"No," Cassius says with authority. "I know that look in your eyes. You cannot bargain with him. His offer as an enemy is worthless."

"You once thought I was your enemy," she laughs.

The king leans in, the corner of his mouth lifting. "Ah, but he is unlikely to negotiate with kisses and compliments."

"It may have just been the power and jewels you offered," I remark to the side.

"Shut up, ghost boy," she snarls.

I step in, close enough to push her back against the door. "How will you shut me up?"

Saying nothing, her eyes narrow, slowly moving down and back up as her tongue presses against the inside of her cheek.

I am entirely at her mercy.

At my silence, she smiles in triumphant victory. "Anyway, I wasn't considering his offer. That would be stupid. It's a bargain. Meaning, we can change the terms and offer him something."

Cassius leans back against the stone, crossing his arms. "Then what do you suggest, my dear reeve?"

"You'll see," she says slyly.

We re-enter the room, Adonis waiting expectantly near a mat.

"Have you come to accept?" he asks with assumption.

"We offer you something of our own," Cassius answers.

Adonis' face shrivels in frustration. "What could *you* offer?" He stalks around Cassius, chains nearly touching his brother.

Both Ari and I glance at each other briefly, nodding and raising our hands. We would no doubt take pleasure in killing him.

At the sight of us, Adonis backs, sitting on a chair and crossing his legs.

"You forget that it is *you* who is a prisoner. Your request to speak to my mother is denied," Cassius replies.

"How about this," Ari begins to persuade, standing between Cassius and Adonis, "you answer three questions, and we'll take the chains from your wrist and ankles. Only freeing you when you are confined to your cell. In turn, we'll add guards outside your door."

He grimaces, but his lips push slightly out. "Why add guards if I am still restrained to the room itself?"

Scoffing, she waves him off as if his words are of little importance. "Does it matter? You can't see outside your door, so what difference does it make?"

He thinks this through, nodding and agreeing to the deal. "I accept your terms. At the release of my chains, I, Adonis, first son of King Elliot, shall answer three questions in full."

Ari reaches into her shirt, pulling the key Kabir gave her from her bra. She unchains Adonis, him shaking his wrist.

"How did you obtain the Stone of Elestial?" Cassius says quickly.

"I had it retrieved for me by someone of Magikal blood. Jefferson was easily willing to part with it."

Ari begins to open her mouth and form the word 'who', but I keep her from doing so.

"Don't ask him. It doesn't matter who it was. We can't risk asking a meaningless question," I whisper into her ear.

Adonis' grin grows, knowing exactly how he is playing us. He's intelligent, expecting us to slip on our own unthought-of impulses.

I know what has to be asked. "You held gatherings for months, possibly longer. How is it that you recruited more members without word circulating around?"

Though Adonis is bound true by his word, I can see that he has ways, like the other Fae, to answer this question fully without confessing portions he wishes to keep out if he deems it unnecessary. "Vows hold a great deal to the Fae, as you can see. Those who loved someone dearly would yield their silence if it meant the promise of safety to those closest to them."

A scheme is formulating in Adonis' head. There's something he is keeping from us, but one misstep will result without answers. "I suppose the former queen can understand this, being that her silence over my existence gave her a crown," he adds, then looking at me. "Just as we have brought you back, I can take your life."

Next, he turns to Ari, licking his lips.

Finally, he turns to Cassius, full of levity and taunt. "Or, I can always torture your witch. She seems up to the task for your answers."

"Careful how you speak to Lady Arabella, brother. Let me say this outright: if you disrespect her once more, I will not stop her from what it is she wishes to do to you," Cassius challenges, his demeanor lull but icy.

Ari pulls Cassius from the room, the king stumbling out in silence. "Luka, wrap this up. We can question him again another day."

The door slams, leaving the two of us.

"Your people are rotting away in the cells, if that brings you any solace," I mention to him.

He looks up, curiosity striking him.

Under different circumstances, I could find humor in how easily I've pulled his attention. "Those that the guards couldn't capture had fled, but I doubt those are ones who were that loyal to you."

"Ask me anything. Whatever it is you want to know, I will answer." His tone shifts, not a hint of derision in his voice.

Suspicion crowds my mind, twisting it into strings of knots. "That would use up our third question."

"No. Consider it a sign of good faith. One you should pay mind to in the future."

I debate on what to ask. There are a multitude of questions going through my mind. Ones that could give us true answers, and ones that are more pertinent to my curiosity.

"Why did you bring me back to life?" After the last word leaves my mouth, I reprimand myself for opting for a question so personal. "What about Arabella's place here carried so much importance that you looked into her personal life and revived me?"

Two questions. Both of which I intend on having answered.

"You seek the answer to questions you ought to not want," he responds caustically. "Why would we not bring back the lover of the witch if it meant her leaving Ifaeris and no longer interfering with our plans? Without her, we would have never been discovered. With you, she would be gone."

"You miscounted for her drive to see something through once she starts it. And the feelings she harbored for the king," I say, an ironic chuckle escaping me.

Adonis clicks his tongue. "Yes, I do suppose that I should have expected their relationship was not a farce to be displayed for the public."

The door opens, Cassius calling for me to join him. "We are needed."

I leave the room, taking away the chairs, Adonis slumping into his mattress. "Until we meet again."

Kabir shuts the door, and the four of us leave the tower, walking briskly towards the palace.

"What happened? Has there been another attack?" I ask through each step.

We walk through the doors of Nexus, Ari shaking her head. "There's a note that was sent to us. It said to return Adonis in two days to the grounds of the meeting spot, or the crown will suffer more than a war."

Despite Ari's protests, a meeting is being held in the council room to discuss the letter that was sent to the king.

The room holds the whole Disaris family, their cousins, Ari, and myself. None are meant to come close to the area while Kabir stands at the door, keeping away from any who may enter.

Esme, the Fae with skin kissed by the sun and a short pixie cut hairstyle, approaches the three of us. "You're late, Cassius."

He pays her comment no attention. "I am not late. Everyone else is simply eager."

The room is full of commotion until Cassius sits at the head of the table, two seats on both of his sides for Ari and me. Everyone goes silent, sits around the table.

"What should we do?" a large man with facial hair and rounded cheeks asks. He's who Ari said is Atticus.

The one named Isadora speaks. "We're obviously not going to give him back. It's a trap."

"I agree with Isa," Esme responds immediately. Her voice is projected with sternness in her tone. "Bringing Cassius to one of Adonis' angry followers just seems like a setup to get rid of another Elemental."

"Then what? We go to war with each other until we capture each Fae who's involved in this?" the one twin with flaming, long hair vocalizes. From the scar at the bridge of his nose and the fuller spread of freckles, this one is Xavier.

Celeste crosses their arms, appearing to kick their cousin's leg. "No. That's unfair to punish everyone when we saw that some had good intentions."

"Or were brainwashed," the shorter-haired of the twin brothers adds. "But I think Xay has a point. This may not end until we have those who were affected by the Stone of Elestial recovered. If not war, something just as destructive."

"I would think you of all people would show sympathy. I saw you protect a man who was cowering in fear and begging for his life," Dyana says, scorning Xavier.

Arguments around the table break out, Ari being suspiciously quiet.

"What say you, my reeve?" Cassius asks, turning his head to Ari.

Biting her lip, she debates her response. "I agree with keeping Adonis prisoner. Keep him and the king away from harm and keep us from falling into a trick. Do nothing, and carry on with what we've done, striving for better treatment for the common fae in hopes it'll be enough."

She responded quickly. Too quickly for my liking.

Celeste, the Fae barely taller than Ari, slams their chair back. "You're lying!" they accuse from down the table. "You can lie to the other Fae and hide whatever plan you have manifesting in your head, but you don't do that with us."

Ari huffs in defeat from the exposure. "Okay, do I think giving back Adonis is a mistake? Yes. In fact, I think it would be better to kill him now. Sever the monster's head, and shut down the rebellion at the source. But anyone who has a cause to fight knows that when one leader dies, another will take over."

"So, do you have any ideas?" Maude asks. "We can't just keep the

Fae who killed our father and brother in that prison if he refuses to answer any questions."

"He has failed to obtain the crown and now rots with the knowledge he will spend the rest of his infinite days trapped behind iron," Cassius explains. "Is there no justice in that?"

Helena rises from her chair, looking at everyone around the table. "We all agree that we are not sending Adonis to whomever sent that note, can we not?"

No one makes any interjections, just nodding.

"Good. That is all we had met for. However Cassius chooses to proceed is entirely up to him as the king, not us." She begins to exit the room. "I advise you all, as the former queen, to follow me and allow Cassius to decide for himself."

The rest of the Fae leave the room. Cassius, myself, and Ari remain, sitting in silence.

"What do you think about all this, mahal?" she asks.

The question forces me to confront the fact that this is no longer an issue I am indirectly involved in. After what Adonis said, I am just as important to advising as Ari.

"I think that everyone is correct in some way with what was said. Not every follower of the rebellion was inherently bad, but returning Adonis would lead to them believing they hold power over Cassius." My fingers tap the wood of the table, pondering what I have to say next. "If we're going to kill Adonis, I want more questions answered."

Cassius begins laughing uncontrollably. He slaps the arms of the chair with an indiscernible emotion.

The two of us look at the king in wonder over what is amusing him, Ari being the first of us to speak. "Cas? Why are you laughing like that?"

"I have become king, Ezra's dead, and Adonis has found himself back on the palace grounds. A terrible turn of events to our father, I'm sure." He pauses for a second, mind wandering. "Not that it matters, being that he's dead."

I should not find what he says so comical, yet I find myself smiling. "Are we going to refer to Adonis as your brother? Honestly?"

"We could call him something by another name." Cassius presses his finger to his lips, pounding it a few times. "Murderer. Damnation of the crown. I personally prefer bastard."

"Cas," Ari calls to him, "you're technically the bastard. He isn't." She giggles, reminding him of that fact.

Despite having the leader of the uprising, there is an awareness that we are now posed with a new threat. One that lies under the surface.

# XL

## *Precorination Indulgences*

Cassius

It bodes ill to drink this heavily when I am to be crowned tomorrow afternoon.

Luka and Arabella have joined me. He lies at the edge of the bed, barely holding himself up by his forearms, while Arabella sits next to me, both of us with our backs to the bed frame.

The three of us relax, exchanging tales and savoring the small moment of temporary reprieve from what we continue to face.

Arabella takes a swig from the glass bottle, then hugs it between her arms. "I still think I should interview your brother alone. I mean, he quite literally said I would be his consort. Maybe he'll let something slip."

"And you think you are coherent enough to get answers from him at this moment?" Luka jabs, taking the bottle from her.

She laughs, throwing her head back and hitting it against the headboard. "Oh, ye of little faith, my love."

"I would assume my brother to give up his life before revealing more to us," I wager.

"Well, maybe I can try something else," Arabella suggests. Her head hangs to the side, eyes unopened. "I think I should question him alone, but if I do it, why not shower him in praise? He already has assumptions about me. Make him comfortable and feed his delusion."

I look at her, considering her idea. "What good will come of speaking to him again, when he offers up no viable answers?"

"We still aren't aware who sent that note," Luka responds. His eyes are nearly closed as well, carrying a wide grin on his face. "There's a chance he could recognize the writing."

"But I doubt Adonis knew every single common fae who attended meetings." She puts her arm through mine, leaning her head on my shoulder. "Who's to say each of them went to every meeting? If his most trusted leaders barely saw him, why would he know a follower's writing?"

"It's smarter to ask than do nothing," Luka counterpoints.

I finish the wine, tossing the glass to the floor. "There still remains the possibility that someone will take over in Adonis' stead. A successor to take lead in this very event."

"Fine," she concedes. "I'll find out if he knows who wrote the note tomorrow." As I am about to interject, Arabella lifts her head, angling up at me. "Before your coronation."

"What about the runaways?" Luka asks, sprawling his body across the mattress. "I'm sure your ideas would be kinder than my thoughts of ripping apart those who took pleasure in planning your death. We have to think of ways to convince them not to hate Cassius."

"That's just something we have to fix over time," Arabella states. "People are going to be upset no matter what Cas does, but minimizing the damage would be the most effective. Their biggest issue was how the king was petty and never sent help to the other lands, right?" Turning to me, her legs rest on mine while she attempts to hold eye contact. She is more sober than I, but her ability to explain herself is still astonishing. "Fix that issue. You have the funds as king and ability to make peace with the other lands. Make sure that not only do the rulers do their job governing, but you do yours in listening when the common fae come to you."

"That may change the minds of those who pledged allegiance to Adonis," Luka adds.

With the way the two speak, I should offer them the responsibilities of the crown and rid myself of the duties that I would never deem interesting.

"Cassius?" Luka says.

"Yes?"

He flips to his side with his elbow keeping his head up. "Explain how your wings work."

This is something Arabella has asked before, though she barely comprehended my explanation. "Just as I summon my shadows, my wings can be summoned. It is similar to how I can shape the phantom of the shadow into weapons at my intention."

"But your clothes. Do your wings go through your clothes? Are they just an extension of shadows too?" Arabella asks. I look at her to see knitted eyebrows and a look of curiosity. "I've been trying to understand the logistics of that for a while."

"My wings have minimal texture. Elliptical and long, similar to angels in human portraits, yes, but they are no illusion. They function just as any flighted creatures do, but after tearing through multiple pieces of clothing as a child, the tailors gave up and glamoured many of my tops to unclasp at the pressure of my wing expansion."

Both listen to me, Arabella grabbing my shirt from the floor, searching for the clasps and shoving the clothing on my lap.

"If some become damaged, it is of little issue to have another made. I am royalty, after all." I take the wine-stained shirt, flinging it onto the pile of clothes. It is then that I realize the three of us are in nothing but our undergarments.

This is the reason I prefer okkaring to flying. There lies no point in wasting the material of good fabric when I can arrive at my destination momentarily and without as much energy spent.

I look at the witch sitting next to me, one giggling as she messages her friends. She is unguarded with the light from the moon kissing her in the way that I yearn to.

Giving in, I tilt her with my finger, claiming her lips for myself, whispering messages into her mouth. She is the sweetest taste. A blow so fatal, it could end worlds.

Laughs of hollow fill the room. She kisses me swiftly, her nose nuzzling into my cheek before gazing into my eyes. "You're so drunk."

"You taunt my state, yet have once gotten so inebriated that I once carried you back to Nexus as you asked me to admit my hatred for you," I purr into her ear, "while I know you had desired the opposite."

Her eyes lock in on me, closing in while an insinuating grin appears. "You're really annoying, no matter what I say."

"Must you wound me with your words?"

She grins at me, twirling her fingers. "I can always use magik if you prefer."

Opening his mouth with closed eyes, Luka begins to speak. I had thought him asleep. "I'm glad someone else understands what she is like."

I press my lips to hers, my mouth lingering on the rim. "You, my dear princess, you are my most decadent form of torture." I run a finger through her lips, a breathy whimper escaping.

Luka crawls up to Arabella's side, the both of us enclosing her. She kisses Luka, then me, grinding herself on my thigh before drifting to sleep between the two of us.

# XLI

## The Brother, the Crown, and the Ex

Arabella

Instead of bringing Adonis to Enthar, I'm meeting with him again. The possible consequences are grim and unforetold, but if he's here, we know the risk.

Cassius is with his sisters, preparing for his coronation, while Luka is with the tailors, choosing his clothing for the night. This leaves the task to me alone. I have Kabir escort me to the tower, carrying the late lunch in a bag.

The whole walk here, Kabir insists that he go in with me, but I tell him it's better for him to stand guard at the door, ready for anything to come.

At the door, I prepare myself, both for objectifying or wrathful comments.

"Hello, witch," Adonis says upon my entrance.

I don't respond. Instead, sitting across from him on one of the steel chairs brought in for us, noticing the barely cushioned mat that's no longer pressed against the corner. Now it lies in the middle of the room.

"I brought lunch," I say, tossing him a sandwich from the burlap sack.

He takes it, struggling to unwrap the food from the paper with a hand and his mouth before eating it furiously. "You're being kind. Where is my brother and the dead lover you pine over?"

"Doesn't matter," I answer. After I unhaul the rest of the food and drinks from the bag, I put his at the foot of a chair. "I came to talk to you. I believe you owe me one more answer."

"Who am I to reject what was promised?"

I need to find some way to flatter him. When it comes to charming men, it's not something I'm great with, but acting interested in him can't be much different to lying. "I have to say, I find it impressive that you were able to develop such a large following in a short amount of time."

He eyes me suspiciously but thinks nothing of it as he continues to eat. "It was not without its obstacles, I promise you. Actually, it was quite the fickle feat, but when those with a common cause group together, a leader is needed."

"And that leader was you?"

"Yes."

"I see." I take a bite from the food, uncrossing my legs and studying his exact movements.

"You had a question," he reminds me as if I forgot.

Smiling, I slowly open my legs, lifting my skirt to dust off crumbs. He watches me tentatively, clearing his throat. "Patience. I want to enjoy a meal with the clever Fae, who had outsmarted not only the king, but me. Months for that matter."

Adonis enjoys the praise. He bites into his food, chewing slowly until he swallows. "I suppose my company has been craved by Magiks more than yourself."

*Another Magik.* That's what he said about who gave him the Stone of Elestial. Jefferson's a fool, but he isn't stupid. He wouldn't have something of such value without taking precautions to keep it safe. This Magik that stole from Jefferson and works for Adonis has better skills than we've been led to believe.

"It's ironic how you gained your following, don't you think?"

He pauses from his food. "In what way?"

"If you think about it, the only reason your father was so cruel to the common fae in the first place was from petty anger towards the other rulers. The war was finished, treaties were being created, and the only reason the other Elementals had been stationed at Nexus the night your mother died was to have ultimate security until the truce was finalized." I wait, allowing the information to process into Adonis' brain, if it hadn't known this already.

There's a look I can only describe as childlike interest. History he's lived through being shown from the other perspective. "I fail to see your point."

Lips pursing, my tongue smacks from behind the front of my teeth. "Your father was chosen as High King because the other Elemental rulers viewed him as a leader. When they weren't able to protect the one woman he loved–the day before announcing she was to be queen, he decided to let down the rest of his people." I snicker, trying to hold his intrigue. "People with power can be such selfish creatures. When Elliot became hardened by his grief, he stopped keeping the rulers in check. And when he couldn't be bothered to help the common fae, they turned to you. Like I said, ironic how him sending you away ultimately led to his own downfall."

"I now see why you are of a special interest to both the king and others before me," he remarks. The food in his hand is finished, the paper that wrapped it cast aside. "I saw the magik you unleashed on the battlefield. My arm is evidence of that. I may have use for you yet when I escape, my little vixen."

It's bold of him to assume he'll find a way to escape, but his odd word usage is what stumps my thoughts.

"I think I'll ask my question now."

He's become fully enthralled, pleased by my praise and fascinated by what I could ask.

"A note was sent to us." I pull the paper from my boot, unfolding it and handing it to him. "We know that you didn't spend much time with those you commanded. You may have thrown someone else like Cato in charge for this very outcome, being that he held the Stone of Elestial. But in any case, do you know who could've possibly written this?"

Adonis' eyes pique with interest, and it occurs to me that while we have retrieved the stone from the battle and locked it in the vault, if there's another like him or another with his power, they have the ability to find the vault and sneak in. He is, after all, much older and could have easily had a child within the past decades.

"I do, in fact, know who wrote this. The creature you are pursuing is much closer to you than you think."

Leave it to a Fae to give an ominous answer.

"Leave while you can, young witchling," he cautions. "Before all that you love disappears."

Scoffing, I mutter, "And leave you to rule? Murdering more Elementals and anyone who opposes you?"

"It is no different than those who ruled before me," he counters, brushing his hand around my cheek. "You only care about the Fae because you were made aware of our existence."

I hate his cocky candor. I hate how much he looks like the man who imprisoned me here in the first place. But mostly, I hate that his disgusting words aren't untrue.

My hand pushes his away from me. I lean in close to his ear. "You'll rot here for eternity. Without a kingdom, and without history knowing your existence. While I got the love of my life back."

Checking the time on my phone, I have to leave. There's less than an hour before Cassius' coronation, and I still need to get ready.

Kabir takes me back to the palace, Adonis hurling curses at my departure. "That sounded dramatic," the guard says, taking my boots from me to be handed to a servant. "What did you say to him?"

"Only a truth," I utter with a smile.

He chuckles. His movement from his laughter pulls me into realizing he's not wearing his normal guard's uniform but is instead shirtless. His legs are covered in dark colors of leather, with a sword strapping to his back. The markings on his skin are more similar to the scarring of those under the general. On his body is a tattoo that covers from one shoulder to the other, meeting at his chiseled chest.

I want to avert my eyes, despite the fact I learned very early on in my stay here that nudity is normal.

"You may be your most frightening when your anger performs through pleasant demeanor," Kabir remarks.

"Then you would've been terrified to see me when I was younger."

After leaving me to change himself, I follow the sound of a piano. It plays a melody that I can identify, only because there's only one person who plays it. The composition is a song Luka wrote. He played it for me four months into our relationship, saying that it was the best way to describe how he felt for me.

I knock on the door, but he doesn't hear. He's too engulfed by his playing to notice. Taking the seat on the piano bench next to him, I kiss his cheek warmly, worried over his actions. "You only play when you're stressed. What's going through your mind, mahal?"

He doesn't stop playing, but he does lift his head to me as his fingers frolic through the keys. "You spoke with Adonis?"

It isn't the words that clue me in, but what he hasn't said. Or rather, what my mind is believing he's keeping from saying. The note promised that without returning Adonis, something worse than war would happen. If Adonis brought him back to life, whatever way he did it can easily be undone if they know how. Refusing to return Adonis means risking Luka's life.

I nod, confirming that I didn't bring him to Enthar.

"I still don't understand," he admits. "I haven't found a source that explains how he brought me back. Everything is still a haze." When making his confession, he presses down on the keys more aggressively with every sentence, the notes now vibrating off the walls.

"Does that really bother you, or is there something else on top of it?"

Many times, I've found it hard to get him to speak his mind. His whole life, he followed what his father said, craving his approval and grieving the disappointment he felt when his dad not once showed him affection. Luka was never accustomed to sharing his emotions, leaving me to guess his intentions until we became exclusive and worked through that.

He shakes his head. "I'm still not sure what I'm doing here. Will I remain at your side, alongside Cassius? Am I going to be the third that Fae whisper about? I don't wish to spend the rest of my life with no purpose."

"You're the smartest person I've ever known." I take his hands from the piano, keeping one inside mine. "You were the top of every class at Lazipeus. Don't doubt your skills and brains when it comes to advising the king with me."

To calm him from his worries, I kiss him passionately. It's soft and gentle and sweet. But at breaking away, we're breathless and laughing.

I still need to change.

"Besides, you're practically royalty among the Magiks. Being here is no different. Unless you've changed your mind and this isn't what you want. You can go home."

Knowing Luka and I would do anything for each other means finding a way to make things work if he decides he wants to go back to our old life.

While looking at me, he must notice I am still not properly dressed. So he takes my hand, okkaring us to my room.

The midnight blue dress I'm meant to wear hangs on the wardrobe. The long skirt puffs in tulle, the top portion with glamoured, invisible mesh and small beads barely covering my nipples. The fabric the beads are placed on cuts in, creating an opening into a V-shape down the upper half of my body.

*There's no way I can wear a bra with this.* I try, but it doesn't work with the see-through material. I'd have to let the weight of my breasts fall with nothing to support them.

I throw on gloves and gold accessories, coordinating with the metal that Cassius prefers.

Luka wears a lacy black shirt with necklaces and rings. If sculptors thought their muses bewitching, a whole museum should be dedicated to this man. Over the shirt, he wears a regal, black trail coat and slacks to match. It's nice that the heat isn't so extreme here, but it's still too warm for Luka to be wearing layers. He wears chains similar to mine, keeping the moon ring from the set I bought us two Yules ago.

After quickly changing and magiking on makeup that matches the dress, Luka helps me braid two strands in the front of my hair, one on each side. I finish the look by adding olive branch clips into both sides of my hair, loosely pinning the braids up by the ends and hanging in loops.

Finally, Luka responds to my previous words. "My home is not a place. It's with you."

Heat rushes to my cheeks at the words, simple and gratifying. "Come on. Let's go see the king get crowned."

In the throne room, Luka, the Aeon cousins, and I stand at the bottom of the stairs, his siblings and Helena standing by the throne. While the other Fae will be appearing in the ballroom within this hour, witnesses are still required to crown Cassius king.

Cassius is in a closed, inky frock coat with sapphire accents which opens at his neck while also in identically colored trousers. His maroon mantle has white fur that coats the shoulder area, hanging down to his knees. On his neck, he wears my rose ring that's strung through a black lanyard, whereas his hands are covered in golden accessories with nails to match his frock.

Per usual, he wears the chains that cuff from the sides of his ears and dangle down to the opening of the piercing. I've never seen him look so regal, other than the night of the ball. Most Fae are all abnormally beautiful, but I swear he was formed by the gods themselves.

Being that Helena is living and the former queen of the Fae, she holds the authority to crown Cassius. Her dress is as vibrant as her eyes, hair tucked back and in a complex bun. The family gathers around, each standing with their mother in the middle.

The king bends down on one knee before her as she lowers the golden crown onto his head. "Do you, Cassius Disaris, son of Elliot, accept the crown and the title it holds?" his mom asks, hovering the piece over his head.

"Yes, I accept the crown."

A smile of pride appears on her face. The crown now rests on his head while a hand keeps him balanced on the ground.

"I, Helena Aeon, former High Queen of Ifaeris, crown Cassius Disaris High King of the Faeries. Long may he reign."

And just like that, the ceremony is over.

Cassius rises, descending down the stairs and taking my arm. We walk through the doors as Luka follows behind with Xavier and Monty. The twins are bantering, claiming how anticlimactic the ceremony was, while Luka says nothing.

Kabir and Gavin stand at the doors, firmly grasping the handles tightly and waiting for a signal to open.

A voice from the other side of the door is announcing our

entrance. The last time I was in here, all eyes were on Cassius and me. I'm no longer his lover in false, but now his reeve. His second in command.

"May I present King Cassius, High King of the Faeries, his family, and his court," the voice from the other side announces.

The guards open the door, and bright lights gleam, puncturing my eyes.

Once inside, the family glides swiftly from the doors, past the dance floor, and to the elevated platform that holds an elongated table covered in cloth. Cassius sits in the king's seat, me on his right and Luka next to me.

The rest of the group falls in, taking a seat where they choose and collecting food for themselves.

It feels like all the Fae are passing judgment on their new king, his family, and his choice of lover. Korine stands at the table nearest the platform, staring me down with a molten look in her eyes.

Unlike the last time, it now feels like a true celebration. There's drinking and revelry all around. The sparkle of their glamour fills the room while others line up to greet Cassius.

I leave with Luka to the floor, dancing with him and the members of the family until the line dwindles. Multiple times we go to the table for sustenance and drink, checking on Cassius each time.

The food for Luka and me is also prepared with seasonings and salts in comparison to the foods offered to the Fae.

I'd probably have to thank Esme for that.

After all have bowed to the king, I'm full of wine and giddy, stumbling back up the stairs to sit at Cassius' side. Luka chuckles as he guides me up, keeping one hand at the small of my back.

Bowing to Cassius, my hand is taken by the Fae's, kissing me through the cloth.

"Princess," he murmurs.

"My king."

Cassius kisses me for all to see. As if showing off to his kingdom that I am his.

I laugh silently, hardly able to control myself from the wine and carmine pink fruit that Cassius calls Etherfruite. "I'm your High Reeve. This isn't very proper."

"You are my lover too," he growls. "Do not forget."

"Remind me again," I hum, kissing him just as intensely as before.

A throat is cleared, the air causing me to shiver as Cassius' name is called. "King Cassius, is it?" Harrison mimics the pleasantries the other Fae had. His eyes are a strange shade of teal, appearing the same as what a child would color the ocean with.

"A bow is typically required," Cassius jokes, baiting his friend.

Behind him is Korine in a periwinkle dress. Her hair is curled and pinned up, gold painted across her cheekbones. She smiles tightly at me. If her mouth goes any wider, teeth gritting any harder, she'll injure herself.

"You look lovely tonight," Cassius tells her.

She extends her hand to him, curtsying, with a gleam of hope in her eye. "You are too kind, my king. I am but your humble servant."

I refuse to give energy to her fawning, deciding on rejoining the festivities with Luka. Drinking until I can barely walk.

We stay until there's no one in the ballroom but the three of us. None of us are sober, but we're not exactly drunk anymore. The musicians have long gone, the servants cleaning around us.

Sometime in the night, the accessories that decorated my hair disappeared from my head along with my gloves. Now, my hair falls loose with my makeup smudged.

"There are more amusing ways to find use of Luka around Nexus. Attempting to seduce me for entertainment for one," Cassius quips.

"Did you just try making a joke? Your jokes are abysmal, Cas," I cackle. The wine's either made its return into my system or I genuinely find the idea of Luka attempting to seduce Cassius hilarious.

Lips curved, his face becomes defensive. "It is not I who laughs at a screen of meaningless words conjured together."

My jaw drops, mouth agape in offense.

"Ari, it's true. You would laugh if you saw a picture of a frog carrying a giant knife and saying to count your days," Luka chimes in, backing Cassius.

He is upsettingly correct, because I begin wheezing to the point that I can barely breathe from the image I can see in my head. Then, I think back to every cryptic message I sent to my friends that made no sense and laugh harder.

"Alright. I can't say that you're wrong." As my laughter dies, I'm able to get out, "I'm serious, Cas. Make Luka a diplomat or something. He's smart and will actually oversee how the rulers run their land."

Luka's hair is messy, the product he put in it no longer holding. "The Elementals would find it belittling to report to a Magik," he says.

"Who cares? You know right from wrong, and you're just as

qualified as Cas is." I pause, looking at the Fae who's barely able to keep his eyes open. "And he was crowned king."

Honestly, Luka is probably more qualified than Cassius is.

Cassius is lying on the table, one leg bent with the foot on the table. "I can see why that role may be important. What shall be done if those in charge are not acting accordingly? Or worse yet, a common fae still demands an audience with the crown?"

I pat him on the head, messing with his hair a bit. "Then you do your sworn job as king and listen to them. Only reason the Elemental Fae had become rulers was 'cause their abilities would provide safety to the common fae. If they aren't doing their job, there would be no need for them to be in charge, and we'd just decide on new Fae to govern. I think you'd prefer them to do their part and have it overseen by Luka than to weigh in on every complaint."

"If your father did one thing right, it was taking time to meet with the common fae when needed," Luka comments.

"And how often do you suppose I meet with them?" Cassius asks. "I would appear before the kingdom as weak if I presided over every small issue presented."

Pushing himself up to face us, I put my arm on his lap, resting my head on it while facing Luka. "Meet with them once a month or every other. The lower courts are in charge of settling petty disputes, and if a Fae feels the need to proceed and bring the issue to you, then I'll stay at your side during the hearings, if it'll get you through them."

"While you never lived a life of royalty, you have become quite the leader in my decisions ruling the Fae." Cassius moves his hand to my chin, pulling my face to peer up at his. "I would have you be my queen. The High Queen of the Fae."

I'm stunned. Half convinced he's joking. He's rendered me utterly speechless.

"Can you even do that?" I manage to ask. I'm not sure I'm breathing. "We aren't married. How can I be queen without us being married?"

He waves off my comment. "I am the ruler of Ifaeris. If I wish for my queen to be a witch, it will be done. Marriage or not, the moon is still full. I can crown you while Luka stands as our witness."

Robbed of my words, all I can do is stare between the two men who wait for my response.

"You've managed to do the impossible. You silenced her," Luka mocks.

For some reason, there's only one thing that I'm able to think of. "How would sleeping arrangements work?"

Cassius finds my question amusing. He takes his crown, glamouring it into one more fitting for me. "I assume you accept?"

I nod, kneeling before them.

Putting the crown on my head, his voice echoes through the room. "Do you, Arabella Huǒ, born of Magik, accept the crown and all that it holds?"

"Yes."

"I, Cassius Disaris, High King of Ifaeris and all of the Fae, crown Arabella Huǒ, High Queen of the Faeries. May she reign until her last breath or retires otherwise." He places the crown on my head, tapping me to rise.

*My gods. I'm a queen.*

I study Luka, his face smiling but inscrutable on how he really feels. "Are you *really* sure you're okay living like this?"

He traces circles on my palm. His hands are cold, but wet from the chilled glasses of water the servant gave us. "My Blossom, life is about adapting, and this just happens to be a change I didn't expect. You've already expressed to me that the two of you ruling changes nothing. The three of us still rule together, despite it being only the two of you who wear the crown."

"His advising would not be suspicious if he is seen as a seneschal," Cassius points out. "It is not unheard of for rulers to take on lovers. Luka is no different."

"Someone has to supervise you two and make sure there's reason in these decisions." Luka swings his legs over the table, now sitting beside Cassius. "As you reminded me, I'm heir to one of the wealthiest Magikal families to ever live. You would have found yourself in power regardless, Ari. If someone takes issue, Magik or Fae, I can buy a way to silence them."

"So, sleeping arrangements?" I remind them.

We leave the room, walking up to the third floor and stopping where the wings part. Cassius hasn't given an answer. He hasn't moved. "I would prefer if the three of us resided in my chamber. The room is large enough, and if needed, space can be made for two more beds entirely. No one resides in the next chamber over, and our servants are more than capable of knocking down a wall."

"We can sleep tonight and decide tomorrow," Luka suggests.

"I'd rather have my things moved tomorrow anyway. It's the middle of the night, and I'd like some rest before the sun comes up," I rasp in a tired voice.

Cassius kisses me goodnight, lightly patting Luka on the shoulder once before walking into his room, shutting the door so that it wakes no one.

Luka grabs me by the waist, lifting me so that I'm his height, our lips moving against each other as he sets me down.

I give him one more quick peck. "Love you. I'll see you in the morning before we torment this house with the three of us sharing a bedroom."

He grumbles, annoyed by the fact that he'll be sleeping alone. I knock on his door, kissing him again, making sure he's smiling before leaving him to his own company.

Once closing my door, I press my back against the door, keeping my eyes closed. I'm in absolute ecstasy with my life. The only problem I truly have to work on is finding the Magik that helped Adonis. That and running a kingdom of Fae who still hold suspicions against my people. There's also the issue of convincing the common fae to accept Cassius as king.

Maybe there's more than I initially thought.

Something wakes me. I swear I hear my door creak open. The thought's confirmed when I see a figure, dimly lit from the lights in the hall. It's Luka or Cassius, but I can't tell through the grogginess of being half asleep.

"We were supposed to sleep in our rooms tonight," I groan, rubbing my eyes.

That's when I hear laughter. It isn't either of them. It isn't anyone from this house's laugh.

Adonis is free.

Alertness springs from me. I shoot my hand, magiking on the lights. At the same time, the door shuts.

"How the fuck did you get out?" My body jumps from the bed, the magik in my veins ready to fire.

I'm too slow. I feel something slamming into the back of my head, and I'm put to sleep.

# XLII
## Missing Witch

Luka

It's past lunch, but Ari has not come down. While I know we were barely able to make it to our rooms after last night, even Cassius came down before her.

There has to be something wrong.

I hurry into her room, only to find it empty. Perhaps she has already left her bed and is walking around the grounds.

That cannot be right. The light is still on, while her bed barely looks slept in. My eyes drop down and see a stain on the rug that covers the cold floor. It's a dark, crimson color, and the gravity of the fact hits me that the stain is dried blood.

Sprinting out the room, I rush down the stairs, searching for Ari throughout Nexus. No one has seen her. Through every open and unopened door, I search until I find Cassius in an office, speaking with Maude.

"Arabella's missing," I panic. "I went to wake her, and there was dried blood on the floor."

He drops what he's doing, color draining from his face. "Maude, summon the guards and have them search the palace. Search all the grounds."

A guard comes rushing in with dread. She is nervous to deliver the news, possibly petrified of the scorn of Cassius. "Adonis was not in his cell this morning. He's escaped." She pauses, terrified to deliver more news. "The Stone of Elestial. It's gone too."

Trepidation coils in my stomach as we all run to Phantom Tower, pushing past guards until we reach Adonis' cell. Kabir stands there, body paralyzed. I grab the paper from his hand, and my horror is confirmed.

Someone took Arabella. I read the note before handing it to Cassius.

WHAT IS IT THAT THEY SAY? AN EYE
FOR AS EYE? WELL MAYBE I'LL TAKE
MORE THAN AN ARM FROM ARABELLA

—DELPHI

The world drowns in a high-pitched ring. I only know one thing for certain. If it takes burning the world to retrieve Arabella back safely, I will set all the lands aflame without letting a single ember touch her.

# Six of Wands

YA_ARIART

North America
North Atlantic Ocean
Ifaeris
South America
South Atlantic Ocean
Pacific Ocean
Searuck

Arctic Ocean
Europe
Asia
Magik Cove
Pacific Ocean
Indian Ocean
Gigantia
Australia

# Acknowledgments

Hello to anyone who actually decided to stay and read this. First of all, thank you so much for deciding to read my debut book! I worked very hard on this and I am so proud of how it turned out. I cannot wait until I begin writing the second book and I hope that you will join me for that ride in continuing the fate of Ifaeris and the journey of Arabella, Luka, and Cassius.

I had come up with the idea at around two in the morning at the end of April in 2022. Firstly I wanted to write this because I love both Witchcraft and Fae and wanted to see what a book about the two opposing sides would be like, but eventually a whole world was created. This was honestly something I never saw myself doing when I was younger, but I honestly don't think I regret it. Reading and being transported into a fantasy realm has been integral to my personality since I was a child, so writing this book was healing in a sense (even if this book had elements I definitely wouldn't have been allowed to read at a young age).

To my wonderful friends and support system, thank you so much for listening to my ramblings about this book while it was in progress. This was the biggest project I've ever worked on, and knowing that there is more to come was overwhelming. Thank you for everything you did to hear about the chaos of what I was working on and giving me encouragement when I was thinking of giving up. You mean the absolute world to me and I cannot wait for you to read both this and my other books to come.

To writers who are thinking about writing your own work, do it. I promise you that no matter what you'll have fun, whether you publish it or not. This whole experience was so freeing and helped me a lot. Be creative. Do something for yourself. No matter what you do with your work, you should pride yourself in the fact you created it at all.

To my book team, thank you for helping me organize this chaos and edit it where I lacked in grammar. I am sorry for the 4 a.m. messages of my indecisiveness and anxiety over nothing. I appreciate you so much and am still embarrassed over some of the stupidity I had when messaging you.

To the amazing artists who did the artwork for this book, thank you so much for helping my vision of the characters come to life! Your hard work truly paid off to me and I am so grateful for the creation you had given for me. Your work is beautiful and I urge you dear readers to follow them on their social media!

Finally, to anyone in my life I care about, I love you all so much and words will never be able to express my gratitude.